# True
# Honor

*Also by Dee Henderson
in Large Print:*

True Devotion
True Valor
Danger in the Shadows
The Negotiator
The Guardian

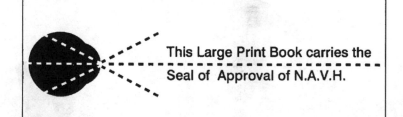

This Large Print Book carries the
Seal of Approval of N.A.V.H.

Book Three in the
Uncommon Heroes Series

# True
# Honor

★ ★ ★

# Dee Henderson

**Walker Large Print • Waterville, Maine**

Published in 2005 by arrangement with
Multnomah Publishers, Inc.

The text of this Large Print edition is unabridged.
Other aspects of the book may vary from the original edition.

Set in 16 pt. Plantin by Elena Picard.

Printed in the United States on permanent paper.

**The Library of Congress has cataloged the Thorndike
Press® edition as follows:**

Henderson, Dee.
    True honor / Dee Henderson.
        p. cm. — (The uncommon heroes series ; bk. 3)
    ISBN 0-7862-6320-2 (lg. print : hc : alk. paper)
    ISBN 1-59415-037-0 (lg. print : sc : alk. paper)
    1. Intelligence officers — Fiction.  2. Terrorism —
Prevention — Fiction.  3. Large type books.  I. Title.
PS3558.E4829T784 2004
    813'.54—dc22                                    2003071165

While I have endeavored to be accurate in both the terminology and tactics of a Navy SEAL and those who work in the intelligence agencies, I was at best only able to capture a feel for what their jobs are like. This is a work of fiction and all errors are mine.

As the Founder/CEO of NAVH, the only national health agency solely devoted to those who, although not totally blind, have an eye disease which could lead to serious visual impairment, I am pleased to recognize Thorndike Press* as one of the leading publishers in the large print field.

Founded in 1954 in San Francisco to prepare large print textbooks for partially seeing children, NAVH became the pioneer and standard setting agency in the preparation of large type.

Today, those publishers who meet our standards carry the prestigious "Seal of Approval" indicating high quality large print. We are delighted that Thorndike Press is one of the publishers whose titles meet these standards. We are also pleased to recognize the significant contribution Thorndike Press is making in this important and growing field.

Lorraine H. Marchi, L.H.D.
Founder/CEO
NAVH

* Thorndike Press encompasses the following imprints: Thorndike, Wheeler, Walker and Large Print Press.

# Glossary

**BLACK OPS:** Military operations that are conducted without public knowledge.

**BOLT-HOLE:** A location arranged as a secure place to hide should a spy be discovered.

**BUD/S:** Basic Underwater Demolition/ SEAL. The name for the initial six-month training program at the facility in Coronado, California, which all men hoping to be SEALs must pass.

**CINC:** Commander-IN-Chief.

**CO:** Commanding Officer.

**COVER BLIND:** A location and occupation created to provide a long-term false background for a spy.

**Cover Your Six:** Slang for "watch your back." Something in the "six o'clock" position would be behind you.

**DIA:** Defense Intelligence Agency.

**GPS:** Global Positioning System. Satellite guidance around earth used to precisely pinpoint aircraft, ships, vehicles, and ground troops.

**IRA:** Irish Republican Army.

**NSA:** National Security Agency.

**NATO Phonetic Alphabet:** Alpha, Bravo, Charlie, Delta, Echo, Foxtrot, Golf, Hotel, India, Juliet, Kilo, Lima, Mike,

November, Oscar, Papa, Quebec, Romeo, Sierra, Tango, Uniform, Victor, Whiskey, X-ray, Yankee, Zulu.

**NVGs:** Night Vision Goggles give good night vision in the dark with a greenish view.

**ROGER:** A yes, an affirmative, a go answer to a command or statement.

**SAS:** Britain's Special Air Service. An elite branch of the British Special Forces.

**SDV:** SEAL Delivery Vehicle.

**SEAL:** One of the elite branches of the U.S. Special Forces operating from the sea, air, or land.

**TANGO(S):** Terrorist.

**TRIDENT:** SEAL's emblem. An eagle with talons clutching a Revolutionary War pistol and Neptune's trident superimposed on the Navy's traditional anchor.

**ZODIAC:** A rubber motorized craft designed to carry SEALs covertly to shore.

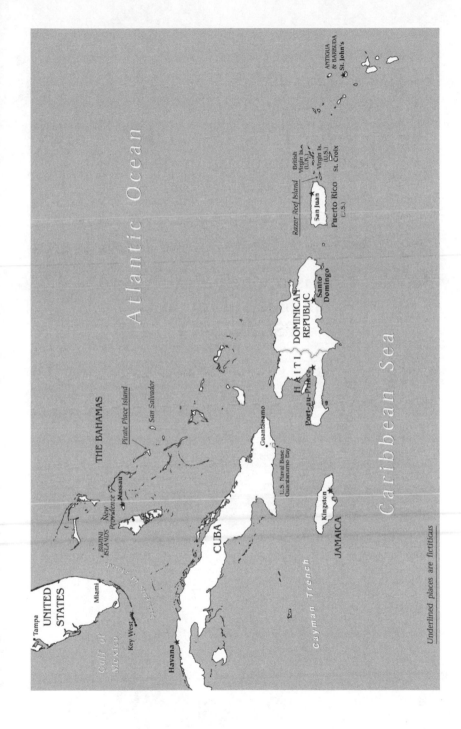

But understand this, that in the last days
there will come times of stress.
2 TIMOTHY 3:1


Behold, God is my helper; the Lord is the
upholder of my life.
PSALM 54:4

# Prologue

September 7
Friday, 6:10 a.m.
Shelton, North Dakota

There was a bounty on Darcy St. James's life, and in the world where she had once worked, having someone come after her was still more likely than not. She rested a booted foot against the lower fence rail shc'd replaced the day before and ran an experienced eye along the length of triple-rail fence, judging how much paint she would need to cover the new rails, while in the back of her mind she wondered if this was the day she would be interrupted by unwanted company.

After weeks of clearing out dead branches and undergrowth, the line of evergreens that provided a wind and snow break for the house had a tended-to look. At least the grounds of the place she called home would return to some semblance of order before winter came, even if the house itself was still torn apart. She loved this place. It was just proving to be a multiyear repair project.

She sipped her coffee and then reached down for the rifle resting against the fence railing. For those who bothered to ask, it was for the prowling coyote that had killed her neighbor's chickens, but in reality it was for her own security. Winter was coming and snow, and this year that was a good thing. It would be much harder for someone to approach the house with a few feet of snow to wade through.

A patrol car slowed on the nearby road, and Darcy lifted her hand to her sister. Amy and her husband Jacob Bond lived down the road. There were worse things than having an older sister with a protective streak who happened to be the town sheriff. And if Darcy did a little quiet watching out of her own for her sister's safety, she kept it to herself. There were some benefits to working for the government that lasted past an early retirement at thirty-five.

This place was beginning to feel like home. It was different living in one location and setting down roots, but she could feel herself relaxing deep inside.

*Jesus, I didn't realize how much stress had built up until I was able to fully stop. The verse this morning from Psalm 54 was perfect: "Behold, God is my helper; the Lord is the upholder of my life." I'm grateful that You brought me back here.*

She looked around the grounds and knew she could use some divine wisdom for the next project on her list. How could she take out that dying evergreen without taking out part of the garage roof? At least while there was work around the house and grounds to fill her days, she could ignore the fact that she still battled boredom when rain or delays in supplies left her with hours to fill.

The phone in her jacket pocket broke the silence. She was tempted to ignore it. The morning was peaceful and hers to schedule. There hadn't been enough such days in her life. She reached for the sheepskin-lined jacket inherited from her grandfather that she'd draped over the fence post and tugged out the phone. "You found me."

"Mornin', dahlin'."

She smiled at the Louisiana drawl that made the words sing. "Does your wife know you still call me that, Gabriel?"

"Marla knows that I reserve it for my

13

one and only partner who saved my life."

It hadn't been much of a rescue. Three years ago someone had driven by and shot at them in Bulgaria. She'd shoved him back into the hotel, picking up a bruised elbow for her efforts. "Flattery this early in the morning?"

"You live too far away. What's North Dakota got that Virginia doesn't? You move all the way out there, and I never get to enjoy your funny face anymore."

She rested her back against the railing and enjoyed the rising sun on her face. "I miss you too." There wasn't much she missed of her former life, but she did Gabriel. "The world blowing up somewhere, friend?" The Central Intelligence Agency had fingers everywhere, and Gabe owned the globe from Europe to the farthest time zone in Russia.

"Have you seen a paper lately?"

"Can't say that I have. I try to avoid such things as news these days."

"I can't believe you've been able to go cold turkey."

"It's not that hard when it's no longer my responsibility to know what, where, when, and how to fix it." She'd retired from the CIA two years ago with an Intelligence Star for Valor. She'd solved enough of the world's problems for one person to tackle in a lifetime.

"I need you."

She finished her coffee. "Now, did you have to go and say that?"

"Sergey wants to talk and he asked for you."

What did Sergey Alexandrov have to share that could only be done in person? He was many things: a former KGB station chief in London, a decorated cold war veteran, a spymaster. He'd advanced to number three in the Russian Foreign Intelligence Service before his own retirement last year. He was a worthy adversary. After a decade of competition between them, she'd call it a draw. She straightened. "Is he going to defect?"

"Doubtful. He's got a nice place in Spain, and he winters in the British Virgin Islands."

"Anyone missing on our side?"

"No."

She leaned back against the fence again. "Then I really don't want to fly halfway across the country to hear about a coming coup, a missing weapon, a renegade agent, or something else equally nasty that means I'd be working for more than a weekend."

"Darcy, you should see some of the new

crowd around here. There's no way I'm going to send one of them to see Sergey. He would laugh and send them back to day care. If you can't go, I will, but this request came through their embassy. Sergey asked for you by name."

And that meant there were . . . rules of the trade in play. The spy agencies of both countries were designed to distrust each other. They built trust on the procedures they agreed to follow, even if they didn't always trust the contents of the passed message. If possible, the Agency needed to honor this request, even if it meant asking her to come out of retirement.

Sergey understood how to handle sensitive information. He wouldn't make an extraordinary request for a face-to-face meeting without good reason. The Russian president trusted him. It could be a private message that needed confidential delivery or information that unless delivered through trustworthy hands would be discounted as not credible because of its unusual contents. Sergey, too, had been called out of retirement. "One weekend and I'm back by Monday?"

"He asked to meet Sunday night at a hotel in Florida. I've got a typed sheet of details. He did his usual meticulous job of laying out time and location."

She accepted her answer was going to be yes and shifted to logistics. "Let's keep this low-key. I'd rather not advertise I'm going to be on the East Coast. Courier me the information and send a guy to check the hotel the day before. I'll make my own travel arrangements between here and Florida. Sergey's news may be time sensitive. See if there's a military flight that can be arranged from Florida, say out of Eglin Air Force Base, on Sunday night so I can bring whatever Sergey has straight to the Agency."

"You want a backup team?"

"I don't think so. Sergey will follow protocol and come alone. I'll get to the hotel early enough to look around, make sure I've got a bolt-hole. If it looks like I need company, I'll call the Miami office. I'd rather not have my name in the system unless it's really necessary."

"It's nice having you back on the job, Darcy."

She'd promised Gabe to give it five years before she wrapped up her cover identity and presence on the East Coast and made a permanent retirement to North Dakota. She was only surprised that he had given her two years before he called for something more than a question, her opinion, or an hour to shoot the breeze. "Let's see what Sergey has to say. I'll see you in a few days."

# One

September 9
Sunday, 8:20 p.m.
Destin, Florida

Sam Houston strolled toward the hotel outdoor pool carrying a soft drink and tugging
at his tie, leaving behind the laughter of the
banquet room. His buddy Tom Yates was
married, and the reception was breaking up
now that the bride and groom were safely
away on their honeymoon. A huge weight
had just lifted from Sam's shoulders.

The breeze from the Gulf brought the
smell of sand and sea. Sam paused at the
steps going down to the boardwalk.
Florida was good to its visitors. Miles of
beach and luxury hotels stretched to either
side. He smiled as he contemplated his upcoming days off. Maybe do some deep-sea
diving and treasure hunting — something
challenging and adventurous. It wouldn't
compete with his last deployment and get-

ting shot at for an adrenaline rush, but it would do.

The past few months peacekeeping in Turkey had put him near a shooting war and turned him a little too serious for his own good. His temporary homeport with SEAL Team Nine was Little Creek Naval Base, Norfolk, Virginia. And while diving in the Atlantic could be fascinating, it couldn't compare to the vast treasures around the Gulf. A little diving, a little getting his priorities back in sync — He planned to enjoy life, not just live it.

"Now you look like a man at the end of a good day."

He glanced to his right and felt a spark of interest. A lady sitting alone by the pool was watching him. He didn't think she'd been a guest at the wedding — he had tried to meet everyone — but Tom and Jill had more friends than he could hope to keep straight. The thick closed book in her lap, the plate set aside on the nearby table, suggested she had been comfortable there for some time. He walked her direction. "Good food, good friends: the definition of a very good evening."

She tipped her head back as he approached. He liked her smile. Her glasses were interesting: oval-shaped with gold frames and a little star in the corner. She slid them off and set them on the table, and he could see through the glass without distortion to read the print on the magazine cover. She must use them and that little star to detract attention from her eyes — no one would forget those baby blues if he got a good look at them.

"You're with the wedding party? I heard the music."

"Best man."

"That explains the tux and the too tight tie."

He tugged it the rest of the way free with a rueful smile. "Hazards of the day." Making a decision, he dumped his jacket on an empty chair and took a seat on the lounge chair near her, turning up the cuffs of his white shirt. Despite being a chief petty officer, he could've used an instruction book for how to give advice to the groom, keep rambunctious buddies in line, trouble-shoot problems, and keep track of more guests under the age of ten than he could remember names for. It felt good to be done and able to consider time his own again. Blue lights shimmered up through the water, inviting a late-night swim. "It's a little dark for reading."

She clicked on a penlight. "Five hundred

and ninety-six pages — I'm going to finish it tonight and find out *whodunit* if it kills me."

He laughed softly. "A committed reader." He liked the sound of her voice and the relaxed humor in her answer.

"I'm recently retired and trying to make up for all the books I missed."

The ice in her drink had melted. His drink was getting low. "Like a refill?" He caught the attention of a hotel employee. He requested a second Coke for himself and she asked for a pineapple ice slush.

It was odd that she thought of herself as retired. He put her age at maybe thirty-five, forty. A glance showed a ring on her right hand, but her left was bare. The watch looked expensive, as did the dress. This wasn't a cheap place to vacation.

"I'd ask, but that looked like a private thought."

"It was." He was single, no kids, with life insurance from the military to bury him. He had a lifelong habit of giving extra money away. Buying stuff just meant it had to be packed and shipped to the next base. But he admired the effort it suggested to be able to retire young. She'd had a plan for catching up on her reading. What other plans had she made for herself now that she set her own schedule?

Their drinks arrived. He signed the slip, putting them on his room tab.

She sipped hers. "Thanks. I love these fruit things."

"My pleasure. The only place where you can get a better one is in Hawaii."

"Really? Have you been there often?"

He nodded. "With work. They're beautiful islands."

"I'll have to go someday. I want to see the fish along the coral reefs, the lush greenery that goes forever. I hear it's good honeymoon country." She lifted an eyebrow.

"They went to the Caribbean on a cruise. Tom and I are Navy buddies. He married a sweetheart in Jill."

She tilted her head. "Did you send them off with a walk under raised swords?"

She had some knowledge of military life; he tucked that observation away to come back to later, even as he smiled. "Our team of SEALs did the honors." The last man had slapped Jill's behind with the flat of his sword in the best tradition of Navy weddings.

"She'll have great wedding pictures."

"I hope so. The photographer certainly took enough of them."

She laughed and the sound was rich, warm, and bubbled. When she spoke he heard a trace of the West and home. He wished he had met her years before. "I'm Sam by the way. Chief Petty Officer Sam Houston." He offered his hand, belatedly realizing the oversight.

"Darcy St. James."

He was careful as he took her hand. His bore rough rope burns from the work he did and had the strength to crush the bones in hers. He found her hand had an unexpected strength. "Pretty name."

She smiled and let the compliment pass, not breaking eye contact but merely not re-acting beyond that slight smile.

That simple fact had him slow to release her hand. Those eyes were the unfathom-able kind, as clear and deep a pool of blue as the ocean when it both welcomed and yet hid its treasures. He had never been one to miss a treasure hunt. "Listen, would you like to get a piece of wedding cake? There's plenty left."

"Actually I've been waiting for someone, but he's running late."

That was either a gentle *not interested* or a simple statement of fact. He held her gaze and what he saw convinced him it was worth taking the optimistic view. Besides, he admired the loyalty and patience she showed in waiting for her date. Too many people in life were impatient, and he'd long ago learned that the best things in life often involved an indefinite wait. "Have a number you could try?"

"I wish I did."

"Then while you wait, let me bring the cake to you." He got to his feet. "White or chocolate? A lot of icing or a little?"

Her hesitation was so slight as to be barely noticeable. "White with lots of icing."

"I guessed that."

She grinned and he got the feeling he'd just made an unexpected friend. Sam walked back toward the ballroom to get the cake, intrigued with her and that tantalizing hint of the West in her voice. If her date didn't show up, he'd enjoy an hour of conversation with her. And if she was interested in learning to dive . . . her company would be welcome. He could hang with the guys anytime; Darcy would be much more interesting.

Darcy watched Sam walk away, leaning forward in her chair to catch a last glimpse of him as he disappeared around the decorative planters, his purposeful stride and posture signaling soldier even in his tux. She wished she wasn't working at the moment. She'd enjoy walking into the reception with him for a piece of that wedding cake and a chance to meet his friends. If there were a few SEALs still walking around in their dress uniforms carrying their swords . . . She shook her head and forced herself to lean back and not follow the thought.

Sergey was late. She could continue to sit here alone and read with her light, but she would be noticed and remembered by passing guests. Sam was her solution. A couple didn't attract a second glance. And if one of them was remembered, it would more likely be him.

Sergey hadn't lost his tradecraft skills. A wedding was beautiful cover. She'd bought her dress in New York the day before and it fit her profile of a guest at this hotel: expensive, elegant blue, cut in classic lines. Sergey would appreciate it.

She shifted the leather portfolio in her lap and reopened her book. It wasn't like Sergey to be late, but she could give him another fifteen minutes. She had contingency plans and a bolt-hole arranged. The contrast of a wedding and the possible danger she was in just sitting here was stark. She didn't want someone making an attempt to collect that bounty while she was focused on her meeting with Sergey. She made herself relax. She'd said yes to this mission, and she was committed to seeing it through.

Was Sam short for Samuel? Maybe she would get a chance to find out. She always appreciated a man who could focus. And he'd focused on her, a pretty nice fact all the way around. The man had wasted no time making a casual scan of her left hand looking for a ring. He wore a unique one with the SEAL emblem at the center and a cross etched into the side. The cross was an unexpected surprise — it was nice to have an early clue as to what he valued.

She'd surprised him. When she interrupted his reverie, there had been just a beat of a pause as he decided how to react before he moved to join her. He hadn't been sure if he knew her but curiosity had him coming over. There were calluses on his hand when he took hers, and she'd picked up the faint smell of peppermint.

He made an impression all right. She had a feeling she would be dreaming about the man and that smile tonight. And those eyes . . . He had a fascinating face. Not a pretty or overly handsome one, but compelling with blue eyes that reflected his laughter and a smile that was quick to appear.

Mid-thirties, six-foot even, fit and tough, he looked well able to take care of himself. Given the amount of trouble in the world SEALs got sent to quiet down, she doubted Sam spent much time in the States. They were Special Operations Forces trained to work covertly from Sea, Air, and Land, and only a few thousand were on active duty. She met SEALs overseas during extractions of spies and occasionally at embassy dinners where just their presence created a layer of security.

*Next time choose the couple from New York,* she told herself, turning pages in the book. They had been seated to her left until a few minutes before Sam appeared, and she could have easily started a conversation with them about the current Broadway plays. Instead she chose Sam and wiped out her concentration.

There weren't many strangers to bump into out in Shelton, North Dakota; a fact that was great for her security but detrimental to her social life. Maybe this meeting with Sergey would fall through, maybe Sam would be around for a few hours . . . And if she didn't stop thinking about him, she was going to end up where most distracted agents did when they were working — in trouble.

Sam walked into the ballroom. Guests had regrouped around a few tables in the center of the room. Someone in the center of that mass of people was about to do something stupid; Sam could hear through the shouts of laughter someone calling off a count. If he didn't know for a fact Wolf was away on his honeymoon, Sam would have predicted his partner would be the SEAL on the spot. He considered wandering over to see, but there were priorities in life and then there were priorities. A lady with brilliant blue eyes didn't smile at him that often.

Special Operations was a small community. He'd trained or worked with most of the men here. Years of sweat equity had earned him a place in this group where respect was earned, not given, and it felt good. The guys had brought their wives and girlfriends. He'd make another effort to talk Darcy into joining him. He'd seen the way her eyes lit up at that idea of walking below raised swords. He wasn't opposed to using the trappings of his career to tip the balance in his favor.

A piece of white cake with lots of icing. Sam studied the table and chose the one with the biggest rose. He picked up a chocolate piece for himself. The evening felt a lot like icing atop an already great day.

"Chief."

Sam turned at the call from his boss. His instinct was to snap to attention but he overrode it. Lieutenant Joe "Bear" Baker was still in dress uniform from the wedding. "Yes, sir. Is Kelly settled for the night?" Bear's wife was five months pregnant, and since she had asked him to be the child's godfather, Sam tried to stay current on the details.

"Asleep, although she wouldn't admit she was tired." Bear nodded to the two pieces of cake. "Found some company?"

Sam heard the curiosity of a friend as well as the care of an attentive CO and smiled. "Yes."

"Then I won't keep you. I want to pass on an invitation from Kelly. If you don't end up with plans for lunch tomorrow, feel free to join us."

"Thank you, sir." It was a night for optimism. "I'm hoping for the plans."

Bear laughed. "Then I wish you luck."

Sam walked back to the pool area, still smiling. Bear was the right kind of boss; it was a twenty-four/seven commitment. The man was responsible for the lives of sixteen men. Keeping an eye out for complications on the home front went with the job. Distractions got people killed. He had smoothed out more relationships with a well-placed word than Sam could count. Even if the advice occasionally came with a bit of a growl for which he was famous – Joe was a grizzly bear early in the morning.

A small pebble bounced down the steps as a couple came up from the beach arm in arm. Darcy looked up from her book and made more than a casual inspection of everyone in sight. She was still expecting her company to arrive. Whatever had held the man up, Sam hoped he appreciated the fact that Darcy was waiting for him.

He walked over to join her. "Here you go." He offered her the slice of white cake.

She turned in her seat toward him and waited until he sat down and had sampled his cake before tasting hers. She waved her fork. "Delicious as I knew it would be." She ate another bite, edging her way around the rose to leave it for last. "You said you are a Navy SEAL?"

"For over a decade now." He waited for the follow-up on what it was like to be a soldier.

Instead she studied him over her fork. "What do they call you?"

It wasn't a question he had expected. Sam grinned. "My friends call me a lot of things. *Cougar* normally. *Chief* when they're razzing me about my recent promotion."

"There's a story behind that name Cougar."

He inclined his head. A complicated, slightly unbelievable, but true story. "A long one."

She lifted the sugary rose from the cake. "Long stories are by far the best kind."

He studied her for a moment while savoring the last of his cake. Darcy wanted him to be the one talking while he was much more interested in hearing about her . . . interesting. Getting beneath the layers of this lady would not be easy. "A cat bit me."

She arched an eyebrow. "I won't ask you where."

He wanted to laugh. Darcy excelled at subtle expressions. Her humor he could come to enjoy as much as her laughter. He pointed to her cake. "Eat."

She glanced past him and her entire expression stilled and then relaxed. "Sam, my late guest just arrived. I need to go. Thanks for your company and the cake."

He took the plate she offered and then turned to see who it was who had kept her waiting, curious to at least meet him, for Darcy was in a hurry to leave. There was no one in sight.

Darcy collected her book and notepad. "Would you give your friends my good wishes when you talk to them next? Weddings are such wonderful events."

"I'll be glad to." He took a chance. "Join me for lunch tomorrow?"

She paused. "I'm leaving tonight." Her hand brushed his arm and she offered a breathtaking smile. "But it was very nice that you asked."

Sam watched her walk past the steps going down to the beach, pause to pick up the champagne flute someone had left on the low wall, and disappear toward the hotel restaurant.

Well, that was a bummer. He'd just seen the last of Darcy St. James. He sat pondering that, looking for any glimmers of optimism to grab hold of and couldn't find one. He knew her name, but not enough other information to track her down, nor any indication that he should try. Sam rose and picked up his glass, then returned the plates to the reception. *It would have been nice, Lord, if You could have held up her date for another hour.*

Rather than call it an evening, he headed down to the beach to take the walk he'd been contemplating earlier. Lunch with Joe and Kelly would be nice, but it would definitely be the consolation prize.

Darcy walked across the patio of the outdoor restaurant, fully attuned to the details of her surroundings, paying attention to the faces of staff and guests alike. She wasn't as worried about Sergey as she was the person who had put that bounty on her head. Splitting her attention between the two concerns was giving her a headache. Too many hotel employees were walking around for her comfort, and out of deference to Sergey she wasn't armed.

"Sergey, it has been a long time."

He rose as she joined him at the corner table. "Four years. You are looking as beautiful as always, Darcy." He kissed one cheek and then the other, the compliment sincere, his smile welcoming.

In his sixties now, he wore the years in his face and eyes. The man looked more like a thug than a gentleman, even in the elegant suit. But looks had never conveyed the real picture. She respected this man, and her partner Gabriel owed him his life.

She answered his smile with one of her own. "Thank you for the champagne." Neither would drink tonight but appearances mattered.

"The least I could offer as an apology for my delay." He held her chair for her. "You should not have waited for me to arrive." He was genuinely bothered that she had. Staying more than a few moments past an agreed-upon time was a cardinal mistake of tradecraft, and he had always been one of the teachers who understood spies lived to be old spies because they followed the rules.

"A risk, but a calculated one. One well worth it for a friend. Gabriel sends his regards."

"Has he forgiven me yet?"

She tilted her head, considering. "Within limits. He wouldn't be so quick to join you at a restaurant." Sergey had arranged to give Gabe food poisoning so he would miss covering a meeting in Sicily.

"You are surprised I asked only to see you."

"Yes."

"It is best," he replied. "Retirement looks like it agrees with you." He circled his index finger on his napkin as he lifted his glass with his other hand, holding her gaze.

The gesture signaled that he assumed they might have unwanted company listening in. His? Hers? She wouldn't put it past either agency. She hadn't seen anyone, and she knew he'd have chosen the table at random. She wasn't too worried about it, for at least spies doing their jobs were not likely to shoot her in the back. "I was about to say the same about you."

"I am a grandfather now. My granddaughter will be one year old next month."

She lifted the champagne flute in a toast. "Congratulations, my friend."

From his pocket he offered a picture. Darcy had seen photos of his family in his file, but this one of his daughter and granddaughter was recent. She studied it and then returned it with a smile.

Sergey's expression turned grave. He gestured toward the hotel gardens. "Let us walk a bit."

With a nod she rose to join him, surprised at the speed he chose to get down to business but also relieved to be away from the flow of hotel staff through the restaurant. Meetings with Sergey had a rhythm, and the time spent reestablishing the relationship was rarely shortened. They strolled through the hotel gardens and eventually back around to the deserted pool area. The deep end of the pool afforded privacy and he paused there.

"How may I help you, Sergey?"

"I have been asked to convey a message to your director."

"I can have it in his hands within hours." A military flight at Eglin Air Force Base was waiting to take her back to Washington, D.C., tonight.

He removed an envelope from his inside pocket.

Darcy slid her thumbnail across the edge of the back cover of her book, opening a hidden slot. The note slid inside. She resealed the edge with a firm touch. "Would you like me to bring you a reply?"

"None should be needed. But if you do need to get in touch, a request sent through the embassy will reach me."

The message in hand, Darcy felt an urgency to be on her way but also reluctance. It might be years before she saw him again. "How is Kendra?" she asked, turning to look back as she heard footsteps.

"My wife is not well." She glanced back at him concerned at the unexpected words and saw Sergey's hand come out from his jacket. "I am sorry, Darcy."

She caught a glint of a blade and reacted to the threat before she understood it, her weight shifting back and her arm swinging the portfolio and book in a sweeping arc to strike it away. The knife caught her. She got out of the way the only way she could. She moved back and was falling. Water closed over her.

# Two

Sam had his shoes off and was shaking out sand from his walk on the beach when he heard the splash. Someone was using the hotel pool. He waited for the laughter of guests to match the late night dunking or for the sound of solitary strokes as someone began swimming. The silence had him slipping on his shoes and changing destinations. With the number of children at the reception, one could have slipped away from a parent and gotten too near the pool.

The pool area was empty. No one was swimming and there was only sloshing water to confirm what he had heard. Then he realized the water at the deep end was stirring. A woman's hand and then Darcy's head appeared, water streaming from her hair and face.

What the . . . He shoved aside chairs in his way and knelt at the poolside to offer her a hand. He liked water, spent most of his life working in it, but one glance told him this lady did not know how to swim. "Darcy, give me your hand." She was almost back to the side of the pool. "What happened? Did you lose your footing?"

And then he saw the cloud growing in the water, shadowing the shimmering underwater light. He lunged, his hands shooting down into the water to close like a vice around her arms. "You're bleeding."

He hauled her out, water streaming from her dress drenching him. She was coughing up water, doubling up on him even as he tried to assess where she had been hurt. He needed better light. The blood was staining the left side of her dress, and he could feel her chest heaving as she tried to expel the inhaled water. Sam tried to move her hand away and she caught him with a backhand across the face, her ring cutting his cheek. "Easy! It's Sam." He pushed back the wet hair blocking her vision, desperate to get her to let him help. Holding her was like trying to grip a live wire — every muscle in her body was fighting his hold.

"Sorry. Stop him," she gasped. Her shoulder dug into his ribs as she clamped her hand against her side then groaned as she struggled to sit up. He looked around again, but for the moment they were alone.

"I will. Let me see." Just as soon as he figured out she wasn't going to bleed to death, he was going after the guy who did this with a fury. Hurting women — The creep needed to meet a SEAL in a dark alley somewhere. Sam closed his hand around her wrist, and Darcy reluctantly let him move her hand. His first instinct had been a gunshot, but this was a knife wound. "What happened?"

"It's not as bad as it looks. He missed."

His gaze shot to hers. "Someone want you dead, Darcy?"

She blinked at him, and the cloud of pain in her eyes crystallized. "Actually — yes. I think the bounty is now a million pounds sterling."

Darcy forced herself to her feet, struggling against the wet fabric of her ruined dress, holding onto Sam's shoulder to keep her balance. *Oh, dear Lord, he tried to kill me.* The shakes were starting. She forced herself not to double up again but to look around for trouble. Sergey had come close to putting that blade between her ribs and into her heart. She was sweating despite the dunking in the pool. This was awful.

*Breathe deep. Think.* She tried, and both hurt to do. She turned her hand away from the cut to look at it. She was going to make Sergey's life miserable. If she had to track him down to the ends of the earth, she would make sure he knew how stupid it was to try to kill her and miss. He'd retired from the job with honor. Why he would destroy decades of reputation in one fool-hardy act made no sense, but at the moment, actions spoke louder than what she thought she knew about him.

"Let's get you to a doctor."

"I'll live," she muttered, ignoring Sam. The gash hurt something fierce, but it was shallow. She leaned down and snagged the portfolio. The leather was sliced down to the thin sheet of steel inside the front cover. It had taken the brunt of the knife strike and kept her alive just as it was designed to do. She slid her finger into the torn leather, disgusted. The blade must have been several inches long.

Where were the book and the message? She'd lay odds it was a blank piece of paper inside the envelope, but she had to know. She'd flung her arm up and to the left and her book would have gone . . . She turned on her bare heel. Wonderful. She walked around the pool and waded into the shallow end to retrieve the book that had landed on the second step. Water streamed from it, the pages already curling and warped. "Sam, if he thinks I'm dead, I'd rather leave it that way." She struggled out of the water. "Forget what you saw. I'm gone." He cut her off and she rocked back on her heels at the abruptness of it.

"Not so fast. What's going on?" The man had planted his feet and the steel in his voice told her he wasn't moving.

She didn't have time for this. He was a SEAL. Every one she had met through the years was inevitably as stubborn as a rock. The problem would be getting him to walk away from the mess now that he'd become part of it. "Fine, then let's go."

He took one step back to let her pass. "Are you a cop?"

She'd give him points for a great question. She wished she could say yes. "No. It would be much simpler if I were. Sergey, the man I was waiting for, is Russian, sixties, gray hair, wearing a tux, and built like a tank. Let's try not to meet up with him."

Sam steadied her with a hand under her elbow as she clipped the edge of a table. "Can you walk without shoes?"

His voice had smoothed out. She knew a shift-to-work mode when she saw it. She had just as much latitude to say what was going to happen as he decided to give her before he'd step in and do what he thought best. She patted his arm and used the movement to slip from his grip. "I hate shoes; they can stay at the bottom of the pool. I want to get away from this hotel."

He led her past the pool to the stairs going down to the beach. "Here." Sam swung his jacket around her. Darcy appreciated the kindness. She was starting to shiver. Pebbles cut into the bottom of her feet and ripped her nylons, yet one more thing she marked up against Sergey's account. She left the walkway for the softer feel of the sand and headed east.

"My car is in that east parking lot. Let's head that way and get you to the hospital."

"Not yet. I know where I'm heading." Time was critical now and she had a plan to execute. She was grateful Sam didn't push harder.

Why had Sergey done it? Spies didn't kill spies. It was an unspoken agreement between nations that insured their most hard-won assets were not lost on both sides. By violating it, Sergey risked sweeping payback. The CIA could drop names in dozens of countries, and Russian operatives would be swept in by governments who didn't have Miranda rights. Sergey had spent a lifetime building up his agency; it didn't make sense that he'd risk everything in one rash act.

The betrayal was worse than the injury. She had thought him a man of honor, but he had proven himself a man of opportunity. Had he done it for the million pounds sterling? It just didn't fit. And he had taken a huge risk to attempt the hit in the States. He had to know the Agency would track him down and bring him in no matter where in the world he hid. What was she missing? She'd been out of the field too long. She should at least have an idea, but there was just the unexpectedness of an attempt to kill her by a man she respected. Did he hate her that much? What had she ever done to inspire that? She angled up the beach to the hotel.

"Sam, when that cougar bit you, did you kill it?"

He didn't pause his scan of the area to look at her. "Since it wasn't clear who would win the fight, we sort of agreed to call it a draw."

"He stalked off?"

Sam glanced over. He gently wiped water off her face. "I suppose I didn't taste so good."

She would have to trust him. She didn't have many options. She needed to find

Sergey, and that wasn't going to be simple. He could have flown in, driven, come in by boat. She could guarantee it hadn't been under his own name. If she called in the FBI, they would make a fuss about not being informed ahead of time about the meeting, and it would take too many meetings to arrange to get people in the field. It would take the CIA at least three hours to get enough people here. "Do you have friends at the reception who might be able to help me do a quiet canvass of the area?"

"At least half a dozen guys. Who put the bounty on your head?"

"It's a long story."

"Try the CliffsNotes version. It seems relevant."

It wasn't public knowledge but it wasn't classified either. "I hunted down Ramon Santigo over thirty-nine months and ran him to ground in Paraguay. He's facing fifteen counts of murder. His family doesn't like me." Ramon had killed two agents; she didn't regret a moment of that hunt. She had been a bit insulted at the first hundred-thousand bounty on her head, but it had grown steadily to a million pounds sterling. If someone didn't collect it soon, it would probably go up again.

"Are you DEA?"

Another good question. Darcy just shook her head rather than lie. He'd run through all the law enforcement agencies before long, and she'd have to come up with something. She pointed out the small hotel where she had another room. She led the way to a side entrance, pausing to reach around the air-conditioning unit for the card key placed there.

"First room on the left," she directed. She let Sam open the door. A Do Not Disturb sign was on the doorknob. She had chosen the room for speed of access in and out. He turned on the lights and led the way inside, looking around.

She'd hoped not to have to use this room, but on the chance she might, she put down a credit card for a nice room. The curtains were closed. On the long dresser were two grocery sacks and a still-packed suitcase. She had come prepared to hole up here for seventy-two hours if needed.

She crossed to the room safe and spun the combination, retrieving the phone inside. "There's a medical kit in the suitcase." She dialed and waited for the security scrambling at both ends to synchronize the call.

Sam opened the suitcase and raised an

eyebrow as he held up a comic book by two fingers. She smiled at him.

"Gabriel Arneau please."

Sam found the medical kit and opened it on the bed. He tore open two of the large sterile bandage packets and found tape.

"Darcy, where have you been? I've been pacing!"

The punch of her partner's words was enough to cost her some of her hearing. "Sergey was late." She sucked in her breath as her dress caught on the cut. "Gabe, here, talk to Sam. I'm bleeding all over the carpet. I need to change."

"What do you mean you're — ?"

She tossed the phone toward Sam and walked into the bathroom, taking the bandages and the top layer of clothes from the suitcase with her.

"Thanks a lot, Darcy," Sam called after her. "Who's this?"

Darcy left them to their conversation. Sam and Gabriel could sort it out.

She closed the bathroom door behind her and turned on the heat lamp above to quickly warm the room. The dress was ruined. She eased it off, blinking away tears. She held her breath as she studied the cut across her ribs, cleaned it, and firmly taped down the bandages. So much for a peaceful return to the field. She leaned against the counter when she was done, gripping the marble edge. Events were catching up with her.

*Lord, thanks for saving my life.* She wanted to go to heaven someday, but not tonight. She wiped her eyes and had the odd desire to laugh at the unexpected relief she felt. She'd been anticipating someone trying to kill her for so long that she was almost grateful that there was something real to finally deal with.

*The last thing I feel like doing is forgiving Sergey, but I'll give You the benefit of the doubt that he's redeemable. Forgive him, Lord, and let him live long enough to realize that he was wrong. I want at least an apology for this when he comes to his senses.*

She didn't want to love her enemies and pray for what was best for them, but she'd do it because God told her to, because she also had a healthy sense of self-interest. If Sergey found God, he wouldn't try to kill her again.

She felt sorry for Sergey. He'd just insured that every morning she was going to pray for him, and every afternoon she was going to hunt him down with every bit of skill she had in order to bring him to justice. Fair was fair. He'd started this. She had been minding her own business, happily retired . . . Well, maybe a touch bored but retired. Now she had a problem to solve. She hadn't earned that Intelligence Star for being easy to shake off.

She reached for a loose button-down shirt. She bypassed jeans for sweats. How was she going to explain this to her doctor when she got home? Shelton was a small town. And since the doctor was married to her sister, there wasn't much chance of keeping this hidden.

A brisk knock on the door interrupted her. "Darcy, your partner is not happy talking with me."

Gabe had been pacing . . . Knowing how difficult physically it was for him to do that these days, she had a feeling Sam was understating things considerably. "Just a minute." She slid on her watch and transferred the cash from the inside pocket of her cosmetic bag to her shirt pocket. She needed to move hotels again later tonight. It was one thing to hide from random trouble, another to hide from another spy. This room would be good for a while, but someone at the hotel would recognize her picture if Sergey started really searching for her.

She walked out of the bathroom carrying

her things and looked with longing at the bed. The adrenaline was fading and being replaced by a pounding headache. She'd love to close her eyes for a few minutes. She set down the wet clothes on a towel and took the phone from Sam. "I'm back. I'll live."

"Darcy, get out of there, get to ground."

The order caught her off guard. This bolt-hole was already a good two or three layers buried in security. "Why?"

"You weren't the only attempted hit tonight. We lost Kevin Wallace and Benjamin Rice."

Darcy threw her brush against the wall. "Who else?" she demanded, quivering at the names of two agents she knew.

"We've got five who haven't reported in yet," Gabe said grimly. "Get out of there."

She looked at the locked door wondering how someone might try to come through it. "Who's behind the hits?" She took a seat on the side of the bed, trying to figure out what immediate threat she was dealing with.

"We're still guessing; both happened in Europe. Give me time to sort out the truth from first reports. I'll have a much better idea in a few hours. I'm sorry, Dar. I should have never let you go on your own."

"Don't, Gabriel," she whispered, knowing how hard her partner would be taking this turn of events. "I'll get moving." She glanced at Sam, leaning against the wall with his arms crossed, watching her. How would she convince him to stay here when she left?

"I'm coming with you," Sam said bluntly without being asked. He didn't need the uniform to make crystal clear she wouldn't be changing that decision.

Gabe heard him. "Don't argue with him, Darcy. He offered, insisted actually, and I don't want you traveling alone. The Department of Defense liaison confirmed his ID and clearances. They'll clear it with his CINC."

She closed her eyes. All branches of the Special Operations worked for the military central command headquartered in Tampa, Florida, and his commander-in-chief there would tell Sam he was going with her. She wished someone had asked her, but she knew better than to waste energy on it. "That simplifies things. What about the hunt for Sergey?"

"Tonight was too well planned and coordinated. He's gone. I can start the search for his travel plans from here. Let's get you out of there first. I need as close to a verbatim record of what Sergey said as you can provide."

"I'll get on the transcript. Let me give you a call from the plane."

She hung up the phone. *Not this. Those men have families.* There would be two more stars added to the memorial wall at headquarters and two new names written in the Book of Honor. She'd hoped not to see another one added during her lifetime. The sadness overwhelmed the anger.

"I'm sorry about your friends."

She looked up. She'd nearly hit Sam with the hairbrush. She had a feeling he'd probably ducked more lethal things. She sighed and tossed the phone on the bed. "It hurts. I knew them from work. Had they been personal friends, I probably would have thrown the phone."

"I know how to duck." Sam rested his hand on her shoulder and squeezed softly. "A spook, huh?"

She was startled by his calm reaction. She'd expected many things, but not a man who took in what he saw, adjusted to new facts, and gently teased her about being a spy. "I really am retired." She hesitated and then lifted a hand to tentatively touch the cut on his cheek. It was small but deep. "Sorry about that." She had a bad habit of hitting the good guys in her life.

"Your reflexes are still pretty decent."

He was definitely teasing her. She blinked. The humor in his voice belied the seriousness in his eyes. This was a SEAL who had been in combat. She had to start thinking, and if humor got her out of this stuck place the better off and safer they were both going to be. If a civilian had been trying to help her, she'd be in a real bind right now.

*I owe you, Sam.* She closed her eyes for a moment and focused her thoughts. She had to get back to Washington, had to figure out who was behind this. Two men dead. Someone was starting a spy war tonight, and she'd somehow made the list. Because she was retired she was considered reachable? Because she knew something?

Sam's hand rubbed the inside of her wrist. "What's next?"

She focused her attention back on him. "I need to leave." She bent over to put on her tennis shoes and stopped as the pain radiated through her chest.

Sam stopped her and reached for the shoes. "I'll do them for you." He knelt and lifted a bare foot, slipped on a sock and then her shoe. "Where do you go from here?"

"Washington, D.C. I really appreciate your offer to help, but you don't know me; you don't know what you're getting into." Darcy was torn between welcoming the help and cautioning him on the reality. Trouble was coming her way in a huge wave.

"You've got a nice smile and you read Mickey Mouse comic books. What's not to like?"

"It's a gift for a friend who wanted to come to Disney World with me."

"Sounds like an interesting friend." Sam neatly tied her shoes and then sat back on his heels. "I'm partial to trouble and you've got some. I'll tag along for a while." He tugged at the sleeve of her shirt. "I'm sorry about your dress."

"So am I. I went to New York to buy that dress. It was gorgeous."

"Indeed it was. I certainly appreciated it."

"Thanks, Sam." He was trying to help her get her equilibrium back. A SEAL for a decade, he'd been around the world long enough to take care of himself. She'd have to trust that. She pointed to the table at the water-soaked book she'd carried back with her. "Can you reach that? Let me see what Sergey passed on."

He handed it to her.

"Got a pocketknife?"

Sam pulled one from his pocket. She used the knife to slice open the safety pocket. She removed the envelope and pulled out a single sheet of paper. The ink on the note was running.

*It was necessary.*

It wasn't an apology or an excuse but an explanation. Whatever Sergey's mission, she'd been part of the groundwork. The implication that killing her had been worth the price . . . What was coming?

She looked up at Sam.

Sergey had failed. It was time to figure out why he had tried in the first place.

# Three

September 9
Sunday, 10:05 p.m.
Destin, Florida

Sam rapidly packed his belongings in his hotel room. How could he have not realized there was something else going on tonight? He got tugged in by a spy and used for cover, had been sitting there during the arrival of her contact, and he hadn't had a clue. *That's what you get for assuming nothing ever happens stateside.* He could have at least insured he got a glimpse of the man she was meeting. He stuffed extra socks in the corner of the bag. Never go anywhere without extra socks.

He was getting mad now that he had the luxury of feeling the emotions. Someone had tried to kill Darcy, had reached out and killed two others tonight. He could have pulled a floating body from that pool rather than just a shaken and angry lady. It was hard to get rid of the image of Darcy dead, those blue eyes lifeless.

He hoped he eventually got to meet the man Darcy called her partner. What had Gabriel been thinking letting her come to this meeting alone? She hadn't been prepared for what happened tonight, and Sam wasn't inclined to trust that same bureaucracy with her safety now.

He packed while Bear worked the phone arranging secure transportation from the hotel and confirming details with Eglin Air Base for the flight to D.C. At least one thing had been arranged right; the Air Force guys could move her at a good clip. SEALs were in the hotel lobby keeping an eye out for Sergey, and a medic from his team stayed with Darcy. Sam had managed to pull together reasonable manpower in an hour. What he was going to tell the guys later he wasn't sure, but like the buddies they were, they had acted and not asked questions he couldn't answer.

"How are you set for cash?" Bear asked.

Sam checked his billfold. "I'm good."

"When I asked if you'd found company, this wasn't exactly what I had in mind."

Sam picked up his bag and smiled at his boss. "She looked like a civilian." It wasn't the first time he'd found himself caught up in someone else's problem, but this was by far the most interesting. He was giving up the rest of his leave to escort Darcy, but he figured it would make for a memorable vacation.

"I'll expect you back in seventy-two hours. If it's longer than that, I'll send out search parties. The Agency has a habit of keeping their assets. And if you need backup, you've got my number."

"I appreciate it."

"Stay safe, Chief."

"That's the plan. I'll see you, boss."

Sam wasn't accustomed to a bodyguard role, but he understood what it meant to go up against a waiting enemy. He was one of two snipers on his squad, his specialty doing reconnaissance, working ahead of the others. He'd get Darcy safely to D.C. and see what developed from there.

The Air Force provided a small passenger jet for the flight. Darcy took advantage of the space to spread out her notes and get comfortable. Sam had somehow arranged for several full-size pillows to be available, and she wanted to hug him for that. They were making this trip bearable. The painkillers the base doctor had given her after stitching the cut were wearing off. They were somewhere over Georgia when

Darcy realized they were flying through a light rain.

She glanced over at Sam, stretched out in a seat across the aisle, his attention on a paperback he'd tugged from the side pocket of his luggage, a cup of coffee in the cup holder. A soldier. It had been subtle, but she'd seen the transformation in his demeanor as they stepped onto the military base where security was better. He was comfortable in military terrain, in the same way she was comfortable walking into the National Security Agency complex or the Central Intelligence Agency headquarters.

He hadn't mentioned what his role was on the SEAL team, just that he was a member. She did know that chief petty officer was an enlisted ranking instead of an officer track. Darcy had a feeling that position in the ranks was by choice. Sam would want to be in the middle of the action. She'd always been partial to the front lines too. Just not this close.

SEALs were known as the quiet professionals. Good enough at what they did they didn't have to tell someone they were good. Their actions spoke for them. How was she going to say thanks when this was over? She instinctively understood part of

Sam's character. He volunteered for a job where he gave up many personal liberties — when and where he worked, even his own life — in order to preserve the liberties of others. His age told her he was career Navy, and that answered a lot of questions about his priorities. And the SEAL trident pin he wore — with its eagle representing air, Revolutionary War pistol for land, and Neptune's trident for sea, all fit across the Navy's anchor — above everything else he'd be a guy you could depend on to do what he said. Honor would be a code he lived by.

He looked up, sensing her observation. He set his book against his knee. She felt herself blush and wished she could tamp down that reaction.

"You should do that more often," he commented.

"What?"

"Look."

She refused to turn away even as she struggled to contain a smile. "What am I supposed to be seeing?"

He picked up his book again and cast one final glance in her direction. "My mom would like you."

Darcy laughed. She had missed this. She'd never had the freedom overseas to totally relax even in social occasions, as it was never quite certain who she could really trust outside of a small circle of people from the Agency.

She reached up and adjusted the light over her head. She bet she would enjoy meeting his mom. She turned her attention back to work.

The pages of the legal pad resting against her knee were soft lavender instead of the normal canary yellow. The color provided good contrast for black ink, making it easier to read her notes later, and told her at a glance the material needed to be stored in the safe. The notes themselves were classified. She had completed a conversation transcript as best as she could recreate it and was working now on her observations.

Sergey is retired; therefore this isn't Russian sponsored, but using Russian assets? The Russian Mafia might be able to exert the kind of pressure to push Sergey into something like this.

Sergey's apology just before he pulled the knife is the strongest indication that it had been arranged by someone else and was not his decision.

If Ramon Santigo's family is behind

this hit, how did they get to Sergey? And if it were Santigo's family, was it a coincidence the attempt happened the same evening two agents were killed?

Why did Sergey make a point of showing me the picture of his daughter and granddaughter? He does nothing without thinking it through beforehand. Were they threatened?

Why was he late to the meeting?

She paused and stared at the page as distress rolled over her. "He tried to save my life," she whispered, stunned.

Sam looked up from his book. "What?"

"Sergey was late. He's never late. He was trying to save my life."

Sam lowered the book. "He would have expected you to leave before the meeting."

"Yes. I put him in an untenable position by staying." She winced as she realized something else. "Sergey circled his finger to warn me he thought others were watching. If I had read the situation better, I would've understood the risk better."

What was coming? She racked her memory for the significance of September 9, but nothing obvious came to mind. They needed to reconstruct Sergey's movements over the last six months and figure out whom Sergey had seen and how he had entered the U.S. They had to get ahead of this intelligence curve. Something she knew or had done was critical to this.

She tossed the notepad aside. "I hate days like this." She had a feeling Sam handled being under threat of a bullet better than she did.

"Why don't you close your eyes and get some sleep?"

"I should." There were certain times in life where God's blessing was very clear. Sam being there to help her tonight was one of them. She picked up one of the pillows that had fallen and settled it behind her. "I'm too old for this job. I should have stayed retired."

He studied her for a moment then pitched a nickel toward his empty coffee cup. "You don't retire in your business or in mine. You just start drawing a smaller paycheck. We make enemies. If you're good in your job, you make a lot of them."

"A reverse incentive for being the best." She grinned at him, realizing the nickels were hitting the center of the cup without his looking at what he was doing. "I wish someone had warned me sooner."

He leaned over and picked up the corner of his jacket on the side seat. He tugged a small medallion from the inside pocket and tossed it in her lap. "The best should be rewarded. You earned it tonight."

She picked up a medallion of a wolf head. "It's pretty."

"They were giving them out at the wedding because Wolf is Tom's call sign. So how long have you been in the spy business?"

"I started in the field two years and two days before the Berlin Wall came down."

"I'd say you don't look old enough to be a cold war player, but instead I'll compliment you on aging very gracefully. You've seen some history."

"Some." The memories were rich and deep, but it was a conversation for another day and time. "What about you, Sam? How do you like being a SEAL?"

"I love the life. I entered the Navy right out of high school and applied to the SEALs as soon as I could. It sure beats being landlocked in a small town in South Dakota."

Her smile widened as he spoke.

"What?"

She held back her amusement. "Nothing." North Dakota was as close to heaven as she'd found, but she wouldn't hold it against him for loving the sea. "I'm going to catch that sleep. Wake me when we're fifteen minutes out?"

"Sure."

She clicked off the light and closed her eyes, holding the medallion in her fist. If she had seen some interesting history, she was willing to bet Sam had probably made some of that history in classified missions not to be revealed for half a century. Life had become complicated enough lately without diving headlong into the start of a new relationship, as attractive as that thought may be. It was better to close her eyes and sleep.

The day wasn't supposed to end like this. She should have flown to Washington and dropped off Sergey's message and then headed back to North Dakota.

It was going to hurt bringing this home and causing her sister more worry. *Lord, being needed isn't worth this, not when it'll touch my family.*

Sam interrupted her thoughts. "What are you thinking about that has you frowning?"

"Home."

"That's normally a good thought."

"I'm regretting the coming explanations."

"Start with 'I'm okay,' " he said. "They'll eventually forgive the rest. Sleep, Darcy.

You need the rest. And I'm not dozing off until you do."

She smiled. "Well when you put it that way . . ."

Darcy slept expecting trouble. Sam watched her hand twitch as the noise of the engines changed tempo. She had a blown mission, someone trying to kill her on U.S. soil, and she had to improvise her plans. Darcy was pretty good at thinking on her feet for a retired spy.

He'd always prayed to meet an interesting woman. He didn't want to spend forever alone, but finding someone who could handle his profession, love of travel, and deal with the danger inherent in his job was tough. Darcy St. James qualified. Did she live in the D.C. area or elsewhere now that she was retired? He'd have to find out. Was Darcy even her real name? He leaned over and touched her shoulder. She was dreaming; he could see it in the movement of her eyes. "We're here."

She jerked as she woke. "Sorry, I burnt the eggs," she murmured.

He laughed softly. "Just a dream."

"More like a bad memory. I got distracted this morning." She stifled a yawn as she sat up.

"You'll crash when this day finally ends."

"That's an understatement." Darcy tightened her seat belt and gathered together her things.

The plane descended and settled onto a runway. It taxied to a far hangar. Sam picked up his bag and Darcy's and led the way down the stairs. She gestured to the car Gabriel had arranged to have waiting in the secure lot. She got the keys from the lockbox and handed them to Sam.

"I need to make one quick stop, and then we'll head to headquarters. Sorry for the late night, but they'll need to debrief you and Gabriel needs my notes." She circled around the passenger side as she pulled out her phone. "Take a right at the light, cross the Potomac River, and head north on Wisconsin Avenue. We'll miss the traffic, such as it is."

He started the car. "What's the first quick stop?"

"My place."

Sam shot her a glance, but her attention was already focused on her call to her partner to let him know they were in town. This would be an interesting visit.

# Four

September 9
Sunday, 11:50 p.m.
Bethesda, Maryland

Sam paid attention to the neighborhood, memorizing the directions on the off chance he'd have the opportunity to pay Darcy a social call someday. The apartment complex she directed him to was unusual. There was a guard and a raised gate at the entrance, and the buildings along streets named Birch, Oak, Willow, and Pine were set farther apart than he would have expected.

"Take the second street, Willow, to the first building on the left. Pull in at the first garage and hold up the badge to the card key reader by the mailbox to raise the garage door."

"Interesting security."

"I'd prefer not to have a bomb in the trunk of my car on the drive to work. The

Agency is a bit paranoid about things like that."

"The government owns this property?"

"No, it's privately owned, but most who live here do work for the government. Some work at the Agency, some are Foggy Bottom experts — that's the State Department — and a few Pentagon short-tour officers. Basically people with heavy travel schedules, hence the security to protect often empty places."

The garage door rose, revealing two garbage cans against the east wall and shelves along the back wall that were bare except for four boxes neatly arranged and labeled. "Lived here long?" Sam asked.

"Twelve years."

"This is way too neat."

Darcy laughed and got out her keys. "Come on up. This won't take long."

Sam retrieved her bag from the trunk. Darcy paused and deactivated the alarm pad before unlocking the door between the garage and her apartment. Stairs immediately turned and went up. "The downstairs of the building is actually another apartment; mine is the entire second floor." She turned on lights to reveal spider plants reaching down from the open banister above to almost touch the handrail. "They grow faster than I can keep them repotted. Watch out for the roller skates."

He nearly tripped on them on the second step before he caught her warning.

Sam reached the top of the stairs. The living room was spacious with a sofa, two chairs, and bookshelves. An oval dining table and open counter led into a long kitchen along the back of the apartment. Darcy dumped her jacket on the sofa. "Make yourself at home." She headed down the hallway toward what must be the bedrooms and bath.

Sam slowly set down the suitcase as he looked around. Light blue carpet, deep blue-and-white fabric for the chairs and sofa, framed modern art on the walls, on the entertainment center with a TV and nice stereo equipment were shelves holding a matching series of progressively larger pottery pieces.

Legos making a half built castle were on the floor in front of the recliner. A stuffed dog peeked out behind the vase of daisies on the side table and a plush bear guarded the phone. Walt Disney videotapes were stacked beside classic Westerns. A child's finger-paint art was on the walls beside the expensive paintings. From the size of the hands, Sam would guess maybe a child about age five.

A man's hat was tossed on the dining room table and a pair of running shoes about size twelve were near the basket where newspapers, magazines, and mail were piled. The well-read magazines on the floor back toward the basket ran to cars and *Popular Mechanics*.

Darcy was married . . . she had a daughter.

Sam picked up Darcy's wedding picture from the end table. She looked happy and young. Her smile was stop-a-guy's-heart beautiful, focused entirely on the man beside her. The second framed photo on the table looked recent, maybe six months old. Her husband had their daughter wrapped up in his hunting jacket that reached almost to the child's feet, and they were together holding up a stringer that held ten good-sized bass. Sam could appreciate the need for a photo to document that catch.

She'd done nothing to warn him, and she couldn't have missed his interest in her. She'd deceived him deliberately. He set the picture frame down slowly. He didn't appreciate getting used.

He looked around the room again, absorbing the full impression and then sur-

72

prisingly found himself smiling and relaxing. This was what he would have expected for Darcy had he not known her real job. This place looked like her, and it felt comfortable. Right down to the spelling book resting on the last cushion of the sofa with a pencil stuck in it to hold the page. She was a woman who would live like this, with her life out in the open, rather than tuck it away in tidy corners.

Darcy walked back into the room carrying a small suitcase, having changed from casual clothes to a more formal red blouse and navy slacks. Power colors. They looked good on her, and as much a part of her personality as the elegance he had seen by the pool tonight.

"You need a kid's bike in the garage."

She lifted an eyebrow as she slipped in an earring.

"This illusion. It doesn't work without the kid's bike in the garage."

She blinked at him, and then a small smile appeared, just at the edges of her mouth. She walked into the kitchen. "You want something to drink before we leave?"

"As long as you don't offer me a juice box."

She poured them both tall glasses of lemonade from a pitcher on the top shelf of the refrigerator. The juice boxes on the second shelf were fruit punch.

She held out one of the glasses. "You're guessing."

"Am I?" He drank the lemonade, studying her, smiling just a little because he was enjoying the moment. "I could look closely at that patio door to your small second-story balcony where you probably keep a small grill and a closed lid box for the charcoal bag. And there will be little handprints on the glass at your daughter's height. The bathtub will have at least a few toys on the ledge and even the medicine cabinet will run to pediatric formulas of cough syrup.

"I bet your husband is the one who enjoys the neatness, and you're the one who clutters the kitchen drawer with coupons and carry-out menus. His razor items will be neatly aligned in the bathroom drawer, but there will be a few whisker hairs along the edge of the floor tiles where the broom wasn't 100 percent thorough. You could tell me all about him and your daughter, but you'll never make the sale."

He reached out and ran a finger down her arm, stopping at her wrist by the new watch she had put on to replace the one that had gotten wet. "If you had a daughter and a husband who loved to go fishing, Darcy, you would know how to swim."

She took one step back and then laughed. "You're good."

"After years training to see things, I sure would hope so." She wasn't married, she didn't have a little girl, but it was a masterful presentation. And at the moment he didn't want to explore why he was intensely relieved that this was an illusion. "You would be a jealous wife and mother. You wouldn't be doing the job you do if you had a husband and daughter waiting for you to come home. You'd want to be spending your time with them."

He'd pegged her, but he didn't want to rub it in, so he smiled and looked around the apartment. "The lack of a wedding ring was also noticed, although that could easily have been explained as a reality of your job so as not to put your family at risk. They're traveling tonight? Your mythical husband and daughter?"

"Her first chance to go with him on a business trip to the city, a day away from school for a father-and-daughter moment," she offered with a smile.

"Yes, it would be a good memory. When was the last time you were actually here?" Why did she even ask him to make this stop tonight, try the deception out on him? She probably had her reasons, but he wasn't nearly good enough to read a woman's mind. Especially not this woman's.

"Six months and seven days ago."

He looked back at her, startled by the time period. He slid his hands in his back pockets, intrigued. "You're what we would call *rated* in my business — very good at what you do that this level of cover would be maintained for such a spur-of-the-moment need."

She nodded at the compliment. "I am very good at what I do but also truly retired. We need to go."

He put his glass in the sink beside hers. "Mention to the woman who comes in to make fresh lemonade every week that she earned her pay."

"I'll do that." She picked up the small suitcase she'd packed.

He shut off the lights behind them as they walked down to the garage. "Is this what you call a bolt-hole?"

She reset the security alarm. "The hotel was a bolt-hole, designed to be a safe place to disappear. This is more of a cover blind, a place to list as my residence that will hold up to the basic levels of a background check. And it is home, as much as any place on the East Coast is. Of course the cover blind in Paris is a bit more interesting." She put her suitcase in the backseat and slipped into the passenger seat. "You'll need to take a left at the light."

"That was your territory? Europe?"

"For the majority of my years in the Agency."

He followed her directions out of Bethesda toward McLean, Virginia.

"Would you mind one more stop?" Darcy asked. "The corner deli up ahead. I need good coffee for the upcoming hours, and I probably ought to drive the last mile to headquarters as security will pitch a fit with you. I don't suppose you're carrying three kinds of photo id and your passport?"

He laughed. "I've got my charm."

"That and waking up the Department of Defense liaison officer ought to do it."

He tossed over his wallet. "There's probably a Navy ID in there somewhere."


September 10
Monday, 12:24 a.m.
Central Intelligence Agency / Langley, Virginia

Traffic circled around the I-495 Capital Beltway to the George Washington Memorial Parkway in Virginia, and a few cars took the exit marked with a small brown sign to the George Bush Center for Intelligence CIA/FHWA. The night shift was already here, but those who worked the European desks often preferred to work Europe day hours and were trickling in.

Darcy found her two IDs as she reached the security gate. She lowered the driver's door window and handed over her ids and Sam's Navy photo ID. She endured the flashlight in her face, then the beam moved to travel around the interior of her car and stopped on Sam. Darcy blinked away the spots in her vision and reached for the coffee mug in the cup holder. "DIA will have called down clearance for Sam." The security checks would take a few minutes.

"That stuff will kill you."

The voice helped her place who was on duty tonight. Dressed in black, walking in the dark, he'd been a man with a flashlight. Darcy blew on the coffee to cool it. "Not in the next five minutes. So far no one has tried to tamper with the coffee bean shipments."

"They do, and this will be a nation of sleepy, surly people. Nice to have you back, Dar."

He stepped into the security booth to

check her ID against the clearance sheet.

The bomb-sniffing dog jumped up to put two paws on the open window. Darcy bobbled her coffee. The German shepherd smelled the cinnamon roll she'd picked up in a moment of weakness at the deli counter. "Henry, you know as a rule I don't share." Her fingers were sticky with melted sugar, but she ignored the resulting mess to rub her hand under the dog's muzzle. "You're cute and you know it." They were buddies even after two years of absence. Her noon jog had her passing his kennel, and he was often allowed out to run with her.

"Down."

Henry obeyed his handler.

"You're clear, Dar. And your friend has an admiral vouching for him so I suppose we'll let him pass. An escort will be waiting at the front door with his visitor's badge."

"Thanks, Kevin." She accepted back the IDs, surprised at the easy treatment. She pulled into the complex and glanced at Sam as she handed him back his ID. "Your security clearance must be pretty high to get you off so lightly on the checks."

Sam lifted his ID and blew off a thin film of powder. "Probably higher than yours," he offered, amused.

"Sorry. I should have warned you they'd lift your prints."

"Don't be. I'm just amazed the Department of Defense agreed to send over mine for comparison."

Darcy tucked her IDs in her pocket and hesitated. "Gabriel didn't make the decision that I go alone to the meeting." She felt it needed to be said. She knew when Sam met Gabe he'd be judging her partner based on what had happened.

Sam tucked his ID away. "He's your partner. He should have been there or had someone else there, if only in the background."

Darcy knew partnership had a unique implication for SEALs. If one went into danger, his partner and his team would be right beside him. "It's not so easy in my profession, Sam. The message Sergey sent through his embassy requested a one-on-one meeting with me. The diplomatic dance over such procedures is part of the foundation of how we function."

"What went wrong?"

"I wish I knew. For the same reason the director needed to honor the request, my safety should have been guaranteed. The fact it wasn't will ripple for years. A spy war may have started tonight and I don't understand why." She worried about the five agents who had yet to report in, afraid the body count would go higher. "Gabriel's a good man. This wasn't his fault."

"Relax. I promise to suspend judgment."

She was overprotective of her partner's reputation, but she didn't want these two men misreading each other. She had a feeling Sam might be in her future, and he had to get off on a good footing with Gabriel or she would find herself in a tough position — stuck between a man she'd trusted for years and someone new she wanted to trust. If forced to choose, she'd come down on Gabriel's side out of loyalty.

She parked beside her partner's car. "Welcome to the place we call Langley, the name itself the first of many myths you're about to walk into. There is no such place on current maps, as Langley no longer legally exists."

"Dar, you haven't seen myths until you start to talk to SEALs about our jobs." Sam got out of the car and scanned the campus. "Should be interesting."

Their escort took them to the third floor of the old headquarters building, and from there one of the four security guards for the floor took them the rest of the way to Gabriel's office in the code-word cleared hall.

The office hadn't changed since her days on the job. Darcy had a habit of beginning her day in Gabe's office, reading the overnight intercepts, debating the importance of news and adding color commentary. Gabe made this job survivable. He understood her often-scattered way of connecting information.

He had his wheelchair up to his desk, his head back, his arms crossed over his chest, apparently napping. She lifted a corner of the towel over his face. "Hi."

"You know, I'm really missing the days when I didn't have a partner. When was that, 1970? 80? When Carter was president? Or was it Ford? The good old days where my age came from fast living and beautiful women, not pacing because my partner got into a jam without my company and took her time calling me."

Darcy grinned down at him. She had really missed him. She'd promised Marla she would keep him alive, and she'd done it for years. Then he'd come home and gotten married. He had been hit by a car shortly thereafter and left needing crutches to walk. When the exhaustion was bad, he accepted the wheelchair to keep his mobility. He hadn't been home today, if his rumpled clothes and six o'clock shadow were any indication. Darcy kissed his frustrated forehead. "Sorry. I missed you too."

"Sam, hi. Join us," Gabriel ordered, his gaze never leaving Darcy as she settled on the couch. Sam took the second chair. "And, Dar, the blouse and earrings from our last Paris trip is a nice touch, but I'm not ready to be distracted even by a subtle reminder of our past successes. What happened to that street-fighter uppercut you were famous for?"

"Professional courtesy. I'd hate to let it be said that I hit first." She stuck her coffee mug in a holder she'd improvised two years ago from a cut off map tube that still sat on the shelf by the couch. "You look good, Gabriel. Marriage agrees with you."

"Marla is an angel, but don't change the subject. I want to be annoyed with you a while longer."

"You can't; I'm too cute," she countered, knowing he'd eventually forgive her for the fright she'd given him. Gabriel laughed. "The doctor swears I'll be fine," she promised. "Is Sam cleared for this discussion?"

"He's cleared higher than me."

They both looked at Sam. "NEST job," he said simply.

NEST as in Nuclear Energy Search Team. They recovered lost, stolen, or accidentally made live weapons. The nasty stuff that gave her nightmares, and Sam was perfectly correct to simplify — she did not want to know details.

She looked back at Gabe. "How bad has it been tonight?" she asked softly.

"The last five have reported in, limiting the losses to two."

"Still unbearable. How's the investigation coming?"

"It's a muddled mess of jurisdictions at the moment. It will be midmorning before we know much concrete. Let's leave those discussions for later, Dar. We'd just be speculating now. What happened tonight?"

She retrieved the soggy note from the portfolio carefully drying out between two Kleenexes. "Sergey left a note."

Gabe took it carefully. " *'It was necessary.'* Is it okay if I swear?"

"About my sentiments too," Darcy agreed. "Necessary for what?"

"Sergey's old school. Maybe he knew someone was going to grab and sweat you for names of contacts and he tried to kill you with kindness first so they couldn't grab you."

Darcy winced as did Sam. "Why don't you start off with the cheerful assumptions here."

"Okay, maybe he wants the bounty on your head," Gabe offered.

"If he was motivated by money, he would have taken the five million dollars I offered him years ago to work for us."

"True. Our Russian friends at the embassy were stunned when they heard about the attempted hit. Given the aggressiveness of their denials and outrage, they probably were in the dark. They've been somewhat helpful in the hunt to find him, although we'll probably find Sergey dead if they reach him first. I'm stumped because we don't have enough on the other two hits tonight to suggest a connection to you beyond the obvious one of timing."

"Any idea where Sergey went when he left the hotel pool area?" Darcy asked.

"Does the business Bluebird Charters ring a bell?"

"Never heard of them."

"Sergey apparently got on one of their boats near Miami."

"He gets seasick."

"I know. It's curious. A gate attendant at

the Tallahassee airport also swears Sergey caught the 11 p.m. United flight to Dallas. He also drove to Georgia, and/or got his picture taken at a twenty-four-hour deli buying red hair dye."

"He vanished."

"Basically. Most civilians want to be useful so they'll remember what didn't happen trying to help out."

"Sergey's good. If he doesn't want to be found, he won't be," Darcy commiserated.

"You have the transcript as best you re-member it?"

She handed him the lavender-colored pages of notes. "Have we been able to lo-cate Sergey's family?"

"The last good intel is from Spain but it's four months old. They haven't been watching so closely now that he's retired. The station chief is checking it out for me." Gabe handed her a stack of inter-cepts. "I pulled everything NSA had. There was one intriguing lead on where Sergey may have been recently."

She started reading the intercepted calls the National Security Agency collected from all over the world. "Guam? What do I know about Guam?"

"Not as much as you're going to."

"That's all I need, another island to add

to my mangled sense of geography." She turned pages. "Did you keep my reading music?"

"Darcy."

"You kept my goldfish." She tapped the glass, then leaned over to look closer at the fish tank. "No, those are smaller than my fish."

"I killed yours; I was hoping you wouldn't notice the switch."

She laughed. "Mine swam in tight circles like a spinning top when someone tapped on the glass. It took months to train them."

"You had too much time on your hands. Your tape is on the top shelf on the left, headphones too. Although how you can think with that noise is beyond me."

"Habit." She got up to get the cassette player.

"She's partial to opera," Gabriel explained to Sam. "Before I read this transcript, would you take me through what you saw tonight? Focus on the approximate times?"

Darcy stretched out on the couch with the headphones on, tuning out the guys' discussion as she read through several months' worth of scraps of information on Sergey and his family. Some were phone intercepts; some were sightings by intelligence services. Some of it was financial records. Gabriel had been able to find a large amount of information in the few hours he had been working the problem. What had Sergey been doing in Guam three months ago? Meeting someone?

The old clock on the wall chimed 3 a.m. Darcy closed the stack of reading material and rubbed her eyes. "I'm missing stuff. It's time I got some sleep."

Sam turned in his chair beside Gabe's desk to look back at her. "You've been quiet for so long I thought you were asleep."

She shifted the headphones and the sound of Verdi's *Rigoletto* at full volume filtered into the room. "I was thinking." She swung her feet to the floor. Gabe and Sam were still going strong. They'd hit it off after Gabe's comment about opera and turned their attention to analyzing the transcript. She'd known the two of them would be like two peas born in the same pod.

"Stay at Marla's place today, okay? Just for my peace of mind?" Gabe asked. "The Brits are there, but they'll make room for you."

Her partner's wife had kept her former

home as they had been in no hurry to sell it after the wedding. The security system there was world-class. Since it would let Darcy offer Sam more than just a hotel room for his stay, she nodded her thanks. "I appreciate that."

Sam got to his feet. "Thanks, Gabriel." He handed back the folder he'd been reading. "This was useful."

"Anytime."

Darcy noted the red stripe on the folder and the code word *Duplicity* in blue on the tab. Sam had been reading about Ramon Santigo. She looked at her partner but didn't ask why he had shared the information. She understood why he was worried about that rising bounty. She personally didn't think they would raise it much above the million pounds. The Santigo's weren't that generous.

If given a choice she wouldn't have shown Sam that information, for it would now factor into decisions he made. She didn't need more people in her life worried about her safety. "I'll call when I wake up this afternoon," she promised Gabe.

"I'll be near a phone."

They were escorted downstairs and Darcy waited as Sam signed out. They walked across the parking lot.

"Gabriel said the Brits are staying at Marla's place. Let's call first. Since they're with the SAS, it's probably best not to drive up to the house and knock in the middle of the night."

Sam held the car door for her. "Don't worry about it. Chances are they're old friends."

"Really?"

"Special Operations is a very small world."

She didn't ask; she knew the British and American Special Forces cross-trained to the point they could deploy to common missions around the world if necessary.

Darcy gave Sam directions. She had fifteen years of history with Gabriel, and she trusted him with her life. He'd given her a safe place to decompress. The options of a hotel or a return to North Dakota both had numerous problems until this was sorted out.

Darcy pointed out the house. The porch light was on. "They're expecting us." Sam pulled into the driveway. A tall man stepped outside moments later, a coat folded over his arm. He wore a black turtleneck and black jeans. Sam stepped from the car.

"Gabriel mentioned you were the escort.

Jolly good to see you again, Cougar."

"Hey, Brandon."

Darcy watched the two men greet each other; it was indeed a small world. "Darcy, my friend Brandon Scott. He's a good tactics man."

She offered her hand. "High praise."

"It's a pleasure, Darcy." Brandon settled the coat across her shoulders as luggage was gathered. "We made up the east guest room for you. And Gabriel mentioned I'm to ask what kind of bagels he's to bring over later."

"Oh, I'm getting spoiled already. Blueberry."

Darcy relaxed as she stepped inside the familiar home. She was glad Marla and Gabe hadn't yet had time to sell this house. It was spacious and comfortable and had a great view as it adjoined a stretch of forest preserve.

Sam came in behind her, carrying her suitcase and his bag. "Why don't you get settled while I fix us something to eat? You'll sleep better if you eat before you turn in."

She nodded and turned toward the bedroom. Darcy took her time unpacking the bag she had picked up at her place. She put her diary on the end table and opened her Bible to read a verse she had underlined. *"For God did not give us a spirit of timidity but a spirit of power and love and self-control."*

Time had always been one of the most overtaxed commodities in her life. She didn't always have time to look something up or have the luxury of taking documents with her. It had always been what she had memorized that kept her safe and alive. Applied to Scripture, it was a habit that transformed her life.

This verse from 2 Timothy was a powerful one. The phrase "a spirit of power of love and of self-control" — what a wonderful definition of balance. Take out any one of the three items and the other two led to extremes, but taken together they make greatness. The words remind Darcy of her sister. *Jesus, thanks for blessing me with great family.*

She left the rest of her suitcase packed.

Sam was in the kitchen building a monster of a sub sandwich. She slid onto a stool and held her hand up, her thumb and index finger an inch apart. "I'd like about this much of that feast."

"From the hot mustard end or plain?" Sam indicated options with the sharp knife he held.

"Hot."

He sliced her a generous definition of an inch and slid the plate over. "Brandon mentioned there's soup in the refrigerator. I can heat a bowl if you'd like something hot."

"This is fine. You build a nice meal." She broke off a piece of the crust. "Can you stay at least a day?" she asked, hoping she wouldn't have to say good-bye as soon as she awoke.

"I'll be here," Sam promised. "Bear gave me seventy-two hours before he'll send out search parties." She raised one eyebrow. "My boss," he explained.

She nodded and took a big bite of the sandwich. She found out quickly that she was hungry. Sam cut her another wedge without asking.

"I owe you a favor."

He considered her over his sandwich. "Probably a couple."

She laughed and leaned forward to rest her elbows on the counter. "Are you going to collect?"

"Eventually. Where do you actually live when you're not hiding out, Darcy St. James retired?"

She speared a black olive that fell from her sandwich with a toothpick. "North Dakota."

She saw him wince when he remembered his prior comment about being landlocked. "It's peaceful," she pointed out
helpfully. "And it snows a lot. I like snow."

"I remember the snow."

"Your parents own a farm in South Dakota, right?"

"More like land with a little bit of everything on it."

"It's beautiful country."

"My mother taught me never to disagree
with a lady when she's right."

"Then why don't you want to go back?"

"I've got two brothers who love the land.
It's enough." He leaned over and wiped a
spot of mustard from her chin. "You're
falling asleep sitting here. Why don't we
continue this later today."

She picked up a napkin as she slid off
the stool. "Where are you going to crash?"

"In this sprawling place? Don't worry
about it. I'll find somewhere comfortable.
Forget the alarm clock and sleep. I'll wake
you if there's news."

"Thanks. Pleasant dreams, Sam."

"It's been an interesting day. Night,
Darcy."

# Five

September 10
Monday, 5:30 p.m.
McLean, Virginia

Darcy paced Marla's home office as she read faxes, commenting as she read to her partner on the speakerphone. "It doesn't make sense, Gabe. Why kill a man who specialized in investigating money transfers?" Twenty hours after the Sunday night attack provided enough confirmed information to outline the scope of what had happened. She was grateful to have a few hours of sleep before she saw this data. It was worse than expected. She bit into her second blueberry bagel as she flipped pages to keep reading.

Kevin Wallace had been killed by a grenade attack as he drove from his home in Stockholm to the U.S. embassy. He worked an overseas desk for the Agency and had good relations with Sweden's bankers, but he'd been out of running agents in Russia for over a decade.

Benjamin Rice had been shot in the head by a sniper round when his car stopped at a streetlight in Munich. Ben's expertise was in transportation and immigration issues as the European Union moved toward open borders. He too was a cold war veteran with experience across Europe.

They were both well-planned hits, not random crimes that sometimes took out an agent. They had happened within thirty minutes of each other. "What is the connection to me? They're friends through our common interests in Europe, but I don't remember you or me working directly with them on a case."

"Neither do I."

She stopped by the blown-up map of Europe on the east wall of the office and looked at the locations. She didn't understand this.

"I see two options," Gabriel said. "First: the obvious threat to you. Maybe Ramon Santigo's family is moving operations into Europe — I can see expert investigators in money transfers and transportation both being threats to their smuggling operations. Sergey came to the U.S. to hit you in retirement. You weren't a minor addition to this list of targets."

"And the second option?"

"This is the opening salvo in something we don't yet understand, something large enough that killing agents is considered worth the fallout. All three of you were seasoned investigators. You have a history working in the eastern bloc countries, and you're familiar with the former intelligence officers of the KGB and the scientists who worked in their military labs. All of you had language skills."

"We're good utility players."

"Exactly."

"Are there any signs of a coming coup in one of the eastern bloc countries?"

"That's what I was wondering. I've got people out on the streets getting a feel for the undercurrents of gossip and rumor." They had both learned the practical value of street intelligence during the months before the Berlin wall came down when Washington hadn't believed what those in the countries were reporting back.

"Anything else on Sergey?" Darcy asked.

"Not much. Security tapes at the hotel, a lead on his car."

"I forgot to ask earlier. Who do you have heading the search in Florida?"

"Neil Fortam."

"He's good."

"You're better. Come back to work full time."

She leaned against the desk and straightened the paperclips. "I'm not as good as I used to be. Retirement dulls the skills."

"Hey, dahlin', you're alive. Our friends were on active duty and they aren't."

"I'll think about it. I do want Sergey found." She crossed over to the safe to store the faxes. "Have you had any sleep?"

"I crashed for a few hours on the couch. We've been getting another wave of threat warnings similar to what happened in July and were already pretty busy when this went ugly."

"Terrorist traffic?"

"Yes. We're working now to figure out if the two are linked. How were the bagels?"

"Wonderful."

"Can I do anything else for you? Want videos sent over or takeout?"

"I'm comfortable, Gabe. The guys are popping popcorn and watching a soccer game. They're good company. I'm planning to finish a book and watch some late-night comedy shows and then crash again."

"Call if you need anything; otherwise let's talk again in twelve hours."

"Sounds like a plan. Talk to you soon." She hung up the phone, then paused.

*Jesus, I know good men and women die in this profession, but it never gets easier to accept, to investigate. If You want me back at the office, I'll go.*

She had always accepted the fact that her life would be spent in service, to country, to God. She poured her life into tracking down Ramon Santigo for murdering two agents. If she was going back into that kind of grueling sweat equity and emotional commitment to tackle another investigation, she would need strength she didn't have right now. *Lord, just help me know if this is a battle for others or one You want me in the fight.*

She walked back through the house. Darcy found Sam along with Gabriel's four British guests settled around a large TV. Brandon had introduced her to the group over dinner. The four SAS officers were over for a seminar and to test out new gear NATO was buying for both U.S. and British Special Forces.

She didn't know much about parachute jumping, but these guys did. Sam talked with Brandon about jumping from twenty-five thousand feet as if it were just another day at the office. She did know that it was cold at twenty-five thousand feet. Cold and you didn't breathe without oxygen masks.

Sam called it fun. She'd hate to ask what he would call a challenge.

"Sam, can I have a minute?" She nodded toward outside.

He set aside the popcorn bowl and wiped his hands on his jeans. "Sure, Dar."

The man's muscles stretched out his faded jeans and were distracting her to no end.

She walked outside and took a seat on the steps, setting down her Bible and notebook. She'd find a place for devotions later. She needed the chance to pull back and think about the last couple days, get perspective before she returned to North Dakota. Sunset in a couple hours would be pretty from here.

Sam had been hanging out with the guys and giving her space; she should be pleased with that. She had work to do and didn't need the distraction. But she'd love to have him acting on that original interest in her and being exactly that distraction. She'd tossed him a few curves though. That cover blind married with a daughter story had thrown him enough she couldn't blame him for deciding that getting involved with a spy was something to think twice about. She'd like to talk more about that ring he wore and the emblem of the cross, find out where he went to church, learn more about him while she had the chance. She wanted to ask but was afraid it would come across as pushy.

Sam took a seat beside her. "How was your call?"

"So-so."

"Maybe tomorrow will be better news."

"Maybe." She studied him and decided it was best to start with the topic of work. There was no good way to do it but to just dive in and ask. "Would you tell me what it's like to be a sniper?"

He hesitated before answering. "What would you like to know?"

"Is it easy? Can someone relatively inexperienced be given the task?"

He shrugged. "Anyone can pick up a gun. It depends on how much you want to ensure success. A sniper who can take a mission and deliver every time . . . You're talking years of training."

"My friends who died last night — one in Sweden, one in Germany — both were well-thought-out hits."

He reached over and squeezed her hand. "I'm sorry."

It was all he said for a moment, and she appreciated the silence.

"There will be a trail to find," Sam said,

his voice matter-of-fact and practical. "It takes planning to watch a person and learn his habits, find a safe place to act, get the right weapon in. Escaping the area takes a lot of planning."

"We're after a team, not an individual."

"Maybe they have two people at each location if there was enough time to plan. Security is key for snipers; they work alone or just with a buddy most of the time."

Sergey had planned his attempt and his escape route. He set the place and time for their meeting. He could have come after her in North Dakota; although it would've been harder to fade into that community. Amy would have noticed. Florida had been a good choice.

"Will you stay another night?" She heard the slight plea in her voice and tamped it down. She'd disrupted this man's life enough. It would be better if her security concerns and what might be a growing relationship between them did not become so entwined that she let one pressure the other.

"I figured I'd head out tomorrow morning." He reached over and stopped her fingers from turning the ring on her right hand. "You don't need to worry about your safety here, Dar. Only a couple people know you are here, and the house has wonderful security." Sam tossed a pebble off the steps. "The Brits are staying another week. They'll make sure the place stays safe."

"I know."

"Can I call you?"

She looked over at him. "I was kind of hoping you would." What did she really want? A friend, a date, a distraction? She smiled. She'd take whatever she could get. "I'm going to be bored here."

"Not with the Brits around."

She laughed. "They do have a few stories to tell."

She relaxed and settled her arms around her knees to watch the skyline. She'd like to freeze this moment. Sometimes the best friendships were found in moments like this, in the shared silence. She rested her chin on her updrawn knees and contemplated the odds he would call her within the first twenty-four hours after he left. What would he tell his fellow SEALs about her? She'd love to have a bug in the room so she could listen in.

He picked up her Bible. "This has traveled a few miles."

"I keep thinking I'll get a new one, but that one is well marked and hard to replace. I got in the habit of memorizing verses years ago since I often had to leave that behind when I went out undercover."

He rubbed the faded inscription on the cover. "Darcy is your real name?"

She blinked then laughed. "Yes. I used Darla when I needed a cover name."

"I wondered." He set down the Bible. "I find Scripture pretty comforting on weekends like this."

She'd always been pretty quiet about what she believed, but she heard a confidence in his voice at talking about the subject that she appreciated. "It has been a help."

"Thankfully, Jesus is able to handle anything that happens. I just wish that hadn't involved you being hurt."

"Unfortunately it's a risk of the job. The pain is down to a dull ache."

"Have you taken the next round of pain pills yet?"

"No."

"I'll be back in a second. Stay here." Sam got up and disappeared inside. He came back in a few minutes with a jacket and a folded blanket. He draped the jacket over her shoulders. "Have you ever had a lemon Coke?" He offered her a can. "It's new."

She opened it. "What will they think of next?"

He offered the prescribed pills and she accepted them with a quiet thanks. He leaned back against the folded blanket, resting his weight on his elbows. "Did I ever tell you the long version of the story about the cougar?"

She turned to look at him. "No."

"My partner is the guy who just got married. Tom goes by the handle Wolf because everyone claims he can track like a starving wolf. He can't, but since his war face is a lot like a wolf snarling, the name stuck. He's pretty tame normally."

Darcy could hear the respect of two guys accustomed to razzing each other. She understood why the bond between soldiers formed and its depths sometimes amazed her — if Tom got in trouble, Sam would get him out.

"We were on vacation three years ago, doing some mountain hiking, and he decides he has to get this photo of the sunrise from a ridgeline for his girlfriend. It's about four o'clock, and he wakes me up rather abruptly because we're going to have to hustle to get there. Anyway, we're packed up and walking, and I'm eating tough jerky and trail mix as we hike. It's a narrow trail cutting uphill on a pretty good grade.

"Wolf disappears around this big rock at a bend in the trail and I've got one hand on the jerky and the other feeling my way around this monster rock when there's this hissing scream. The next thing I know I'm sliding down a chunk of the mountain I just climbed up doing a somersault dance with a cougar. He's big with these piercing eyes, and he's buried his teeth in my shoulder."

Sam shook his head. "I wallop him one in the nose and his ears flatten back against his head, then we slam into this tree trunk that about breaks my back and gives him a huge thump on the head. He lets go of me with this swallowed growl, and I've got him in a grip that would do a lion trainer proud, and we just stare at each other. About that time I realize he's shedding on me and I start sneezing. You should have seen the annoyed offense as he tugs to get back: Hitting is okay, but don't sneeze on me. He stalks off with this swish of his tail that quivers with his outrage.

"About this time my partner comes stumbling down the mountain and about lands on top of me. Wolf decides I lost my footing and am making up the cat. He's not buying the holes in my jacket so he takes off to track this mythical cougar. I'm standing there shedding cat hair and he's having to see the thing to believe it."

Darcy bit her thumb as she struggled not to interrupt him. She wanted to howl with laughter. Sam was allergic to cats.

"That giggle is going to crack ribs if you hold it in much longer."

"You're a born storyteller." She could just see the scene. It was a wonder he'd been able to walk away from it.

"Only true ones. No one believes the made-up ones."

"Did Tom ever see your cougar?"

Sam shook his head. "It remains a debatable legend."

"Before that, was your handle something to do with Texas? Your name just begs for one related to Texas."

"Sam Houston is a pretty colorful figure in history. He was both governor of Tennessee and of Texas during his lifetime. The guys tried out a few handles over the years, but they said I never lived up to them. Then the cougar incident happened and that name stuck. What about you, Dar? Did you ever acquire a handle?"

She wrinkled her nose. Sam laughed and reached over to tip up her chin. "What?"

"I'm kind of tenacious going after my objectives. They call me *Hound Dog*."

Sam considered that name and smiled. "You've even got an Elvis Presley theme song. Not bad." He studied her. "How come you can't swim?"

"Who said I can't?"

"Darcy, you can't even do the guppy stroke."

She wasn't sure she could handle being teased by a SEAL about water. They were born and formed in it, in a Basic Underwater Demolition training / SEAL course where a man's mental and physical strength were both tested to the limit. He loved water; she could tolerate it. "There wasn't a YMCA anywhere near where I grew up."

"You need to learn."

"Maybe someday."

"I could teach you," Sam offered.

"Somehow I doubt you'd start with blown-up flotation rings."

"I'm actually a pretty good teacher. We could start with windsurfing, and by the time you climb back on the board a few dozen times, you would learn the basics of closing your mouth before you go underwater."

She laughed. "You're enjoying this."

"You bet." Sam glanced at his watch. "The guys should be about ready." He got to his feet and picked up the blanket. "Let's go take a walk. I want you to see something." He offered her a hand up.

Darcy took a deep breath and forced herself to go with the flow, wondering what he had arranged. Sam led her into the trees a short distance to where a fallen tree on a rise overlooked the road. He spread out the blanket and encouraged her to take a seat. She pushed her hands into her pockets and did so while he perched beside her.

"What do you see?" Sam asked.

"A road." The sun was beginning to go down and the shadows were shifting around.

"The four Brits are out there. Somewhere between that telephone pole and this one. No one more than fifty feet away."

She paid sharper attention, searching the area. There was nothing moving, no sign of where a person stood or lay on the ground, nothing to indicate someone was there.

"You need to understand the problem with facing a sniper. He's not like a street thug who wants to get close to you with a gun. Distance and patience are a sniper's tools. If he sees you stand still for an instant, you're dead. They don't miss at two hundred yards, and a really good sniper can hit from a thousand yards away. That's ten football fields out, farther than you can see."

"Why show me this?"

"You can't see a sniper when he's amid trees and grass, the most unnatural environment for a man to hide in. You'll be even less aware of him when his perch is an upper-story window a block away or a car parked down the block from your home. Snipers have to be stopped before they are sent, or you are betting your life on him making a mistake. And most snipers don't make mistakes."

In other words, if they came against her again, she wouldn't be alive. "You made your point."

"Have I?" Sam asked softly and lifted his hand. Darcy jumped, startled, as Brandon moved away from a tree seven feet in front of her. His face was painted in green and black and his clothes were woodland cammies with two draped bands of cloth like a long scarf hung over his shoulders tucked with leaves and twigs. He stood on the slope going down to the road. The other Brits rose from the ground, two beside the road and one near Brandon.

"That was with less than twenty minutes to disperse into cover," Sam remarked. "With planning, it gets better."

"Is there any way to counter and stop a sniper committed to a mission?"

"You can provide a blanket of security that makes it hard for a sniper to find a location he likes. You can use counter-sniper teams during an event to watch for one setting up for a shot. Technology that can pick out heat sources from a distance can change the equation drastically. But in general, no. The best option is to disrupt planning before a sniper is sent or to catch him before he reaches a target site.

"Darcy, don't make the mistake of getting slowed down tracking the shooters when it's the man sending them who is the core danger." Sam squeezed her hand. "I don't want you getting hurt because the risk wasn't adequately understood."

It was rare to know the moment in time when someone decided you mattered, and she'd actually heard it from Sam. She didn't have words to say just how much it meant. She'd always been lousy with words. She so wished she had them now.

Sam ruffled her hair. "Don't let this freeze you, just be aware."

Ignoring the fact they still had interested third parties around, she leaned her head against his shoulder for a moment. "Okay. I appreciate what you arranged."

She straightened and got to her feet, then stepped forward and thanked the four officers. She knew when she was in over her head, and this was one of those times. And when in this position, the best tactic was retreat so she headed back to the house. She'd talk to Gabe about joining the investigation; Sam was right. They had to find the guy sending these shooters.

And when Sam went home, she hoped he thought about her and remembered to call. She would be waiting for the phone to ring.

Sam woke in the middle of the night, not sure why, but very aware something was wrong. He slid from the office sofa and grabbed his shirt. He had slept in jeans, the situation suggesting being ready for trouble would be prudent. Brandon was already in the hall, his handgun at his side. He clicked on the safety and with a quiet hand signal gave the sign for Darcy, and he gestured to the living room. It was an indication of the tension that they had both reacted to someone simply getting up. Sam buttoned the cuffs of his shirt and nodded that he'd handle it.

The TV was on and an end table light on low.

Darcy was curled up on the sofa, the bowl of leftover popcorn beside her. "Hey, slide over." Sam settled beside her. "What are you doing up?"

"Reading."

The book in her lap wasn't open.

Sam took a handful of the popcorn. A nightmare? A flashback? Something had driven her in here to watch television at 2 a.m. It wasn't because she wasn't sleepy. He'd seen hibernating bears more awake than her. She just didn't want to close her eyes that final slit. "What are we watching?" So far it had been a number of commercials.

"Carol Burnett."

"A wonderful comedienne."

"Laughter should be mandatory after every stressful day," Darcy said.

A car drove by and he came close to choking on his popcorn at the suddenness of the transformation in her as she tensed. She must be having a flashback while awake. Sam set his hand on her arm, afraid she was going to bolt from the sofa. She finally relaxed.

113

"He's not going to come through that door at you." He'd flatten the guy if he did.

"Easy for you to say."

He tightened his hand.

"Sorry."

He relaxed his hand. "Don't be."

"I also dreamed about being underwater. I'm fond of being able to breathe."

He was definitely going to teach her to swim. "I can understand that."

He pulled the comforter down from the back of the sofa and rearranged her multitude of pillows so he could settle his arm around her shoulders. Darcy was scared. He didn't like this image at all. "You know, this is an awful lot like a late night date. Popcorn, show, pretty lady."

"And you've got a gun tucked away on the shelf of the side table."

"Okay, a cop-type date then." His personal handgun, a SIG Sauer, was still back at the Norfolk base, but he'd borrowed the Browning from the Brits.

The show came back on. He felt when she shifted and let her weight rest back against his arm. He ruffled the edges of her hair.

"Quit. That tickles."

He did it one more time to get another smile then rested his hand on her shoulder.

Darcy wasn't in the mood to talk, and he didn't feel a need to break the silence. He was relieved to hear her soft laughter as the half-hour show concluded. Credits rolled by in a type font not used in the last decade. One mercifully brief car commercial gave way to the opening logo for a late night movie. He looked around for the remote but couldn't see it. He didn't feel like getting up to change the channels.

"Do you ever think about dying?" Darcy asked.

"I think about heaven." He rubbed her shoulder, calibrating his answer to her serious mood before continuing. "I think about how hard it would be on my family if it happened. How hard it would be on them to hear the news, have to deal with wrapping up my affairs given the fact I live on the other side of the country. How stressful it would be to plan my funeral if I happened to die while on active duty and the media descended, wanting their reactions and televising everything. It hurts to think about what the first holidays would be like for them."

She was quiet for a while. "I've just got my sister and she's pretty tough. Amy's a sheriff in North Dakota, married to the town doctor. Once a year we have a morbid file exchange with current wills and a list of accounts and phone numbers for everything from insurance policies to credit cards down to who handles trash collection in case Amy and Jacob die in a car crash or someone collects that bounty on my head."

"There's nothing wrong with being well prepared for death."

"I know. It's comforting that the Bible defines heaven as such a beautiful place, because the transition through death kind of spooks me." She hugged one of the pillows and leaned her head back. "I'm so tired of spending my life fighting for peace and having so little to show for the effort. I retired, Sam. I wanted to stay retired and out of this violence."

He'd guessed from the worn Bible and the personal way she said grace before dinner that her faith had deep currents, but it was reassuring to hear the words. "No one said life would be easy, Dar."

"I want it to be."

He brushed her bangs back. "Are you prone to pity parties late at night?" It got him the smile he had hoped for. Her expression cleared.

"Only when I can't sleep and someone wants me dead."

He leaned over and kissed her forehead. "I like your optimism." He wished he could wrap up the events of the last couple days for her and put them behind her. "You can't retire from the battle between good and evil in this life. No one can."

"It's just a battle we never win. Two more agents are dead, and I've got to decide if I'm up for another fight and manhunt. I've been there; it costs an awful lot from me."

He hesitated to answer her. He wasn't sure if she needed words or simply someone to listen. It was likely the stress of the flashbacks were simply triggering this discouragement. But it worried him; it sounded deep with a lot of history behind the emotion.

"What?"

Words were all he had tonight. "Part of your problem is perspective. You assume people are the source of this fight, and you get discouraged because you defeat one then another takes his place. Good and evil is a more fundamental fight."

He wanted to ease the weight she felt but didn't know how to do it in easy platitudes, only in the harder truths on which the real answers rested. "When Satan rules in men's hearts there is war. There's really only one adversary, Darcy. And as long as men follow him, we're going to have violence and war and all manner of evil to deal with. It's not that God isn't the more powerful of the two; it's just that so many men remain blind to the fact they have a choice of which master will rule in their lives."

"I know. It's comforting to know that one day Jesus will enforce the full victory He won at the Cross. But the years of God's patience with mankind so they have time to repent . . . If it had been my choice this would have ended long ago." She turned her head to look at him. "You've thought about this a lot. Did you originally plan to be a preacher, Sam?"

"It's an honorable profession. But no, I'm a soldier, Darcy. And part of that means knowing who my enemy really is. Pray for peace, work toward it, but understand that it's not going to come by another treaty or another conference or a few more bad people being arrested." His hand rubbed her shoulder. "A fallen world can't redeem itself. It's painful to watch sometimes, man's futile attempts to fix things. Only Jesus can do that. Somewhere on earth there will always be war and rumors of war. We've just been lucky it hasn't been in our corner of the globe lately. You're as much a soldier as I am. You can't retire from this fight. You can only decide how close to the front lines you want to be."

"I tended to prefer the front lines before I retired, which is why it's hard sometimes to keep a perspective on who's winning. Thanks, Sam. You're good at putting facts into perspective so eloquently. That's a gift." She pushed to her feet. "Since I'm not awake enough to think this hard tonight, it's best if I call it a night." She picked up the pillow she had brought with her. "I liked the company."

He caught her hand to stop her departure. He adored that smile and was not looking forward to leaving tomorrow without definite plans for when he would see her next. But that was a conversation for the morning. "Sleep well, Dar. And this looks like an interesting movie. If you can't sleep you can come back and finish it with me."

She hugged the pillow she was carrying and laughed softly. "Deal."

# Six

September 11
Tuesday, 8:45 a.m.
McLean, Virginia

Darcy found it hard to concentrate on the report she was reading. The sunlight streaming through the large bay windows warmed her flannel shirt and jeans, making work the last thing on which she wanted to focus. Not much had changed over the last twelve hours beside Sam scaring her with that sniper demonstration. He'd done a good job of making his point.

The Brits were out running, and Sam was with them. The man should be declared dangerous to traffic, for women drivers would watch him rather than the road. Even half asleep with eyes barely open she'd stopped when she saw him in cut-off shorts and a gray T-shirt, stretching in preparation for his run. The muscles in his legs were sculpted; there was no other word for it. And his shoulders — she didn't have to ask if he worked out. He looked over and smiled at her, that knowing smile accompanied by a wink. If she'd been able to quit gawking, she would have had something sassy to say. She settled for a strangled excuse me as she slipped past him to go to the kitchen for the coffee.

Sam's bag was packed and by the front door. A rental car had been delivered a short time ago. When he got back and showered, she'd be saying good-bye. She still hadn't figured out the right words to say. She would have to plan a trip to Norfolk in her near future and come up with an excuse to be in his neighborhood. She should be good at coming up with that kind of cover, but she hadn't come up with one yet that he wouldn't see right through. It had been too long since she tried to mix dating and her job.

Her coffee had grown cold. A glance across the room at the muted television showed the top-of-the-hour news update would soon be on. She'd wait to get a refill. There was comfort in the morning routines she tried to maintain regardless of her location.

She returned to the report. If she went

back to work officially, she'd have broad access to imagery, signal intelligence, human intelligence, and open-source data. Despite sophisticated software, watch lists, and powerful computers, the job still came down to the skill of someone putting together small bits of scattered information in order to read the enemy's mind.

Three days. If they didn't have a solid lead in three days she was going back to work. She owed it to Wallace and Rice to try.

The television flashed to breaking news. Darcy heard the logo and looked up.

Smoke was billowing from the north tower of the World Trade Center. A fire? More like an explosion from the smoke pattern. She grabbed for the remote and turned up the sound, searching for context.

A plane had hit the World Trade Center.

It didn't make sense. It was a sunny, clear day in New York. How had a plane hit the tower? Diverting a plane even when it was gliding without power was basic flying: a move of the yoke and the plane would have missed the building. Had the pilot not been conscious and at the controls when this happened?

Darcy crossed toward the television as

she flipped channels, searching for more information. Tuesday morning in New York. The financial district began work early. That tower would have been fully occupied. She watched and bit her lip, memories of the World Trade Center car bombing in '93 replaying in her mind. How were they going to get people out of the upper floors of that tower with a fire raging?

A second plane hit the south tower.

The shock of seeing it was like a punch to the gut. *Oh, Lord, it's happening again. Another terrorist attack.* Her hand shook on the remote.

Two planes, two towers. A deliberate attack. Her mind began to race with the implications as stunned reporters replayed the tape to confirm what they had just seen.

*Pandora's box just opened and evil was spilling out.*

How many more planes were out there? What else had they targeted?

The counterterrorism desks would be desperately trying to answer those questions, even as they struggled to deal with the horrific knowledge they had been caught blind. The CIA's New York station was at 7 World Trade Center. The case officers could literally look out the window and see the buildings burning.

Two planes in a well-planned and coordinated attack — there would be more. A second wave had to be coming.

Darcy felt such helplessness. She was shaking as the cold reality of what she was watching settled across her.

She'd seen the sniper who killed the German finance minister in 1987 and hadn't been able to do anything with the knowledge in time to stop it. Arresting the man responsible had been less than adequate to alleviate the fury about what he'd done. The same sensation enveloped her now.

She walked outside to the back deck. The birds on the feeder took flight. The day had not changed — yet everything had changed. The carefree America she had grown up in was gone. The treasured peace she had thrived in had just imploded. She saw Sam and his friends running at a steady pace near the tree line. She shouted for them. They saw her and changed directions, coming back at a sprint.

Tears streaked down her face.

Liberty came with a price. They just hadn't had to pay it for a few decades.

They would have no choice now but to fight. Whoever was behind this was killing civilians. The U.S. would have to look at the monster that was this evil and out think it. They would need good intelligence and good warriors to act on it.

She headed back inside.

The door flew open behind her moments later. "Darcy?" Sam asked.

She just pointed to the television. As the images registered she saw Sam stiffen. The Brits crowded into the room, a soft murmur of reactions as they saw the image.

"Maybe eight minutes between the two planes," she said softly.

"This is war."

"Yes." She felt so old as she said that word. She watched the towers burn, unable to look away. "Those who did this are already dead. And those who sent them wanted the martyrs." This terrorist act had just ripped the underbelly out of the U.S. financial district.

"We'll find them." The solemn assurance in Sam's voice told her it had already been decided in his mind. They'd find them and justice would be swift. She reached over and squeezed his arm. The nation would need and ask much from men like him.

So many were already dead. So many more would die before this was over. More tears formed. She didn't want to face this. Sam tugged her toward him, and she rested her head against his chest, grateful to share his strength. His pager went off. She didn't have to ask what the codes meant. The Department of Defense would be calling back SEALs as first responders for the retaliatory strike.

She went to find her security IDs. Someone was waging war on her homeland. That anger would provide the endurance she needed for this fight. This battle she was going to win no matter what the cost.

# Seven

*Four Months Later*
January 15
Tuesday, 4:35 p.m.
Hamburg, Germany

Darcy tore the page off the secure fax. NATO had provided the plane and the world map display on the wall showed their location as currently over Hamburg, Germany, heading west to Spain. She was traveling with a military contingent and was one of five intelligence officers on this hunter team. Dozens of teams like this one existed around the world tracking different terrorists. They were able to translate and assess information at the source where it was recovered, allowing immediate military and police actions to be taken.

Whoever had thought America wouldn't hit back had badly misjudged them. She was still angry, and it drove a nonstop European travel schedule as she focused on the task at hand. She was rebuilding her network of contacts across Europe and turning those assets into a formidable force. Even former enemies were now working with her, offering information and leads and taking her calls at all hours of the day.

*Jesus, am I missing anything here that will help us? I don't want more civilians to die because I overlooked something subtle in these documents that will give us another thread to tug. Please provide the wisdom I need to do this job.* Darcy knew just how much depended on her efforts, and it was scary at times to carry that burden.

Gabriel joined her from the teleconference that had been going on at the front of the plane, taking the seat across from her and laying his forearm crutches by his feet. "Are you ready for the brief?"

Darcy held up a photo of Luther Genault. "He knew September 11 would happen in advance, he profited from it, he's the scum of the earth, and we want him."

Gabriel smiled. "You're ready."

"I want this guy so bad I can taste it." He wasn't a terrorist out to blow up people; he was worse — a former Czech intelligence officer who used the evil he learned others were planning to carry out for his own profit. She handed her partner the fax. "They located another brokerage firm in Sweden that he used to short stocks before September 11. We're looking at close to half a billion in profits from the trail of accounts we've been able to uncover so far."

"Any leads on where he moved the cash to hide it?"

"Lots of brick walls we're knocking down, only to find the next account already bare as well. He had time to prepare his plans for spreading out the profits. He's evil, but I'll give him credit for his tactics. He's the Lex Luther of evil."

Gabe gestured toward the men he'd been on the conference call with. "If we find him, the guys in the front of this plane will drop a bomb on his head."

"I'm still looking for the first good lead. He's in Ireland, Switzerland, Canada, or the Caribbean Islands. Those are the current guesses." Darcy held up the second picture in the briefing book. "His wife Renee — French, cultured, with a love to shop. I'll lay odds she's going to surface at a nice hotel or major fashion or art event this year. I've got a standing half-a-million-dollar offer of your money out there for the first paparazzo that takes her picture. Tabloid photographers are wonderful snitches to have when it comes to going after someone like her."

"It will be worth every dime," Gabe agreed. "Luther is flush with money, and he's falling in love with this idea of profiting from the tragedy caused by others. The latest from the Russians is that Luther's number two has been actively trying to hire retired snipers from their army. The suspicions we've had appear to be true — terrorists are turning to Luther to try and slow down the soldiers and intelligence officers chasing them."

"More blood money." The death of two agents and the attempt on her on September 9 had only been the beginning. Twenty of the best investigators in Europe were now dead, as were nine high-ranking military officers from across NATO countries. Someone had killed a French officer assigned to Interpol last night. Luther could easily be the one accepting cash to make hits like those happen.

Darcy turned pages in the briefing book to the photo of Luther's number two man: Vladimir Kurst. "If you want security, kill those who oppose you," she murmured, remembering his motto. Luther had hired a ruthless man as his number two. She sincerely wished Sergey was still alive to help her track this Russian down.

Belgian authorities had found Sergey's family murdered at a chalet weeks after September 11. When she had a moment to grieve for the thousands who died during the initial terrorist attacks, she'd also let herself grieve for Sergey. The man was likely dead now too — his body not yet found, his family part of what had been used to pressure him to act against her. When this was over, she promised herself that she'd track down what happened to Sergey's family and bring justice for them. It mattered. Sergey had been an enemy but also a friend in a profession where respect for the craft connected them.

And whoever had collected the bounty on her head on the rumor of her death was going to get a knock on the door. The CIA had fostered that rumor to add to her safety. She appreciated it. But it was only a temporary answer until there was time to go back and track down those responsible. Someone out there was a million pounds richer, and it did not sit well.

"What do we have on Luther's number three?" Gabe asked.

Darcy looked through the briefing book.

"Peter Dansky, their operations man. Other than the fact he likes explosives and probably was born in Belgium, we don't have much. Russian intel may have more; they are forwarding what they have." She stared at the grainy photo, frustrated. "Luther has an organization of exactly three people and his wife. And apparently they don't travel together very often. They keep their distance from events they help foster. If we get lucky and spot them, we can take 'em down. If not we'll just be spending our time investigating crimes they have already done."

"Relax." Gabe stretched out in his chair. "It's not an accident we drew Luther's name. I asked for the toughest assignment they had on the list. Luther's good, but we're better. We'll get him. All we have to do is find one of them, and we'll be able to roll up the rest."

Darcy closed the briefing book and forced herself to relax, taking the moment while she had it. "Were you able to get a call through to Marla?"

Gabe smiled at the mention of his wife. "She's going to fly to Brussels and meet us when we head back to NATO headquarters in a couple days. We'll get a weekend away. Were you able to get ahold of your sister?"

Darcy held up a cassette tape. "Even better, a care package Amy sent caught up with me. Tapes of the hometown radio station, only a week old in its news and weather reports." It was nice to hear a voice with a Western accent. Darcy had returned the favor last week with a new pair of night-vision binoculars, another large thermos, and a collection of gourmet coffees.

Amy didn't have to deal directly with the open border with Canada, but major highway routes through the state came through her territory. They were still considered the front lines for finding unwanted items brought across the border. Darcy would join Amy as a deputy when she was next invited if only to give her a helping hand. This war had definitely moved to the home front.

"I want to go paint my fence." She didn't care if she had to shovel out snow to get to it.

"When this is over, I'll slap some paint around for you."

She unwrapped a sucker that had come in the care package. "Promise?"

"You think the Agency is going to want me around after I spend them into bankruptcy?"

Darcy smiled at him, knowing he was already on the short list to be the next deputy director of intelligence for the Agency. He might have pegged her as a rising star early on and helped along her career, but Gabriel had long ago become one of those stars. "We have hired just about every private eye we can find in Yemen and Turkey, not to mention a multitude in Europe," she agreed.

"Eyes and ears walking around the streets are wonderful things. You want to locate a skunk, ask the neighbors." Gabe pushed back his seat rest. "I'll give this guy six months at the outside, then we'll be drawing a line through his name."

"It's kind of nice being the spotters for a very big stick. The British and Australian Special Forces are as good as some of ours." She glanced around to see who was near, then smiled. "Almost." There wasn't much difference in training or execution, but there was in motivation. America had been hit, and it showed in the focused intensity of the U.S. military to win this war.

Where was Sam now? He'd deployed less than ten days after the September 11 attacks, and she had heard only rumors. SEALs were on the front lines of this fight, not only on land, but also at sea. She'd helped sort through numerous documents, notebooks, scraps of paper, and other items recovered from missions deemed too classified to even name. She didn't have to be told what they were doing; she could see the results. The number of names and faces on the terrorist most-wanted list was dropping fast. As long as her days were now, at least they were relatively safe. Sam's were not.

# Eight

January 15
Tuesday, 9:23 p.m.
Lebanon

A bug crawled under the back collar of Sam's uniform as he lay stretched out on rocky ground in Lebanon. He had no choice but to ignore it. The audio mike had to be kept directly on target at this distance or the conversation streaming to tape would be interrupted. A hand rested on his collar and firmly pushed, squishing the creature. Sam rolled his eyes at his partner Wolf in thanks.

He'd had easier assignments during his years in the SEALs. Lebanon was not a friendly place to attract attention. They had spent the last six hours inserting to this position: moving from the sea to the beach, creeping into a town bombed by decades of war to watch two men meet on a strip of land near a destroyed school. The meeting broke up, and Sam followed the taller of the two men with the directional mike as he walked back to his car. Battihi was a smart man. The Egyptian explosives expert didn't use phones. He conveyed instructions face-to-face. So they came to listen to him. The cars with the principals and their security details pulled out. Sam watched until they were out of sight. *Next time, gentlemen . . .*

Sam nodded to Wolf. They began the slow process of inching their way back into the rubble. Next time he came to Lebanon, Sam hoped it would be with orders to put a laser dot on Battihi's car and guide a five-hundred-pound bomb down onto it. Walking away from a terrorist under indictment for six bombings and a train derailment in Europe was the pits even if it was necessary. They needed to know what was coming, and that meant listening in on Battihi a few more times before they moved in to take him. The Brits had taken down a cell in Algeria based on the last such taped conversation.

"I'm getting to know this guy better than my own brother," Wolf whispered. "I hate that feeling."

"You don't have a brother," Sam whispered back. "And what I find pretty annoying is how I can't understand a word he's saying. I hope we've got a decent translator waiting for this tape."

"The other man sounded European."

"Battihi actually sounded respectful. First time I've heard that," Sam said. It was time to get out of here. They continued to creep back.

Sam followed Wolf through bombed-out buildings, their path parallel to the road as they made their way back to the sea. They reached the secure site they had set up and Wolf moved concrete debris to retrieve their hidden cache of gear. They had slipped off their wet suits and went in wearing desert camouflage to allow them to blend in with the concrete and dirt rubble, risking the time to strip off gear for the safety of being able to merge into the landscape. Sam secured the communication equipment for transport underwater. He pulled on his wet suit and picked up scuba gear and his air tanks. The beach was in sight.

Sam nodded to Wolf and they sprinted across the sand. They lost the cover of darkness for that short distance to the sand, and then they were back into the welcoming arms of the sea. They touched water, waded in, and dropped below the surface. Out there in the blackness was their pickup team of three SEALs and a submersed SDV, a motorized underwater SEAL Delivery Vehicle that would take them another two miles to the very big, black, and bad USS *Dallas*. The nuclear submarine had become this war's black ops flagship for assaults that sprung from the sea.

The swim was not a safe one. A few floating mines still hid along this coastline. The silence beneath the water was complete. Sam swam hard, relieved to be near the end of a successful mission. The tape would be worth this. That fact allowed him to push aside the reality that he was cold, hurting, and looking at another three hours before he'd be dry and warm again.

What was Darcy doing right now? He thought about her every time he went underwater, wondering if she'd changed her mind and learned to swim. It wasn't easy to get in touch with her. He'd managed to call the number she had given him and left a message on her machine twice over the last months, but he hadn't been in a place where she could call him back. He couldn't just call the CIA and ask for a supposedly dead person, and he wasn't sure mail would reach her. He missed her . . . intensely. He felt like he was fighting this war for her, for he knew that opening attack against agents on September 9 had probably been part of this mess, and she'd been one of the first hit.

Wolf touched his arm. He pointed to the beacon of the waiting team members. Sam nodded and they changed directions to intercept.

January 15
Tuesday, 8:35 p.m.
Madrid, Spain

Darcy had a secure office down the hall from Gabe's in one of the military planning buildings NATO had built in the eighties and never fully occupied. It was a mix of both very high-tech equipment and cast-off furniture. The place was cramped, had no windows, and was probably going to be hot during the summer, for it was icy during the winter so that her toes froze when she walked around the office without shoes. She'd stuffed in three computer terminals and a reel-to-reel tape deck. She even squeezed in a couch. As a home away from home it wasn't bad; if truth be told she loved the place. Tucked as it was at the dead end of a hallway, interruptions were minimized.

A secure Internet physically separated from the public network let her connect to classified web pages at agencies around the world. She started with the U.S. Treasury Department to see how the hunt for Luther's accounts was progressing.

The Treasury Department had spent years developing the software that could sort through millions of transactions and generate a graphic picture of the money flow. The money in Luther's brokerage accounts had been routed out of the first accounts within hours, and it had been done in a systematic way. Only with the review of four months of history was the plan he had used apparent.

Luther believed in diversification. Within two days he had spread his bounty into a hundred different piles of about fifty thousand dollars in size. Then over a two-week period the majority of those accounts had shrunk to smaller amounts. What cash they had been able to trace had ended up in bank safe deposit boxes and assets like diamonds and cars that could be quickly resold. Luther had done most of it by bank wire transfers. They had recaptured only about thirty-two million of what was known to be in excess of 550 million dollars.

Luther had taken a chunk of cash off the top and probably stuffed it in his mattress. He laundered a huge amount more, and the rest he moved around accounts between banks like a shell game, slowly hiding it behind walls. He probably rightly assumed he wouldn't need to touch one of those accounts for at least a decade. Darcy looked at numbers that were blood money and she wanted him.

She focused on the items they knew had been purchased. She was willing to bet one of the diamonds was going to turn up as a gift to Renee. An expensive stone — likely having its characteristics recorded in the international registry of gems — prestigious, possibly named, and sold to a private collector. Word would get out. She'd know what she was looking at when she saw it.

*"The love of money is the root of all evil . . ."* The Scripture fragment came to mind and was personalized by the data she looked at. Luther was the embodiment of the pursuit of wealth destroying conscience.

"Darcy?"

"It's open." She'd stuck a piece of cardboard in the doorjamb to prevent the lock from closing.

Gabriel joined her, carrying dinner. "Eat."

She moved aside papers to make room for the china plate. "I could get used to being back in Europe; meals are rarely fast food." She pointed with her fork to the chair beside her. "Sit. I want to run something past you. Luther's third man, Peter Dansky, what are his habits?"

Gabe had been working with the Russians to get a profile figured out. "It's an educated guess: gambling, Russian vodka, and fast cars."

"Does he strike you as a careful man?"

Gabe thought about that. "Yes and no. He plays with explosives; he's the operations man in the threesome. Luther wouldn't have hired him if he was careless or wasn't extremely good. Dansky believes in planning and security, but he's also the ultimate kind of risk taker. He thinks he's invincible."

Darcy nodded. "I'm thinking it would be worth digging into European luxury car dealers for about the time Dansky showed up on the radar screen. A really expensive custom car bought with cash sometime between September 11 and December 31. A show-off piece. It won't be in Dansky's name, probably not even traceable money back to one of these accounts, but how many new car owners do you think we would have to covertly photograph and check out? A couple hundred?"

"We don't know if he's in Europe," Gabe pointed out.

"Luther's money is primarily in Europe, his wife is French, his second in command is Russian. Dansky is probably from Belgium. They are going to hide where they're comfortable. I'm betting the Caribbean if they do leave Europe."

"I'd put my money on Canada," Gabe suggested. "We're still turning up safe houses the Russians set up during the cold war. Luther came through the same KGB school Sergey did. We lost Sergey more times than I can count when he'd slip away from the UN in New York, drive up to Canada, and disappear."

"The Siberian express. Skirt around Alaska and you're in Russia," Darcy remembered with fondness.

"Luther's a planner like Dansky. You can bet he already had every place he and Renee would live and visit for the next couple years arranged before September 11 ever went down. He'd have stayed with things and places he trusted." Gabe got to his feet. "I'll get people looking into cars.

It's a good idea for Dansky. Got plans for tonight?"

"I'm going to catch up on my reading."

"Stick around and grab a catnap on the couch. Defense has a lead on the Egyptian Battihi. He may have been spotted in Lebanon last night. A transmission will be coming through in a few hours. They'd like us on the translation feed to see if we can help with IDs."

Darcy looked over, intrigued. "Number eight on our terrorist list? He's trying to move those explosives we've been hearing about?"

"We'll find out. It would make a great evening if we could take him out."

"Come get me when the transmission comes through."

January 16
Wednesday, 1:20 a.m.
Lebanon

Distances in the ocean at night were deceptive. The SEAL delivery vehicle began to slow. Sam strained to see ahead. In the murky darkness forty feet below the surface of the water came the realization the blackness ahead was not water but metal. Lethal, powerful, with technology far in advance of what had sent men to the moon, the submarine rested motionless in the sea, waiting for them. In port it looked huge, but seen underwater it became the biggest thing in the sea, so massive Sam couldn't see to the diving sail at the sub midpoint.

Riding on the back of the submarine was a dry deck shelter, about forty feet long and nine feet in diameter, stuck atop the submarine like a long metal canister. It was loaded with special SEAL gear, and it allowed them to deploy men and equipment while the submarine remained submerged.

Two SEALs in scuba gear came from the hangar to meet them. Working by hand signals and lighted wands, the SDV was guided onto the track running atop the sub and rolled inside the shelter. It had three interlocking compartments inside that could be independently pressurized. The forward compartment sphere became a hyperbaric chamber to treat injured divers. In the middle was a transfer trunk allowing entry and egress to the USS *Dallas*. The third compartment hangar stored the SEAL delivery vehicle or when it was out, up to twenty SEALs in full gear. Sam moved into the middle sphere with Wolf and Bear. They were sealed inside, it was pressurized, and the water began to pump out. Sam removed his SCUBA gear and gratefully took a normal breath.

"What do you think, Chief?" Bear asked, as he too stripped off his gear.

Sam confirmed a look with Wolf before answering. "The tape should be good. And I'm going to bet the conversation turns out to be explosive, sir."

"Let's hope so."

The light turned green and Bear opened the hatch.

Sam descended the ladder after Wolf and entered the USS *Dallas*. Ninety-seven men lived and worked in this submarine. It was an isolated and self-contained world. The sub rarely if ever surfaced during its six months at sea. The *Dallas* was an attack submarine, and it hunted other submarines. It could gather shipping and signal intelligence as it cruised the shore of a hostile country listening to every transmission. Its location when at sea was carefully guarded.

Sam handed over the recording to the waiting SEAL from his squad. The conversation would be compressed and made ready to transmit to the Defense Intelligence Agency over burst encryption. The SEALs would send the audio tape along with digitized pictures taken through the nightscopes, add their action report, and while the package streamed over, they would answer via text message any questions the interpreters who were taking the feed live had about the meeting. The process meant it would be another ninety minutes before this mission was complete, but at least it meant he'd get to see the first rough translation of the conversation he'd just risked his life to gather.

"Get the pictures queued first, Frank," Bear requested. "Find the clearest ones for each tango. Let's see if we can get a confirmation of identities before linguists start translating the conversation."

"Will do."

Time was tight. Bear motioned him toward the stateroom, and Sam started dictating the action report to him as they walked.

Passageways aboard the submarine were tight, and two people couldn't pass each other easily. The boat had never been designed to carry extra passengers, let alone the numbers and the amount of gear a SEAL team brought with them. On some submarine trips they had bunked down in the missile room, the sleep feeling a bit strange when it was inside a room full of explosives. On this trip the sixteen SEALs shared a small stateroom; a hot bunk schedule allowed them to sleep with only nine bunks.

Sam stripped off his wet suit. He was so exhausted it was a struggle to lift his arm to peal off the material. Cold fingers hurt. "What bit me?"

Bear lifted off the remains of a big black squished bug Sam hadn't been able to shake off earlier. "Ouch."

Sam was grateful it was dead. "It felt like an ugly critter. Battihi was meeting with a European," he continued. "It looked like a big deal just given where they talked and how nervous the security guards with each man were." Sam gratefully accepted a mug of coffee from a yeoman. "I think we got good photos; it would be nice to get an identification on him."

"Any problems getting in?"

"There was a lot of activity in the area, but the rubble along that road has increased since the last visit, and it wasn't hard to stay out of sight. It was a lot of climbing through destroyed buildings. Any problems on your end?"

"Two boats got a little close. They were fishing trawlers, but neither was actively searching with sonar. It was just a cold night in the water."

Sam settled a towel around his neck, wishing for a hot shower and a meal. He followed Bear through the boat to the communications center.

Wolf had the sequence cued up. Sam handed Wolf the mug of coffee and the towel and watched the sequence play. "I agree on the picture choices; that looks good. Audio ready?"

Frank shifted tapes in the compression mixer. "It's ready."

Bear passed word to the executive officer of the boat that they were ready to ascend to periscope depth.

Sam took a seat at the console beside his partner. The captain would lift powerful antennas and listen for anyone around or anyone listening in. And then if they had clear surroundings, he would raise the powerful transmitters and send this package in bursts. At the other end the time lags in the transmission would disappear as the audio and video were decompressed.

The captain sent back word they were ready to transmit.

"Send it," Bear ordered. "Let's see what DIA has to say."

# Nine

January 16
Wednesday, 1:35 a.m.
Madrid, Spain

Darcy settled on her office couch with the stack of the latest intercepts and the file she'd built on Luther and read in no particular order, just looking for patterns. She had stopped writing reports. The number of people with high enough security clearances to read them was so small it was faster to brief verbally. She read, she thought, and when she had something Gabe agreed was solid, the military went in. Synergy was the name of this game. The terrorists were beginning to understand the terror of being hunted.

She was interested in the basic question of logistics. Luther had to talk and move, and so did those who worked for him. Fifty dollars to an airport worker gave her plane tail numbers and the amount of fuel pumped, twenty gave her a copy of the disk from a security camera in the parking garage, ten bought her a copy of a taxi company dispatch book. When she was looking for patterns over time, it was money well spent.

Her computer was wired to control everything in her domain from coffeepot to CD player. It began to play the strains of Elvis Presley's hit song "Hound Dog." Darcy reached back and punched in the code to unlock her office door.

"I wish you'd get a key lock on this door instead of an electronic keypad. You die in here, it's going to be a pain getting in to haul you out," Gabriel commented, shoving the door to close it again so he would have room to pull out her desk chair.

"Considering the amount of your coffee I'm drinking, I'd be self-embalmed." She turned her head to look at him and winced, reaching back to move around the pillow she had brought from home to help ease the stabbing pain.

"You need to see a chiropractor for that neck."

"It's the strain of all the office work. I prefer being on the road somewhere, traveling."

He tipped his head to read the title of the report she held. "Have something?"

"Right now it's just a whiff of smoke, not much substance." She studied her world map on the wall. "That cell in Morocco we've been watching? They went shopping today and bought Russian Vodka. We've been watching them for four months, and they've bought a lot of items but never that."

"Someone is coming for a visit."

"Dansky drinks Russian Vodka." That was one of the tidbits she'd noted from the Russian files on the man.

"It's thin."

"But we know he's looking for a new group to hire. The Brits took out the cell in Algeria he'd been talking to last month. Dansky may be going to Morocco as a second option."

"Flag it so the guys watching Morocco will know we're interested in lots of pictures of any guests."

"Will do. Has the defense feed come in on Battihi yet?"

"It's setting up now." Gabe connected them to the Defense Intelligence site and entered the security codes to join the pool taking the feed. Darcy recognized several names of the translators, some of the National Security Agency's best linguists among them. The screen split into sections as the DIA set up the package transfer of audio, digital pictures, and text.

On the second terminal, Darcy logged in so she could search their database.

The first picture painted to the screen. The green of night-vision photographs allowed better elimination of possible matches than identification of one. "That's Battihi," she concurred as image specialists noted a visual match probability at 74 percent. She'd studied his face over the last months; she knew him.

The audio of the conversation began to play as the second photo painted to the screen. Whoever had crept in to capture this had a lot of guts. Who would the DIA send into Lebanon covertly? CIA? SEALs? Battihi was incredibly hard to get close to. She listened to the conversation as it streamed in, watched the live translation begin to appear on the side screen as translators worked, and read the action report below from those who had captured it.

Who was Battihi meeting with? "Gabe, that almost looks like Dansky." It was hard to get a clear image through the night-vision camera, and the photo they had for comparison was grainy at best. "And the

154

voice may be a match; it's European. Could Dansky have slipped into Lebanon?"

She added a question to the queue: DID THE MAN TALKING WITH BATTIHI HAVE A LIMP?

"Dansky's knee surgery was just a rumor," Gabe remarked, seeing the question.

"About everything we have on him is a rumor."

The operative on the other end eventually reached her question in the queue. YES. LEFT LEG.

"I'm on it." Gabe began hunting through old records to find the information. "Here it is," he said moments later, tapping his finger on the monitor to note the success. "Not much, but at least it's from an intercepted phone call between people suspected of working for Dansky rather than a snitch trying to make points. 'Dansky's unavailable; you'll have to handle it yourself.' 'There's cash on the line; where is he?' 'I heard he needed knee surgery.' That's the extent of the reference."

"When was that dated?"

"Four years ago, June."

"Surgeons take X rays, photos. We find Dansky's doctor and we've got a good thread we can pull."

155

The pictures of the two men shaking hands and parting appeared. The transcription was finishing up. Darcy added a final note to the queue with her call sign after the others signaled they had no more questions. I OWE YOU A FAVOR FOR THE GUY WITH A LIMP. COLLECT SOMEDAY; I'M GOOD FOR IT. HOUND DOG. It flowed out at the end of the queue of traffic.

"If that guy with Battihi is Dansky, we've hit gold," Gabe said. "What's the best visual they got of him? We'll need to firm it up."

The last photos were coming across. Darcy set up to see the sequence again, when the screen flashed a note in the text section.

DARCY?

The question sat there in the lower quadrant of the screen, flashing, lingering.

She struggled to know what to do.

Gabe leaned over her shoulder and typed: SAM?

YES.

"While the final pictures transmit, use the side bandwidth," Gabe said. "I want to talk to DIA about this for a minute." He picked up the secure phone.

Darcy nodded and took a deep breath. CHAT ROOM 2.

The secure chat room opened moments later.

HI DARCY.

HI SAM.

She had no idea what to say. He was on the other end of the transmission, and his presence meant he'd been one of the guys sneaking into Lebanon to spy on a terrorist. She might know in her head that his job put him at this kind of risk, but it was different to know about a specific mission. *Samuel, you are going to get yourself killed and then what am I going to say? I don't have that many really great friends in my life that I can afford to lose one.*

Sam didn't have a problem knowing something to say; letters were appearing on the screen. STILL DEAD?

She smiled. *Oh, friend, you and I have some talking to do. I've got four months of news.* She rested her hands on the keyboard and continued typing, grateful she had learned to type fast over the years. YES. OKAY FROM MISSION?

A-OK. DO FAVOR? CALL KELLY — MSG: JOE OK, ILY. JILL — MSG: TOM OK, ILY. MY FOLKS — MSG: GOT LETTERS, ILY.

"What's ILY?" Darcy asked Gabe, rapidly jotting down numbers, names, and

157

messages. Sam was typing this? The words were flying faster than she could scrawl notes.

"Subspeak for *I Love You*."

DONE. Darcy hesitated before she typed: I MISS YOU.

THANKS, D. I MISS YOU MORE.

I'M SERIOUS ABOUT THE FAVOR. COME HOME AND COLLECT.

I PLAN TO. PROMISE.

The last photo came over. She typed the direct phone number to her desk here as rapidly as she could, trying to beat the cut off of the satellite link. It had been so frustrating to get Sam's message on her answering machine in the States and have no way to get in touch with him. The link dropped on her before she got an acknowledgment on the transmission.

"A SEAL team sneaking into Lebanon . . . interesting," Gabe commented.

"Did Sam get my number?"

"It's impossible to tell. You'll know if he calls you." Gabe turned the other terminal screen toward her, and she forced herself to think about work again for a moment. "DIA will see if they can enhance the visuals, but they agree it's probable. While they see if they can get a voice match, let's proceed as if that is Dansky. Dar, print out the transcript of Battihi's conversation with him and come down to my office. Let's see if we can figure out what he's planning. We may have a shot at actually getting ahead of Dansky and anticipating his next move."

"I'll be right there."

He struggled to his feet. "I'm glad it was Sam."

"So am I."

Gabe tugged the door shut behind him.

Darcy queued the document to print.

*Sam.* She reached over for one of the oranges in the fruit basket on her desk. She wasn't ready for the surge of emotions she felt. *I'm so glad he's okay.* She rarely let herself step back from the day-to-day fight to take a deep breath and think about life before September 11 or what it would be like after this war was over. She still hoped for a chance to explore a relationship with Sam. The distance of several states had to be easier to manage than the present reality of countries and oceans.

She kept oranges around as a reminder of him. *"Take courage, do the work, and peace will once again flourish."* Sam's note had arrived at CIA headquarters the day after the attack tucked in a basket of Florida oranges, the package hand delivered to her by Brandon. That note now folded in her wallet had helped relieve the stress of the last few months.

*Jesus, please bring Sam safely home. I want to have a night out to celebrate with him.*

She tucked the piece of paper with the phone numbers and messages into her pocket. She would gladly make those calls for him.


January 16
Wednesday, 5:10 a.m.
USS *Dallas* / Mediterranean Sea

The main mess area located in the center of the submarine was crowded with SEALs catching dinner in the early morning hours. Sam fingered the piece of paper with what he hoped was Darcy's phone number. It had two digits missing, but that could be solved with a little deliberate dialing. A hundred numbers wouldn't take that long to dial. It was a European country code prefix. Where was she? Did she realize he'd been on a sub during that conversation? He wanted to be somewhere he could call her, but that wouldn't be happening anytime soon. *Dar, I hope you're being careful. Stay safe.*

160

"Sir? Did I get your steak too well done? Would you like another put on the grill?"

He glanced up at the helpful sailor doing his best to make their lives easier by making sure the food was first-rate. "The steak is great. Thanks, Ensign." It was tough to distract him from a meal, but Darcy had managed to do it.

"You got her number?"

He looked up from the paper over to his partner. "Most of it."

"She sounded pleased to hear from you."

"It was a pretty short conversation to draw that conclusion." He wanted to think it would be possible to pick up the promise from that early meeting. He wanted a chance to collect that favor, spend some more time with her, find out if the feelings so profoundly stirred in a matter of days had lasted through this separation. Darcy was a lady he thought could handle being in a relationship with a SEAL, and he intended to find out.

"Be optimistic, bud. She certainly turned your head."

Sam smiled at his friend and tucked the slip of paper in his pocket. If he encouraged his friend's speculation, the topic would never subside. "So when do you think we'll be going home?"

161

"I'm betting we'll spend Thanksgiving in the States."

That idea was one Sam hadn't even let himself seriously consider. Holidays at home . . . it would be wonderful.

"Thanks for asking Darcy to call Jill."

"My pleasure. Thanksgiving?" Sam confirmed.

Wolf smiled and pushed him the coffee. "Eat your steak, man. It's prime rib. You'll see Darcy sooner rather than later."

January 16
Wednesday, 10:10 a.m.
Madrid, Spain

Darcy tossed an orange back and forth between her hands as she listened to the conversation again. They had the translation now on audio, a dubbed tape that gave them the original conversation, a pause, the provided translation, and then continued playing the recorded conversation. The overlapping playbacks allowed the emotion in the voices to still be part of the factor in the analysis. "Play that segment again, Gabriel."

He leaned over and rewound the tape.

"Dansky doesn't want Battihi moving

162

the explosives through Yemen. Interesting."

"Do you think Dansky has an inkling of the kind of network we've got in Yemen?" Gabe asked.

"He knows. Why else ask for this meeting to happen in Lebanon, the one place it's hard to observe?"

"The SEALs were there."

"But you have to admit, it was high risk to send them in." Had Sam volunteered for that mission? She had a feeling he may have. She could remember his voice, his expression on September 11, and she didn't think he would back away from anything that would help end this war.

Gabriel started the tape again.

Darcy was disappointed by what was not on the tape. "There is very little about an upcoming mission. Just that reference to the urgency in moving the shipment. Just before they part company, when Battihi is speaking, play that again."

*"Check out Thatcher. You'll need to bring a deep pocketbook."*

"Who's Thatcher?" she wondered. "The money reference suggests Battihi is suggesting someone else Dansky should look to hire."

Gabriel checked the latest updates on-line from the team working this conversation. "*Thatcher* doesn't show up as a name or alias of a terrorist in our database. The Brits and the Russians have checked their files and come up blank. It's a common European name."

Darcy peeled the orange. "Battihi is not expecting to be overheard; he's not trying to be obtuse. It's in the casual part of the conversation after the business concludes. We need to find this Thatcher. He sounds like another player."

"Maybe if Dansky follows up on the suggestion we'll be able to put a face to the name." Gabe ejected the tape. "Dansky is planning a mission, and for the first time we've got clues for its setup. The explosives, Battihi. We watch them, and we're going to get Dansky."

"Take down Danksy, and that leaves Vladimir and Luther." Line them up like dominoes: They would take out number three, then go after number two and ultimately number one.

"Get out of here for a couple hours and get a break while I pull in people. We'll talk around options for how to proceed."

She nodded, knowing she needed the break. She hated hours like this where they had information but weren't sure what the information meant. *Jesus, I could really use some help and wisdom now. Who's Thatcher? How do we find him?*

# Ten

January 16
Wednesday, 11:30 a.m.
Madrid, Spain

Darcy went back to the hotel just to get a chance to walk a bit, using her Walkman to play a tape. Listening to the opening aria for *Madame Butterfly* while walking in Spain — it was a wonderful break. She would tell Sam about it in a letter, but somehow she didn't think he'd appreciate the moment like she did. She slipped off the headphones as she reached the hotel.

Her room at the hotel was a comfortable suite with a sitting area and a small kitchenette. She fixed a peanut butter-and-jelly sandwich from her private stash sent over in a care package while she listened to the phone ring in North Dakota. She got her sister's machine. "Hi, Amy. There's nothing new. Just calling to say hi. I put a package in the mail to you today, so expect

166

what looks like a box of books. It's not books, and don't open it until your birthday. I wanted to be early with the gift for a change. Hope you're well. Talk to you later. I'll have my pager with me."

Darcy retrieved the slip of paper with her jotted notes from Sam. She poured a glass of milk. Kelly or Jill first? She had seen Jill very briefly when she passed by the wedding reception. She dialed her number first. The phone was answered after the third ring just as Darcy expected a machine to kick in.

"Hello?"

Darcy had woken up the lady. She winced. "Is this Jill?"

"Yes."

"My name is Darcy St. James. Sam Houston asked that I call you. I apologize, I don't know Tom's last name. Is your husband Tom currently in the Navy overseas?"

"Yes."

Darcy heard the uncertainty and fear in Jill's voice in that simple word. "It's good news," she rushed to explain. "I have a message for you. It's brief, I'm afraid. I'll read it. *Call Jill — Tom OK, ILY.*'" It sounded so small as she read it. "I'm sorry, that's it. Sam was on a limited transmission."

"Oh, if you only knew how sweet that message is." Jill's voice came alive with joy. "Do you know where they're deployed?"

"On a sub somewhere in the Mediterranean Sea, but I'm not sure beyond that."

"You said your name was Darcy?"

"Yes."

"Sam met you in Florida after our wedding reception."

It was her turn to hesitate. "That's right."

"I thought it was so romantic that Cougar took off with you."

Darcy had to laugh. "I don't think you heard the whole story."

"Probably not, but I heard the important details. Feel free to call with great news like this anytime. If you hear from them again, would you repeat the same message back to Tom?"

"I will." Darcy said good-bye and hung up, smiling. She dialed the second number and was able to pass the message about Joe to Kelly. The third number gave her pause. If Jill had heard about her, what had Sam told his parents? She was sure they would have asked where he had been when September 11 happened. *Sam, what did you tell them?* She dialed.

"Hello?"

"Is this Mr. Houston?" A man answered, but the voice sounded too young to be Sam's father.

"Which one are you looking for: Ben, Christopher, or Scott?"

"Umm, I'm not sure. Sam's father."

"You want Ben. Hold on." The phone was covered. "Dad, grab the phone." The man came back on. "He'll just be a minute. We're working down at the barn. Are you a friend of Sam's?"

"I have a message from him."

"Oh, even better."

"Hello?"

"Mr. Houston? Ben?"

"You've found him."

"My name is Darcy St. James. I'm calling on behalf of Sam. He asked if I'd pass a message on."

"Hold on, his mom's going to want to hear this too." Darcy could hear another phone pick up.

"Yes, hello. You heard from my Sam?!"

"He's fine, Mrs. Houston. I've got a short message from him for you."

"It's Hannah. And you must be Darcy. You really talked with him?"

"Only by text message, I'm afraid. But it was this morning. The message is very short; he was on a limited transmission. He said: 'Got letters, ILY.' "

"Oh, this is wonderful! He got the letters. I sent a huge bunch from a local school class for all the guys. Do you know if he's coming home?"

"I'm sorry; I don't know his unit's schedule. He's on a sub somewhere in the Mediterranean Sea, but I'm not sure beyond that."

"If he can at least come home for the holidays, to Thanksgiving dinner, have him bring you with him. I always like to say thanks for good news in person."

Darcy laughed. "He mentioned I'd like you. He was right."

"What else did he mention?"

"Besides an aversion to snow?"

"Darcy, honey, you do know my Sam." Hannah's laughter filled the phone line. "And you sound like you're a neighbor. Where did you grow up?"

"Just outside Shelton, over on the Cannonball River."

"Our place is just north of Timber Lake. Now you have to come for a visit. The world is so small."

"If I'm out to North Dakota to see my family over Thanksgiving, I'll give you a call," Darcy promised, taking the only gracious out she could come up with, knowing the odds she would be able to travel later in the year for Thanksgiving were slim.

She was finally able to say good-bye. It sounded like Sam had a wonderful family. Darcy bet before long Amy would be calling to mention she had spoken with Hannah. A couple hundred miles apart in the Dakotas meant the two families probably had half a dozen friends in common. Hannah would mention something to a neighbor, who would mention something to a neighbor, and Amy would get word.

She loved the small-town world. It was why she had moved back to North Dakota. But she could also understand why Sam might have found himself dreaming of going to sea.

Darcy knew she should catch a nap while she was able to do so. The idea was strong enough she went to stretch out on the couch.

What were the odds of Sam being able to get home during the upcoming months? He'd probably rotate home during the first of the year. If he could get home, she'd have to figure out a way to be there to see him.

She wanted someone like him in her life, who would be able to understand her unusual past and put it in perspective. As much as they tried to understand the world of working overseas, of following international diplomacy, civilians missed the ongoing intensity that went with this life. Sam spent his life on the front lines of international hot spots, he had traveled much of the world — they had a shared history in that kind of past. Unfortunately she wasn't going to be the lady Sam remembered. The months had added a lot of gray hair and permanent shadows under her eyes.

*Lord, sometimes I wonder who I would have been if I had followed in my sister's footsteps and become a cop instead of choosing the CIA. Would I have had a chance to meet Sam? Would he have been interested if I had been a beat cop?* She wished she knew sometimes if there had been an easier path in life. Amy was married and settled and Darcy still had that season in life to figure out.

She tugged over her Bible. She had begun to reread Psalms the last few months and found them comforting. Her morning had begun in Psalm 34. The verse she had underlined had been easily memorized. *"I sought the Lord, and he answered me, and delivered me from all my fears."*

*It's a great verse, God. You've delivered me*

172

*from a number of nights where the stress was so heavy and the fear so great it was all I could see. I'm grateful You don't change and that You're sovereign. I wish men would choose You, get to know You, rather than keep fighting. If there's anything I can do today to help move peace forward, please let me find it.*

She closed the book, the binding worn through years of travel. Faith in Jesus was the one consistency in her life. She was so thankful she had that to hold on to, could share it with Sam. At least her family and her faith hadn't been shaken by this war.

Her mind drifted back on the subjects raised by the tape. Sam had risked his life to get that conversation. She owed it to him and the others on his team to figure out everything in that message she could. *Check out Thatcher.* The suggestion sounded like someone telling a pitching coach to check out an up-and-coming player. Battihi was trying to make a good impression on the man he had just agreed to work with. He was making a suggestion he thought Dansky would appreciate.

She wanted to lock up all the loose ends, and it sounded to her like another player was out there. Dansky knew what the reference meant. That was the one fact that was very clear. Somewhere in Dansky's past he had learned who Thatcher was.

She was not going to sleep, so she got up, locked her hotel room, and walked back to work. Dansky's habits, places he had traveled in the past, something would be the connection. She had it if she could just put the pieces together.

Two hours later, she burst into Gabriel's office. He bobbled his soda. "Darcy —"

"A horse race." She nearly leaned over and kissed his frustrated face. "There's a horse race in Morocco, and a two-year-old is running named Thatcher." She felt like laughing her joy was so overwhelming. "That's what the reference is about. It's a betting tip. Thatcher plus Russian vodka seals it: Dansky is the one heading to Morocco, and he's going to stop by the racetrack. We can get both the cell and Dansky if we move fast. But we've got less than four days to set it up."

They had the golden jewel of intelligence. Future knowledge of when and where a target was going to be.

Gabriel looked at her and the twinkle in his eye that she remembered from the times they had gone behind the Berlin Wall reappeared. She smiled at him and waited.

"A principal's meeting will be held in

three hours. If I'm going to sell it, give me the bullets I can use, dahlin'. Then get your briefing books in order. I'll want you on lead for the brief."

She grabbed the dry eraser. "This one is going to be an easy sale. Once I knew the dots to look for, I found some more interesting pieces to the puzzle."

# Eleven

January 17
Thursday, 10:10 a.m.
Mediterranean Sea

Sam had become accustomed to fitting his life into small spaces. The USS *Dallas* was a big submarine, but after missiles, sonar, nuclear propulsion, and flood-and-fire suppression systems, there wasn't much room left for the sailors who ran the boat, and even less for their Special Ops guests. His bunk had six inches of storage space under it, and he was splitting the space with Wolf. He had enough personal space to pack in three paperbacks and his Bible. Sam settled on the bunk with a Western he had bought especially for this underwater deployment and let himself go back in time. Old West justice had been tough and built around the man who was sheriff, but it had been direct justice that got the job done.

Someone bumped into the stateroom

door. Sam glanced up. "Watch the peaches, Wolf." The passageway had become lashed-down storage space for the extra provisions to accommodate their presence on the boat.

"It's like living in a grocery store."

"At least the chef has good taste in fruit. Been running?" Wolf was dripping sweat.

"Five miles on the tread mill, listening to just as many tall stories from the guy who mans the firing station on this boat."

"George? Did he tell you about the octopus they found draped around the conning tower?"

"He disappeared and came back with the photo. A monster of a thing, and he tried to convince me it was only half grown."

"It was." Sam stuck a page marker in his book. "I'm enjoying this tour. These guys have been around the block a few times. Next time ask him about the last time they crashed through the ice cap near the North Pole."

"Gentlemen."

Wolf looked around as Bear came into the stateroom. "We just got a heads up. That conversation you two went beach crawling to get is apparently turning up gold: We're heading to Morocco."

"Morocco?" Sam looked at Wolf. "I've never been there."

"Neither have I. Sounds interesting. We volunteer, Bear, if you're asking," Wolf offered for them both.

Sam laughed. "At least ask what you're volunteering us for first."

"There's going to be plenty to do on this one," Bear assured. "We've got a green light to take out a cell they've been watching in Morocco."

Wolf stood a little straighter. "About time."

"Darcy came through," Sam noted.

"Check gear; in about five hours we'll be meeting up with the Brits on one of the flattops they're sending our way. We'll get an intelligence brief there."

January 17
Thursday, 6:40 p.m.
British Carrier / Mediterranean Sea

Darcy did her best not to look outside as the helicopter flared to come in for a landing atop the deck of the British carrier. A day of travel, first by NATO plane, then by helicopter out to sea, had left her longing for firm ground. That wasn't going to happen aboard a ship at sea. She saw sailors coming forward with chains as the helicopter settled to the deck.

"Where's your adventuresome spirit?" Gabe asked as the door slid open. The wind whipped inside.

The weather was threatening and she had a return flight through it to look forward to. "I didn't want to give the briefing this bad."

"You know the information cold. Trust me, Dar. You'll be glad you came."

She stepped down to the flight deck. The other helicopter bringing four NATO planners landed to their left. Her part in this day would be to brief on background, and then she and Gabriel would be on their way back to shore. Doing a snatch on Dansky in Morocco with only four days to pull it together would be a logistical feat. It wouldn't be a small operation. The British carrier was racing to cover the distance to be in position for the attempt.

Two sailors met them and provided an escort from the flight deck to the door leading into the ship's vast superstructure.

"Brandon." She was delighted to see the SAS officer coming to meet them.

"Welcome aboard, mates."

Gabe shook hands with his friend. "Your other guests arrived?"

"Forty minutes ago. You've got perfect timing." Brandon turned to Darcy with a smile. "Cougar's here, and the other chaps from SEAL Team Nine. We met up with the USS *Dallas* to give us some escort coverage."

"You knew and didn't tell me, Gabriel?" Darcy asked, as her day went from stressful to joyous. Of all the spots in the world, she'd managed to land in the same place as Sam. "Does he know I'm coming?" she asked Brandon.

"I doubt it. They're setting up gear in the hangar. Come on; you've got about twenty minutes before the briefing gets under way to say hello."

Sam opened new packages of batteries, systematically replacing them in all the communication equipment. He wasn't having any preventable equipment failure interrupt this operation. Beside him Wolf set down the laser sight he was cleaning, only to still as he reached for the next one.

"Wolf?"

Hands covered Sam's eyes before his query was finished. He tensed, and then the softness of the hands registered and the fact Wolf had started to smile before it went dark.

"Hi, Navy."

He got a whiff of her perfume as the voice registered. "Darcy." He pivoted on his heels, not rising, slipping around in her hands. The flight jacket she wore was several sizes too large and her hands were cold, but he'd never seen a more gorgeous sight. "Dar, what are you doing enlisted in the British Navy?"

"I've got twenty minutes before I have to give a brief on why you all are here. It's nice to see you, Sam."

He got to his feet, taking both her hands in his. She'd changed. Darcy's blue eyes were still captivating, but the sparkle in them was now subdued. She looked like she had endured the weight of this war on her shoulders until it pressed into her soul. Sam leaned down and kissed her cheek, wishing he wasn't surrounded by others so he could greet her properly. "You're more beautiful than I remember," he whispered.

"And you've been underwater for a while," she demurred back.

He laughed. "True." His hands slid over the jacket sleeves to rest on her shoulders. She hadn't changed, not in the way that mattered. He grinned like a fool, overwhelmed to have her here. Her blush hadn't changed. It appeared as her gaze held his and her bearing turned just a touch shy. "It is so good to see you, Dar." He had a thousand questions but settled for a simple one. "You've been traveling around Europe?"

"Racking up frequent flyer miles." Her cold hands rose to cover his. "Your mom was thrilled to get your message. I talked to your brother, your dad, and your mom."

His team crowded around to meet their first visitor in months. Sam accepted he would have to share Darcy's limited time with his friends. He wrapped an arm around her waist and introduced her, simply enjoying listening to her voice as she answered questions about home.

"Wolf, your wife asked me to return your message back to you. And Joe, Kelly's doing great. She's sending a video for you; I'll expedite it now that I know where to send it."

Someone handed her one of the water bottles they carried as standard parts of their packs, and she subtly shifted her weight to use Sam as a wall to lean against as she laughed and shared news of home. She had come to brief them on their upcoming mission. Sam knew what that suggested of her importance in this war. Europe was a big place; if Darcy and Ga-

182

briel had even stopped in the last months for a day off, Sam would be surprised. He was so proud of her he could burst.

Her cold hand slid into his and she turned the ring on his hand in an idle motion as she talked. Someone needed to get her a strong cup of coffee to warm her up. One of the huge elevator lifts brought down a Harrier jet from the deck above causing a swirling rush of wind. He lifted his arm and shielded her from the worst of it. She must have had an interesting flight out here.

She glanced up and back at him. "I'm not looking forward to the flight back."

"You'll do fine. The pilots here are the best."

"You speak from experience?"

He smiled down at her upturned face. "Trust me; as long as you don't have to jump out of one of those helos intentionally, you have no need to worry."

"I missed you, Sam," she whispered.

"Same here." Words just didn't cut it. He wrapped his arms around her and hugged her, the too-big coat, his buddies, and the fact that they were standing in a hangar pushed aside so he could enjoy the moment. In wartime, you took what you could get and appreciated the time rather than regret its brevity. "Someone find me a camera."

Whistles met his words.

Darcy picked up her briefing book and perched on the table at the front of the squadron room as the British SAS and U.S. SEAL Team Nine members assembled. "Gentlemen, my name is Darcy St. James. I'm a U.S. national intelligence officer working on one of the hunter teams NATO has deployed across Europe. We need a cell in Morocco taken down and one particular man snatched. I'm here to provide the background on who and why."

She took a drink from a water bottle, settling comfortably into this briefing. She'd done many presentations over her years at the Agency, and by far briefing soldiers was one of the most straightforward and enjoyable parts of the job. No matter the rank, branch of service, or even country they came from, her task was the same: tell them what you knew, what you thought, and be clear on differentiating the two. Since they were the tip of the spear, the information she provided would lead directly to action. Long months of work on her part were about to be used to bring justice. It was why she did the job. She did her best to avoid looking at Sam, knowing that would be enough to break her train of thought.

She turned the projector on and put up the first photo. "Luther Genault. A former Czech intelligence officer. He knew September 11 would happen in advance, he profited from it, he's the scum of the earth, and we want him." Her frank assessment earned her a few smiles; each man studied the photo.

"He has two men working for him. This group is different; they are not terrorists seeking to implement their own agenda through violence. They seek to profit from the fact terrorism is happening in the world and, where they can make money, encourage it. Think of them as black market profiteers. And profit they have, to the tune of half a billion dollars, most through stock market manipulation."

She clicked the pointer and put up a picture of Dansky. "This is the man we want to snatch. Peter Dansky is the operations man of the outfit. We believe he is heading to Morocco to meet with a terrorist cell we've been watching for some time. He's facilitating a deal for the explosives the group is seeking to acquire. In doing so he'll make a tidy sum and learn when and where they plan to strike so he can profit on the turmoil that results."

She put up a photo of the compound they had been watching in Morocco. "We believe he will be at this location on January 20. He's planning to attend a horse race and then travel south to this compound. Dansky is a cautious man. He depends on anonymity. He won't be traveling with a big group that could draw attention; historically he's had one driver who also acts as his security. He's not known for disguise or changes in appearance beyond dress that would fit in among the locals. Dansky limps from surgery on his left knee."

She put up a map of the area around the compound. "If he senses danger we believe his escape routes will be made through tapping into the old Russian network of contacts in Morocco. I've highlighted the few safe houses we know of, and the Russians will have a full list here by morning. Dansky cares about one person — himself. The groups he meets with are interchangeable to him. Last month he worked with that terrorist cell wiped out in Algeria. If he runs, he's likely to go in the opposite direction from the group."

She replaced the map with the picture of

Peter Dansky again. "This man, gentlemen. We want him."

She quietly handed the pointer off to Gabriel who would be presenting details on the Moroccan compound. She could see it in their faces — this group of men wouldn't fail. And that was exactly what she wanted to see. She caught Sam's gaze and held it. In situations like this one he'd be key; the snipers always were. She'd done her job; now he'd do his. She was so proud of him. She was grateful he was one of the soldiers the military had prepared for just such an assignment. They couldn't afford missing this opportunity.

January 19
Saturday, 4:10 p.m.
British Carrier / Mediterranean Sea

Sam knelt beside the huge satellite maps spread out on the hangar deck next to two Harrier jets undergoing maintenance, mentally going over the plan one more time against the best visuals they had of the situation on the ground. The SEAL team had been working this plan for a day and a half side by side with the SAS team. It was unusual for their teams to work so tightly coupled in an active mission, but given the men and equipment in position to act within the time constraints, this was a very smart pairing. He had to admire the intel Darcy and Gabriel had provided. They knew this compound inside and out.

She'd gone before he could say good-bye. She'd briefed them and left by the time the four NATO planners finished up their tactical briefs. Some things war didn't allow, and the luxury of time was one of them. At least he had her picture. And a reminder. She had left the medallion he had given her from the wedding reception in the pocket of his jacket, a finely braided chain showing she had worn it for some time.

"What do you think, Chief?" Bear asked, kneeling beside him.

Sam glanced at his CO and pulled his thoughts away from Darcy back to the job at hand. "Brandon's got a good plan. The house and compound are set back from civilian homes; the road is cut into the hillside on a pretty good grade. Terrain works in our favor. We've got good divisions of responsibility. Three teams — one to take the house, one to take the back of the compound and garden, and one to secure the road." He outlined the plan on the map.

"The helos land here and here for egress, then we dash to the sea. The huge risk is the fact that it's a daylight action, but that appears to be the only way to grab Dansky."

"We want him alive, but it's not an at-all-costs mission parameter."

"We'll have close parity in good guys/bad guys ratio, we'll have surprise, and we'll have the tactical advantage. We act when the meeting is breaking up. That gives us the best intel on how many people we're dealing with. It lets them be at their most relaxed at the end of their big meeting. The plan is to divide and conquer as Dansky leaves. We cut him off on the road and isolate him from the compound. That allows us to minimize the risks to the team going in and hauling him out. We hammer them with suppressing fire and have snipers doing the critical work of pro-tecting our guys. The helos bring the big firepower just before egress. We want Dansky. It's worth the risks."

"It's a good plan, Chief." Bear got to his feet. "Come see the bigger picture we've worked out for this."

Sam rose and joined his boss.

"The CIA has a team of three men watching the compound from a house located here, halfway up the hillside as it curves around. They also have access to a second vantage point, here, that provides coverage of the back of the compound. We'll put recon teams in at dawn to both sites. I want you and Brandon going into this one to confirm the situation on the ground." Bear indicated on the aerial map. "Spotters will set up at these perches before the mission starts and get video in place so that all three teams will have full visuals on the compound. If Dansky doesn't arrive, if we are dealing with more tangos than expected, if there's a question about being able to execute the snatch, we'll have three alternative plans: fall back and wait for night, strike with air power, or from the ground take out specific individuals. Washington will be viewing the spotter feeds and making that call."

Sam nodded. "If they decide against a snatch and just want to take out the cell, this gets straightforward. It's a fortress but that's also its biggest weakness. The Brits proved that in Algeria. We wait for night then sweep in."

Bear slipped his pen into his pocket. "I want you to plan one more option for me, Chief. Assume the worse and one of our teams gets discovered — we have a firefight from the compound, a firefight coming toward us on this road, and our helo for egress can't get in."

Sam judged the lay of the land in the maps and let it suggest an answer. "Fall back to . . . here, snipers close this area to all comers, and we acquire transportation to get us to another extraction point, say by boat from here."

"Okay," Bear agreed. "Get the pieces together so they're in our back pocket if we need 'em. I don't trust the weather, helos coming in at low altitude, the direction of street signs . . ."

Sam laughed. "I'll get on it, boss."

January 20
Sunday, 6:27 a.m.
Morocco

Sam went in with one of the two reconnaissance teams at dawn. They inserted into Morocco by sea along a deserted stretch of beach, were met by the CIA station chief, and driven to the safe house being used to watch the compound. Perspective changed when the area was seen from the ground. Resting on a mat, Sam stretched out on the roof of the house and used binoculars to scan the area. "We need to move the team handling the road a little farther south to take advantage of that foliage. It blocks line of sight to the house. We move when Dansky's car clears that point. It's a natural fire zone, the street narrows, not allowing the vehicle much movement once it's blocked in."

Brandon beside him studied the setup and nodded. "We set a charge behind that wall and the debris will close the way forward. Four guys coming around the wall in the car's blind spots race up either side, disable the driver, and yank Dansky from the car. We can land the helo forward of that location."

Sam turned his attention to the compound. "When you blow that wall to stop the car, we lay down fire into the front of the compound; that forces people back. They'll have a hard time getting fire out the front of the building without making themselves visible. Snipers pick off any who try. The helos come in, land, and the snipers fall back to egress."

"Weather is good; visibility is good."

Sam nodded. "Signal Bear. The mission's on."

# Twelve

January 20
Sunday, 3:15 p.m.
Madrid, Spain

"Why don't you sit down," Gabriel suggested. Darcy paced. She couldn't sit, not while the SEALs and the SAS were going in based on her intelligence. It was a daylight raid and incredibly dangerous. The video feed was dark. "How long before we get something?"

"Would you relax? We'll get copied on the feed. The director put through the approval personally. And we're going to owe him favors for the next decade for it."

"We set up the mission intel fast. What critical items have we missed?"

"Dansky is there. He was spotted leaving the racetrack and driving toward this town. Thatcher won his race; Dansky will be in a good mood. This is going to happen, and the guys on the ground know how to think on their feet and adapt if necessary."

The live feed came on, the camera image facing an adobe wall. "Yes!" The picture bounced around. She tilted her head to the side to right the image. "Those are chocolate chip cammies and an SAS insignia. We've got a feed from the Brits. All right, guys." She collapsed onto a chair in front of the set, leaned close, and tried to absorb every impression, hoping she would see Sam.

"We've got to get you into the field more often. You're going four-wall crazy," Gabe punched the record button to capture the feed for replay.

The image shifted and looked down at the front of the compound. She wanted to be the one on the ground collecting those early surveillance pictures. "When we go after Luther, I want in on it."

"Keep dreaming, dahlin'."

"Do we get the U.S. feed too?"

"If there is one, we'll get it," Gabriel reassured. "There are at least forty specialists at Defense and NSA watching the feeds to identify people, but Chip said he'd like your best guess on IDs as well." The DIA officer was coordinating this live transmission.

"He knows I would tell him anyway."

The pictures stabilized and telescoped in to focus on a compound some distance away. "A clear day, this is good clarity."

The second video came up, showing images from the back of the compound area, giving a full view of the garden.

She settled in to try and identify the members of this terrorist cell as they moved from the house to the gardens and back inside. "They're getting ready for a meal and a meeting. There doesn't appear to be a great hurry."

"Notice the fact they are serving themselves? There isn't any house staff around." One man appeared to carry what looked like a torchlight into the garden seating area.

Over the next forty minutes Darcy sighted each of the six men who were part of the Moroccan cell in the compound. "Good, everyone is there."

The guards settled into what looked like a fairly regular security patrol of the compound grounds, containing a house and a walled-in garden with what looked like a parking area on the east side that had a higher wall around it. "Interesting that in an hour of watching, there are no signs of a phone call or radio message."

"They've learned," Gabe agreed. "Communication is face-to-face."

"Here, we've got something happening."

Two trucks arrived first, and several men bearing automatic weapons spread out to provide security. Cars, interspersed by several minutes of quiet, followed the trucks as men providing security tensed with each arrival.

"I can't believe this," Darcy finally said as they watched the fifth car pull away.

"Believe it," Gabriel replied. "We were due a lucky break at some point in this war." He had picked up the phone to check in with DIA on this unexpected turn of events. More cars kept arriving.

"This is like a convention of the terrorist who's-who list." She circled her finger on the screen identifying men now standing around the inside walled garden, greeting each other. "That man was behind the USS *Cole* bombing, those two Russians have been indicted for their embassy explosion, and the Swiss want this man for the downing of an airline last year." The SEALs and Brits had to pull this off. This was the first major break in months.

"DIA agrees. They're rapidly changing plans. Dansky is celebrating his horse winning, and he invited some friends over."

"Thank you, Dansky. Who else did you

invite?" She could feel her excitement building. "The war could take a major step toward being over today, and we're watching it happen. Can they adapt to this?"

"This kind of chance opportunity has been on the CINC's mind since this war began."

A car with tinted windows arrived, and one of the two men guarding the house stepped forward to meet the guest. Darcy watched the back door open and leaned forward to study the picture, hoping the man would glance left and give them a direct visual of his face.

"Battihi," she breathed. "He rarely travels outside of Egypt. He came along with the explosives?"

"I don't think he brought an armored truck with him to be subtle about it." Gabe grabbed the secure phone as they watched the armored truck pull into a secure area of the compound.

Darcy was on her feet. She watched Battihi look around, walk up the path, and disappear into the house. "The assault team has to wipe out that shipment. Can they take Battihi along with Dansky?"

"Chip, it's Gabriel. That last guy is Battihi. Yes, we're confident. Can they adjust to try to take that shipment of explosives that just came in?" Gabe stayed on the phone as the military planners sorted out options.

The second image covering the back of the compound showed the men beginning to move and sit down. "The meeting is starting. Battihi must have been the last expected guest."

"Thanks, Chip." Gabe hung up the phone. The second image zoomed in tight and brought Battihi's face into focus. "The guys on the ground have word he's there. He's on the list of prioritized targets to take out. This mission is on the clock now."

The camera focused there for about thirty seconds and then pulled back and began to review the entire area in a systematic sweep. The men she knew that were part of the Moroccan cell were not part of the meeting but were standing as security at various points within the compound. The camera moved to a wide view and stabilized.

She watched as discussions, some of them animated, continued among the group. "I would love to have a few bugs in that compound."

"Same here."

Gabriel watched the growing list of

people being identified. "This is a coordinating meeting between different terrorist groups. They are finally deciding isolation makes it harder to act. They don't realize just meeting together also makes them all vulnerable."

"We've been financially squeezing the groups individually; they have to work together to survive." Men began to rise to their feet. She tensed. "The meeting is breaking up. They're going to be leaving any moment."

"A few minutes yet. It's becoming social, and now the real power brokers will be talking in small groups."

Darcy leaned forward to try and see who was talking with whom. She blinked at a sudden movement of white across the screen. The house blew up, imploding from the inside. She jerked back. "What was that?"

"Justice," Gabriel replied coolly. A second flash appeared in the dust cloud. He studied the two different angles of the compound as rubble began to appear. "The building collapsed in on itself. A crater marks the remains of the garden. Notice the compound wall absorbed the blast wave and toppled outward? It looks like minimal damage around the area. You wanted to know what the CINC would do given the unexpected guests. There's the answer. Two smart bombs hit the house and grounds and took them all out."

"It's cold."

"They're combatants in a war they declared, and they've spent their lives killing civilians. My only regret is that we didn't stop them months ago," Gabe replied.

"The armored truck was just buried in the rubble. It didn't explode."

"The problem with smart bombs is sometimes they don't do enough collateral damage."

"What will our guys do?" Darcy asked.

"My guess is they were falling back long before that missile hit. I wouldn't want to be across the street when it came in. They'll get out while the Moroccan police try to figure out what just happened. If that shot came from offshore, the missile may not have even shown up on radar."

Darcy hoped he was right, that everyone who had gone in for this mission was safe. She watched the images from the observation perches tilt as they were moved and caught a glimpse of soldiers kneeling and methodically breaking down and packing equipment before a steady hand turned off the camera. The movements from the soldiers on the ground weren't desperate or hurried as if they were dealing with trouble. They were packing up after a job accomplished.

"We just put a huge crimp in Luther's group." Gabe pushed himself to his feet, pausing to make sure his legs would take his weight. He ejected the tapes and put them in his safe. "Go lock up your office and grab your keys. We don't have Dansky to interrogate for information, but I'll take this exchange. That strike probably permanently eliminated some planned operations for the first anniversary of the World Trade Center attack. The fallout of this is a problem for tomorrow."

"I want to wait until we get the after-action reports."

"They aren't going to come for several hours. CIA will go in quietly with the police to collect whatever documents they can from those crushed vehicles and make sure that the armored truck and its contents are secured. I'm guessing we'll have weeks of work ahead of us going through all the intelligence collected." Gabriel held the door open for her. "The interesting part of this will be how cells around the world react. There'll be internal battles for leadership happening in numerous cells over the next weeks."

"Luther is going to be annoyed," she said, understating the obvious. And Vladimir. Luther's impenetrable wall had just been breached. If they could get to Dansky, Luther knew he himself was at risk. There would be a reaction from him, movement, something that could be tracked.

"We'll get him," Gabe promised. "After tonight, it's inevitable."

# Thirteen

*Four Months Later*
May 21
Tuesday, 11:22 a.m.
Little Creek Naval Base / Norfolk, Virginia

It felt good to be back on U.S. soil. Sam slipped on his sunglasses, as his eyes struggled to adjust to the brightness of a gorgeous day. The military base was more than just homeport; it was home. And the Stars and Stripes were flying in welcome.

"Gear."

Sam leaned down and caught the strap of the bag Wolf lifted up. Unpacking a submarine meant everything came out of a hatch. The sailor assigned to help the SEALs unload their equipment reached to take the bag from him.

"It's heavy, son." Sam released his grip. The sailor staggered a bit as he took it. Sam reached down for the next bag.

He was tired, but it was a good tired.

There was a lot to do during this return stateside — a trip to South Dakota to surprise his folks and an expedition to find Darcy. He'd heard through friends that she and Gabe were back in the States. He was taking her out for lunch somehow. It was time to collect on at least one of the favors he was due.

"Cougar."

"Sorry." He reached for the next satchel.

Wolf climbed up the ladder after passing it up.

"You've got lipstick on your collar," Sam felt obliged to point out. Jill had marked him good.

"Why in the world they would let wives come for joyous reunions and then turn around and say you're on duty another three hours to unpack is beyond me. I've never seen more distracted men in my life."

Sam laughed. "For two weeks' liberty in a few hours, I'll put up with first-year kids stumbling over their own feet. What time are you and Jill taking off?"

"Six. We'll probably go as far as North Carolina tonight, just as long as I'm far enough away I can't be found easily by phone. You?"

"I don't know. I'll probably head north."

Wolf laughed. "Have you even called her yet, or are you just going to go?"

"I'm still debating."

"Team Two said they'd handle the gear in the dry deck."

"Nice of them." Sam picked up their scuba gear.

"Would you go call her? I'm not taking off until I know you've at least got plans for your two weeks off."

"Just because you're not going to be around to keep me out of trouble . . ." Sam replied and ducked Wolf's good-natured shove.

May 21
Tuesday, 11:42 a.m.
Central Intelligence Agency / Langley, Virginia

In the months since the World Trade Center attack, Darcy had taken up running as a way to maintain her sanity and stay in shape. The music contained by the earphones was Big Band at full volume. She ran without counting the laps she made of the path that wove around the 225-acre complex looping around the CIA headquarter buildings and parking lots to the woods by the power plant. She was thinking. She would stop running when she was done thinking or her legs gave out.

The off-duty dog from the bomb squad running beside her crashed through a pile of dried leaves then circled around to do it again, barking at the fun. She pushed back the earphones and jogged in place, laughing at him. "Henry, they're dead."

He rolled in the leaves and then scrambled back toward her. She picked up her pace again.

How was it possible for Luther and Vladimir to simply go quiet and stay quiet? She hadn't even caught a glimmer of a bank account transaction in the last four months. The places on earth she couldn't snoop were so few they could be numbered on one hand. Even China and North Korea were under constant electronic surveillance. Tracking down Ramon Santigo had been much like this. Chasing something she couldn't see. It was making her mad.

Luther and Vladimir had both gone to ground. Even the contracted killings of agents in Europe had stopped as suddenly as they began. Where would Luther hide? And where was his money?

They were four months away from the anniversary of September 11, and the stress in the pit of her stomach was growing. They didn't have a year to chase this man. They needed Luther and his money wiped off the map so it couldn't be used to spawn any more evil.

She was under no illusions. The loss of key leadership in so many terrorist groups would make retaliatory actions by followers more likely than not. Without the infrastructure behind them, the attacks would be less organized, less destructive, but there would be something to mark the anniversary. She needed Luther and his source of capital taken out sooner rather than later.

She worried about Luther learning the names of those in the assault teams. The next months hunting Luther and Vladimir would be the most dangerous of the entire fight. He knew he was vulnerable, and you didn't back an angry cat in a corner and leave him means to strike back.

*Lord, I can't take more civilian deaths happening on my watch. What am I missing? You've opened doors and provided leads in the past, given wisdom to put together the pieces. What has to happen next to break this case open? I'm stuck; I need help.* The pressure of her job was burying her under weight that never eased up.

In one of his few letters to reach her Sam

had pointed to 1 Peter 5:8 about their adversary, the devil, prowling around like a roaring lion as his way of putting what was happening in perspective. She wished she had the ability to put into words the reassurance Sam found so easy to do. She knew the verses, but at times it was hard to transfer what she knew to what she felt. She had to daily seek the peace that God was in charge, whereas it seemed Sam lived under that reassurance all the time.

Her nerves were stretched to their limits as the months passed without a good lead to work. She was getting beat by Luther, and she hated that feeling. She hadn't lost a fight in her years with the CIA, but this was beginning to feel like defeat. Some days she felt like she was trying to run away from the burden. She was clinging to the verse: *"Cast all your anxieties on him, for he cares about you."*

"Darcy!" The security guard at the main gate got her attention, and she removed her headphones. "Your partner is looking for you. You've got a call he thinks you'll want to take."

She changed directions to stop by the security station; it would be a ten-minute run to get back to her desk. Kevin slid open the door for her from the inside.

"Line four," the guard directed, pointing out the phone.

"Thanks, Kevin."

She snapped her fingers for the bomb dog to settle down near her feet. "This is Darcy."

"It's good to hear you're still alive."

She nearly dropped the phone. "Sam?" She laughed, delighted. "Where are you?"

"Little Creek. You want to have dinner tonight? I can be in your neighborhood in four hours."

She looked down at the sweats and the beat-up tennis shoes. "I'd love to; only I've got a late afternoon meeting that may drag out. Can we do it late, say eight o'clock?"

"Eight it is," he promptly agreed.

"Find a pen; I'll give you a refresher on the directions."

Darcy leaned against Gabriel's office door, wiping perspiration from her face from her run. Her partner had his reading glasses pushed up and his attention focused on a satellite photo that was part of the city of Aden, Yemen. She knew the streets in that town better than those around her own apartment building. They were chasing down a rumor that Vladimir had been there recently.

Darcy chewed on the sucker stick she was working on. "Who's his new number three? Luther has to replace Dansky with someone. Who is it going to be?" She posed the most interesting of the questions she had been pondering since the takedown in Morocco.

"It's not like there are many options. Vladimir will probably assume operations as well as security."

"He won't let himself be that exposed, out traveling and meeting people who he knows are watching and hunting him. After what happened in Algeria and Morocco, I bet he figures someone is selling them out. Without seeing our cards, it looks like too much of a coincidence that we got both cells in a matter of weeks. I'm betting Luther's new number three is going to be someone not on our radar screens."

Gabe leaned back in his wheelchair. "The way Luther has gone quiet, I'm betting he'll be looking to settle in and restore security around a new home before he makes any attempt to rebuild his organization and anoint a new number three. We may not have knocked him out, but we stunned him and it shows." Gabe exited the Yemen page and logged out of the secure site. He reached for his stack of phone messages. "How was your call?"

She smiled at him, surprised it had taken him that long to ask. "You knew it was Sam. Why didn't you warn me?"

"And ruin his surprise?" Gabe asked, returning the smile. "He was trying to get a call to your desk here, but no one would admit you were alive. The operator had actually tagged security to a possible problem." He held up his hand. "I took care of it. So what's the verdict? Going to see him?"

She rocked her foot on the edge of her tennis shoe. "Maybe dinner. Since I'm still rumored to be dead, it's a bit awkward having him come this direction, but I'll work something out. I'll probably take him to Chin's. I want a good grilled swordfish."

"He's at Little Creek?"

"Just got in."

"I figured that. He sounded like he was seeing daylight for the first time in ages. Why don't you visit him there? You haven't had a day off in months, and it would do you good to get away. Besides, the seafood is better that direction."

"I've got a meeting with the Mideast desk at three."

"I'll take the meeting. Take a few days now. It's a quiet window. As it gets closer to September 11, we'll be working around the clock again. I'd like you fresh for that. You'd better go while you can."

"Gabriel —"

"Go. Luther is quiet. We're watching everywhere we think something might appear. You owe Sam a favor, so go surprise him."

She wanted to get out of here with an intensity that surprised her. She wanted to forget this war and the fight and have a few days truly free. "Your wife and I were going to go shopping tonight, but this means I'll have to cancel on her. Will you surprise her with dinner since if I cut out early you can do the same without me knowing about it?"

He grinned at her. "Probably."

"Then I'm going. But only if you promise to answer my phone while I'm gone and call if there's anything interesting. And be liberal on your definition of interesting."

"I predict you'll be in news withdrawal within a day. There's a great bed-and-breakfast in Norfolk on Route 60 — that's the scenic highway, by the way, which I strongly suggest you drive and enjoy the scenery — the bed-and-breakfast is at the corner of Independence Boulevard. I'm sure one of the thousands of directories this place owns can give you the name."

"Or I could type bed-and-breakfast, Norfolk, Virginia, in my know-it-all search engine and get the phone number."

"That would work too."

"I'll call you when I arrive," Darcy offered.

"That was a preemptive decision because you knew I was going to ask."

She grinned at him and picked up one of Gabriel's decoder rings he kept in a bowl beside his phone to give out as jokes and slipped it onto her little finger.

"Get out of here, Dar, and enjoy the time away."

She started toward her office and then came back to lean around the doorway. "What are you getting me for Christmas?"

"Darcy, it's May."

"It's exactly seven months and four days to Christmas. A useless fact, but I tend to remember those kinds of things. I want a guppy for my new fish tank. A fancy one. Sam says I don't know how to do a guppy stroke. I want to be able to tell him that I have a guppy." She grinned at him and then headed to her office.

She had to figure out a way to head off Sam. He might have already left to come north, but she'd said eight o'clock, and she was counting on the fact he would at least be stopping by his place to look through the mail first.

Where was that note with his friends' names? Her desk was clear, the papers in the safe, and the slip of paper she had kept with his messages for friends was no longer tucked on her keyboard where she kept it for weeks as a souvenir. She finally found the slip of paper in the paperback she was reading and picked up the phone.

"Kelly? This is Darcy St. James. I called a while back with a message Sam asked me to pass on."

"Yes, hi. How are you, Darcy?"

"I was hoping you might be able to do me a favor. Sam just called, and he was thinking about coming this way for dinner. I'd like to head your way instead, but I need some help."

May 21
Tuesday, 4:17 p.m.
Norfolk, Virginia

"Kelly, she's beautiful." Sam carried Bethany over to the couch and carefully sat down. His goddaughter was five months and four days old, and she'd already stolen his heart. He'd seen her this morning as Joe showed her off around the pier but it hadn't been nearly long enough. Her eyelashes were perfectly curled and the little fingernails had grown. She had good muscle tone and even in her sleeper outfit with its little feet she was quite mobile. Joe had been back in the States for two weeks for her birth, and photos had been regularly posted on-line to let the entire team stay in touch. But it wasn't the same as holding her.

"Here's her bottle. I so appreciate this help, Sam. Joe got hung up for a few minutes, and it's critical that I get this packing done before he gets home. We're leaving at eleven tonight and driving straight through while Bethany sleeps, and Joe has to get the insurance and will paperwork signed at the lawyer's office before six. What a time for the sitter to be late."

Sam tucked the bottle comfortably in place against his arm but found Bethany was more interested in flirting with him than eating. "I'm glad you caught me. Go and pack. I'll keep Bethany occupied. I've got a little time before I need to leave." Darcy had said eight, and if he left in the next twenty minutes, he could probably make it on time without getting a speeding ticket.

"You've got a date."

"Not exactly."

Kelly leaned over the back of the couch to look down at him.

Sam smiled up at her. "Okay, maybe a small date."

She patted his cheek. "Relax, I talked to Darcy. There's been a slight change of plans. She's coming here to meet you."

"You talked to Darcy —" His surprise had Bethany succeeding in winning their tug-of-war for the blue plastic donut ring.

Kelly slipped in her earrings. "I like her. It was supposed to be a surprise, but since I'm extra partial to you and you don't handle surprises very well, I thought I'd give you a little warning."

It took Sam a moment to catch up with the information. "Darcy's coming here." He looked down at Bethany now happily swinging the blue plastic donut back and forth. "The missing baby-sitter was a ruse? You were supposed to figure out how to keep me from leaving?"

"Oh, it's real enough. The baby-sitter isn't going to show in ten minutes. And there is no way you would turn down Joe if he asked you a last minute favor to stay and help us out. Not when it also involves your goddaughter."

"You're thinking of having me baby-sit?"

"No. I'm thinking of having Darcy baby-sit Bethany. You're going to watch her and learn." Kelly laughed. "You are adorable when you're speechless." The doorbell rang. "That should be Darcy; she's right on time. This is called neutral territory. I think she's nervous. No, don't get up. You look totally charming so out of your element."

Sam got up anyway as Kelly went to get the door. This wasn't what he had planned. He should at least have flowers.

"Darcy, hi. I'm Kelly. It's great to finally meet you. Did you have any trouble finding the place?"

"None at all. You give great directions."

Sam was hungry for the sound of the voice he had thought about nearly every day.

Darcy stopped in the living room doorway. "Hey, sailor."

The worn-out picture in his pocket didn't do her justice. Darcy had been rushing; her cheeks were flushed and her hair a bit out of place. He wanted to say something profound but instead he just stared, absorbing the fact that the months away had only intensified the pleasure of having her company. "Hello, Darcy."

They stood smiling at each other until Kelly bustled through the room to answer the ringing phone. "Darcy, did Sam tell you he's that angel's godfather?"

"No, he didn't."

Sam walked over to introduce them. "This is Bethany."

"Oh." Dar's entire face softened. "She's beautiful." She gently rubbed Bethany's arm.

"I hear you're helping me baby-sit."

Darcy looked up at him and a small smile appeared. "I have to admit, the last time I baby-sat I was sixteen," she whispered. She held up a piece of paper. "I've got a list of baby experts in town if we need help."

"We'll manage," Sam replied. He leaned over and kissed her, a soft brush of his lips against hers. "Hi, beautiful," he whispered. He moved his head back just enough to enjoy the depth of blue in her eyes.

"I'm glad you came." Sam realized suddenly that there was very little he could add to tonight to make it more perfect. Her blush turned her cheeks a beautiful rose color. Kelly was right; Darcy was indeed a bit nervous. He wanted to stop that subtle biting of her inner lower lip with another kiss but instead he just smiled. He was going to make tonight the best night of her life.

"Kelly," he asked, not looking away from Darcy, "you and Joe need about an hour for the errands?"

"Better make it two given the traffic. I've set out baby food jars for Bethany. She likes the peaches best. Diapers and supplies are by the changing table." He took one step back from Darcy as Kelly rushed back into the room. "My cell phone number." She tucked it in his shirt pocket. "Joe had a change of plans; I'm to pick him up."

"He's the boss, all the stuff lands on him as soon as we dock."

"I know, and it's okay. I get him for the next two weeks. Is there anything else I'm supposed to tell you?" She tickled her daughter who laughed back.

Sam settled the infant more comfortably in his arms. "We're fine. Do you still keep spare house keys in the dish by the microwave?"

"Yes. If Bethany fusses, turn on the tape in the player and walk with her. She loves her daddy's voice."

"Will do."

"Darcy, it was great to meet you. Sorry to be rushing out. I'm normally so organized. I'll tell you all about Sam later, I know *everything*."

Darcy laughed. "I'd like that."

"Okay, I'm going." Kelly kissed her daughter one more time then grabbed her jacket.

Sam pointed out the baby bag. "Snag that, Darcy."

"Where are we going?"

He slid on his sunglasses. "A walk down the block. I'd like you to meet Wolf's wife, Jill." He took the spare set of house keys and picked up Bethany's blanket to tuck around her. Sam realized the direction of Darcy's gaze. "Would you like to hold her?"

"I was wondering if you were ever going to offer."

He chuckled and gently transferred the child into her arms. "I think I'm going to enjoy being a godfather."

"I think you will too." She snuggled with Bethany.

Darcy looked wonderful holding an infant. Sam stayed in her space on the pretext of helping with the blanket. Sam figured Darcy would get along great with Jill, but if they needed an icebreaker,

220

Bethany was a perfect one. She would create instant common ground. "You must have left the office shortly after I called."

Darcy nodded without looking up at him. "Gabe kicked me out and said go."

"You couldn't have given me a more special welcome home than meeting me here. Do you have a place arranged to stay already or should I make a couple calls?"

"He recommended a bed-and-breakfast. I'm set for a few days."

Sam held the front door for her. "How long can you be gone before Gabe sends out search parties?"

She stepped outside and waited as he locked the house. "I don't have to be back until Monday."

"I've got two weeks off," he offered, walking backward on the sidewalk, hopeful.

Darcy smiled at him. "We'll start with dinner first."

"Playing hard to get. Okay. You know a SEAL likes a challenge."

"And a spy likes to decide the ground that's played on."

He laughed. "I noticed that. My boss's place. Not bad, Darcy. It kind of guarantees good behavior."

"I thought it was pretty clever myself."

She glanced down at Bethany. "Besides, if you're boring company, I've still got a couple perfect hours coming up."

"Ohh, you slay me. I think I'm going to enjoy tonight."

"I know I am."

# Fourteen

May 21
Tuesday, 6:15 p.m.
Norfolk, Virginia

Darcy sank deeper into the couch, letting a sleeping Bethany settle against her shoulder. She should have kept baby-sitting into her thirties instead of leaving that practice behind as a teen. There was nothing more soothing in life than to cuddle an infant whose only priorities in life were to eat, sleep, and play. The stress of war hadn't touched Bethany, and in just sharing that there was a reason to relax. Darcy couldn't remember the last time she had truly stopped and let everything go. She handed the nearly empty baby bottle to Sam. "She's asleep."

Sam traded her the baby bottle for the blanket. "She's grown up so much in the months we've been away. You should have seen Bear down at the pier this morning when he brought her around to show off."

Given how proud Sam was to be this little girl's godfather, she could imagine what it must have been like when Joe saw his little girl for the first time after months away. "Proud daddy?"

"Oh, yeah. He's also a great boss."

"I think so. He got you home alive," she added softly. "Jill is a sweetheart." She and Sam hadn't stayed long as Tom and Jill were also getting ready to head out for a vacation over the leave, but they had stayed long enough to convince her Jill was indeed the perfect wife for Sam's swim buddy. Wolf and Cougar: The two men stood beside each other and it was like an invincible wall. It mattered to Sam that she meet his partner's wife, and Darcy found that touching. "To get married and two days later send your husband off to war?" She shook her head. "I don't know that I could handle that."

"You handle what you have to."

Darcy leaned over to retrieve her glass of iced tea. Sam looked ready to handle whatever came. She studied him stretched out in a nearby chair. He'd been in great shape before he left. Now that physical toughness had been honed by months at war. She enjoyed just looking.

Was he a friend, a date, something serious and permanent? She looked at Sam and hoped this relationship would have a chance to grow. From his kiss in greeting, he was clearly thinking the same way. She helped herself to a handful of the Cheerios Bethany had been eating. She was ready for dinner. "What's it like being on the front lines? I only know of a couple places you've been."

"I can do better than Cheerios. How about Chex mix?"

"Hand it over."

Sam passed her the dish. She picked out the peanuts first.

"I've seen just about every terrain God created short of tropical jungle. Cold and heat, tough living conditions, carry in your own water and food, lots of miles walked in boots, lots of sneaking around in towns you don't want to be seen in." He sorted out Bethany's blocks by color. "Are you handling the work overseas okay? You've been busy. I'm glad you were able to get back to the States for a while."

It was a hard question to know how to answer. "I walk away from the office every day wondering what I missed, what I should have seen." She wished she could put in words what those long evening hours when she couldn't sleep were like. "It's a struggle to learn enough to head off the next attack. I know we aren't going to be able to stop them all and it haunts me." She knew what could come next, the rumors of what different terrorist groups planned, and she feared the phone call that would come in the middle of the night. "And Luther is still out there waiting to profit on that terror, to even fund it if he can make money doing so."

"I'm sorry we weren't able to grab Dansky. It —"

She stopped his words with an extended hand. "It's okay. Morocco disrupted so many groups it's considered the most successful strike of the last months. We'll get him."

"Dar, the weight of the last months is visible. I'd like to think you could get your life back at some point. Have you at least had a chance to get back to North Dakota?"

Just the thought made her smile. She dreamed of getting back to work on her house. She'd love to have Sam's help digging the new fence posts. "I've been too busy to get home. I do talk to my sister several times a week though, and she shipped some of my stuff out here."

"You need to get home."

"I don't want to drag this stuff back there, you know? Amy will take one look at me and read me like an open book."

"She can do that?" Sam asked. "I'm going to have to meet her and ask her secret. Are you at least going to be able to get home later this year for the holidays?" The sound of a car door slamming caught his attention. "Hold that thought. That sounds like Joe and Kelly." Sam got up to open the door.

Darcy liked Sam's apartment. It was definitely a bachelor pad with only a few soft touches in the decor. It didn't look like he had lived here all that much, but it was quite interesting to see what he had collected. Not many guys had a kayak in the hallway. There were more family photos on the tables and hanging on the walls than she had expected. His two brothers were easy to pick out and his parents. "How big is your family?"

"With cousins?" He paused to count. "Thirty-two, but I may have missed a couple." He handed her the soda she'd requested. "Give me twenty minutes to shower, shave, and change. Make yourself at home."

"Do you mind if I use your phone?"

"Feel free."

Sam went to change for dinner. Darcy wandered for several more minutes, absorbing the images. Sam was a family man down to the guts of who he was. And his home vibrated South Dakota from the art on the wall to the rugs on his floor. He might love the sea, but he was also still deeply attached to the place he had grown up and where his family called home.

The family ranch must be huge. There were photos of guys on horseback moving cattle, bringing in hay; there was timber, a lake, and pictures of elk. She smiled at the photo of Sam with his arm draped around his mom. It was good to see his roots. He'd grown up in an area where the sheer scale of the land and the effort it took to live there led a man to have big dreams.

She picked up the cordless phone in the living room and walked outside to the patio to call Gabriel and let him know she had arrived.

Sam nudged open the patio door with his foot. He'd been dreaming about a steak and lobster dinner for a long time, and sharing it with Darcy would make this evening perfect. "Okay, what are you thinking about so hard?"

She looked back at him and smiled, but it didn't reach her eyes. "Just thinking."

The phone was closed but still in her hand. He studied her face for a moment and motioned her over. "Well think harder this way."

She rose to join him. He settled her wrap more firmly around her shoulders. It was windy out tonight and a bit cool as it threatened to rain. She didn't need someone taking care of her. She could handle herself briefing soldiers aboard an aircraft carrier and could probably sneak in and out of enemy country undetected if needed, but Sam rather enjoyed the fact that she was letting him take care of her anyway. "Let me guess, you checked your messages."

"A compulsive bad habit." The smile reached her eyes this time.

He leaned down and kissed her, smiling as her hands entwined with his holding the wrap and she leaned forward against him. He eased back and let them both breathe. "Trouble?"

She had to think a moment. "The call?"

He smiled, enjoying her confusion. "Yes, the call." He kept the question light as he sought the information he needed, for he knew better than she probably realized just how much she had to balance in her life. Darcy coped in a world of flash traffic and classified versions of twenty-four hour news television and live satellite feeds. She dealt with real-time horrors and heard threats that would destroy thousands should they be carried out. She might leave the office but the job stayed with her. It was a unique pressure, and one he prayed about daily that she'd have the strength to cope.

"Then yes, it may be trouble," she whispered, taking a small step back. "There's a package coming in. Gabriel needs me back on Friday."

Sam brushed back her hair. Her disappointment wasn't far beneath the surface of her calm words. "Here six hours and you've already lost three days," he remarked lightly, determined to take it in stride. He knew she was probably making a tough decision for his sake to stay until Friday rather than head back in the morning. It must be sensitive information since the package was being hand delivered rather than transmitted electronically. His hands slid down to take hers. "Don't worry about it. We'll just plan things hour by hour." He tugged her toward the door. "Come on, Dar. Let's go to dinner."

He had made reservations for them at a local restaurant, a quiet place near the beach where the food was good and it would be comfortable to linger over the meal.

"You could have spent tonight celebrating your homecoming with fellow teammates and their families," she said as they walked into the restaurant.

"Trust me, Dar, we've been living on top of each other for months. We've seen plenty of each other. It's tradition to scatter far and wide during the first days of leave. In about two weeks when we come back on duty, the platoon will gather their families together for a big picnic to catch up on everyone's news."

Sam was welcomed back to town by the owner, and they were led to a quiet table at the side of the restaurant. Darcy looked around the room, paying special attention to those at tables near theirs. Sam knew without being told that she was still living carefully. The rumor of her death had been greatly exaggerated, but there was always a day where the personal threat could return. The number of agents killed during the last month had to weigh on her and at least make her movements more cautious.

While he knew exactly what he wanted for dinner, he took his time to enjoy the breadth of the choices. They ordered and he settled back in his chair to study her. "Back to the question I asked a couple hours ago, will you be able to get home over the holidays later this year?"

She shook her head as she broke a hot roll to butter. "I'll be working. The holidays are inevitably a high threat time."

"That's unfortunate."

She looked up and forced a smile. "Even if I could get away, there's no way Amy could. She's one of six officers for a huge territory. She doesn't have a day off now, and the holidays and bad weather will just increase the demands on her time. It won't be the first time we've shared the holidays at a distance."

The expression that shadowed her eyes was beginning to have a name. Darcy was still grieving. She'd been part of the opening salvo of this war and had been focused on the fight every day since then, accepting a separation from her family as one of those costs. When the subject was her family, it was safe to show her emotions.

"I am sorry," he said gently, relieved to

have stumbled onto her safety valve. Work was her professional mode; her home on the East Coast more of a CIA cover than a place to be herself. The one thing Darcy had that was just hers was her family. "Tell me about your sister. She sounds like a wonderful person."

Darcy laughed. "Sam, you have to meet her. Think town sheriff meets Grace Kelly."

"Why do you love the sea?" Darcy asked.

Sam settled his arm around Darcy's waist and kept her upright as the sand dune shifted and threatened to take her feet out from under her. "You know, we could walk the beach in the daylight. It would be safer."

She laughed and kept going. "The moonlight is supposed to be beautiful on the water."

"The cloud cover is threatening rain," he replied, amused with her. Whatever had touched her funny bone had lingered for the last hour. "I love the sea because it's incredibly huge and the exploration never ends. There are all kinds of creatures in it, and the seabed is still a vast mystery."

"It's also a graveyard for ships." She stopped at the water's edge.

He watched her for a few minutes, his hands pushed in the pockets of his slacks. She walked close to the water only to scramble back when the waves rolled in. "Darcy, you want to tell me why you got so nervous at the restaurant that we left in a bit of a rush rather than linger over dessert?"

"It was getting crowded, and a bit noisy."

"Uh-huh." He walked after her. "Who'd you recognize?"

She stiffened but didn't look at him, didn't even acknowledge the question. He was annoyed that she ducked the question but also impressed. A nonreaction in place of a denial — now that took skill.

"You remember months ago, a Carol Burnett show at 2 a.m.?"

"Sure. You looked a lot like a hibernating bear who didn't want to go to sleep."

"Thanks a lot." She skipped a rock into the water. "I still flashback to being under the water occasionally, and sometimes . . ." she shrugged — "an older man in a tux is a bit too much of a reminder."

He frowned. "It's been months, Darcy."

"I've been quietly looking into what happened to Sergey's family, trying to figure out who killed them. It revived the memories."

"They'll fade again."

"Yes . . . eventually."

Her energy ran out and she walked over and took a seat on the steps between the boardwalk and the beach. Sam sat down beside her. He'd watched Darcy swing from lighthearted moments when her attention was focused on memories of family or Bethany to moments like this when the animation in her died. The haunted look was back.

"What's going on, Dar?" he asked gently. A heavy conversation was not the way he wanted to end this evening, but the war and the toll it had taken had been a subject skirted many times tonight by both of them. They had to talk about it at some point. It hurt to see how much this fight had cost her.

"That conversation you recorded in Lebanon?" she said. "I was the one who cracked what the reference to Thatcher meant. It gave us that rare find in intelligence and future knowledge of where the enemy is going to be. I made it possible for Morocco to happen."

"You have to be full of mixed emotions." He reached over, took her hand, and wrapped it in his.

"I watched Dansky die, and those other men. It was cold justice, merciless, but it was a relief to know they were gone. They earned that fate; I know that. We recovered a shipment of high explosives capable of punching a hole in a nuclear submarine. Now . . . I'm just so tired, Sam. I want this to go away."

"This is war, declared by them and fought on their terms. A fight to the death. Don't feel guilty over the fact we're good enough to be winning."

"I know it's simplistic, but I just want to shake them and say wake up and come to your senses. You declared war and you are losing. Give it up." She twisted the ring on her right hand. "It's hard, Sam. My emotions know that every day I go to work, I'm dealing with life and death for a lot of people. If I'm good at my job, bad guys die. If I'm not, civilians die."

He understood her pain, for he'd seen both friend and foe die on the battlefield. "You've got a tender heart, Dar." In the past she had dealt with the threat of war, but this was her first experience with the reality of it. He couldn't protect her from it, even though that was the one reason he had entered the military — to keep war away from those at home.

He squeezed her hand. "Wishing these men would go away won't make it happen. They started a war, and now everyone has to live with the consequences of that. Let yourself grieve over what you lost, Darcy. Your peaceful retirement, time with your sister, the right to live without fear of an attack, the right not to have to deal with those life-and-death decisions. There is a lot to grieve. Peace was taken away from us, and it's one of the most treasured possessions we had."

He had no wisdom to offer her, no way to make it easier. War was brutal even on those who were winning. He tried to explain how he lived with it. "It's hard, because there are very few choices. You can deny terrorists' intentions and decide they really won't do what they threaten, and you'll spend your life hoping they won't prove you wrong. You can retreat and say I can't handle it and let others step in to try and do your job. Or you can accept the weight of it and do the best job you can. What you can't do is abdicate responsibility. You live in a time of war. You didn't choose it, but you must deal with it."

"How long is this war going to last, Sam? Another year, two?"

"It won't go on forever. Don't give up

hope. Peace will return." He tightened his hand on hers. "Think about God. He's holy and perfectly good. He has to deal with people who have chosen to wage war against Him. He didn't choose it, didn't want it, but look at how He handles it. He doesn't say it's My fault they made the choice they did. He says to mankind stand up and take responsibility for your actions. Turn from your sins and I'll forgive you. Keep resisting and I'll let you experience the consequences of your actions. He's blunt about it: 'The wages of sin is death.'

"Dar, you would do well to let go of a stress you were never designed to carry. Men choose war and they die. Pity them, pray for them, but don't make their decisions your responsibility. Even God doesn't do that. He says here it is: life and death. Choose. And He lets people make that choice. It's false guilt to feel responsible for someone else's wrong choices."

"How do I put together those facts I know with the emotions I feel? I don't want to be in this fight. I pray for strength and courage and wisdom, but inside what I'm really crying for is simply relief. I just wish God would make this war go away," she whispered.

Sam wrapped his arm around her and

hugged her. "Endurance is part of this fight, Dar, a vital part of who will win in the end. God is strong enough to get you through this." He rested his chin on her head and simply held her. She could have walked away. After the attempt on her life, she could have packed her bags and left to hide out somewhere in anonymity. Even her partner would have understood why she did so. Sam found it revealing that it hadn't been considered. She stayed.

"I wish I was comfortable putting this experience into words like you are. I loved getting your letters."

"I don't need many words to figure out your emotions, honey. You're pretty transparent and your actions are words enough. I've enjoyed writing the letters."

"Would you do something for me, Sam?"

"Anything."

"Tell me I'm okay."

He rubbed her back, smiling at her request. "You're perfect."

"No, perfect is too much pressure. Okay will do."

He tipped up her chin. "You've got nothing to worry about. You are perfectly okay."

She blinked and her smile grew. "You're good for me."

"I know."

"Seriously. I know I'm pretty quiet most of the time about what I believe, but I just wanted to say your words really mean a lot. God has never failed me. I know that, have lived it. I've been blessed to get out of several tight situations when I was working overseas. But this is the first crisis where it's so obvious that part of God's plan to help me out was through a person — you. I'm really grateful." She leaned back. "Did I just embarrass you?" Her hand tweaked his shirt collar. "I did."

He smiled at her laughter. "Maybe a little."

She grinned and turned her attention back to the water. "You know how I'm doing. How are you handling this war?"

"I don't have your questions. The men we fight are committed to destroying us. My only regret is that we still haven't flushed them all from the shadows. I just wish I could make this end tomorrow. I can't. But I promise you this: There is no better friend than the American military and no worse enemy. Our adversaries forgot that. We'll remind them. My goddaughter will live in peace, Darcy. I'll stake my life on that promise. It's one of those big, worth-the-price purposes in life."

She reached for a handful of the sand to

run through her hand. "I already had my big purpose in life — to win the cold war. We won that. And the peace we fought for slipped out of our hands like this sand and was suddenly gone again."

Sam got to his feet and held out his hand. It was time to shake up this conversation. It was enough for him to know evil existed and ultimately the good guys were guaranteed to win in the end. "Come on, Dar. Let's walk. I want to hear about the last movie you saw, the last book you read, the last sports event score you heard."

"Boring."

"We'll see which of us can be the most dull." He tugged off his tie and slid it in his pocket. "I read an old Western while cruising the Atlantic. Didn't finish it yet, but I at least creased the spine."

"Why do you wear the tie if you pull it off the first chance you get?"

He looked at it. "Mom drummed it into me as the polite thing to do. It's habit."

"I think it's a nice habit. Maybe I'll buy you a tie." She led the way down to the beach. "I read my friend's comic book while I shared a macaroni-and-cheese dinner with him. He thinks it's cool that I'm dead."

"Does he?"

"It's not that cool. I still have to pay taxes."

The laughter felt good. "Tell me about this house you're remodeling."

"You could bomb it and it would probably look better. Think eighty-some years old, pounded by wind and weather, with plumbing and electric that has to come out. I think it was my security plan, something huge I had to do so it would be easier to accept that I didn't know what I wanted to do after I left the Agency."

"You weren't planning to leave until someone put a price on your head?" Sam asked.

"I thought I'd be in for years. I had tentative plans to work my way up to the Chief of Disguise job."

"You're kidding. You have to be making up that job title."

She laughed. "Nope. It's a very high-tech job these days, straight out of Hollywood. If I wanted to walk up to you and not be recognized, I could do it easily."

He could hear the teasing, and he was absolutely confident he would recognize her, if only her eyes. "Maybe after a day of makeup work."

"Five minutes. Fifteen if I've got the luxury of time."

"I'd love to see that."

"The techniques are classified. And it does take some preparation work before I head to the field."

"Meaning you could be telling me a tall tale and I'd never know it."

"True."

Sam enjoyed seeing the smile. "I'll trust you. But I still want to see this someday."

"The Agency doesn't pay that well, but it's got really great toys."

"You should see what the military has. We get to spend the big bucks."

"Can you see around corners yet?"

"Better than that, Dar. I can see through walls."

"Now you're joshing me."

"Classified toys are by far the best." Sam went back to a point that needed to be stressed again. "When this war is over, I want to see this house you're remodeling." He would enjoy helping her on such a project if only to see how she handled being a carpenter.

"I had the bathroom tile partially ripped up before this all started. Months later and I still have that job waiting for me. I wish it had been something like laying new carpet instead."

Sam saw her glance back behind them

again. "Are you sure there's not someone looking for you, Dar? You're skittish."

"It sounds like someone is crying. Don't you hear it?"

"It's the sea breaking across the shoals back there."

"What?"

"Listen."

She stopped walking to stand and listen. "How long has it sounded like that?"

"Sometimes the sea sounds peaceful. Tonight it sounds sad. The only thing more memorable is when it sounds mad."

She turned to look at him.

"We occasionally fight in bad weather," Sam simplified.

She searched his face but didn't ask. "Tell me about that Western you were reading."

Sam told her his version of the story, stretching out the tale. He doubted she could understand just how good it felt to have her company tonight, just how much he appreciated moments like this. He'd missed her. This was the life he fought to keep safe, an evening with a lady he really liked.

Nothing was simple about Darcy, from the job she did to the way she struggled with the implications of it. He admired what it showed about her spirit. Despite the cost, she poured her whole heart into the effort and did not back away.

A romance in a time of war; he never would have planned it this way, but there were small blessings in it. He got to see her under stress, and he was learning what she really valued.

The animation was returning to those blue eyes as she laughed at the stories he told. Darcy paused in her wandering of the beach to look up at him. "What?"

He hugged her. "I'm just enjoying the laughter."

"It feels good." She looked ahead. "Where does this beach end?"

"New Jersey."

"I don't think I want to walk that far."

He turned them around. "So we'll wander back toward the car."

"Slowly, Samuel."

He liked the sound of his name when she said it. "Who's in a hurry? I'm the one with two weeks off."

# Fifteen

May 22
Wednesday, 6:15 a.m.
Norfolk, Virginia

The bed-and-breakfast pampered its guests. Two newspapers were set outside the door along with a carafe of coffee, and the buffet breakfast started at seven. Darcy tugged on her tennis shoes to go running before breakfast, feeling more lighthearted than she had in days. Sam had offered her a day enjoying what the town had to offer. He had missed out on a lot of things in the months away, and she was looking forward to joining him for a day with no particular objective, maybe ending it with Chinese takeout for dinner and a video store for the best of the movies he had missed.

She laughed and took off her shoe to shake sand out into the wastebasket. She loved this time off. Sam made her so happy — last night had been an oasis in the middle of war. She could share the pressures of work and know she was understood.

Darcy relaced her shoes. The phone rang in her room as she confirmed she had her keys in her pocket. She leaned over to grab it as she danced around on one foot to get the old tennis shoe from curling at the heel. "Hello."

"Hi, partner."

"Hey, Gabriel. I love the bed-and-breakfast. It's a great spot."

"There's a theory that bad news always comes when it's least welcome."

Her smile faded. "What's happening?"

"Luther's number two was in Yemen. He's not anymore," Gabe said carefully, for the line was unsecured and the message was in what he didn't say.

Her hand curled into the bedspread. She didn't need the words. Vladimir had been in Yemen, and when he left, he hadn't been alone. He wouldn't have been there to hire a bookkeeper or a chef. "You're sure?"

"I want you to put the puzzle pieces together to confirm what I see, but yes."

"How soon do you need me there?"

"Get breakfast, then head this way. We're going to be working against the time zones on this one. My guess is he's got a twelve-hour head start on us."

She already wanted to find two aspirin. "I'll pack."

"Did you at least get to enjoy dinner?"

"Yes."

"Be grateful for small blessings. I'm sorry but I need you, Dar."

She knew they were words Gabriel did not say lightly. "I'm on my way."

She hung up the phone and bowed her head, then reached over for her bag to start packing. She'd have to call Sam and cancel their plans. As much as she regretted that fact, she accepted it. Whatever disruptions in her life she had to pay were minor to getting the job done. They had to get Vladimir. If he was moving, she was chasing.

Sam had forgotten how nice it was to make a mess in his own kitchen. Eggs for an omelet were simmering as he diced ham when the phone rang. He wiped his hands and reached for it. "Hello."

"Sam."

He knew as soon as he heard the tone of her voice that their plans would change. "Good morning, Darcy." He turned off the heat under the skillet. "You're calling to say you've lost a few more days."

248

"I leave as soon as I can pack."

He reached over and made a pyramid of the oranges. "Glum doesn't suit you," he teased, trying to take the disappointing news lightly.

"It's necessary."

He knew that; she wouldn't be going otherwise. "Want a chauffeur?"

"It will be a long drive with some lousy company. I've got a lot of stuff on my mind."

"All the more reason to let me drive. I'll take you home then catch a cab to the airport, head west to see my folks."

"You can arrange a flight that easily?"

"Flights heading west are hardly fully booked these days. It won't be a problem. I don't need a direct flight, just the next one heading the right direction." *Come on, Dar. Let me in. These are the moments that make a relationship stronger.*

Her hesitation was brief. "I'd like the company."

"Pack. I'll be over shortly."

Sam set the items for his breakfast back into the refrigerator. The toast he buttered and put together into a sandwich to take with him. Darcy would learn not to be so worried about calls like this one. The military was built around accepting changes in

249

plans in order to get the mission done. He spent his life on call, never knowing when he might get word of trouble and within an hour be on a plane heading somewhere into danger. Adapting was something he had grown comfortable with. One of the many reasons he liked Darcy was her unconventional job. He'd take a rain check on a day with her and make sure he collected with interest.

She was waiting for him at the bed-and-breakfast, her bag already packed. He paid the cab driver, then transferred his bag and hers to her car trunk. She offered him one of the two cinnamon rolls she held. "What time is it in London?"

*Time in London* . . . He opened the passenger door for her. "They're five hours ahead of us, so coming up on noon."

"Just checking."

He paused in closing her door. "Darcy."

She licked sticky fingers. "I really need one of those world time watches. You enter the country code and get the current time, adjusted for daylight saving time of course. Mine disappeared sometime after I retired."

He'd asked about birthday ideas last night, and she had been unable to come up with anything better than a book. The date was months away, but he liked to be prepared. "The suggestions are getting better."

"You still haven't given me one yet."

"I'm working on it," Sam promised. He slid on sunglasses and checked the map she offered him. He accepted the car keys. "What's the name of your perfume?"

"What?"

"I like it. What's the name?"

"Kodia. It's made by a small company in Poland. They grow the most wonderful flowers in their greenhouse as a laboratory for fragrances to inspire their perfume creators."

"I'd recognize you in disguise, Dar, if only by your perfume." He caught her small smile as she opened her briefcase. "What?"

"Why do you think I wear a perfume that is so distinct from what someone might be able to buy in America? Your subconscious knows me, so when I want to disappear, changing perfumes is as much a part of the disguise as changing my appearance."

"You choose it because you love it. But like everything else, it gets used in your job."

"Basically." Darcy opened her portfolio. "I'm afraid I'll have to work while we drive."

"Don't worry about it."

"You were fast getting here."

"I always keep a bag packed." He turned on the radio. "Are you okay with a news station or do you want music?"

"News, please," she replied gratefully.

"Missing your morning briefing?"

"The world news in the local papers can be measured by a few column inches."

He drove them north. Darcy hummed as she worked, and she kicked off her shoes soon after the drive began. She filled nearly a full legal pad with notes before she paused as they came near the Virginia border. "How well advertised is the fact your team has returned stateside?"

He looked over at her, surprised by the question. "It's not advertised, but it's also not a secret. Anyone who wanted to know we were home could figure it out with a little looking around Norfolk, either the base or the community. We travel as teams. See a few men and you can correctly guess which teams are stateside."

"So if someone wanted to pay you back for Morocco it wouldn't be that hard to find you."

"Besides British SAS guys and some classified analysts like you, it will be decades before anyone links SEAL Team

Nine to Morocco."

"I wish I had that same confidence."

"Assume it is known. What are the odds someone who plans attacks against soft civilian targets is going to try and hit a hardened target like a Special Ops unit in our own backyard? It's possible but not likely. Too many of us walk around armed and ready to defend ourselves. I worry more about you."

"Compared to the risks of war, the rumors of my death and the bounty that was paid are dormant concerns. I'll be warned if something there changes." Darcy pointed out the upcoming turn. "Why don't you head toward the airport? We can grab lunch along restaurant row, and I'll make sure there are flights heading west and drop you off."

"I've got your direct number now," he remarked. "When's a good time to call?"

"Whenever you happen to think of me."

He laughed. "Remember you said that. I'll be calling." Sam saw the restaurant options ahead. "How about pizza for lunch?"

"Sure."

He pulled into the parking lot. "When life slows down a bit, block a day off on your calendar. We'll try a day out again."

"I'm looking forward to it."

They didn't linger over lunch. When they parted at the airport, he made a point of keeping the good-bye casual. Sam knew her thoughts were already on work, and it wasn't fair to complicate the departure. He planned to do some reconnaissance when he reached South Dakota. It was near enough to North Dakota to allow him to do some looking around on Darcy's home turf.

"Call me when you get in?"

"Will do," Sam promised. "Take care, Dar."

She hugged him and buried her face against his shirt. "You too, Samuel. Watch your back."

He relished the hug and squeezed her tightly. This relationship had found its footing. They'd build on it from here. "You too, Dar."

May 22
Wednesday, 1:38 p.m.
Central Intelligence Agency

Darcy read the notes as she sat in Gabriel's office, having not yet gone to her own. Luther's number two, Vladimir Kurst, had indeed slipped in and out of

Yemen. Seeing the evidence for herself left little doubt about that fact.

The plane tail numbers and fuel loads showed a small commercial jet leaving Yemen for Egypt. From there it appeared the flight had departed for Greece. Darcy studied the Athens airport security tape the NSA had scanned. The images were grainy, but it was Vladimir and behind him a man she had reason to fear. "Jerry did a pretty good job of changing his appearance: maybe nose, eyes, and a little chin work? Still clean shaven, styled haircut, and a European suit. He looks more like a rich tourist than a hit man." Jerry Summit was one of the best snipers who had ever come through the American armed forces. He'd gone rogue nine years ago.

Gabe rolled his wheelchair toward the bookcase and brought down a reference file. "I was hoping the guy was dead. I suppose it was too much to wish for two lucky breaks in one war. Vladimir must be arranging something that will happen either in Europe or America. He hired the one sniper who can blend in there and bide his time."

Darcy nodded. "Jerry is also a highly wanted man. Why draw the added lightning? Wherever he's hiding, Luther must truly think he's safe again to take the chance of sending Vladimir out to make this contact."

"He probably calculated that it's worth the risk. Luther is out to hire the best."

"Who's the target?"

"You don't hire Jerry if you want to shoot the local drug dealer."

Darcy studied the logs. "Yemen. We had the ports covered. Why couldn't he have taken a boat like we expected? And what happened to good airport security?"

"Ten to one, bribed and threatened," Gabe replied. "This isn't all bad news. Vladimir is vulnerable for the first time in months," Gabriel said. "He's on the move. Dansky went out to talk to people and he's dead. You can now hear the clock ticking on Vladimir. Luther will be the tougher one to get. He's probably shifted entirely to secondhand communication now. Something sent to a dead drop, a message passed through Vladimir."

"His wife will break that silence eventually." It was the one thing Darcy thought would give them the lead they needed for the man they most wanted. "So how do we track Jerry?"

Gabriel smiled and tossed her an apple from the sack on his desk. "Think. That's why I called you."

★ ★ ★

Darcy stretched out on the couch in her own office, the lumps and taut springs against her back uncomfortable in a familiar way. She'd often slept here. Someone had painted over the smoke-stained tiles on the ceiling. The building had caught on fire a year ago August, and it had taken a long time to catch up with the minor cleanup. Darcy tipped her head to see the direction of the brush strokes. She missed the gray smoke. It could be cloudy when she needed something else to be cloudy besides her thoughts. Her computer began to play the song "Hound Dog," and she reluctantly reached back to release the door lock. "Go away."

"You don't have to find Jerry in the next hour," Gabe said.

"Do too. And I've got a headache."

He tugged a lock of her hair. "Sam will call."

"I hope not in the next hour. I'm in a bad mood and I'll snarl at him." She held up a sheet of a paper for Gabriel to read. "The Athens cops think Jerry may have gone toward the ports. A cabbie recognized the photo."

"We can find out every boat that has left during the twenty-four hours after his arrival at the airport," Gabriel said.

"Already did. Two passenger cruise liners, sixty-two personal crafts, and eleven cargo ships from the docks. That's assuming he isn't sleeping and playing solitaire in the cabin of a boat still moored in the harbor just to make our lives difficult. You know how hard it is to track where boats go?" Darcy asked.

"Let the guys at NSA map it out."

"They already groaned and asked, 'How many boats?' They'll try but no promises." It was yet another lead where they were a step behind being able to do anything with it. *Jesus, I'm tired of the missed opportunities. Really tired.*

Gabe settled into her desk chair. She thought about ignoring him until he went away, but he had more patience than she did. "You've got something else."

"The package the Brits were sending over arrived earlier than expected."

She swung her feet to the floor and shoved her hands through her hair. "It's a day for puzzles. Keep this one simple."

"They raided a safe house on the coast of Ireland near the town of Bangor. They found the man they expected to find, a retired sniper for the IRA, who unfortunately died during the exchange. They also found a few items that were a surprise to them. He had cash, a lot of it. And this." Gabriel handed over a folder.

One eyebrow raised as she saw a photo of a piece of paper laid out beside rulers to show its dimensions, the page filled with lines of numbers in neat rows. "What is this? Connect the numbers?"

"It's got Luther's prints on it."

She looked over, startled.

"That was about the Brits' reaction too. They now think Vladimir had hired the IRA sniper to do some work in London. Luther's sending encrypted messages now to the men he hires. The Brits couldn't crack this one."

"Luther doesn't have state-level quality code encryption. And the Brits are as good as any at NSA. I can't believe they couldn't break it."

"They concluded it was an open code," Gabriel replied.

This was the last thing she needed today — another puzzle. Open codes were simple. Two people agreed on how numbers would be turned into letters, and while the two of them could decode the messages easily, it was incredibly difficult for others to do it. Her favorite open code used *New York Times* crossword puzzles.

The numbers one and four became the first question, fourth letter. The next numbers in the code, eight and five, became the eighth question, fifth letter. The fact the open key was a public document that changed weekly made it difficult if not impossible to find that key unless one of the two people who used it revealed it. "Was there anything in the house that suggested what they were using as the open key?"

"The Brits spent a week going through the house. They sent over videos of the walk-through they did of the rooms and photos of everything they recovered. They were hoping we'd have better luck spotting it."

"Are you sure they weren't just hoping to keep us busy for a while? And what's Vladimir doing hiring an IRA sniper and then hiring Jerry mere days later?" Darcy asked. "How many hits are they setting up?"

"Luther has a plan and we're seeing it begin to unfold."

"We need more guys on this."

"We'll get as many as we need," Gabriel promised.

She closed the folder. "I hate puzzles."

"You love puzzles, dahlin'." He struggled

to his feet. "You've got clearance to take the package of materials home, just lock the stuff in your safe. We need to know what he was hiring this guy to do."

"And find Jerry."

"That too. I've got a meeting with the Brits this evening to find out what we can about this IRA sniper's background," Gabe said.

"Check and see if he ever did any fundraising in the States, if he had been here before. I'd like to get a sense of where he was being sent — Europe or here."

"Will do."

"Who do we have at NSA looking at this puzzle?" Darcy asked.

"There is a team of five on it; the fact the Brits couldn't crack it has the NSA boys determined to show they can."

She looked at the numbers. "In this case a little friendly competition is a good thing." She was tired just looking at the page. She'd prayed for an answer. She had one. She just had no idea how to read it.

*All I've been doing lately is asking for wisdom and help.* Faith is the evidence of things not seen . . . . She'd read that somewhere. *Can You guess what I'm asking for in this prayer, Lord?*

May 22
Wednesday, 5:38 p.m.
McLean, Virginia

Darcy took the four videotapes and the photos of recovered items home with her. She wished she had stayed on vacation another two days. She needed to be fully rested for this kind of job. She sat at her dining room table and looked at the numbers. It was an aggravating puzzle. She knew the message was staring at her, but she didn't have any idea how to approach it.

Lord, I don't want to be doing this, but it's got to be solved. What is this? And who's going to be killed if I don't figure it out?

A note to a sniper in Ireland. Maybe there's also a note to Jerry in Yemen? What would a guy in Ireland and a guy in Yemen both have easy access to? Darcy turned to a blank page on her notepad. She looked through the photos. Items were displayed on the table: newspapers and what looked like a television guide. She started listing what she saw. They would have to be considered one by one.

The phone rang. She reached around to answer it, even as she tried to make out the name of a newspaper.

"I tried your office, but you had already gone home."

"Work came home with me," Darcy said, relieved to hear Sam's voice. "You got home okay?"

"There's a party going on to celebrate. I wish you were here, Dar."

"It would be better than here." Maybe the key was a book? The numbers could be page references. She tried to figure out if they were a page number only, a page number followed by a line number, or a page number followed by a line and character number.

"Mom asked me to say hi."

"Tell Hannah thanks." She chewed on her pen. "Sorry, I'm pretty distracted."

"Is there anything I can do to help?"

"Pray that I get a big dose of wisdom. I'm stumped." She set down her pen and pushed the work away. "So . . . they're celebrating your return."

"You're always in my prayers, Dar. You'll figure it out. It feels good to be home. We party tonight, move hay tomorrow."

"I'm glad for you, sad for me. I wish you were still here," she admitted.

"Hugs are good from a distance."

"I'll take one."

"You've got one."

She smiled at the noise in the background. "Go cut the cake, Sam. It sounds like a good party."

"And I really wish you were here with me."

"Call me tomorrow, okay? It's nice just to hear your voice."

"Guaranteed. Don't work too late."

She looked at the photos across the table. Late was relative. "I won't."

# Sixteen

May 24
Friday, 6:30 a.m.
Timber Lake, South Dakota

Sam understood why Darcy had come back to this part of the world when she retired. Open land, wide vistas, a place to breathe. He drank his coffee while watching the sun come up.

His brothers had done an excellent job in preparing for the summer. He felt the soreness of moving hay. It was a good hurt, though, from hard productive work. His brothers planned to have the third barn under construction finished by midmonth to allow this fall's hay crop to be stored nearer the cattle. The screen door behind him opened, and he turned to glance over his shoulder.

His mom joined him. "Blueberry muffins. They're hot."

He set down his coffee and accepted a

muffin from the towel-covered basket, tossing it between his hands as it was still steaming. "Thanks."

The rest of the muffins and coffee carafe she would take to his father down at the barn in a morning ritual that went back to his childhood. The routines of home were comforting, familiar, something he could depend on to be here when he came back from his travels. "Mom, you mind if I borrow your video camera today?"

"Feel free. I think it's still in the living room." She looked at him, curious. "Heading somewhere?"

"I was thinking of taking a drive and heading a couple hours north." Darcy could use a taste of home. She hadn't had a chance to really relax and breathe in months. He couldn't change her situation, but he could help her out.

"Going to see Darcy's home?"

Sam nodded. "Meet her sister if possible. It shouldn't be that hard to find the local sheriff."

"That would be a good idea. Darcy makes you smile, Sam. And you've been mentioning her in letters for months. I can think of worse distractions for one of my sons to have. I'd love to have a daughter-in-law."

Sam laughed. "So you've been saying for a decade. She's got more layers than any other lady I've ever met."

"You don't need someone simple, Sam. You would be bored. Go take your drive and make some tapes for Darcy. She'll appreciate it."

Sam hugged his mom. "Okay if I invite her for Thanksgiving this fall?"

"I would love it."

He didn't know if Darcy would think a soldier in her life was a good thing, but he was beginning to think a retired spy in his would be.

There was a lot of time to think on a long solitary drive. This land was home, and while he drove, Sam understood just why Darcy chose this place to live the next season of her life. She would be comfortable here, with her house, her family, a chance to have deep roots again surrounded by people who had known her growing up. For her the struggle over the years had been overseas. It was now centered on the work she did on the East Coast. This was the heartland of America, as far from the touch of terror as she could go.

The idea of coming back here for part of

the year was taking hold. He loved the sea and the travel, but a few days at home had reminded him of everything here he had missed. For the first time in years, he was feeling a tug to come back toward his roots and find the permanence that so marked his parents' lives.

He loved it here, in a land that stretched for miles, home to only a handful of people. He would retire from the SEALs in a few years, for it was a young man's profession, and he wouldn't want a desk job when his days in the field ended. He'd spent years exploring the world, and the idea of coming home no longer felt restrictive.

He had a feeling Darcy had gone into her profession because she was just as much an explorer as he was. She sought out knowledge, places, people. In a civilian life he bet with a little prompting that she would make a world-class adventurer.

The sound of a siren interrupted his thoughts. He looked up, surprised to find a police cruiser settling in behind him with lights flashing. A glance at the cruise control showed his speed was steady at the speed limit. He was the only one on the road, and the cruiser was definitely signaling him. He tapped his brakes, and when it was safe to do so, pulled to the shoulder of the road. The police car pulled to a stop behind him.

The one officer inside got out from the squad car.

Sam slid off his sunglasses. It didn't take much study in the side mirror as she approached to see the similarity to Darcy. He'd been looking forward to meeting Amy, but this wasn't quite what he had planned. "Is there a problem, officer?"

"Could I see your driver's license and registration, please?"

He handed them over, keeping his moves to a minimum. The badge said Bond. He hadn't known her married name. "I didn't realize I was speeding."

"Excuse me."

She stepped back from the car toward the trunk and lifted her radio, looking at his IDs and then at the car plates. He didn't like the tension in her voice as she approached again. "Mr. Houston, would you please step out of your car."

"Amy, what's the problem?"

"Please step from the car." The tone of her voice said she expected the order to be obeyed. Other than stepping back out of the way, she simply waited for him to comply.

He shut off the car, picked up his billfold from the dashboard, and stepped out.

She motioned back toward her patrol car and he followed the silent order. He saw the relaxation creep in as he moved away from his car. "What's going on?"

"You picked up this rental car at the Bismarck airport?"

"Yes."

"Did you ask for this particular car by model?"

"I requested a large car with leg room."

He saw a small smile as she looked him over. "Yes, I imagine a compact would have been a problem. Where were you September 11?"

Now he was more confused than ever. "With your sister in Virginia."

She studied him for a moment and then gave a small nod. "I figure her read of character is still pretty good." She stepped away and lifted her radio. "Jim, send a tow truck. The car is at mile marker 8, Route 6, just inside the state line."

"Will do, Sheriff."

"I gather there's a problem with the car," Sam said.

"Yes."

"A problem for me?"

Amy smiled. "Not unless your prints are

270

on the stash we think is inside that wheel well."

Sam blinked. "I've been driving around contraband?"

"Despite the war, most crime around here is still the normal kind. We arrested the kid who put it there two days ago, only he had managed to confuse the car he put it in. Process of elimination, we made it out to be yours. We'll get you another rental car." She leaned against the side of the squad car and tugged open a pocket. She offered him a butterscotch candy. "Sorry about the welcome; it's going to be a boring twenty minutes."

"I've done boring before."

"I thought you were down at Timber Lake. What are you doing up this way?"

He let himself relax. "Looking for you."

"Truly? Well you found me."

May 24
Friday, 11:18 a.m.
Central Intelligence Agency

Darcy studied the timeline tacked on Gabriel's bulletin board. "Luther hired snipers to go after our guys on September 9; he just hired Jerry and a former IRA

271

sniper. We think Luther was behind the wave of sniper attacks across Europe. Looking at that picture, it's pretty obvious we need to get a better handle on snipers who are out there for hire. I don't see that pattern ending."

"It looks to me like he's hiring just the sniper and letting that man choose and provide his own support team," Gabe agreed.

"If only we could get an idea of his target list."

"We need to focus more on squeezing Luther's money," Gabe countered. "We find his money, then his ability to hire snipers of this caliber disappears. The diversity of his targets suggests he's not the one with a master list. The names are being given to him by different groups, and he's simply facilitating the contacts."

Gabriel tacked a new picture of Vladimir to the board. "We've got this down to Luther, his wife Renee, and Vladimir. We get them, and the people they've hired will die on the vine."

"Add an unknown person to replace Dansky," Darcy said. "Luther's new number three has to be several things: trustworthy, a good planner, and probably experienced at moving money."

"Add acceptable to Vladimir. He's hiring the help and will be thinking about his own safety as much as Luther's. He won't want someone he doesn't trust to know their movements."

Darcy nodded. "Not a small point." The calendar on the wall haunted her. The September 11 anniversary was out there and coming closer. "Luther's got a hit list, and it scares me that the Brits or the Special Ops guys that hit him in Algeria and Morocco will be on it. On the opening day of this war he attempted three hits in the space of an hour. Can we at least put together a list of names of who might be vulnerable and warn the guys?"

"I've already talked to the Defense Department. They understand the risks this new information represents. Don't worry about that, Dar. They'll take care of their own. My guess is the team will be tucked away on some military base out of sight, and they'll have arranged security for the families. A sniper has to establish a base of operations, has to know the terrain. If you're new to town, it's not easy to move within a town like Norfolk these days and not be noticed. There are too many military personnel at the numerous bases who are already looking for trouble."

Darcy had experienced a taste of that security on her brief trip to Norfolk. She knew it was good, but she still didn't like the threat out there.

The phone on Gabriel's desk rang. He leaned back to answer it. "Hello."

"Yes."

Darcy looked over and saw a strange look cross his face.

"What's the address?" He reached for a pen and paper.

"We'll be there in less than twenty minutes."

Gabriel hung up the phone.

"What?" Darcy asked.

"The FBI has something we need to see. They may have found one of Luther's hired snipers."

May 24
Friday, 11:50 a.m.
Shelton, North Dakota

Sam walked around Darcy's home, feeling a combination of envy, wonder, and sheer disbelief. She had called this house a multiyear project. There was some truth to that. The plumbing and electrical probably needed to be totally gutted. The outside was weathered and would need substantial work to go with the new roof she'd put on. But the house . . .

Sam leaned over the stair railing to peer down at Amy. "She's planning to what?"

"Rip out that staircase and put in a spiral one and open up this part of the entryway."

"This is pure walnut."

"I told her that," Amy said.

"How's she going to get furniture upstairs with a spiral staircase?"

"She says she'll just never change it."

"Amy, she buys a masterpiece and she wants to modernize the heart out of it?"

"She's bored."

The house must have twenty rooms; it was huge. He found the bathroom Darcy had mentioned she was remodeling. Half the floor tiles were pulled up, tile that must have been custom made given the scripted $J$ in each tile. A few were chipped and they showed the yellowing of age, but still . . . "Who built this place?"

"An old guy who found a gold mine and wanted the town to remember him."

"They will."

"But not for the reason he hoped. He drove his car into the creek and drowned."

"Ouch."

"Darcy was a favorite of his. He left her first rights to buy the house."

"This is a spectacular house. She owns all the land too?" He looked out the stairway landing window to get a good view. The grounds reflected an enormous amount of Darcy's energy. The fence bounding the property had been repaired and the underbrush cleared. An out-building had been torn down and the ground leveled. There was enough wood chopped to keep a fireplace blazing for a full winter season. Darcy had been working from the outside of the property in.

"She owns just over a hundred acres — all the surrounding land plus the land down to the creek."

Sam descended the stairs, letting his hand slide down the banister. "With a lot of work this will become a great place."

Amy perched on the window seat over-looking the huge front yard. "I think I'm starting to really like you, Navy SEAL Sam Houston. You'll be good for Darcy." She offered a book of wallpaper samples. "She chose this one for the kitchen."

"She was pulling your leg."

"I sincerely hope so."

"She was smart enough to buy a wonderful house; she'll fix it up right. And she's got to be joking about the spiral staircase." A multiyear project — Darcy had certainly found that. It told him a lot about the future she planned for herself: a place with space, freedom, work that would keep her outdoors. This was a decision to return to her roots of her hometown and family. They were good priorities. "What does she talk about doing once she gets the house fixed up?"

"Besides wandering into my office to see what's going on that might be interesting?"

"She mentioned she was a bit bored."

"That's the understatement of the year. Darcy has to be in the middle of the action or else she's out somewhere making the news." Amy picked up another paint sample strip. "Actually, she has been seriously exploring a few options. Our dad was a biographer, a rather good one. He used to go to these obscure towns to look up the house where someone had been born, visit neighbors who might have lived in the community for decades, dig out school yearbooks and talk to fellow classmates. Darcy used to help him with the research. I think she was exploring writing some history of the cold war from her firsthand perspective. She also talked about buying the ice cream parlor when Sandy retired. Personally I'd bet on the ice cream parlor with a few tall tales for the tourists who come to town."

"You actually have tourists visit your spot-in-the-road town?"

Amy laughed. "A handful every year. And the town is big enough to have its share of troublemakers." She got up. "My husband and I live in the ranch house down the road. You want to come to lunch? You can spend the afternoon making a video that is guaranteed to make Darcy homesick. Your new rental car should be here by then."

"I want you on the tape."

"I wouldn't miss it."

"You don't need to get back to the office?"

Amy shook her head. "One of the pleasures of being the boss. Jim will call if something urgent crops up." She locked the house behind them. "I'm glad you came by, Sam."

"Can you not tell Darcy I came to look you up?"

She laughed. "Tell her what?"

# Seventeen

May 24
Friday, 12:05 p.m.
McLean, Virginia

Darcy walked up the carpeted stairs of the condo, following Gabriel and the state police officer who had become their escort. They had already passed through two checkpoints and ducked under yellow police tape just to get to the building. She was not accustomed to walking into a crime scene. She saw information about events like this in reports, occasionally saw photos, but it didn't exude the sight, smell, and punch of the reality.

Given the number of Fairfax County sheriff and Commonwealth of Virginia police cars blocking off Great Falls Street, the lack of people inside the condo was surprising. The upper level of the condo had only one FBI agent and two men from the crime scene unit present.

"Sir, they're here."

The FBI agent turned, finished his phone call, and came to meet them. "Special Agent Mike Sands. I called."

"Gabriel Arneau; this is my partner."

Darcy endured the curious look and quietly returned it. The agent nodded his thanks to their escort, dismissing him.

"What we have is a murder and a message left for you, Gabriel. As soon as the sheriff reported what they had, the director tapped me to handle this one. Since the scene context seems critical to figuring out what happened, I've held things for the moment rather than let the crime lab guys move in. I've worked a few cases with Agency connections, and they haven't been the smoothest experiences in my life. I'd like your cooperation."

Gabriel shifted both forearm crutches to his left hand and raised his right hand to rub the back of his neck. He looked over at Darcy. "What do you think?"

She'd summed up the agent in his first two sentences. He'd already proven he was more interested in getting information to solve his case than protecting it from an interagency turf war, and the FBI director trusted him. Darcy smiled back at Gabe. "He's not wearing a tie, those shoes haven't been spending much idle time behind a desk, and he was smart enough not to ask for my name."

The agent winced at the mention of the tie.

Gabe rested his weight back on his crutches and nodded. "Mike, how do you define full cooperation?"

"A seat in your office."

"Since she monopolizes the couch, you're welcome to it. We'll figure out how to expedite the code-word clearance to make it happen."

"Oh, I've already got the code-word clearance, not that it's much of a blessing; hence the director's call."

Gabriel laughed. "Show me what we've got."

Agent Sands led the way to the room at the end of the hall. The layout suggested it had been intended for use as a large bedroom, but it had been turned into an office.

"You want to clear the room so we can talk freely?" Gabe suggested.

Mike nodded to the two technicians photographing the scene, and they left the room.

"They rushed a set of fingerprints through the system. They identified him as a former Russian army officer," Agent Sands offered.

Maps on the wall, photos. Darcy had never seen a sniper rifle up close, but she put two and two together and the open gun case on the bed made it obvious that the weapon wasn't used to hunt deer. Darcy stood just inside the doorway and simply absorbed it. The blown-up photos on the wall were taped at eye level in a line. She was looking at the images of people she knew, agents now working at CIA headquarters. The street map of this area had also been blown up, and one-way streets were marked in red with on-going construction points highlighted.

A man was dead. He was slumped over the table near the window, his face turned away. From the look of the pool of blood, not much remained of his head. He wore a tailored suit, and at the wrists she could see white shirt cuffs. Pinned to his back was a white piece of paper with a message.

Even from across the room she could read the words written with a red marker. *Call Gabriel Arneau, CIA.* The message was so startling. Darcy accepted the image she would have to wrestle to forget and walked across the room to join Gabe beside the body. "Your desk phone number."

Gabe knelt to study the note, not touching anything.

"Tell me what you know, Agent Sands."

"We think his name is Mikail Provosta. Immigration didn't know he was in the country. We're guessing he's been dead about eight hours. He had one lethal sniper rifle in that case."

"You shoot some?" Gabe asked.

"Enough to know what I'm seeing is some well-developed planning."

"Darcy, check out the signature on this note," Gabe warned softly.

She looked and had to brace her hand on his shoulder to keep her balance at what she saw. "Sergey." She knew that signature as well as she knew her own. "He's still alive?" She took a shuddering breath as she absorbed that. It shouldn't surprise her. He had taught her over the years to withhold assumptions, but she really had thought he was dead. What did this new development mean to her?

"Sergey was here a few hours ago." Gabe squeezed her shoulder. "He said Gabriel, not Darcy. Maybe he thinks you're really dead."

"He knows I'm alive; he's too good to miss that. He probably figured you'd be the more forgiving of the two of us. How did he get into the country?" She held up her hand, waving away her own question.

"Forget I asked." He could do it easily. He'd shown that over the years.

Gabe looked around the room. "Sergey did us a favor. The question now is why?"

She was trying to restructure her mental list of facts to deal with the reality that he was still alive. "Sergey's family was murdered. He's running on his own agenda, probably with the cash from the bounty collected on me. He'll be after payback. And not just payback — vengeance." She studied the insignia ring the dead man wore, recognizing the Russian unit emblem.

Gabriel stepped back. "I'll bet you good money this is the man who killed Sergey's family. Sergey waits this long to show his hand, he's going after the man who did the crime."

"And then he's going after the man who ordered it."

"I gather you two have met my most likely suspect." Agent Sands said, standing back and simply listening to the exchange.

"Sergey's Russian, in his sixties. We've got a reasonably good picture of him in the files; although if he doesn't want you to recognize him you won't," Darcy replied. "He's former KGB and very good at what he does. This past year he's been a little hard to find. We thought he was dead."

She looked around the room. There were too many photos to suggest which individual had been this man's central target. More planning documents were on the second table. "May I?" Darcy held up her capped pen.

Agent Sands nodded. "The table surface has been photographed."

She used the pen to nudge the top page aside to see what else was in the stacks of papers. Restaurant menus. Bus schedules. She took in a deep breath. "We've got another encrypted note. A partially translated encrypted note." The first four words had been transcribed from the numbers. At least there was one item that would be immediately useful. "Sands, this page needs to be fingerprinted and handled with a great deal of care."

Gabriel came over to look. "Longer than the first one. Possibly listing more names?"

Darcy started looking for the open key. The note wasn't on top of the pile of papers, but probably sometime in the last hours before his death, he'd been working on it. There wasn't anything obvious. She glanced at Agent Sands. "We'll need copies of everything in this room. And I mean everything."

"Better make that the house," Gabe suggested. "You'll also be looking for a large sum of cash, probably in the low six figures. If it's found, we need it checked for fingerprints."

"So far I'm hearing sniper, Russian agents, secret messages, and what sounds like a conspiracy. For now, why don't I let them remove the body, start the autopsy, and dust the place for prints. We'll leave the room and its contents sealed until we're both comfortable moving something isn't going to disturb a lead."

Darcy smiled. "I'm beginning to really like you." She pointed to the line of photos. "Who do you think he was after?"

"Given the number, I'd say there was one primary target and lots of targets of opportunity."

"Gabe, this sniper is dead; Luther will just hire another one. Can we pull in Sam on this?"

"What are you thinking?"

Darcy was trying to connect what she could see to what she suspected. "This guy is going to prove to be a military trained sniper. We need someone looking at this planning who can take it apart at a glance and tell us what the focus was. As good as the Agency guys are, they may miss something that a military man wouldn't. The key to stopping this next round of sniper attacks is here, if we can solve it fast enough and figure out who Luther is planning to hit."

"Agent Sands, can you handle one more guest to this?" Gabe asked.

"Unofficially?"

"Very unofficially. A little technical advice."

"As long as I'm present to hear his ideas," the agent agreed.

Gabriel looked at her. "Why don't you take a walk, make a few calls, and see if you can locate our good buddy. Just stay out of public sight in case someone is watching this gathering."

She nodded, grateful to get out of the room. She paused on the landing and called headquarters to have Gabe's secretary get Sam's numbers from Darcy's office. While she waited she looked around the hall and listened to Gabe and Agent Sands.

"Got someone in your team who can read Russian?" Gabriel asked.

"The New York office has a couple decent guys."

"You'll need one. Tell me how you think this shooting went down."

The on-hold music cut off as the line

was picked up. "Yes, I'm still here." Darcy wrote the numbers on her palm. "Thanks." She left the two guys talking, walked down the stairs, and after a moment of thought for where to find the best privacy, stepped outside to the back patio.

She dialed Sam's cell phone number.

May 24
Friday, 2:20 p.m.
Shelton, North Dakota

Sam decided about midafternoon that Amy had been born in the wrong generation. She would have made a great Old West sheriff. He changed tapes in the camera as they walked from the bank toward city hall. She knew everyone in this town. "Can I see your office?" He turned the camera back on to continue recording the actions on the main street.

"There's a desk and a chair."

He swung the camera toward Amy. "Do you have the Most Wanted posters on the wall?"

"I have a calendar of cats."

"I'm allergic to cats."

"I heard about the cougar story. You made it up."

"Amy, you wound me."

She laughed. He could hear an echo of Darcy's laughter in her sister's.

His phone rang.

"Hold this." He gave Amy the camera and retrieved his phone. "Hello?"

"Sam, what are you doing at this moment?"

He was surprised to hear Darcy's voice. "Talking to your sister."

"Amy?"

He smiled at Amy. "You have more than one sister? Would you like to talk to her?"

"Maybe. This is a surprise. You're in Shelton?"

"Yep."

"Let's come back to that later. Can you find somewhere private for a minute? I need to ask you something."

The stress in her voice began to register. Sam lifted his hand and had Amy lower the camera. "Sure, Dar. Give me a minute." Sam covered the phone.

"What's wrong?" The seriousness he had first encountered when Amy pulled him over on the highway was back.

"I'm not sure yet. Where's a quiet place I can chat with Darcy?"

Amy was already pulling out her keys. "My office."

Sam followed her to the town hall where the sheriff's office was located. There was one deputy and a secretary in the outer office. Amy unlocked her office. Sam got his question answered. Amy kept missing person's pictures on her bulletin board.

She motioned him toward her chair. "Let me talk to her before you hang up," she said softly. He nodded and Amy closed the door to give him privacy.

"Okay, Darcy. I'm alone."

"I've got a situation here."

"Describe it."

"Another sniper, this one in Virginia, stopped before he could act. I've got planning documents, photos, maps, and a very dangerous-looking weapon. The FBI is running the investigation."

"How'd you get pulled in?" Sam asked.

"Sergey was likely the man who killed this sniper. He left a note for my partner."

"He's still alive?" Sam asked, feeling a chill at the news. "He's in your area?" He rose from the chair, the urgency kicking in.

"It's just starting to sink in but yes to both. Sergey was here within the last day."

"Are you somewhere safe?"

Darcy hesitated on that answer. "Relatively. I don't think Sergey is after me this time. Frankly we think he helped us out on this one. We're still trying to figure out what is going on."

Sam paced. "How can I help you?"

"We're trying to figure out what this sniper was planning in case someone else is sent to complete this job. How would you feel about being an honorary spook for a few days? In order to think like this guy, we need an expertise here we just don't have. He's military trained. Informal and off the record, just tell us what you think."

Sam looked at his watch. "I can get a flight and be there by late tonight."

"I'm taking up your leave from work. I'm sorry about that."

"Don't be. If I'd heard about this event days later, it would have been hard to take. I'm on my way."

"I appreciate this."

She was nervous about asking for his help. He wanted to shake her for wondering how he'd react to her request. He would be there for her no matter what it took to convince her to let him help. "Dar, don't make assumptions about Sergey. Please. Stay at the office late tonight, make sure you have security drive by your house."

"I'll be careful."

He had to take her word for it, but he

291

knew reality. If a sniper pinpointed her as a target, time was already against him. He looked at the clock, knowing he had to get on the road right now. "Your sister would like to talk with you for a minute." Sam opened the office door and signaled Amy.

"Before you pass me to her, how's your family? I'm sorry I didn't ask earlier."

"Fine, and I've got lots of stories to tell. I'll catch you up on the details when I see you," he said, rushing her a bit because he had a few urgent calls of his own to make. "Here's your sister." He handed the phone to Amy.

Sam joined the receptionist to give Amy some privacy and asked for a phone book so he could look up the number on the East Coast. *Lord, I need to get across the country quickly and figure out what's going on. This threat is too near Dar for comfort. Please keep her safe.*

Amy rejoined him and handed him back his phone. "She'll be okay, Sam."

"It must be tough having Darcy as your sister."

"She can take care of herself; I taught her that. But she knows if the world gets too hot and something goes wrong, she can always come home. Right now it would be nice to have her here."

"I need to get back East. What's the fastest way to make that happen?"

Amy picked up her hat. "I'll drive you to the airport. Leave the camera and the rental car keys. I'll make sure the camera gets back to your mom and the car gets returned."

May 24
Friday, 11:40 p.m.
McLean, Virginia

Darcy walked the concourse at the airport, carrying a book. A look at the incoming flights board showed that Sam's flight was expected to arrive in another twenty minutes. Amy had called her with the flight numbers, and there was no way she would let him take a cab, not when he was flying halfway across the country because she called him.

Sam was worried about her. She didn't know what she could say to change that, but she hadn't been one of those portraits on the wall and didn't see the need to assume the worst. Sergey's reappearance was unsettling, but Sam and Gabriel were overreacting. Nevertheless, she found herself looking over her shoulder when she drove, feeling uneasy. She was tired of being suspicious of cars that turned out to be driven by old ladies.

She spotted a corner seat where she could see the walkway and settled in to wait for Sam. She found herself looking up at every sound and finally calmed her nerves by refusing to be distracted from the story. She was determined to read and to wait, showing patience even if she didn't feel it. The story was good; the words eventually absorbed her for real.

"I seem to remember you reading that book when we first met."

She glanced up, startled, to find Sam smiling down at her. She looked past him; the board showed that his flight still hadn't arrived.

"I shaved twenty minutes off with a change of planes in St. Louis."

She closed the book, feeling caught off balance. "I'm actually trying to finish it this time. I never did figure out whodunit." She rose to greet him.

"Come here." Sam opened his arms and wrapped her in a hug.

She relaxed into it, comforted by the strength and breadth of him. The tension flowed out of her. Just by his presence, he made the situation better. "I'm okay,

Samuel," she whispered.

He stepped back and lifted his hands to brush back her hair and study her face. "We'll talk about today in the car."

Darcy nodded and tried to remember how to be an organized hostess. "I got you a room at a nearby hotel. Would you like to stop and get something to eat first? You must have flown out shortly after I called."

He turned them to walk the concourse toward the parking lot. "Amy and I grabbed a sandwich at the airport, but I'd go for some drive-thru on the way to the hotel if we pass something open. I like your sister."

"She said nice things about you too; although I'm intensely curious to know why you were up my way."

He smiled and pulled a videotape from his carry-on bag. "Since you couldn't get away to see home, I decided to bring home to you."

She stopped walking. Sam caught her arm and pulled her out of the way as she was nearly overrun by a luggage cart.

"Your sister, your town, about fifty hellos from your friends we met up with on the street. Dar, we've got to talk about your house. That's a fabulous house. Hey —"

Unexpected tears pooled and she tried

to blink them away.

He wiped them away for her. "It was fun to do, and it wasn't that big a deal."

"Yes, it was," she whispered.

He wrapped his arm around her and hugged her again. "I didn't mean to make you cry."

She wiped her eyes. "I guess I'm more tired than I thought."

"We'll watch the tapes when you have a couple hours."

"Tapes?"

"Two, plus a bit of a third."

She slid her hand behind his neck, tugged him down, and kissed him. She was falling in love with this man. He went to North Dakota and made tapes of her friends and family. She'd never had someone do something so wonderful. She didn't care how emotional she got or how obvious it was that her heart was on her sleeve. She had a treasure in this man and she knew it.

He leaned his forehead against hers. "When you're not so tired you're swaying a bit on your feet, kiss me again okay? I think my heart stopped. I could go for a repeat during daylight."

She had to laugh. Her hand settled on his shoulder where it had to rest because she couldn't splay her hand wide enough across the muscle and bone to actually hold on. "I really missed you."

"It's mutual, big time, huge." He ducked to quickly kiss her one more time. "And the sound of those boots coming this way is my partner with a lousy sense of timing."

Sam let her move to look around. Wolf was coming toward them, dressed in a Hawaiian shirt that screamed tourist. "He came with you?"

"Actually, he's been watching you for the last several hours."

She looked back at Sam, startled.

He wrapped an arm around her shoulders and nodded to the sunglasses Wolf was twirling as he walked. "So he's not subtle unless he wants to be. Call him my insurance. He's been tailing you since you left work at seven."

"You sent me a bodyguard?"

Sam shook his head, his expression grim. "No, I sent a hunter to see who was hunting you."

# Eighteen

May 25
Saturday, 10:40 a.m.
McLean, Virginia

Darcy stood by the doorway to the condo bedroom and watched Sam study the crime scene. It was kind of spooky watching the intensity of the man. The hard-to-ruffle, smiling man she was falling for was gone, and in his place was this focused soldier with distance in his eyes and assassination on his mind. Sam was in front of the wall where the maps and photos were taped up. He'd been standing there just looking and absorbing information for the last twenty minutes. Planning sniper hits was one of the things Sam did for a living.

She would have been just fine skipping this glimpse into his work. This room was giving her the creeps. The body had been removed, fingerprint dust covered most open surfaces, but the rest of the room contents remained undisturbed.

Sam moved over to study the documents on the table.

Darcy looked at where the man had died. *How many did you kill over the years? Who were you sent to kill this time? And why did you spend your life murdering for money?*

It was inevitable that he would be stopped eventually. What went around, came around. She'd been reading Psalm 75 that morning, and its words provided a glimpse into this — "At the set time which I appoint I will judge with equity. When the earth totters, and all its inhabitants, it is I who keep steady its pillars." There was still justice in the world. But for all the evil that men do, there was still a good God keeping it checked, choosing to use evil for His own purposes to bring men to know Him. If the earth remained comfortable in sin, it would keep people blind to the death in their spirits.

Sergey had stopped this act of great evil, but it raised an interesting question: How had he learned it was coming?

Darcy stepped aside as Gabe and Sam's partner Tom came up the stairs, accompanied by Agent Sands. The way Tom and Gabriel had been huddling together earlier, she had a feeling she would have someone tailing her until they found Sergey. The guys were closing ranks and making decisions without asking her opinion.

Last night she'd ended up getting a hotel room for the night at the place Sam was staying just so she wouldn't have to hear that Tom spent the night in his car watching her place.

Darcy let it go. She wouldn't be talking any of them out of it. About the only course of action was to figure out what had happened here. She looked at the partially decrypted note in her hand. What was the open key? The note had to be deciphered. If it contained names and hers wasn't on the list, she'd have something to point to that would lessen the stress around here.

This man wouldn't have hidden the key. He wouldn't have felt the need to do so. The note had been on the table, with only a few words decoded. If he went to all the trouble to start, why not finish? Had he been interrupted, set it aside, and it got buried under other items?

She walked back to the table where the note had been discovered and looked at exactly what was visible. On top of the encoded piece of paper had been a bus schedule. On the wall was a calendar turned to the correct month. A soda can on a coaster. A mug being used to keep pens. A ruler. She closed her eyes. She was making this too hard.

She went over to her locked briefcase and retrieved the pictures recovered from the house in Ireland. She flipped through the pictures comparing what she saw in common between the two places.

Books. Both men were snipers, both had been stopped during the planning portion of their assignments, and both were reading popular fiction. It didn't make sense that they were reading for pleasure when time was that tight. "Sam, do you read a lot?"

He looked over at her. "In general, yes."

"Do most snipers?"

"Being well read on current events is an occupational necessity."

That suggested newspapers, not fiction. She went looking for all the books she could find. She found two popular thrillers in the bedroom on the side table beside the clock. The price sticker on the back of the mystery was priced in euros, not dollars. Was it bought at an airport when he had extra time?

Were the numbers in the notes page numbers? She looked through the books trying to match up the numbers on the partially decoded message with some page numbers and letters. There wasn't an obvious match.

"Darcy?"

She walked back to join Sam.

"Who's this?" He pointed to a photograph on the table.

She hesitated. "Dr. Ellen Sandford. She's one of our in-house experts on trade, particularly with Canada. She handles grain, fish, livestock, timber; that kind of thing."

"She was the primary target."

Sam motioned to the documents on the table and the maps. "Think of this as a layered plan. You need to peel back layers. His primary mission is where he started his planning, and then he added layers to see how many other targets of opportunity he could pull in."

"What did he have planned?" Gabe asked, joining them.

"He would hit at her home probably the night before and then move during the cover of night to his next target. I need to get out and see several places he has marked, confirm this sequence is possible. My guess is three phases, maybe four, with shooting perches at each. This one looks like an ambush over the highway going to the CIA headquarters. This looks like a fallback perch near the high school, this one at a subdivision entrance. He intended to get as many of those targets as he could. He would use the chaos his first actions created to predict where people would then go, and that's where he set up fallback locations. Be very glad he was stopped. This planning is good."

"Are these all outdoor perches?" Agent Sands asked.

"They appear to be. But I'm beginning to wonder if he doesn't have another weapon stashed at one of these sites. A couple of these look like they're within walking distance, and he's not going to be taking a weapon with him. He would want to be up high. I found gravel on the soles of his shoes in the closet, maybe the fine gravel from a roof. Look around for keys. He won't want to slow down to break into a building. He'll have rented other apartments, offices. But why Dr. Sandford?"

Darcy shook her head. "I don't know. I never would have predicted it based on Luther's past activities."

"Go back and look at the data. A trade expert. You said Luther liked to profit from terrorist acts," Sam said. "What would happen if U.S. and Canadian trade is seriously disrupted?"

"It would make the economic hit of September 11 look like the ripple of a pebble in a pond next to a boulder crashing into a lake."

"Exactly. Profitable if you knew the disruption was coming. Darcy, go back to basics. You don't have to figure this out; Luther is going to tell you in advance what will be hit. Follow his money. It could be anything from a bomb in a shipping container to a significant number of arson forest fires across the West getting planned. Ellen knows something that would either help minimize the damage or would cause the plan to fail."

*Follow the money.* A simple suggestion that would be difficult to do. She'd add to the risk list telecommunications, power transmission, trains, banking, gas pipelines, for the two countries were interconnected in some very fundamental ways.

Gabe pulled out his phone. "The first thing is getting someone baby-sitting Ellen. Sam, can you and Tom take Agent Sands through those sites? Let's find out what's out there and get it wrapped up. Darcy and I will camp out at Ellen's until we know everything she knows."

"Done. And Darcy, don't head home until Wolf or I are with you."

She nodded rather than have the debate here. She'd be tied up for several hours with Ellen anyway.

May 25
Saturday, 6:18 p.m.
Central Intelligence Agency

Where was Luther putting his money? Darcy sat in her office and pondered the great question Sam had asked and couldn't figure out how to answer it. The Department of Treasury had three guys chasing Luther's money. He was going to arrange to profit from whatever was coming. And if the timing of the sniper attacks was as eminent as Sam believed based on the sniper's preparations, then the money should already be in play. But it was like looking into a black hole and trying to see light.

Darcy picked up another of the reports Ellen had written in the last year. Gabriel had taken half and she'd taken half. Timber shipments. She scanned the table of contents. The U.S. and Canada were close to a trade-sanction war over pine. This report focused on the projected market effect of opening the Tremont Forest Preserve to limited tree harvesting. Darcy read, but frankly it didn't make much sense. She'd stayed as far away from economic espionage and intelligence assessments as she could. Why would Luther care what Ellen thought about timber, fishing, or the like?

She went back to the treasury report. Luther had profited from shorting airline stocks, insurance stocks, and he had made a chunk of money just betting the market was going to sharply correct downward. He'd had the advantage of surprise on September 11. He had been able to make a lot of large bets in the market and yet not get noticed ahead of time by the regulators. This time Luther would have to be subtle. He'd buy the stocks and sell short; he'd buy some futures.

She switched to the secure SEC Web site where software monitored for trends. Luther could quietly put a few hundred million into bets like that, and there would be no way to see it in a trillion-dollar global market. Oil and gas stocks, paper stocks, shipping, nearly every sector Ellen watched was under selling pressure. Would he stay away from the stock market and play the commodity market directly? Darcy rubbed her eyes, then closed the screens. She could be looking at Luther manipulating items and she wouldn't understand what she was seeing. The guys at the SEC would have to give her those answers.

Maybe Ellen wasn't targeted because of her current work. Darcy went back to Ellen's work biography. Did she know someone who would raise a red flag today? Had she traveled somewhere and maybe seen someone or something that would lead to trouble? Had she crossed paths with someone they were interested in? Was she targeted simply because she would hear about the crime and instinctively think about a culprit's name?

Ellen had degrees in agriculture; she'd traveled extensively to Europe last year when the foot-and-mouth disease crippled the beef export industry; she'd done her thesis work on Mad Cow Disease; she had four recently published studies on the interactions of the Endangered Species Act and the North American Free Trade Act.

"You need to go home, dahlin'."

Her knee slammed up against the corner of her desk. "Gabriel, scare me out of a few years of my life, why don't you." She rubbed her aching knee as she turned around.

"Ellen is a forty-four-year-old economist whose only logical enemy is probably her neighbor who dislikes all the animals she keeps as pets. We're chasing the wrong thing."

Darcy leaned back in her chair. "What?"

Gabe leaned against the doorjamb and bounced a tennis ball against the floor in a steady rhythm. "Try thinking domestic — a disgruntled former CIA employee who wanted to kill as many others as he could from his former employer. Had September 11 not happened that would've been our first guess as soon as we saw that set of photos. Besides agents in the field, the photos contained everyone from analysts like Ellen to assistants in the personnel department."

"So why would Luther be involved then?"

"A sniper hit is a sniper hit, and Luther will take money from anyone. All it takes is one disgruntled former CIA employee who worked in Europe at some point, and we can explain how he knew to look up Luther when he wanted something nasty to happen."

She leaned her head back and looked at the ceiling. "How many people have been fired since September 11 happened?"

"Several, even if it was quietly done. This sniper was hired to kill a lot of people. Ellen could have been chosen to lead the list for a twenty-year-old grievance."

Darcy thought about it and shook her head. "A disgruntled employee wouldn't have the kind of cash needed to hire this hit." She frowned. "At least an honest employee wouldn't."

She looked at Gabe and hesitated to run that idea to its conclusion but reluctantly did so. "But a spy in our midst might. A spy working in this building is one of those fired, and he's not sure if his espionage will be discovered now that he is not present to cover the evidence of what he's done? That could explain the breadth of those photos and how the cash was obtained to have Luther hire a sniper of this caliber."

The fact that Gabriel didn't reject the idea told her a lot. He was senior enough in the CIA hierarchy that if there were suspicions of a spy being quietly checked, Gabe would know it.

He nodded. "We put the word out we're looking for a disgruntled ex-employee, and we may just get the small observations from coworkers needed to discover a spy. The key would be not to let the apparent lack of resources eliminate a candidate."

Darcy swiveled her chair back and forth, thinking through the pieces they had. "What about Sergey's involvement?"

"What you originally speculated. Mikail was the sniper who killed his family. Sergey hunted him down and paid him back."

"You know, it does fit, which is almost scary."

"I'll take this idea upstairs." Gabriel caught the tennis ball. "Sam's here. Go home."

"I don't need to be baby-sat."

"Yes you do. Besides, I think he views it more as an excuse to hang out with you."


May 25
Saturday, 7:40 p.m.
McLean, Virginia


Darcy settled on the couch at her apartment, letting Sam have the floor. She fished loose french fries from the bottom of the sack. "How's the shake?"

"Still very thick and frozen." He held it back so she could taste.

"That's definitely mint."

"It's good." Sam added turrets to the Lego castle.

The place she thought of as her temporary home still had remnants reflecting her
cover story lying about. She didn't need
the cover now and didn't envision picking
it up again. The desire to be an agent in
the field was gone. She was more convinced than ever that when this war was
over, she'd go back to being a landowner in
North Dakota and not miss this work.
"Did Tom get off okay?"

Sam glanced at his watch. "He's probably back with Jill by now."

"I still can't believe you called him."

"He's my partner; on things like this we
call each other."

"Sergey wasn't after me this time. He
wouldn't have left a message for Gabriel if
he were."

"I'll believe that when we find him.
Ready to watch movies?" He moved aside
his cheeseburger and selected the first
video he'd made.

"Sure. I'm so glad you did this." She
snuggled down against the pillows she'd
piled up. She wasn't sure how good of
company she'd be tonight, but just the fact
he had gone to so much trouble on her behalf mattered more than she could put into
words.

"You need the break. You don't smile as

much as you used to."

She looked at Sam, trying to read the depth of that statement. She hoped it was only an observation and not a comment opening a deep conversation. Sometimes the guy was too perceptive. "There hasn't been a lot to smile about lately."

"You can't grieve for three thousand people."

"Sure I can."

"It doesn't help. You're letting yourself get depressed, Dar."

She knew he understood what it was like to get caught in the weight of a crisis that never let up. If she made a mistake, people died. "I'm just tired. There's a difference."

Sam studied her face. "SEALs learn early to sleep when war is going on around them, to trust their buddies. You've got a good team helping you out. Walk away from it when you leave the office. You can't carry this war as your own personal fight."

"I don't mean to. It just feels like stuff is piling on, you know?"

He reached back and rubbed her arm lightly. "I know, and I'm worried about you. In 2 Timothy it says that there will be times of stress. Not a thing is going on here that caught God by surprise. You've just got to learn to let it go."

Stress was like the five-letter word around the office lately. She tugged her Bible off the end table and searched to find verse he referred to. "It's in chapter 3: 'In the last days there will come times of stress. For men will be lovers of self, lovers of money, proud, arrogant and lovers of pleasure rather than lovers of God.' " She closed the Bible. "It sounds like today."

"It is today. Step back and get your perspective. If God wants you to be the one to figure this out and stop Luther, you will. If not you, maybe He has someone else in mind. He's sovereign, Dar. There's a lot in the Bible about trusting Him in times of trouble. There's nothing that says, 'if Darcy doesn't accomplish $X$ all is lost. I can't sustain the world without her.' "

She had to smile, for Sam had pegged her. "You made your point."

"I want the Darcy back whose smile reaches her eyes."

She found relief just in the kindness of his words. He cared, and he was watching her closer than she realized. She envied him the easy ability to apply what he knew about God, his steadfast faith. Too much of her days lately were spent carrying burdens she needed to be reminded to put down. "How about one who falls asleep watching a videotape of home?"

"You can sleep right there. It looks comfortable, and I'll lock the door on my way out and turn the security on."

"You're good for me, Sam."

"Of course I am, honey." He leaned back and kissed her. Passion skimmed beneath the surface, and she wanted to wrap it around them both and follow where it would go. This was so much better than the stress going on in life, but she put on the brakes and eased back so the memory didn't end tinged with frustration for both of them.

She loved this man. She blinked back tears as the kiss ended. "Nice," she whispered, watching his eyes already soften as he smiled at her. "Do you feel like you're getting pulled under right now? I do."

Sam stroked her cheek. "I think we've got something between us that feels more like a powerful current than a playful wave," he agreed. "You are so beautiful."

She grinned. "I like hearing those words."

His thumb rubbed her bottom lip. "And you're nervous. One of these days I'm going to stop your habit of nibbling your lip with a kiss."

"That wouldn't help my nerves much. They feel like live wires right now."

Sam laughed. "A fact that pleases me more than a bit. Tone back the gorgeous smile just a notch so I can turn around and get this tape in."

She tugged over a throw pillow and hugged it to her face. "You've got a minute."

He took advantage of the moment and tickled her. She doubled up on the couch, nearly rolling off it with the laughter.

"That's better. No more serious face."

She swatted him with the pillow. "Go put in the tape."

He move back and took his time getting the tape in and the channel set. "It's in. You ready?"

"Hit the play button and we'll find out."

The video began to play showing the grounds of her house, her sister walking ahead of Sam giving the commentary. Darcy fought against the tears. "Oh, she looks wonderful." The times hadn't changed Amy. She still walked with a comfortable command in her steps, that big white Stetson her husband had given her perched on her head.

Sam settled on the floor by the couch and reassuringly rubbed her arm. "I really liked her, Dar. She reminds me of you."

The fence still needed to be painted, and the inside of the house was just as she had left it. The house was waiting for her to come back and resume work. It was home.

Darcy reached her hand forward and let it rest in Sam's as the tape played. "Sorry I don't have any popcorn or anything."

"You're looking at a man quite content with where he sits."

From her house, Sam had traveled to town with Amy, the roads and the fields and the sheer beauty of the place captured on tape was much as she had remembered.

Her eyes closed as the walk down Main Street played and Sam stepped into the diner filled with her friends. As hard as she fought sleep, it was taking over. She tightened her grip on Sam's hand, not wanting to lose contact in sleep. She wanted North Dakota back, but with Sam still in her life. Having that would take some figuring out. She drifted to sleep keeping her grip on his hand.

Her beeper going off woke her. She was alone, the apartment was dark, and an afghan covered her. Darcy groggily fumbled with the beeper. Sam had left; she wished sleep had held off and given her another hour with him. She called the number back. "Yes, Gabriel."

"NSA came through. I'm reading two decrypted messages."

May 25
Saturday, 11:50 p.m.
Central Intelligence Agency

Darcy stuck her coffee mug into the cutout map ring on the shelf beside Gabriel's couch and held up her hand as he started talking. She wasn't done with breakfast yet, but she wasn't going to start work at midnight on a Saturday night without at least a bagel to soften the blow. She'd put enough cream cheese on this one that it was hard to hold. And Sam wondered why she was tired. She wondered if Luther got this tired on the other end of this fight. He had to know one mistake would bury him. Gabe handed her sugar packets for the coffee.

"Okay, tell me about the open code first."

"The partial note shows two digits turn into one letter, with that and a list of books found at each location it was easy to solve." Gabe handed her a book. "Take the first two-digit number. Start on page one

317

of the book, count that many letters, and circle it. Take the next two-digit number, turn to page two in the book, and count the letters. The letters circled become words. It looks like they were using whichever book was at the top of the bestseller's list."

"What did the two notes say?"

He handed her a folder. "Luther doesn't believe in being verbose. He was sending the IRA sniper against a British intelligence officer. The Russian sniper had been given a list of nine names with Ellen's at the top. Sam was good in his read of this."

Darcy looked back at Gabe, judging his mood. "Jerry's still out there."

"I know. The question is who he'll be sent against."

She looked at the next list of names. "If we discount the one here as domestic, that leaves the British intelligence officer. What do we know about him?"

"He's essentially your counterpart, a troubleshooter who worked most of Eastern Europe and spent the last decade tracking where people have ended up as the USSR dissolved and Russia created herself. In the past he worked cases with both Kevin Wallace and Benjamin Rice."

A fact that tied this sniper hit all the way

back to the initial hits on September 9. "An interesting lead." They had never been able to come up with something solid behind the reason Kevin and Benjamin had specifically been targeted. "What kind of special projects did this British officer handle?"

"Some euro counterfeiting cases, investigations into the source of the Foot-and-Mouth Disease outbreak that decimated the British beef industry, several smuggling cases where immigrants were found locked in shipping containers. He's a good coordinator when something is hot."

Darcy got up to look at the timeline of events posted on Gabriel's board, each written on a three-by-five card. The number of agents and military officers killed across Europe was staggering. "Luther's playing a blocking game, Gabe. If there's a pattern here, it's not the people he's striking at, it's the roles. We've been making this too complicated."

She tapped the first card. "Look at how it started. Luther knows September 11 is going to happen, he's planning to profit from it, and he knows there's an extensive file out there on him because of his years in Czech intelligence. He can't do much about destroying the records, but he can encourage them to become dusty and forgotten. Ever since September 9 there have been attacks against individuals here and in Europe who had firsthand knowledge of how the Czech intelligence service functioned."

"He's got a list of names and he's taking individuals out as he has the opportunity."

"Basically. Luther is still a planner, thinking in terms of what intel he has and what intel the other side has, but now he doesn't have rules for the game beyond his own survival. He's hitting people who have reason to know him. All Luther did was pause for a while when we got close enough to kill Dansky." Darcy picked up Gabe's tennis ball. "And if his interests and someone else's overlap, he lets them pay for the hit."

"He's out to limit people who could hunt him down."

She nodded. "It doesn't matter which person gets hit when, only that they do." She picked up the overnight summary. "Have the FBI tracked down anything on where Sergey went?"

"They found the murder weapon in a drainage ditch two miles from here, suggesting Sergey headed north after he stopped this sniper."

"I'm glad Sergey is not dead. Maybe it's a case of knowing the enemy too well, but I feel like he's as much a pawn in someone else's game as we are." She picked up her coffee mug. "We've got to find Jerry. Otherwise someone else will be dead soon."

"The last lead was Greece."

Darcy would be the one putting an ocean between herself and Sam. She hated the idea, but maybe it was best to test the relationship with a little distance right now. Given Sam's job she'd have to get used to it, and her emotions were so involved it was hard to think.

"Get us a flight, Gabriel. I want to talk to the people on the ground who last saw Jerry Summit." She would miss out on a chance to spend time with Sam over the last days of his leave, but it couldn't be helped. She wouldn't have another intelligence officer's death on her conscience if there was something they could find that might stop it.

# Nineteen

June 12
Wednesday, 9:40 a.m.
Athens, Greece

Darcy loved Greece. She flipped pages in the guidebook at her hotel room while she waited for Gabriel to join her. She'd spent long days walking around the Acropolis and the Agora, taking pictures to show Amy. She wanted to see the Philopappos Monument even if only by taxi before she left. They had a late morning meeting with the CIA station chief at the embassy. Days spent chasing Jerry had given them all the information available. It was time to head back to the States.

Her phone rang as the coffee percolated.

The caller ID she had on the secure phone told her it was Sam's cell phone. She knew he was in Coronado, CA, at the West Coast SEAL headquarters. She answered the call with a smile. "It's incredibly late out there." She was about nine hours ahead of him.

"We're just getting back from a night jump," he replied, sounding a bit distracted. "I wanted to give you a call before you headed to work. It's quiet in the world, Dar." He'd been touching base with her daily. Over the last two weeks, she'd come to set her morning around his call. It was so nice to hear his voice.

"Starting that way." She poured herself a cup of coffee and picked on a bagel. "How was the training exercise?"

"A couple minor injuries. The wind turned out to be marginal for the jump."

A couple injuries . . . She set down the bagel. "Sam?"

"I bruised an elbow. It happens."

She frowned as she realized Sam had covered the phone and was coughing. It didn't sound like he had a cold. "Where are you?"

He paused before he answered. "The hospital. It's no big deal. Wolf landed on me. We try to avoid things like that."

She winced on his behalf. "How many ribs did you crack?"

"Maybe one of his, although he swears it isn't so." A voice in the background added, "Is too." Sam sighed. "That's Joe. He's ragging us both. A weapon misfired complicating things a bit. Otherwise Wolf would have probably been a little more graceful about his crash landing. I just bruised an elbow and got the breath knocked out of me when I tried to block him."

Sam didn't sound badly hurt but he did sound more than a little frustrated. She leaned against the counter cradling her coffee mug. "Can I help?"

"You already have. I'm just blowing off steam."

"You're allowed."

The phone got covered again as Sam barked at his partner, "Wolf, shut up and take the needle."

Darcy covered her end of the phone to hide her laughter.

"Dar, you want to remind me why I haven't retired yet?"

"You love it too much."

"I'm rethinking that."

"Tough it out, sailor."

"Wolf is really annoying me. Call me about six your time tonight, okay? I think we'll be heading back to Little Creek tomorrow."

"I'll call you," Darcy promised.

"This day is going to pass peacefully."

"We'll know in twenty-four hours. I miss you, Sam."

"Still going to be back in the States by this weekend?"

"I hope so. I seem to remember we have a date."

"Definitely. Bring sunscreen because we're going sailing."

"I'm looking forward to it." Sam loved the sea. It was time she learned to share his passion for it. "You're too far away."

"Tell me about it. Don't work too hard today, Dar, and skip the worry."

"That's a promise. Go take care of your partner, Sam."

June 14
Friday, 9:18 a.m.
Central Intelligence Agency

Darcy picked up another letter. She was trying to wade through the mail that had piled up while she'd been overseas. The fan rotated and blew papers on her desk, forcing her to grab for her calculator to use as a paperweight. The air-conditioning for the old CIA headquarters building was out. She had her office door propped open and a fan moving air but it was still stifling hot. Most of the mail were paper versions of things she'd been able to review on-line or had verbally been briefed on. Classified pages went into the burn bag, and the rest went into a blue recycling tub.

"I brought you a refill." Gabriel joined her.

She took the large iced tea her partner held out. "Thanks, Gabe. What's with the bomb dogs roving the halls?" She wasn't that interested in bailing out of her office for a trip to the parking lot where a sniper might be watching, but it was kind of disconcerting to find the dogs passing by. Henry and his handler had been by three times in the last forty minutes.

"Yet another phoned-in bomb threat. Don't worry about it."

The threats had apparently been happening with regularity while she and Gabe had been overseas. "You would think this place could trace a phone call."

She slit open the next letter with her sharp-edged knife. The irradiation process to kill anthrax or other hazards turned the pages brittle. Mail was now a pain to deal with.

Gabe relaxed against the doorjamb. "Canada found a safe house in Ottawa they think Sergey had been using during March and April. It's been abandoned."

"Send Neil to take a look?"

"That's what I was thinking."

"The safe houses seem to have the same pattern for hiding cash boxes in the floors and tucking documents behind ductwork. How long was this house owned?"

"It was purchased over thirty years ago. You have to admire the KGB for its long-term commitment to infiltration. They were good about giving themselves places to go that would attract no attention. Money was hidden in places they might use once or twice in a decade."

Darcy tugged open the next envelope. It was a refresher document on the meaning of the code words stamped on reports. Learning them was one of the necessary evils of working in a place that used letters to cloud even what they wanted to say. She scanned the document for new code words, feeling she should at least attempt to remember them. *GAMMA* was highly sensitive signal intelligence; *ZARF* was intelligence picked up from eavesdropping satellites; *VRK* — Very Restricted Knowledge. She flipped a couple more pages. "Do I need to know the latest ways to confuse us?"

"Just read what I give you. You'll be fine."

She pitched the report in the burn bag as the report of names and acronyms was itself red-striped and stamped classified.

Darcy slit open a pale blue envelope. She saw the first of the text on the page as she took it from the envelope and stopped, leaving the page half inside the envelope. "Well, well. What is this?" She pushed the box of mail aside and the recycling bin back under her desk. She elbowed aside the papers on her desk to clear a space.

"Something interesting?"

"What was Sergey's authentication code during his embassy days?"

"K7942 and the date of the postmark."

She turned over the envelope to check the cancellation stamp. "He sent us a note. It's postmarked the day we found that sniper." The delay caused by the irradiation process to keep the mail safe had just badly disrupted a priceless lead.

"Gloves."

She was already tugging open the side drawer of her desk. She kept a box of latex gloves available, using them most often for the film work she did on the light board where fingerprints clouded images.

She pulled the piece of paper carefully

from the envelope and gently laid it open. "The brittleness is going to be a problem." The page crease cracked under the mere pressure of her fingers. "It's his signature."

Gabriel read over her shoulder.

We need to meet. I propose one month from today, June 24. The Fairmont Mall in Fairmont, Florida, at noon, the rare stamp and coins display of our mutual friend Thomas. I'll bring something worth your time. I'll be alone, bring all the security you like. I'd like five minutes face-to-face, just you and me. They had my granddaughter, Darcy. Send someone else, and I won't show.

Darcy read the note twice. "It's an interesting offer, Gabe."

"I'm not sending you to meet with him again."

She leaned back to look up at him. "That's your emotion talking not logic."

"He broke his word last time; I don't trust him. If he has something to share, he can do a dead drop and pass it to us. He wants to cut a deal, we can talk on the phone. He knows our number."

She read the note again. She waffled on

whether she trusted Sergey or not. She wanted to know what he had to say. And she wasn't interested in leaving him out there. "He broke his word to us, so we're not bound to keep ours. Let's pick him up. All it will take is me as the bait."

# Twenty

June 24
Monday, 9:40 a.m.
Fairmont, Florida

For days leading up to the meeting, FBI and CIA agents had been slipping into the hotel across from the Fairmont Mall. Darcy would make contact, and FBI officers would move in and arrest Sergey. In theory it was simple; in reality no one in the room expected today to go smoothly.

Darcy slipped on the watch the technician handed her. It told the time but it was basically all microphone. It was so sensitive the problem would be filtering out all the background noise from shoppers around her. It would pick up Sergey's every word on tape.

Darcy leaned against Sam for balance as she worked to slip on the white sneakers that were tagged to track where she went. "You'll be roving?" Sam hadn't given her a choice about his involvement. After barking at her for the mere idea of meeting with Sergey, he said he was coming. The problem with having a relationship with a SEAL was his protective streak was about a mile wide. She'd protested for form, but it was kind of nice to have him here. She trusted the agents brought in, but they had other objectives as well as her safety on their plate. Sam would have only one, and Gabriel couldn't attempt a foot race if it was required.

The cops couldn't do much but give their agreement, for unless they detained Sergey the mall was a public place. The blueprints on the table showed not only the stores and the various dressing rooms, bathrooms, and elevators, but also the employees only areas and corridors behind the stores where merchandise was moved.

"I'll be near you and Wolf will be above us scanning the area from the food court."

"You have to give Sergey credit; a craft fair with booths cluttering the mall hallways gives him optimum safeguards: dense public traffic and numerous ways to approach the meeting place."

"Just stay in your assigned box, Dar, and let him come to you."

"He's not going to be easy to identify.

You can guarantee he won't look anything like that photo." There were still two hours before the meeting, and ten agents were already throughout the area.

"I'll spot him," Sam replied. "You still owe me a day sailing."

"When this is over I'm taking a week off."

She slipped on glasses and looked at the monitor. "How are visuals, Gabe?" There was a thin wire camera in the frames of the glasses. Her partner was already in the command post van in the mall parking lot, tracking cameras that monitored every inch of the meeting area. She had audio with him through a small earpiece and a miniature microphone in her flag lapel pin.

"Tiny. I get about fifteen degrees directly where you are looking, but it's the best that lens can do."

"I'll look around a lot," she promised. Sam handed her the shopping bag she would be carrying. It contained her special gift from the Chief of Disguise to be used if needed. "Gabriel, I'm coming to join you at the van. Shut off the video for a minute."

"Why?"

"I plan to kiss Sam good-bye."

Her partner chuckled and she heard a click.

"It's been kind of crowded around here

lately," Darcy said, smiling at Sam.

"It has indeed." Sam rested his hands on her shoulders. "You enjoy this field work."

"More than I do sitting behind a desk."

"You'll play today by the book?" Sam asked.

"I'll get the job done."

"I note the change. I'll be close by. If anything goes wrong, you look for me."

Darcy rested her hands against his. "That's a promise." Sam and Tom would both have audio, hearing everything that was going on.

"Come here, gorgeous." Sam drew her to him and claimed her lips in a quick kiss. "You probably won't see me very often, but you'll never be out of my sight."

She squeezed his hands and stepped back. "Gabriel, I'm on the way."

It was time to go to work.

The rare stamp and coin booth was set up in corridor $E$ of the mall. On the left side of it was a booth selling customized painted mailboxes, on the right a booth selling sculptured candles. The stores in corridor $E$ included two small clothes boutiques, a Hallmark card shop, a candy store, a music store, and was anchored by a department store.

Darcy entered the area ten minutes before the prearranged meeting time, carrying with her the shopping bag with her gift from the Chief of Disguise and three packages bought from stores as she walked through the mall. A backup microphone was built into the handle of the shopping bag. The packages purchased during her walk through the mall let her control space around by simply where she set them down.

The rare stamp and coin display was owned and managed by Thomas Youst, a mutual friend of both agencies. He was a Canadian, used by both sides over the years as a trusted courier for documents. His business gave him a reason to travel wherever he was needed. The CIA hadn't told Thomas they were coming, and she doubted Sergey had either. But if for some reason Sergey was not going to show, Darcy figured Thomas would be holding the message.

She stopped at the east table of the three tables that made up his booth and looked at one of the stamp books. Twenty bucks for a stamp, all the way to several stamps priced in the hundreds. If she'd been a collector, Thomas's booth would be a fascinating stop.

"Have a favorite era?"

"I collect by topic. I love butterflies," she mentioned, "and dogs."

Thomas didn't even blink at the message, he just reached for the other photo album and turned it back four pages. "Have you seen Scotty, President Truman's dog?"

Maybe she would start a collection. The stamp was gorgeous.

She set down her packages. "May I?"

"Sure."

She tagged the sheet with one of the Post-it Notes provided and turned pages in the display book, looking at what else he had.

Thomas stepped over to the cash register to serve a customer buying a silver eagle.

Now these were pretty. She studied a set of four puppies that were on a Danish stamp.

"It's overpriced," Gabe's warning came softly in her ear.

She smiled but didn't answer him. She turned back to the Scotty. Christmas was five months and a day away. And they wanted Thomas to stay in business. She reached for her purse. Her company credit card came out. "Would you wrap these two please?" she asked Thomas, selecting both the terrier and the puppies.

"Darcy. Quit shopping. You're on the job."

She brushed back her hair and smiled again, knowing a camera was perched in the decorative ferns beside the staircase that had her face in view.

She had picked out four of the agents in the area, but Sam still escaped her. Most of the agents would be shopping within the stores in the area, awaiting word to move on Sergey. She didn't bother to look at her watch. Sergey would not be late this time, knowing she'd leave rather than linger.

"Report in," Gabe said, as he had done regularly since before she entered the area considered her box. One after the other agents reported in that they had seen no sign of Sergey.

Darcy signed her name on the credit card receipt and accepted the sack. "Thanks."

She picked up her bags. She paused by the table of coins on the west side of the booth, admiring the gold maple leaf coins, and then walked toward the department store.

"Darcy, stay in your box."

"I see him," she murmured.

Two men heading toward her immediately found reasons to slow, pause, and window-shop so they could see what she did then head back the way they had come.

Her heartbeat quickened as she contemplated what she was about to do. Where was Sam? She needed to know his location if she was going to pull this off. A man rose from the bench to her left and she realized somewhat startled that it was Sam. He'd changed clothes and was in a suit and tie talking with a woman. At first glance she had placed him as a businessman on his lunch break. Okay. She picked up her pace ever so slightly and angled to her right to skirt between two teenagers and a woman pushing a double stroller.

"Where's she going?"

Sam heard the intensity of Gabriel's words and felt the same concern as Darcy left her assigned security box and crossed the hallway into the department store. The agents were arrayed around the coin and stamp booth. By entering the store she was cutting down to a quarter the number of agents around her.

"Darcy, stop. Don't follow him."

Sam caught a look at the side of Darcy's face as she entered the department store and turned toward the women's dress department. The determination in her face meant she wouldn't be stopping. She was heading somewhere intentionally. What had she seen? Sam hadn't seen anyone he thought fit the basic profile of Sergey.

"Talk to me, Darcy," Gabriel demanded. "Did anyone see what she saw or what she was passed?"

Darcy paused to allow a mom stepping off the store escalators with a toddler to pass by.

"Stop her. She just dumped the glasses and the watch," Gabe demanded.

Sam was still thirty yards behind her, and the only two agents closer were on the wrong side of the traffic flow. Darcy disappeared from his sight as she turned into the congested area near the cosmetic counter leading into the women's clothing department.

He never saw her again.

"This better be worth the official reprimand I'm going to get, Sergey." Darcy set her tray down on the food court table.

"You haven't left the mall," he pointed out reasonably, sampling one of her nachos. Today he was a three-hundred-pound short man in a custom-made suit with a bold blue tie. Sitting on the table beside him was a salesman's display case of fine writing pens. "You have to admit, the cheese makes the nachos. We don't have as good a cheese sauce in Russia."

His tray showed he'd already had two cheeseburgers and a plate of cheese fries. "I have to keep up appearances, you know," he said, eyeing the tacos she bought. "The man you had in the bird's-eye seat, watching the stamp and coin booth from here at the food court? He's good. It took me almost an hour to realize he was also one of yours."

"A friend of a friend."

"Yes, I saw the others pick up your tail when you unexpectedly left. Sit down, my dear. Resting against that walker has to be tiring."

She lowered herself to the seat, moving with the speed of a seventy-year-old. She'd dumped the glasses and watch in another woman's shopping bag. Her tennis shoes with their tracking tags had been abandoned in the women's dressing room along with the flag pin. The key Sergey had slipped her worked perfectly to the storage room door behind the rack of dresses being returned to the showroom floor. The walker was waiting for her beside a baby stroller as Sergey helped her to go either young or old. Darcy's own shopping at the mall gave her the change of clothes. The Chief of Disguise at the Agency had given her the critical last item. The female FBI agent sent in to search the changing rooms had been too late to catch the metamorphosis.

Darcy had walked right by the agents canvassing the department store to find her. It was embarrassing to realize she could fool Sam as well. She had honestly thought he would recognize at least her eyes, but he'd not only stepped aside to give her the right of way in the aisle, he'd held the elevator door for her and asked if she was going up or down.

Darcy looked at Sergey and took a sip of her diet soda. "You're as good as you used to be, but you are begging to be caught." He had slipped the directions and the key into her pocket as she paused by the display of hand painted plates.

"Eat. If you want to take me in when we're done with lunch, I promise to go with you quietly. But you and I need to talk."

"Where did she go?" The latest officer to enter the van and ask that question got several nasty looks in reply. The van was crowded with men. Sam stood behind Gabriel, watching the tapes he was replaying. They had to find her before Sam let his anger boil. Even knowing the danger, she'd still ducked out on them. On him.

"There was the pass. Look at that. Slick as a professional pickpocket." Gabe stopped the video and replayed frames one by one. The man was twenty years too young to be Sergey — bald, wearing a U.S. Hockey Team shirt and jeans with high-tops unlaced and shoelaces trailing. It couldn't be Sergey, but it was, and something had clearly been given to Darcy.

"Come on, Darcy, when did you read it?" Gabriel asked, hitting the play button.

She continued window-shopping as she made her way through the mall, wandering, shopping, so she would end up at the coin and stamp booth at the agreed upon time. "Your patience is killing me, Dar," Gabe muttered, hitting the fast-forward button.

"Whoa." Sam's hand tightened on Gabe's shoulder. "There."

Gabe stopped the playback. Darcy's hand came out of her pocket. The view from the camera in the frame of her glasses remained on a pair of shoes in the display window while the security camera tracking her captured her hand coming up and resting against the glass briefly, then going back into her pocket. "She used the glass. Darcy, we are going to have words. Peripheral vision. She put the message on one pane of glass and read it in the other. Exactly like that sales poster reflects into both panes."

"So we have no idea what he told her."

"Only that she had a good forty minutes to think about what she was going to do," Gabe said grimly. "Whatever was in that message, it was enough to have her breaking decades of trust between us. Would someone please tell me we've got Darcy's sister on the phone and that she's fine?" The possibility that the note said "I've got your sister" was a reality Gabriel had immediately jumped to as he saw his partner breaking with the plan.

"Her office says Amy's out somewhere chasing a stolen truck, but they swear she's fine."

"I want her voice telling me that."

"We're working on it."

Gabe rolled back his chair and tossed his earphones on the table.

Sam recognized extreme stress when he saw it. The man was at his limit. "You know her best, Gabe. What's she likely to do?"

Gabriel punched a button to print the image of the man who had passed Darcy the note. "Not leave the mall. Sergey wants to talk with her and not get arrested, that's one thing. But she's not stupid enough to be alone with him again. Even if the worst case has happened, she wouldn't leave the mall with him."

Gabe picked up the image. "The odds Sergey still looks like this are nil, but get it out to the guys and let's start combing that place end to end, starting with the second floor."

"You have to know what Darcy looks like."

"No one sees the disguise she travels with unless she needs to use it. She's superstitious about it. I doubt I'm even going to recognize her." Gabe pushed himself to his feet. "I knew today was a bad idea."

"We've got Amy on the phone. It's patched in by radio."

Gabe held out his hand for the mike. "Let me talk with her."

Darcy lifted her drink to sip through the straw. "I'm sorry about your family, Sergey." She could see the anger and grief in his eyes.

"The man who did it is dead."

"And the man who ordered it?"

"We both want Luther, Darcy. I just plan to get to him first."

She dipped her head, acknowledging his statement as fact. He'd try to get to Luther first, to kill him, no matter what the price. "Why try for me?"

"You haven't figured it out yet? All the sniper hits? Darcy . . ."

She quirked an eyebrow to ask him to get to the point.

"You won the cold war, he lost, and Luther didn't want to accept it. He's killing those who were awarded the Intelligence Star for Valor for the cold war victory. Protecting himself, by eliminating those who could find him. The fact terrorists are paying him to remove investigators — He's just putting those he hates most at the top of the list."

She thought of the names of those who had died. There had been so many more significant events, so many awards and commendations in the files that it had never clicked. "That's why you came after me?"

"He had my family, Darcy. And as awful as it is, I knew I could use the bounty collected for your death to give me a chance to get to Luther. I am sorry. My family was all I had left. It was necessary."

Forced to choose between Amy and a Russian agent, she wouldn't have thought twice if there was no other way to deal with the situation. "Why didn't he just send a sniper after me?"

"Logistics. September 11 was a moved-up date, and I was someone he knew could get into the U.S., could get you to meet me." Sergey waited until she nodded. "Luther knows I'm after him, and he hired Jerry to kill me before I kill him."

Darcy set down her drink. "We assumed Jerry was coming after one of us."

"No. Vladimir went to get Jerry for one reason. Luther is a scared little rat hiding behind the two men he hired," Sergey smiled darkly, "or so my Russian friends who turned down the money offered to kill me said."

"At least Jerry's going after you takes one thing from my worry list. I was afraid he would target one of our people. You're good enough it would be a fair fight. You said you had something for us — you were right. This was very helpful, Sergey." And more than made up for the past.

"Oh, that one was free. We both want Luther. Agreed?"

"Yes."

He took a manila folder from his fancy writing pen case. "Find this boat. I departed Miami on it with Vladimir and spent two days aboard. I'm confident Luther owns the boat." Sergey tapped the folder. "I was bored; I took many pictures." He slid it over to her. "I would like to know what you find."

"That's fair."

"My friend at the embassy will pass me a sealed note. Assuming, of course, I walk out of this meeting still a free man."

She didn't know yet what she thought was best. This man was on a mission to find Luther. If he accomplished his goal, he would remove a problem for them. A problem big enough that it was worth letting him walk. "Do you have any idea where all Luther's money went?"

Sergey laughed. "Still typically Western in your priorities, chasing the money. Shall we continue with your schoolwork, Darcy? Another free lesson in tradecraft?" He nudged the tray of food she had bought for lunch. "How do you hide a lot of money if you wish not to leave it in a bank to be confiscated?"

Sergey let her think about it, and she felt like a blind fool. "You buy something very expensive."

"Very good." He inclined his head. "He bought an island. Or an island and a tourist charter firm, or a hotel on a private island. My sources were not clear on the particulars." He leaned against the table. "That is the best lead I have on Luther. I just do not have the resources to prove it."

"Which is why you asked for this meeting."

"A boat —" he waved his hand at the folder — "I can find a boat. Eventually. An island, buried under so many layers its purchase is hidden, that takes someone with sophisticated resources. That takes the U.S. or the Brits."

"So we trade information, a boat and a lead, for a location and his new cover name."

"Correct."

"Who's to say we won't act on what we find, long before we bother to tell you about it?"

"Honor. And the fact Gabriel still owes me a favor for tipping him off that his cover in the Ukraine was blown."

Darcy picked up the folder. She wanted Luther, and the information was worth the price. "We have a deal. For what a retired agent's word is worth."

★ ★ ★

Sam stopped by the fountain in the center of the mall. The sick feeling in his stomach grew worse with each passing minute. She was gone. Had she been snatched, kidnapped, killed? *You just had to walk away, Darcy. You just had to do it.* When he found her he was going to slowly murder her. A relationship with a spy wasn't worth this. He looked at Gabriel coming back from a walk of the opposite concourse. "I sent Wolf to check receipts at the stores she visited and confirm what Darcy bought. We're assuming she's changed clothes."

"A given."

"If she's still in the mall, where is she? We've looked everywhere."

"Right here."

The soft words came from his right.

Sam spun on his heel, searching the faces of those walking by. Darcy was nowhere in sight. On the nearest bench a mom was feeding her son Cheerios and shaking a bottle of juice, an elderly lady flipping through a packet of photos from the camera shop, and a teenager trying to get his girlfriend to pay attention to a music track.

He was going crazy hearing her voice;

that was all there was to it. It was the third time he was sure he'd heard or seen her. He had about scared some schoolteacher to death when he stopped her near the mall exit, mistaking her for Darcy from behind.

"We go back to the van and check the security tapes for those entering the mall, we find Sergey, then we try to backtrack through the tapes to the car he was driving when he arrived," Gabriel suggested.

"It's worth trying. We've got to find a lead somewhere on him."

The mom got up to take her son to the fountain to toss in a coin; the teenagers headed toward the music store.

The elderly lady patted the bench beside her. "Sit down, Gabriel. You've been walking a long time."

Sam narrowed his eyes at the gesture and the words.

Gabe took two steps over and laughed. "Why don't you just sit there eavesdropping, Darcy."

She lowered her head, reached up to her face, and a thin film no thicker than a piece of paper floated into the air. Darcy reappeared. "Like I said, Sam. You wouldn't recognize me."

# Twenty-one

June 24
Monday, 7:30 p.m.
Fairmont, Florida

Darcy sat in a chair in the hotel room suite, watching Sam throw his gear into his duffel bag. He had given her a cold, arms-crossed look when she reappeared at the mall and then walked away. His reaction hadn't improved much since then. "Have you forgiven me yet?" They had the suite to themselves. The others had left with the last of the surveillance equipment, and Gabriel was down at the office handling the bill.

"What do *you* think?"

She'd put her job ahead of staying safe, and he'd taken her actions personally. She didn't know how to deal with his reaction. "You're angry."

"Give the lady two stars."

The sarcasm hurt.

Sam paused in his packing to glare at

her. "What do you want me to forgive? Your recklessness? Your total disregard for your team?"

"I didn't mean to scare you like that," she said. "I'm an intelligence officer. This is my job. The situation unfolded fast and I did my job." She didn't know what else to say. She didn't want to defend herself; she just wanted him to understand.

"You totally miss the point. You were part of a team, Darcy, and you rashly decided to abandon that. You went out there on a quest of your own."

"Yes, I slipped your coverage to meet with Sergey. Your training and experience teaches you to stay with the team at all costs. Mine is the opposite. I'm trained to be flexible and keep focused on the information I'm there to obtain. It was worth the risk. I'm not impartial in this fight. I want Luther. And I want it more than I do staying in your good graces or Gabriel's, for that matter."

"You let Sergey walk away in exchange for some information. We could have had him, Darcy, and his information."

"Sergey gives me something; I give him something. It's better that he stay free and out there because people will talk to him who would never talk to us. It's smart business not to wrap up an intelligence source that is providing useful information when you know you need more than you have. And frankly if Sergey gets to Luther first, I'd consider it a blessing because then it won't be you or another Special Forces soldier sent in to try and apprehend him."

"There were choices, Darcy. You had over an hour to tell us of the change in plans. You know Gabe would have accepted your recommendation to let Sergey leave. You were showing off."

She got to her feet, getting angry herself, and walked over to the window. It was the illusion of peacetime outside — the streets busy, shoppers going to the mall. "I wasn't showing off. It was tradecraft, Sam. I met Sergey on his terms. I know him. It's the only way he would have shared what he did."

"You scare me, woman."

"There are times when it's mutual." She turned to stare at him. "Do you think I like knowing you were sneaking into Lebanon?"

"At least I had a partner with me. If this situation happened again, you'd do the same thing."

She reluctantly nodded, her emotions draining away. The idea hurt him and she wished she could give him what he sought but she couldn't. "I'd probably do the same thing. But I *am* sorry my actions today hurt you."

"I don't like being left out of your life, and that's what you did today. You left me out when I was there to protect you." He crossed to where she stood and settled his powerful hands on her shoulders. He sighed. "You're special to me because of who you are, but I'd like you coming back at the end of a workday rather than have Gabriel call me with bad news."

She leaned against him, hugging him. "Sam, it's mutual. It isn't easy knowing what you do for a living — SEALs get shot at."

"Only if the enemy can spot me."

"Are we okay?"

He rested his chin against her hair. "No, but I'll give us time to sort it out. You need to remember you're part of a relationship now and that decisions you make affect both of us, not just yourself."

She understood the trust he expected. This man was leading their relationship toward something permanent and putting boundaries in place so it could stand a chance. "I'll remember; I promise."

He tipped up her chin. "You'd better."

June 26
Wednesday, 11:30 a.m.
Fort Walton Beach, Florida

Darcy followed Sam down the steps from the Parker & Son Boats office to the marina. White rock formed the steep banks to the water, and a wooden pier with segments resting on flotation barrels stretched out into the Gulf, providing walkway access to over a hundred boat slips, most in use. These expensive boats were used for multiday jaunts at sea and designed for deep-sea fishing.

Their planned day of sailing had turned into an exploration of boats instead. Her knowledge was minimal, but she was getting a crash course from an expert teacher. This was the sixth boat dealer they had visited. They walked through so many models her notebook was filled, and she carried fact sheets on thirty personal luxury craft models.

Sam stepped onto the deck of the show model and offered his hand to help her across. Darcy looked at the reference sheet they had picked up. "Four cabins, three baths, an onboard grill, and teak furnishings."

"Good horsepower in the engine, a live

well for the fish, and the best in sonar technology," Sam added.

She flipped through the photos Sergey had given her, comparing them to this craft. "This is pretty close to the boat Sergey was on."

Sam opened the live well. "My guess, you're looking for a forty-five or forty-six footer, and from the style of the trimmings in those photos, probably a late '90s model."

Darcy walked down into the cabin. She was learning the differences between models: the cabinets, the placement of the sink, the type of table and bench seats, and the storage areas for gear. Some had coffeemakers and communication and navigation equipment in the galley area, others had it in a side captain's area. She took photos of the boat interior for her reference book and then climbed back to the deck. "I'm on information overload. What's next on the day's agenda?"

"Two more boat dealers and then a trip to the marina where Sergey said he met Vladimir and the boat the night of September 9."

"Let's skip the boat dealers and retrace Sergey's steps that night. I want to talk with the FBI guys now investigating Bluebird Charter." The CIA had suspected that was the charter service used from their own investigation of September 9. There was a slim possibility that they already knew the charter service Luther had bought and not realized the importance of the lead they had.

"Fine with me." Sam offered her a hand to step from the boat to the pier. "I find it interesting that Vladimir was the one piloting the boat that night. A Russian captain of an expensive fishing boat — it might be a fact a harbormaster would remember in parts of the world where they don't get many guests from Russia."

Darcy jotted herself a note. "Good suggestion."

"You'll find this boat."

It had been months since Sergey had been on that boat. He wouldn't be asking her to locate it if it was out in the open somewhere and easy to trace. "I wish I had your confidence."

## Twenty-two

July 22
Monday, 10:18 a.m.
Central Intelligence Agency

Darcy tossed wadded up pages of a report at the boat photos tacked to her bulletin board. Sergey had given her copies of fifteen of the most illustrative pictures from the interior and exterior of the craft. She was sick of boats and islands and leads that went nowhere. If she had to read one more harbormaster report on boats docked overnight, she would pull her hair out. Bluebird Charters was one of many cold leads.

*Lord, this is making me crazy. Just one boat. Why is this so hard?*

Gabe appeared in the doorway, and she hit him in the chest with a paper ball. "Do you know how many forty-six-foot cruisers are registered in this world?"

"So we're looking for a needle in the haystack."

"It's July and I'm stuck inside. I want my summer back."

Gabe hit a bank shot off her calendar to land the paper ball in the recycling bin. "What do you have from the maintenance shops?"

She tossed a wadded-up page at the map of the British Virgin Islands, just one set of islands in the huge string of them around the Caribbean. "I'm spending your money to buy copies of repair manifests, parts orders, insurance claims . . . You name it, we're getting it. Data is raining in." There wasn't a boat in use in the world that didn't need occasional repair and maintenance work. Luther probably had his boat stored in dry dock somewhere.

Even knowing whom they wanted to find, where he might have his safe haven, and one of the boats he might own, they still couldn't find Luther. She had put every Caribbean land transfer for the last year into the possibility list and was eliminating them one by one. But beyond finding a few rich men trying to hide a land transfer to avoid paying taxes, she was hitting dead ends.

"Search islands around Ireland and Greece next. Luther didn't have to go to warm weather."

She made a face at Gabe for the suggestion. "One part of the globe at a time is enough."

"Sam didn't call?"

"I'm not sure if he's back at Little Creek yet. His last message had a Georgia area code. He's spending his summer climbing mountains, jumping out of planes, and working at sea; I'm behind a desk. What is wrong with this picture?"

Gabriel laughed. "Join the Navy."

"Don't think it hasn't crossed my mind. Fieldwork is where the fun is, not this analysis stuff. I never thought I'd say I missed the cold war, but slipping across the Black Sea stowed away in the cargo hold of a smelly fishing trawler is beginning to sound like something fun to do again."

"You find a lead on Luther, and I'll buy the plane tickets so we can check it out," Gabriel said.

"Luther buys himself a nice island and settles back to watch the world. I need his shopping list, what magazines he subscribes to, what papers he reads, what his habits are. Something that will stand out as an unusual item for that part of the world. Russian vodka was a good lead on Dansky. I need something I can hook Luther to, and so far our bios on him have given next to nothing useful."

She had seven weeks until the anniversary of September 11. The days were being crossed off her calendar in big bold red marks. She wanted at least one significant success to look back on before she faced that day of memories. Darcy tossed the report in her lap back onto the desk where it joined a mountain of paper. "If I have to get new reading glasses, Gabriel, I'm going to submit a bill to the Agency. This paperwork is blinding me."

"You've needed them for months, dahlin'. You keep moving the documents around to find the right distance to read the type." Gabe knocked the rolled-up file in his hand against the doorpost. "I came down with some news, but I don't know if you can stand the excitement."

"You mean something interesting is happening in this world and you haven't told me? What do you have?"

"You know Ramon Santigo's family who paid out all that money on the rumor of your death?"

"They found out the truth . . . they're here . . . I'm back to watching my back?"

Gabe held up his hand. "They're dead. They got into a fight with the national army of Paraguay over a piece of property, and the army literally decimated their compound during the assault. You're in the clear at least on that front, Dar. The threat is gone."

Darcy blinked. "Gone." It had lingered over her head for so long, she didn't know what to feel. "Oh, my."

He held out the report. "It's classified, but you're welcome to read it if you like."

She shook her head. "I'd rather not."

"The good guys won this round."

Darcy took a deep breath and relaxed. "Okay, thanks. This is good."

Her computer played "Twinkle, Twinkle, Little Star." Darcy leaned over to grab the phone, relieved to have work to divert her attention. She pushed Ramon Santigo to a corner to think about later. "There's my buddy."

"Halfway around the world and he's more prompt than my mother in her weekly check-up calls," Gabe commented.

"You're just jealous that my network of snitches is deeper than yours."

"Tag me if you get something."

She nodded and he closed the door to give her privacy for the call.

There was no better contact for the inside scoop on boats than the warranty officer at the factory headquarters for the most prestigious line of personal pleasure craft out there. Someone filed paperwork on a claim, transferred ownership, and she knew all about the owner and the boat the same day. All she needed to find was one link to a name, an address, or an account on her watch list, and she would have a lead she could work. All it cost her was a hundred bucks per call. She loved this part of the hunt when it worked out and was incredibly frustrated when it didn't. She started taking notes about the boats he had seen paperwork on recently.

Her computer played her school's fight song and a red flash traffic warning flag appeared in the corner of the screen. Darcy reached over and opened the code word area. An oil refinery in Mobile, Alabama just exploded.

July 22
Monday, 10:45 a.m.
Norfolk Naval Air Base

The noise was deafening as another transport plane took off, straining to get enough lift to climb into the sky. Soon this plane would be taking off. Sam heaved the case of swim gear to the back of the pallet being loaded aboard the transport aircraft. SEAL Team Nine was deploying to join up with the amphibious task group now refueling in Puerto Rico, their team replacing SEAL Team Five doing ship interdiction missions.

"Cougar."

Sam turned and took the heavy case Wolf passed him. "This is getting old fast." They were loading their mine detection gear.

"You need the weight training," Wolf pointed out.

Sam shoved the case into place and turned for the next one, only he took his time checking the tag numbers.

"Hey."

"Got to get the paperwork right." Sam let Wolf come close to dropping the case before Sam took it. "Now who needs the weight training?"

Wolf laughed.

Sam secured the case. Persistent intelligence reports suggested someone planned to mine major seaports in an attempt to cripple international shipping between North America and Latin America. Sam didn't relish the idea of swimming around a harbor trying to find explosives without setting them off, but it had to be done.

Blow holes in and sink one of those huge cargo transport ships and the insurance rates would skyrocket and cripple trade through the region.

"Are you going to get a chance to say good-bye to Darcy?"

Sam took the next case from Wolf. "I hope to see her Thursday night."

Two months stateside. It was more than he hoped to get, but it was still too short. Sam signaled the load master that the pallet was ready to pull in. He was beginning to ask himself whether the separations were worth it. He'd been a soldier a long time, and his time in the field with the SEALs would end soon, for it was a young man's job. More time to visit his parents while their health was still good, time with Darcy — He cared more about her than he did the Navy. That realization paused him midmovement.

*Lord, what do You think? After this deployment, should I do a little quiet asking around about options?* It was time to think about life after being a SEAL. He wanted Darcy in his future.

"Chief." Wolf jerked him out of the way before a forklift bringing in a massive pallet of replacement fuel drums hit him.

"Sorry."

Wolf slapped his chest. "Distracted guys on the flight line get dead."

July 22
Monday, 3:18 p.m.
Central Intelligence Agency

Darcy pushed the button on her phone that signaled a hot alert to Gabriel for the third time in less than a minute. He was down the hall. She was getting close to rolling her chair back to the hallway and shouting at him to get down here.

"I heard you the first time," he remarked mildly from her doorway. "And security frowns at the newspaper stuck in the doorway to keep the lock from engaging."

"Rag at me later. Sit."

"I'm deep into trying to figure out how a confirmed accident at an oil refinery in Mobile, Alabama, results in the director of the Agency asking me to chase down a wildcatter who worked to put out the Kuwaiti oil field fires. The man is somewhere in Siberia at the moment, and I'm supposed to get him back here overnight. I'm trying to negotiate with the Russian military to provide a helicopter for transportation."

"Ask an Alaskan charter service to dart over and get him. For the right price, they'll do it. Look." She turned the screen toward him and showed him the data she was studying. "Would you say after that 10:18 a.m. refinery fire the lines on the graph in red went up faster than the lines in blue?"

"That's clear."

"Red lines are brokerage accounts the Treasury Department thought might be tied to Luther but couldn't prove. That oil refinery fire just shot up gas contract prices, yielding Luther a profit of ninety million. And the profit of these suspicious accounts far exceeds what experts who invest in oil and gas accounts have done: Those blue lines are our control group."

Gabriel studied the data. "Luther couldn't have known an accident was coming. He must have known a terrorist attack was coming that would disrupt gas refining capabilities and has quietly been making his bets. The accident had the effect of tipping his hand to even a blind man, leaving Luther dangling out here with a huge spotlight on him."

Darcy tried to spin in her chair with joy only to come up against the open file cabinet drawer. "The only way Luther can remain hidden is if he disavows all of these accounts and never touches the money. But given his personality, he won't be able to walk away. Luther will try to move the money from these accounts. The minute he does, we'll have him."

"Nicely done, Dar."

She let herself soak in the relief that she had a solid lead to work, then turned serious. "They must have been planning a refinery or pipeline attack as a September 11 anniversary hit."

"A threat we can work now that we have a reason to put it at the top of the threat list," Gabe said. "Trail that money, Dar. And tell the Treasury guys to be as discreet and as fast as they can on those taps."

"Bring in pizza for dinner tonight. I work better on a full stomach."

The phone rang at Darcy's desk at 10 p.m. She glanced at the Caller ID, turned down *The Marriage of Figaro* playing at full volume, and picked it up. "Hey, Sam."

"I call your home thinking it's late, but I want to hear her voice so I'll wake her up. And lo and behold, you're not only awake but sitting next to the phone."

"I wouldn't want to miss your call," she replied, smiling as she turned the pages of a report. "Actually I'm still at the office; I forwarded my home phone here. My workaholic tendency is showing itself again. Did you know there are 168 barbecue stands in Dallas, Texas?"

Sam laughed. "No, can't say that I did."

"The trivia struck me as interesting. And don't ask me why someone bothered to count them." She rested her feet on the corner of the open file cabinet drawer and reached for the next report on her desk.

"I see, you collect trivia to compensate for all the heavy stuff you read. Did you get dinner?"

Darcy looked at the remains of her dinner in the box. "The pizza is down to nothing but crumbs but at least this time Gabe was the one who ate most of it. He shared his pizza crusts with the bomb dog. You know that oil refinery fire in Alabama? It triggered a lead on you know who."

"A good one?"

"Really good."

"Part of SEAL Team Nine flew near the refinery site on the way back to Little Creek tonight. They said the fire was still visible."

She looked at the television at the end of her desk. Flames and glowing heat with heavy black smoke still rose into the air.

"It's going to be tough to extinguish."

"They'll do it."

"Did you get your gear packed for the deployment?"

"We're loaded," Sam confirmed. "The plane is going out ahead of us, so others will get the pleasure of unloading the equipment and transferring it aboard ship. How late are you going to be at that desk tonight?"

She looked at the computer screen, watching the U.S. Treasury taps on the accounts. Already Luther had moved money out of one third of the accounts. They still hadn't cracked the second tier of accounts, but it was only a matter of time. Luther was moving money, and the money would lead them to him.

"As long as it takes." She watched another account move to the transferred column. Because this oil refinery accident had tipped Luther's hand before the date he thought something would happen, there was a chance he wouldn't have as many blinds and cover accounts set up that they would have to penetrate. "I had some news today."

"What's that, Dar?" he asked, his serious tone matching hers.

"Ramon Santigo's family is dead. There

is no more threat from that quarter."

"An answer to prayer."

"I'm still trying to sort it out in my head."

"My body is still on Mountain Time. I'm wide awake; you want to talk a while?"

"I'd appreciate it. How about you get today's crossword puzzle and a pencil, fix yourself one of your milkshakes, and call me back? I'd like your company. I'm watching others work at the moment and waiting for something I recognize to cross the screen."

"Sounds good. I'll call you back in twenty minutes."

Darcy said good-bye and hung up the phone, relieved she would be able to talk with him tonight as she sorted out the implications of at least this threat being gone. She loved the fact that their phone calls during free moments were now the pattern for their relationship rather than just an occasional thing. She would miss their daily contact when he deployed. She tried not to burden him with her sadness. It was part of what she had to adjust to in having a relationship with a soldier.

*Lord, please keep him safe. I'm falling deeply in love with that man. I want our relationship to survive this deployment. I'm slowly learning to leave this stress and burden with You, but it's a profound one, wondering if he'll be safe through this deployment.*

Luther was one of the threats still out there. She'd promised Sergey a message when they had something; this lead on Luther qualified. Sergey might be in a position to act on it faster than they could. When to make the call was a decision to be made by others. But if it were up to her, she'd give him as much of a head start as she could. She didn't want Sam or one of his friends going after Luther if Sergey could do it for them.

She picked up the next report on the stack while keeping an eye on the money transfers. Peaceful nights at work, with leads they could pursue . . . This was why she loved this job.

And at least for the moment she didn't think her name was on anyone's hit list.

# Twenty-three

July 31
Wednesday, 4:18 p.m.
USS *Hailey* / Caribbean Sea

The surveillance ship USS *Hailey* sailed into the warm waters of the Caribbean Sea. The lights in the ship's command center were dimmed as sailors manning sophisticated monitors tracked every ship currently at sea within six hundred miles through a combination of satellite and surveillance aircraft. Sam watched with Bear as a ship with a manifest claiming a cargo of wheat, cotton, and spices tracked north of St. Croix Island near the British Virgin Islands. If intel from the Colombian port where the ship had last docked was right, it was also carrying twenty cases of high explosives.

"When do we hit it?" Sam asked.

"Defense Intelligence is still trying to figure out who purchased the explosives and where it's heading," Bear replied. "For now we watch. They think the transfer will happen at sea. The cargo ship is easy to track, but anything smaller than a fifty-foot trawler will get lost in the wave clutter." Joe pointed to the map, which showed in three dimensions the thirteen islands in the area. "There has to be a reason the cargo ship has left the normal deep water shipping lane and is tracking to the east. One of these islands is probably the intermediate destination for those explosives. It makes sense that the smugglers are using one of those uninhabited islands as a way station of sorts."

Sam studied the water depths. "The cargo ship can stay on this present course probably another day before it has to move back toward deeper water."

"There's no moon tonight, and a transfer like this would not be something you would want to do during the day. I want to fly out ahead of the ship and position four of us about . . . here," Joe indicated a point that would put them at equal distance between the islands and where the ship would pass. "We don't know where the smaller boat might originate, but we know its destination is to meet up with that cargo ship. We sit and watch what's moving in the area." Joe signed for a copy of the map printed for the SEAL Team Nine full briefing.

Sam looked at the map. "I volunteer Wolf, sir, to be one of those forward observers."

Joe laughed. "Accepted. You and Wolf, Frank and myself, doing the reconnaissance, with two teams of six on standby in helos ready to raid the boat if we get a green light to take the shipment tonight."

July 31
Wednesday, 10:18 p.m.
Central Intelligence Agency

"Darcy."

She was trying to sleep on her couch, but it was at best a doze. She moved the pillow from atop her face to look over at her partner. Gabriel had taken over the thread of a lead she was working on. "Got something?" Luther's money had disappeared into a black hole twenty-four hours after the refinery fire, and nine days of chasing it had simply given her a headache.

"I'll qualify it to a maybe."

She sat up and pushed aside the jacket she'd been using as a cover because the air-conditioning in the building was freezing her out.

"We found the first pool account," Gabe said.

Darcy studied the screen. The Treasury Department had cracked the stubborn third layer of shell accounts. Five transfers had all eventually ended up in an account in the Bahamas. As she watched, a sixth deposit was made. "What's the bank name?"

"First Capital Bank, Nassau."

"Not one we had suspected before."

"A bit of a surprise there," Gabe agreed. "And the location is a little farther north than I would have expected to find Luther. I figured he would be down among the Lesser Antilles Islands, maybe using Barbados or Venezuela for one of his major bank stops."

"Twelve million. This is going to be serious money soon. Who do we have in Nassau?" Darcy asked.

"The Agency has two guys who were down there on vacation. For now we're asking them to find a place to watch the bank on the slim chance a withdrawal is made from there rather than another transfer. We risk tipping our hand if we inquire about the account too soon."

"Look at the pattern of movements — four transfers from the initial accounts until it reaches this pool account. And the accounts being transferred to this one are all high account numbers in that original list. There is at least one other pool account out there," Darcy guessed. "Can we get a list of accounts in the Bahamas accepting multiple transfers in the last seventy-two hours that are now above ten million in assets?"

"If we can't, some serious diplomatic pressure needs to be applied." Gabe picked up the phone to call their counterparts in Treasury. "How do you feel about going to the Bahamas, Dar?" he asked as he dialed.

"My suitcase is packed and in the trunk of my car."

"If the money is still in this account in three hours, I want us on a plane going south."

Darcy lifted an eyebrow at the fact Gabriel was ready to make that kind of forward move, but she nodded and reached for the other phone. They would travel under their own passports but would carry optional documents to let them switch names if needed to long established covers. Sometimes it was beneficial not to travel as Americans.

July 31
Wednesday, 11:10 p.m.
Caribbean Sea

Sam was stretched out on his stomach against the tough black rubber of the 6-by-15-foot Zodiac, finding comfort in the familiar texture as the boat rode four-foot sea swells. He searched 180 degrees of the horizon with thermal-vision sights. Wolf, stretched out on the other side of the craft facing the opposite direction, scanned the other 180 degrees. Bear and Frank were in a Zodiac craft a quarter mile to the east doing the same type of search.

The huge cargo ship was like a lumbering elephant on the horizon; it would pass by in half a mile. The two Zodiacs were black spots on the water in a black night, only twenty-eight inches from the surface of the sea. They were invisible even when someone knew they were present. It gave them the advantage. The craft they sought had to be able to transport heavy if not voluminous cargo. The engines of such a boat would be glowing heat sources through the thermal sights.

This was the type of work Sam liked best — the surveillance, the stalking, catching the bad guys when they didn't know they were being observed. And it was much better to be busy than on the boat with too much time to think. It would be at least four months before he saw Darcy again, and it stretched like an eternity. Did she feel these separations as strongly as he did? They'd never talked about the distant future after this war was over. They talked about the logistics of the here and now. Was she as afraid of trouble disrupting this relationship as he was?

"I've got movement on the water, grid 92C," Wolf whispered.

Sam checked what Wolf saw. The speed of the movement was uncharacteristically fast for a boat sailing safely at night, and the most telling sign of something unusual was the lack of running lights. The boat was clearly visible with the thermal-vision sights, but only darkness was seen through normal binoculars. Sam touched his radio. "Bear, this is promising." He gave the grid coordinates.

"Possibly a drug runner," Wolf said.

"Affirmative." They had seen several during their last several days watching movement around the islands.

As soon as it was clear the boat was angling toward the cargo ship, Bear signaled for them to move in closer to try to identify the boat. As the massive cargo ship slowed and the boat drew alongside, they shadowed the transfer. A night-vision long-lens camera captured the first silhouette of the vessel and the two men aboard. A netlike boom lowered a case over the side. Against the huge cargo ship the smaller boat looked like a dot.

Bear gave word for them to pull back from the area as it became clear the transfer over the side of the huge cargo ship was complete. "We track this boat to where it originated. We want the buyer, not just the couriers."

The boat put on speed. It came between the two Zodiacs full of SEALs, its wake adding another layer of rocking to their rubber craft, the closeness giving them a bonanza of close-up photos. Water washed over the side of the Zodiac as they cut through the waves, trailing the boat. The distance between them grew with every minute, but the heat signature made the boat easy to track with the thermal scopes.

Land appeared on the horizon as a sliver and then it became bigger, a deeper blackness than the surrounding sky. "Razor Reef Island," Wolf whispered. Only a number officially named the uninhabited island, but locals called it Razor Reef Island. The coves were unattractive to visiting boats due to the razor sharp volcanic rocks that circled the island, and there were only two short stretches of beach with clear sand attractive to visitors, the rest of the small island was overgrown vegetation or steep drops of rock to the sea.

"Not a place to stay." Wolf remarked as they took bearing marks for how the boat had approached the island. It had managed to enter one of the coves that turned inland.

"A quiet place to hide something you wanted to stash," Sam agreed.

"How much did that transfer just cost?"

"I'd think you could start in the millions and you'd probably be close."

"Watching this stash is going to be an interesting challenge."

"We won't be doing it from the water during daylight hours," Sam said. He changed rolls of film. "Air surveillance, satellites, a spotting team put on the island. It's more a matter of intelligence now to identify the buyer. As long as we know where the stash is, we can get it whenever they decide the time is right."

Bear passed word that it was time to fall back to the pickup point. It was a long ride in the Zodiacs, for they wanted a good distance from the island to mute the sound of the helicopter extraction. Sam hoped the information would lead to a decision to send in the SEALs soon. He didn't want those explosives making it off the island.

July 31
Wednesday, 11:20 p.m.
Central Intelligence Agency

"What did Luther just buy that cost ten million? A cargo ship?" Darcy asked. The funds had transferred in a block precisely at 11:15 p.m., to an account that to all appearances looked legit. The cash had transferred to a shipping company with over eighty years of history moving cargo around the world in its huge fleet. A search of the CIA's files on the company showed it had few safety problems and even fewer criminal problems.

"Even a decommissioned cargo ship would go for more than ten mil just for the resale value of the cut-up metal hull," Gabriel replied. "My guess is Luther just facilitated his first deal since we shut him down in Morocco. Either arranging a shipment or a quiet passage for someone."

"Five million is still in the account,"

Darcy pointed out. "Luther created this pooled account and used it within hours. Why pool more money than he needed?"

"A second transfer or withdrawal is imminent," Gabe guessed. "I still want us to travel south, Dar. We know the date the money transferred; we know the shipping company Luther paid. The DEA has good surveillance around this area of the world. Let's go ask some questions and see what else can be learned."

Darcy reached for the phone to finalize the travel arrangements. "I'm all for getting back into the field."

# Twenty-four

August 1
Thursday, 10:14 p.m.
Nassau, New Providence Island, Bahamas

The vacationing CIA agents had taken two rooms on the ninth floor of the hotel directly across from the First Capital Bank, Nassau. Darcy stepped to the camera focused on the front entrance of the bank, pleased to see the surveillance they already had in place. "What time does the bank open in the morning?"

"Nine o'clock."

She looked at the secure computer feed coming in by satellite. It was linked into the web site back at Treasury headquarters, letting her see the latest data. "The five million is still sitting there." She had expected the money to move by now.

"We'll know the minute a withdrawal occurs. If anyone accesses that account in person, we'll have photos of everyone entering and leaving the bank. Tracking devices and bugs are ready to go if we need to tag and follow someone so we don't tip our hand too early."

She looked over at the equipment and nodded. They could walk across the street and tag a car under the bumper with a transmitter before someone entering the bank could reasonably finish their business and come out again. It would be a bit more challenging to plant a small bug inside a car to pick up conversations or place it in someone's bag or briefcase, but she had done it before, and these guys were both experienced field agents. They had options. "What if the money is transferred from here electronically?" Darcy glanced back at her partner, not sure what he intended.

Gabe opened a bottle of water. "Then it will be another quick plane trip to chase it. We stay with this money. Whenever Luther accesses it, whatever he tries to buy, wherever he tries to move it, we're going to know real time. He can't let it sit there for fear we'll seize it. You want the late shift or the early one?"

They were taking no chances that an official had been bribed and this transaction like the prior one would be handled after hours. "I'm going to crash now. Come wake me at 5 a.m."

Gabe handed her a room key. "Sergey often wintered in the British Virgin Islands with his family. It would be worth tracking down that information, see where he stayed and if he ever came through the Bahamas. If we tracked Luther to Nassau, chances are good Sergey has as well. He probably knows this area better than we do. I'll see what I can find tonight."

"Good idea, Gabe."

Darcy took her bag with her and settled into the hotel room, not bothering to unpack beyond what she needed for some sleep. She'd only been able to leave a message on Sam's machine to let him know she was traveling. She hoped he understood why the message had been so vague. She didn't want to worry him again.

*Jesus, I miss him. I have no idea where Sam is right now, but You do. Please encourage him and give him a reason to smile and laugh, lighten a moment of his day as a gift from me. Please give us a future together, despite all the logistics involved.*

She had to trace this money to Luther, locate his island, and apprehend him. She closed her eyes. *It's time. Help us find Luther and end this.*

It was getting easier to trust that this would work out.

Sam brought over the latest weather report as Bear laid out the satellite map of Razor Reef Island on the table in the briefing room. SEAL Team Nine crowded around the table as the meeting began. "Surveillance shows no movement around the island in the last twenty-four hours," Bear said. "The boat came into this cove, remained for shortly over an hour, and then left the island and went toward St. Croix. From that time track we can infer the cargo was stashed somewhere near the inlet. If we're asked to go in and recover the shipment, how is the best way to do it?"

"Constraints?" Wolf asked.

"We have to go in, pick it up, and leave undetected."

"What kind of detection resources do we think the other side has?" Sam asked.

"Assume the worse: Things like a sensitive microphone set up near the shipment

387

that transmits everything it hears to someone on a boat or another nearby island; the ability for them to trigger a blast to take out the shipment if they think someone is trying to take it. Probably decent tracking of boats traveling near the island."

"A helicopter approaching the island would be heard," Wolf commented.

"Yes. We have to get in quietly, locate the shipment, get around any monitoring or trip wires, and then haul the shipment out of there either by air or sea without tipping off someone that we've snatched it," Bear replied.

"Even the simple jamming of their signal will indicate we are there. Why not set up on the island and simply wait for someone to come and get it?" Wolf asked.

"My guess is the chain of command will decide to do an intercept at sea after someone recovers the shipment," Joe agreed. "They'll want the investigators to have as much time as possible to find out who arranged the shipment, not just who's hoping to use it. For now their goal is to simply put together options."

"Getting into that cove unseen is straightforward. We swim in at night and give ourselves the daylight hours to locate the shipment and figure out what type of monitoring we have to defeat," Sam proposed. "If we need special gear, we bring it in after sundown. Sound monitoring can be defeated if we tape the night, slip a soundproof hood over the microphone and play back the tape, letting them hear only what we want them to hear. Cameras can be defeated with a view screen playing back what we want them to see. We wait until the early hours of the morning when anyone monitoring this site may miss any minor glitches."

"And if we take the shipment out packed in underwater containers we can tow them out with us so there won't be a surface vessel to see," Wolf suggested.

"All good ideas," Bear replied. "Let's work up details and figure out how to minimize the risks."

August 2
Friday, 9:07 a.m.
Nassau Hotel / Nassau, New Providence
 Island, Bahamas

Darcy counted nine customers in line by the bank front doors when it finally opened at 9:07 a.m. She studied faces, not

389

sure who she was looking for but hoping Luther would try to take the money from the account rather than transfer it. The money was still sitting there for a reason. The odds increased with every passing hour that someone was coming for it.

"You've had too much coffee," Gabe remarked.

She stopped drumming her fingers on the table. "Where is he?"

"Patience, Dar. We sit and watch." He had moved a chair near the window and made himself comfortable for the day of surveillance. Gabriel snapped more pictures.

"Luther, Renee, Vladimir, or Jerry. Would he entrust someone else to act as a middle man when it involved this kind of money?"

"I doubt it. And given five million is more than just expense cash, I suspect he's got something else to buy."

"Any more leads on what he bought Wednesday night for ten million?"

"There may be something developing south of here in the British Virgin Islands. A very large shipment of explosives is being tracked. The CIA station chief called this morning and said he'd bring by what he had," Gabe replied.

"That makes sense. It won't be the first

time we've had Luther trying to buy a large quantity of explosives to facilitate a terrorist act."

"And it means the odds are at least better than even that Luther's in the area," Gabe agreed. "We're going to get another chance to grab him. Now this is a surprise."

Darcy focused her binoculars on what Gabriel had spotted. "He sent his wife Renee."

"So much for her being the little lady he marries, spoils, but keeps in the dark."

"Where did she come from?" Darcy asked.

"She walked coming from the north." Gabe queued his radio and alerted one of the CIA officers watching from the street to follow her into the bank. "With whom did she travel?"

Darcy searched every face on the street. She backtracked several times as she came up against several maybes for Luther, but none that held up to a longer scrutiny. "There! Vladimir. He's at the end of the block sitting in the outdoor café. He's wearing a hat, sunglasses, but you can't disguise that build."

She searched the area around him, turned, and searched the other end of the block to see if they had someone watching from both directions. "He looks to be alone. No sign of Luther, no sign of Jerry." She picked up the backup camera and used the zoom lens to get several photographs of Vladimir.

"There goes four million of the money in the account," Gabriel said, monitoring the U.S. Treasury real-time web site.

"Four million is an expensive check to hand a lady who loves to shop. Renee is here. Is Luther also on this island? Did Renee fly in to pick up the money? Did they come in by boat?"

"Great questions. It's clear she came with Vladimir to provide her security. How do you want to handle tailing the two of them?" Gabe asked.

"I want to tag her with a transmitter. I can get to her as she comes out of the bank and she'll never think twice about getting bumped."

"The odds are good she's seen your picture."

"I'll wear that floppy straw hat and I'll be passing her as she emerges. She'll never see my face. If we're going to avoid Vladimir's attention, we need to be able to tail from a distance, and the only way to do that is with a transmitter," Darcy said.

"If they split up?"

"Vladimir is your problem. With two agents and yourself, you might be able to keep a general sense of where he's going — the docks, the airport, staying in the city. I'll stay with Renee."

"Get the hat."

Darcy nodded and rushed back to her room. She had worried if Gabriel would hesitate to let her go back out in the field after having slipped away from the agreed upon plan for meeting with Sergey. She was going to earn his trust back with this one. She came back and took the transmitter Gabe had checked. She left the hotel and walked across the street toward the bank, just one of many tourists using the bank for her currency needs. She reached the glass doors as Renee emerged.

August 2
Friday, 11:07 a.m.
USS *Hailey* / Caribbean Sea

There was more room to bunk down aboard the USS *Hailey* than a submarine; the SEALs shared four staterooms. There was still an upper and lower bunk, and having lost the coin toss Sam had settled on the top bunk to get some sleep. Feet against the underside of his bunk pushed his mattress up. "Cougar, you awake?"

"I am now," Sam assured Wolf, pushing aside the pillow over his face. They were going back on duty at sundown, and he had been looking forward to the rack time to get some sleep.

"Did you see my letter from Jill?"

"You showed everyone the letter from your wife. I saw her mention that Darcy hadn't returned her message. Dar's probably in the field somewhere." Darcy said she had a promising lead she was trailing. Maybe it had panned out.

"Is that good or bad?"

"I know she wasn't enjoying being stuck in the office." Sam wasn't sure what to think about her being back on the front lines. He'd gotten involved with an intelligence officer. He had to trust her job skills just as she had to trust his. But it didn't make it any less hard not to worry though.

A tap sounded at the cabin door and then it opened. The red light, used in the room letting some men sleep while others moved around in something better than the darkness, gave way to the brighter light from the hall. Bear leaned in.

"Chief, Wolf, DIA needs us in Nassau.

Grab your gear; there's a transport flight we can catch. They may have found the buyer for this shipment."

"We're on the way, boss," Wolf assured.

The door closed.

Sam leaned over to look at the bunk below. "You volunteered us again?"

"It beats staying here doing maintenance checks on diving equipment."

"I was looking forward to sleeping today," Sam protested mildly. Several hours on a noisy plane was not what he'd had in mind.

"A minor problem." Wolf laughed as Sam nearly stepped on him as he came down from the upper bunk.


August 2
Friday, 3:45 p.m.
Nassau, New Providence Island, Bahamas


The car they were using to navigate the Nassau streets was more than small; it was tiny. Darcy had to turn sideways to lean across the backseat to see around Gabriel. "Where is she going now?" The transponder Darcy had slipped in the side pocket of Renee's purse was working beautifully. Since Vladimir was still with her, she and Gabe were only making occasional visual contact as they trailed her around Nassau.

"Another jewelry store."

"She's carrying around a four-million-dollar check while she shops. It makes you wonder what she's thinking."

"At least it ensures she keeps her purse close to her."

Renee's numerous purchases were being handed off to couriers to deliver for her. Gabe had the other CIA agent trying to follow one of those deliveries to locate where Renee was staying on the island or if the packages were being delivered to the harbor.

"Gabe, the way she's shopping — designer dresses, shoes, jewelry — I don't think she's been in Nassau for long. We need flight manifests and harbormaster reports for the last few days. If we find out how she arrived, maybe we can backtrack where she came from."

"The CIA station chief is working his contacts to get the lists now. And the Department of Defense is trying to get a pickup team in place. Jerry is high on their list, not to mention Luther." Gabe's phone rang. "Hello." He smiled. "Excellent. Get rooms there; sit tight. We'll join you shortly."

Gabe hung up the phone. "Renee sent her packages to the Pierre Hotel, a fact that suggests she's staying local for at least one more day."

Darcy tugged out her copy of the city map to determine where the hotel was located. If Renee was staying there, it would be in the expensive part of town. "A fact providing the one thing we need most right now: time."

The Pierre Hotel was a vast step up from the hotel they had stayed at the night before. Darcy was grateful she didn't have to check in, for she was woefully underdressed for such a hotel. A CIA agent had arranged a block of rooms on the seventh floor, and their team went upstairs by the back stairway, avoiding the public areas and the elevators. It was dangerous to set up surveillance in the same hotel as the target but there were no good vantage points around the hotel. And should the decision be made to act, taking Renee and Vladimir inside the hotel would at least contain the problem to a particular floor and room.

Darcy set her bag down on the bed and walked into the bathroom to wash her face. She had her choice of three different colors of plush hand towels, designer soaps, lotions, and shampoo. She hoped Renee settled in for a long visit. A few days staying here would be a vacation while at work.

Three distinctive knocks on the hotel door told her it was Gabriel. She opened without checking the security view hole. "Do we have a room number for her yet?"

Gabe pulled out the chair at the small table and glanced at the notes he had made. "Renee is four floors above us on the penthouse level. She's traveling under the name Karen Norvost. It doesn't look like Luther's here. There is talk at the front desk that the entire penthouse level was booked for the next month. It contains two large suites and four luxury rooms. Vladimir took the room across from the elevators. The other rooms are unoccupied."

Darcy finally started connecting the dots. "Her birthday."

"What?"

"Renee's birthday is this month, the sixteenth. She will want to celebrate it in style with a few of her friends coming to see her."

"She has been known in the past for some lavish birthday parties," Gabe said.

"Luther isn't here yet, but he's coming," Darcy speculated. "Renee is settling in early to enjoy herself." She added ice to her glass of water. "What do you think Renee is going to do with four million dollars?"

"You can bet she wasn't shopping those jewelry stores for their counter display items. Do you want to set up the surveillance equipment in here?"

"Might as well. It's a corner room; we can cover the approach to the hotel entrance from here as well as a piece of the marina. We need to arrange to have someone else at the airport watching for Luther's arrival."

"I'll make sure it's covered. Now if we can just get enough time to get a snatch team assembled," Gabe said, getting slowly to his feet.

"It sounds like we have a few days." The biggest problem would be Luther showing up and leaving before they were ready to execute a safe takedown. Rushing a plan in this situation meant someone could get killed. "We want him, Gabriel. This time it feels like we may have him."

"Sergey is the big unknown."

"Do we call him?" Darcy asked, ambivalent about it.

"If a sweep of the harbor turns up the boat, we'll call him," Gabe proposed.

"How hard are we going to look?"

Gabe smiled. "You know me too well."

# Twenty-five

August 2
Friday, 11:37 p.m.
Pierre Hotel / Nassau, New Providence
  Island, Bahamas

Darcy shifted her stool to the side of the small table so she could reach the piece of paper she had taped to the picture frame. For a temporary place to stick important notes, it did the job.

"Darcy, can I borrow your luggage? I need to get the security monitor off the floor," Gabe asked.

She pushed back her earphones and the muted refrains from *Carmen* so she could turn. "Sure." She turned to point out where she had pushed it under the bed.

Gabriel, with the help of two technicians, was turning the room into a command center. Good video surveillance of the lobby was set up through a tap on the hotel security cameras. Views from their hotel suite windows were now appearing on monitors. The logistics for the next seventy-two hours of surveillance were a nightmare. She pulled over the blueprints to see how food and housekeeping went back and forth to the penthouse level. With Luther reserving the entire floor, Vladimir had good physical control of the layout.

She heard Gabe open the door in answer to a soft knock and invite in more guests. "Make yourselves comfortable wherever you can find room; we're going to brief in twenty minutes. We've got a problem to sort out with the satellite link to get the video feed with Defense Intelligence up, but otherwise we're ready to go."

Darcy added a note to check on what kind of helicopter transportation the hotel arranged for its special guests. Luther would want quick ways to leave the hotel if needed.

"Guess who?" Hands slid across her eyes from behind. Darcy instinctively brought her elbow straight back, hitting solid muscle and causing her fingers to momentarily go numb from the collision. The hands across her eyes fell away.

Sam coughed. "You do have a habit of hitting the good guys in your life."

"Sam!" She turned on the stool. "I am so sorry." She reached toward his stomach to soothe the place she had struck, her hand covering his.

"I'll learn not to interrupt you when you are working." His hand turned and captured hers. "Want to try this again? Hi, beautiful."

She surged to her feet to wrap him in a hug; his embrace felt so wonderful. She laughed. "Not that I'm not thrilled to see you, but what are you doing here?"

He chuckled. "Tracking a shipment of explosives. I hear you may know who bought it."

"You actually saw the shipment?"

"Twenty cases of deadly explosives, enough to take out something very big."

She winced at the image. "We're pretty sure Luther is behind it; we saw the cash transfer. His wife Renee is upstairs."

"That close?" He shook his head. "Details can wait; I don't want to talk about work at the moment." He picked her up a few inches and kissed her, then slowly released her. "I thought you might have a bit of a tan as you're in the Bahamas but alas, no."

"Gabriel isn't letting me out of this corner room."

He looked around the crowded room. "Captive again, huh?"

"I'm afraid so." Privacy was virtually nonexistent in this stakeout.

"This is going to be a problem."

Tom wrapped his arm around Sam's shoulder and leaned around his partner. "Who's this? Darcy — I thought I heard your voice. Small world."

"Hi, Tom. Keeping Sam out of trouble for me?"

"I volunteered Cougar for this briefing."

She grinned at him. "Good job."

"Now is it worth the lack of sleep, buddy?" Tom teased.

"Don't tell me you knew she was here."

Sam's boss entered the room. Sam reluctantly released her.

Gabriel called the planning meeting to order. Sam and Tom took up station leaning against the wall on either side of her chair. Gabe began the discussion. "We're dealing with two topics tonight: the location and capture of Luther Genault and laying plans to deal with a shipment of explosives we believe he arranged to purchase for someone else. Since the two are intricately linked in their timing, tonight we figure out how to make both operations happen successfully and safely. Let's talk about the explosives first. Joe, you have the floor."

Sam's boss unrolled a large satellite photo taken hours before and taped it to the wall for all to see. "The explosives are currently being stored on Razor Reef Island, somewhere near this south inlet. There are radio burst transmissions happening at regular intervals, suggesting there is at least some real-time monitoring of the shipment."

"We can block that monitoring and blow up the shipment," the defense analyst suggested.

"We want the guys who plan to use those explosives; otherwise they'll just find more to buy," Gabriel replied.

"Which means we can't take Luther until after we pick up the people coming for the explosives," Darcy pointed out. "And as soon as there's trouble with the shipment, Luther runs. We'll have to be prepared to grab them simultaneously. Right now we don't know where he is. If we are forced to choose, which has priority? Luther or the shipment?"

"Luther," Joe replied. "We can track the shipment for days if necessary before we hit it."

Darcy looked at Gabriel. "For a short

window of time Vladimir, Luther, Renee, and probably Jerry are going to be inside this hotel during the days leading up to her birthday celebration on the sixteenth. We need to take Luther and the others while they're here. Is there a way to make sure the explosives are picked up during that same time?"

"Weather may help us for a few days," Tom suggested. "The rain front passing north of the British Virgin Islands tonight is churning up the sea, and it's not safe for a small boat to enter that cove. It would be tossed onto those razor reefs and ripped apart. They won't try to access the explosives for at least the next three days."

"We could plant news of a Navy exercise in the paper, a ruse, that will let them know they don't want to be around that island after, say, the seventeenth," Sam said. "We can box in the dates."

"Do one better than that," Joe suggested. "Put a boat in distress, even sink one, and mount a rescue effort to find the survivors. Stage it right outside of Razor Reef Island and station a military cutter leading the search right there at the island. Don't declare the search ended until we know Luther is here at the hotel. We can use that Navy exercise announcement to box in the other end of the timeline. The buyers will be so eager to collect their explosives, so relieved the stash wasn't stumbled upon that they'll move in to get them as soon as we move away."

"I really like it," Gabe agreed. "When the buyers pick up the explosives, we simultaneously take them at the island and Luther at the hotel. It just leaves the question, will Luther show up at the hotel? We're betting he will. Let's get down to details and figure out how many people we need where to make this happen."

Darcy picked up her notes. It would help if they could improve the odds that Luther would be here. Sergey could get Luther to this hotel. This was a case of the enemy of my enemy is my friend.

It was time to call Sergey.

Darcy found Sam a tube for the satellite maps. One by one those at the meeting had slipped out to make sure they were all away from the hotel before an early riser might notice them. She had a brief moment of privacy with Sam, but she wasn't sure what to say. *I've never said a harder good-bye.*

Sam studied her as he slid the maps into the tube. "You'll stay in this command center, Dar? You'll let the tactical guys be the ones to go in and take Luther and the others?"

She rested her hand on his forearm. "I'll stay on the intelligence side of this," she promised. "I have no desire to be part of the takedown team."

"I'll hold you to that."

She smiled at him. "I know; I'm glad you care."

He picked up his gear. She could read the fatigue in his deliberate movements, the huskiness now in his voice. With the preparation work SEAL Team Nine had already done to take these explosives, Sam had been awake close to forty-eight hours.

She wanted to keep him here a few more minutes, but it was best if he got going so his long day could end. She stepped forward and hugged him. "Take care of yourself."

The map tube hit the back of her knee as his arms closed around her. He sighed and leaned his forehead against hers. "The next two weeks are going to be the longest of my life. I want to be here."

"I know." She tugged him down to kiss him, putting months of emotion into it. "I love you, Samuel," she whispered. "This is my last mission. We get Luther, then I'm

407

going home to North Dakota and work on my house. From now on, I promise I will always be very easy to find."

His hand slid behind her head to hold her close. "Do you want to come to Thanksgiving dinner with me? I've got a few obligations to finish up before I can ask about dates farther out than that. So we'll start with Thanksgiving and just kind of work out the following decades from there."

Tears welled in the corners of her eyes. "I would be delighted to join you for Thanksgiving dinner."

He rubbed her back. "I love you too, Dar. I didn't come looking for you, but I never was so blessed as the day you crossed my path."

"It's mutual." She rested her head against his chest, happy that the corner had been turned to this becoming something permanent. She was going to be one of the best SEAL girlfriends a guy could ever have. She stepped back. She had to let him go. He was a soldier, and he had a job to do. "Stay safe out there."

He picked up the plans. "We both need to go to work, but when this is over . . ."

She loved that twinkle in his eyes when he smiled. "I can't wait for those first days off."

# Twenty-six

August 5
Monday, 2:32 a.m.
Razor Reef Island

The sailboat was a beautiful craft; it was too bad it would soon be at the bottom of the sea. As captain of the vessel, Sam leaned back against his safety line and brought the last sail down. Without the captured wind to counter the force of the waves, the sailboat turned broadside. The deck pitched thirty degrees to starboard as the boat was battered by waves. The sound of sail ripping was ugly. It was a shame to ruin a perfectly good boat. "Are we set, Wolf?"

"We're set," his partner hollered back.

*Lord, don't let a rogue wave hit us now. I want to live to enjoy Darcy's company for the rest of my days.* He had a ring to buy her when he was next on dry land.

Sam jammed the tiller. Adrift at sea, the sailboat would be driven relentlessly toward Razor Reef Island. He made the final radio call to the local authorities reporting a boat in trouble. They would respond as normal but would be quietly told not to risk lives during the days to follow searching for survivors.

"I've done a lot of crazy things in my life, but up 'til now blowing up a civilian boat was not one of them." Wolf turned on the flashlight to signal the other SEALs that they were ready for the final act of this carefully scripted play.

Sam wrapped his gloved hands around the thick rope threaded through the final knapsack of explosives and struggled against the pitching deck to join his partner. "Let's go."

Wolf stepped off the deck into the sea. Sam followed, letting gravity win.

The water swallowed him, tugging him down. The current took them quickly away from the boat and the danger of being slammed against the hull. As his final act as the boat skipper, Sam released the final satchel of explosives on their weighted line.

It wasn't that easy to make an intentional act appear an accident. They wanted to leave behind a wreck still essentially in one piece so television pictures would make this story linger longer in the news cycle. If the small blast through the engine room didn't bring the boat down, the final satchel of explosives was a depth charge, the concussion of the blast designed to rip enough leaks in the hull to flood the boat. They wanted the boat to go down as near to the point of the last radio call as possible.

Wolf swam over to join him and clipped his safety line to Sam's combat vest to connect them. Wolf laughed against the force of the waves as he tried to turn away from the wind to be able to speak without getting clipped by breaking water. "You have to give Darcy credit. The name of the boat is a stroke of brilliance."

The boat *Kendra* would be in news updates for days to come. Sergey's wife was being memorialized in the mission that would capture the man who had arranged her death. "Let's get out of here."

With powerful kicks, they swam away from the floundering boat. They could hear the Zodiac before it appeared. The black rubber craft materialized from the darkness, slamming against the waves. The SEAL guiding it turned so they had to swim to the craft rather than have it run over them.

Sam caught hold of the netting draped over the side and pulled himself up and over the taut rubber, flopping onto the bottom of the raft. Wolf landed beside him. The boat turned and raced to the north. The sailboat was only a bobbing light against the sea as the running lights still flickered.

Wolf tugged out the remote activation pad. "You want the honors?"

"Go ahead."

Wolf turned the key.

The explosives aboard the sailboat blew through the engine compartment, sending a huge plume of flames into the night. It was followed moments later by an underwater blast that shook the Zodiac and left it quivering in a fine vibration.

They watched the sailboat sink in less than a minute.

"We did that job right."

"Hooyah, Wolf." Sam brought the captain's logbook from his inside pocket and dropped it into the water. "Rest in peace, Kendra."


August 7
Wednesday, 8:12 a.m.
Pierre Hotel / Nassau, New Providence
    Island, Bahamas

Darcy leaned over to the small table in the command center suite and picked up the remote. She turned up the volume on the TV. "The search is now fully underway for the missing sailors off Razor Reef Island."

"A boat sinking off the island where his explosive shipment is stored." Gabriel said, passing her a bagel with cream cheese for breakfast. "Luther must be pacing right now at the ill-timed hand fate has dealt him."

Sam and Wolf had done a good job with the demolition; the first pictures from the sunken sailboat had been broadcast today from divers going down to see if the ship had become the grave for the two missing sailors. "I wonder what his buyers will think if they're thwarted from collecting the shipment when originally planned."

"I hope they give Luther sleepless nights. What is Renee doing?"

Darcy looked at the second monitor. "She hasn't been seen yet, and no breakfast has gone up. I somehow doubt she will sleep this late once Luther arrives; he's a morning person." They were falling into a routine for this surveillance. She took the early morning hours, Gabriel took the day, and over breakfast they relayed any observations with the night crew.

Gabe wheeled back to the window and

picked up binoculars to look at the café at the end of the block. "Sergey is just sitting out there, drinking his coffee." The note passed to the Russian embassy had brought him to the scene.

"You know word has filtered back to Luther that Sergey is here. He's daring Luther to send Vladimir or Jerry after him," Darcy said.

"You have to admire Sergey's cool nerves. If Luther wants to give Renee her wish to stay here with some friends in the penthouse, he can't have the police investigating a sniper murder right outside the hotel. So Sergey sits there and makes a statement. And while he does, they aren't paying as much attention as they should to who else is around watching them."

"Sergey knows the British Virgin Islands; he knows the Bahamas. You notice he showed up twenty-four hours after we passed the note to his embassy. He was probably already in the area." Darcy got up. "You want to watch the place for a while? I think I'll pay a visit to an old friend."

"Darcy, you promised Sam not to do another solo."

"Sergey is no threat to me; he's after Luther. We need to know what he has found out. One last time before I end this career."

"I agree with your assessment on Sergey. You still determined to retire again when this is over?"

"Absolutely." She walked over to her case. "Should I become old or young?"

Gabriel considered the question. "Keep with the setting — go young."

Darcy took a seat at the table across from Sergey, setting down her second bagel and coffee. The book she was determined to eventually finish if it took this entire war to do so she placed on the table. "Thanks for coming."

"My pleasure, Darcy."

She accepted the section of the paper he offered. It was in Russian, but with a little reading the words came back with ease. She turned to the international news. "Do we need to talk about what's coming?"

"I've already planned the ending."

"So have I," she said softly. "Probably a different one than you."

He smiled at her. "Read your paper, my friend."

"Are you sure, Sergey?"

"It is time to have this end. I agree with your note, 'What is the enemy of my enemy, but my friend?' I brought some of my own friends along this time. Friends with debts to settle." He looked over. "We're on the same side in this. No matter what happens."

"Sergey —" She didn't know what to say at the intense focus she could see in his eyes, his expression. "It would be best not to get in our way."

"My family were not the only ones killed; I was not the only one pressured. A few others also want to see Vladimir and Luther dealt with. Luther is coming in on his boat Friday, Darcy. Sunset."

She absorbed the news he offered so matter-of-factly. "You're not going to let him arrive."

"Not if I can help it."

There were times she knew things that were hard to bear. The weight of this one . . . "Be careful, Sergey."

He set down his orange juice glass. "Please tell Gabriel I appreciate the note."

"I will."

He got to his feet and picked up the cane he was using. "Why, Darcy? You didn't owe it to me."

She didn't understand Gabriel's reasons, but she was honest enough to admit her own. "I'd like Sam to live to see retirement."

His expression softened. "Yes. I thought there might be such a reason." He touched his hat. "Until Friday."

She nodded and watched Sergey walk away.

*One of us will find Luther in the coming weeks: Sergey, Gabriel, Sam, myself. Lord, I pray for strength to get us through the next days, for safety. Don't let me shirk from completing this task.*

There was a time in every investigation when the work was essentially done and the waiting began, for the pieces to fall into place and the ending to play out. This one was playing out on its own momentum now.

*Lord, I've never felt less ready for the end game. Please don't let me make a mistake that costs us capturing Luther.*

# Twenty-seven

August 9
Friday, 5:15 p.m.
Nassau, New Providence Island, Bahamas

Darcy took a seat on the bench overlooking the marina. The day had been a scorcher and it was ending humid. She raised binoculars to look around the crowded piers, searching for Luther, praying and hoping to see Sergey. Only one of them would likely show up here tonight.

Gabriel set down his phone beside her. Four men were watching the hotel. Renee had been busy today: a haircut, a stop to have her makeup done, multiple calls to the hotel caterer bringing a special dinner for the night. Renee expected Luther to arrive tonight. Vladimir was with Renee at the Pierre Hotel; Jerry was probably with Luther. "Do you think we'll be able to get Jerry too?"

"Maybe. Luther is at the top of the list, then the explosives shipment, and then I'd call it a tie between getting Vladimir or Jerry," Gabe replied. "I know Defense really wants him."

Darcy straightened on the bench. "There's Luther." It was earlier than she had expected; they still had an hour till sunset. Visibility was good.

"Where?"

"The boat just clearing the buoys." She felt a sinking sensation in her chest as she watched the man steering the boat into the marina.

Gabriel studied the man. "I agree."

"What happened to Sergey?" She was afraid just to voice the question. Luther was here; Sergey was not . . . It wasn't what she had come down to the marina expecting to find.

"I don't know, Dar." Gabe searched the other boats preparing to enter the marina. "Sergey is nowhere to be seen."

Sergey was dead. She didn't want to accept that, but the evidence before her was stark. Sergey had failed to stop Luther. So many friends had died in this war, now an enemy she had respected, maybe even cared about. "Can we quietly inquire with his embassy? A mutual friend?"

Gabe nodded. "I'll see what I can find out."

Darcy focused back on Luther. The man was confidently standing at the controls of the large motorboat. "Jerry isn't with Luther."

"He was hired to take care of Sergey," Gabe noted.

"So did Jerry do it, or did Sergey at least manage to kill him before he went down?" Darcy hoped Jerry was out of this. "Sergey said he brought friends with him this time. Maybe one of them will get in touch and tell us what happened."

"If they're still alive, I bet they'll try to complete what Sergey started, go after Luther again."

They watched the boat approach a free slip. Gabriel sighed. "We adjust to this, Darcy. We have no choice. Sergey's dead, possibly Jerry too. What's Luther going to do now?"

She struggled to shift her thinking to this reality. "Luther will join Renee; he'll make arrangements to move the explosives. As long as we don't attract attention, he's going to relax now that he thinks Sergey has been dealt with. He's going to get expansive, maybe take a few risks he wouldn't normally take."

"Luther's on borrowed time. All he has to do is walk through the doors of that hotel, and we'll have him bottled up. Just as soon as he's at the hotel, the SEALs can grab the shipment."

August 9
Friday, 5:20 p.m.
Razor Reef Island

Members of SEAL Team Nine slipped onto the island under cover of the search for the missing sailors. With a number of helicopters doing an aerial search and several search boats roaring through the area, they were able to have a helo drop them off on the slim strip of beach without drawing undue attention. The search for the sailors was to end today in the solemn words to the news media that there had been no survivors. The ruse had served their purposes well.

In two-man teams, the SEALs spread out to search the inlet for the stash of explosives.

Sam was grateful for the Nomex gloves. The terrain was as much up and down as level, and under the tropical foliage was black volcanic rock, still rough and ragged, not yet smoothed by time and weather. Sam deposited a piece of rock in his pocket to add to his collection, then struggled up the incline. This island was pocketed with caves, some no bigger than a tree and some as vast as caverns. Sometimes the lava had flowed around obstacles and hardened, while at others it had burned up what it swallowed. The number of holes a man could step in where there had once been trees were numerous.

"Cougar, this is not fun."

Sam stopped his partner's slide down the bank by grabbing his shirt. "I seem to remember in BUD/S training they promised us days of this exact kind of 'fun.' Try walking *with* this island's terrain and not attacking it. The more you hurry, the slower you actually go."

"You really think someone hid explosives on this side of the inlet?"

"Not hardly. They followed the sand and used the first concealed cave they came to."

"But we're looking here anyway, just in case."

"We were due to draw the hard assignment eventually." Sam looked around the area. "Besides, this view is worth it."

"I prefer to see my flowers in a vase."

Sam laughed.

Bear's call interrupted their discussion.

The explosive cache had been found.

By the time he and Wolf worked their way back to the inlet and around to the other side where the team was gathering, the initial inspection work was already completed.

Bear briefed the team. "The cave is halfway back that path on the south side of the bank. It's deep and the opening is shrouded with netting and foliage. We checked it with a pole and mirror and saw all twenty boxes stacked along the far wall. What looks like a couple different types of trip wires are set up, with one actually tied to the netting. Move it aside without thinking and a grenade goes off in your face. Pretty effective security. There's a satellite transmitter farther up the hillside where there's good line of sight."

The shadows were beginning to stretch across the island as sunset came. "Once Luther arrives at the hotel and is securely on the penthouse level, we'll get a green light to take anyone coming here to pick up the explosives. We take them before they can get to the cave, here along the trail where they will be naturally squeezed into walking single file. I want six men here; I want another six men ready to take those remaining on the boat. Your task is to make sure the boat does not leave the inlet.

"Wolf, Cougar, find somewhere you can see any approaching boats. I want at least two minutes' warning of any craft trying to come into the cove. While they may come at night, the critical hours are now while there's still twilight to guide them or at dawn. If for some reason the men arrive before Luther is contained in Nassau, I want everyone to just keep out of sight. We'll take pictures and call in air assets to track the boat, but we let them go. Questions?" Bear looked around at the men. "Let's get to it."

The men dispersed to find their new homes for the night. Sam looked at Wolf. "Back to that crest where we were a few minutes ago?"

Wolf winced. "Yes. It's got the view. The mattress is just going to be a bit rough."

Sam knew what he meant. "You can take the first shift if you want. When you're tired, you don't notice the rocks as much."

"Two-hour watches?"

"Sounds good to me." Sam led them back the way they had come. It was worth the effort to get the right spot for the lookout perch.

Twenty minutes later he and Wolf had

settled in for the night. A huge pile of leaves created a cushion against the rocky surface. Sam began scanning the water with night-vision goggles to get a fix on what was out there.

Wolf answered Bear's half-hour check-in call.

They searched for an hour, as the sun lowered to the horizon.

Sam queued his microphone. "Heads up, guys. We've got company."

The small craft was heading straight into the cove. Coming in at sunset was risky. It would take them longer than expected to load the explosives, and the boat would have a tough time getting past the reef in the dark of night.

"I don't have clearance yet that Nassau is ready. Everyone hold. Acknowledge that."

SEALs acknowledged by number.

"Cougar, I need a count."

"Standby."

Wolf was already working on it. "Two at navigation, one on the bow, one at the stern. The boat could carry eight. You think anyone is below deck while they're trying to cross that razor reef?"

"Everyone is on deck watching for trouble and backseat driving for the

425

skipper," Sam guessed. "Call it four, plus a possible fifth."

Wolf called the news into the team. Sam started searching the boat for signs of what type of weapons the men were carrying.

The boat made it across the reef with a lot of shouting between the men on deck. SEALs stationed around the cove began talking among themselves, assigning team members to specific individuals aboard the boat so that every man would be taken down in the opening assault.

Bear's voice broke in. "We hold. Repeat, we hold. Luther hasn't made it to the hotel, and they can't risk moving against him at the marina. Let them come ashore and move the cases. Luther is moving, so stay sharp. Status could change any minute to a takedown."

Wolf and Cougar kept the boat in view until it entered the back of the cove. They listened to the action in the cove reported by other SEALs while they continued to scan the horizon for any signs of a second boat. The first of several trips to the cave and back to the boat began.

All the SEALs waited for Bear's word they had clearance to act.

It never came.

Forty minutes after it arrived, the boat

made the dangerous journey back across the reef and out to open waters.

Bear broke the silence. "Surveillance aircraft has them. The weather is clear; the boat is being tracked. We'll get another opportunity, gentlemen. Reassemble on the beach and let's call in a ride home. We'll see what the holdup is in Nassau."

# Twenty-eight

August 11
Sunday, 6:49 p.m.
USS *Hailey* / Caribbean Sea

Sam studied the weather maps for the upcoming seventy-two hours. They had to let.
the shipment go. All that coordination and
the plan had come apart on the smallest of
problems.

Bear joined him and handed him a
coffee mug. "Where is the boat?"

Sam located the coordinates for his boss.
"It's making steady progress north into the
Bahamas."

"A direction that suits us. It was simply
bad luck that Luther lingered at the harbor
rather than reach the hotel in time for us
to act Friday night. This is a delay, not an
unrecoverable setback."

"For us, but what about Nassau? They
were set up to act, and a glitch stopped
them from taking Luther. The next time

they'll be that much more eager to go even under a less than optimal setting. Someone usually gets hurt in situations like that."

"Right now they have no choice but to wait. I hear Renee's birthday guests have begun to arrive. It complicates the planning. The plan now is to move in after the guests go home, tentatively the nineteenth. That should put this boat of explosives about . . . here, nearing Florida," Joe judged. "It's workable from our end. If weather looks like it's going to change, we move in sooner. It is not critical that the two actions be coordinated so tightly now that Luther thinks his part of the explosives transfer is done."

"Bear, you won't need all of us to stop that boat. It's a small craft, and even with a full backup team, there will be a few in the platoon just watching from the sidelines. I'd like to join the operation in Nassau."

"Are you sure?"

"Yes."

"I'll talk to DIA for you," Bear agreed. "And I volunteer Wolf to go along to watch your back."

"Thank you, sir."

"I can understand your desire to be there."

August 14
Wednesday, 10:12 a.m.
Nassau, New Providence Island, Bahamas

Sam took his duffel bag off the helicopter and nodded his thanks to the pilot. Wolf stepped out beside him and slid on his sunglasses. "Where to first, Chief?"

"Find the assault team, get us a slot solving this mess, then the reason we're here — Darcy."

Wolf smiled. "You protect her back; I'll protect yours."

"Sounds like a good plan to me."

"Who knows we're coming?"

Sam pointed to the car just pulling in the lot. "DIA. There's our ride."

"Do we need to wait until tonight to slip into the hotel?"

"I hope not. Be inconspicuous."

Wolf laughed.

Their DIA escort popped the trunk and waved them to dump gear.

"Who's leading the takedown team?" Sam asked.

"The Brits. I understand you've met Major Hamilton at least once before."

"Brandon's friend who plays jolly good piano?" Wolf asked.

Their DIA escort laughed. "That's him."

"A good man." Sam remembered him from Morocco. "Where are they at with preparations?"

"Waiting for the word go. They took over a local warehouse and laid out a model of the penthouse floor to practice in. The planning is done; the rehearsals are running three times a day. I'm surprised how well the pieces have fallen in place."

Their driver took them through town and to the warehouse. Upon their arrival the warehouse door raised, allowing them to pull inside to park out of sight.

Major Hamilton strode over to be the first to meet them. "Joe called and said he was sending his Bear Cubs. Jolly good to see you Wolf, Cougar. We can always use two more shooters." He and Sam shook hands. "I understand you've got a personal interest in this one, mate."

"You might say that." Sam slipped Darcy's picture taken during the carrier visit out of his pocket and showed it to Hamilton.

"St. James, a fine lady. She briefs us every morning on happenings during the night and is one of the more pleasant voices in our ears conveying security camera images."

"Luther tried to have her killed."

"The man must be daft." The major looked between the two of them. "We can use two men in the tail if you're interested."

It was a better offer than Sam had hoped for given the circumstances. "We accept." Sam was glad to be in the action, even if it amounted to securing the stairwells. This was a frustrating war, with many missions gathering intelligence, a few assignments where they had been given the green light to act, and a lot of waiting. It was hard to maintain his patience. They had a few thousand opponents spread around the world. It wasn't often they got one pinned down like this. Sam wanted Luther.

"Major."

The man turned at the call. "Excuse me. I need to take this phone call straight-away."

Sam left his duffel bag beside Wolf. "I'm heading over to the hotel. Stay with the guys and get acclimated; I'll be back for the run-through."

Wolf was already checking out the new communication gear. "You sure you don't want me to cover your six?"

"I appreciate the offer. Stay, it looks like some interesting toys."

Wolf rubbed his hands together as he smiled. "I'll say."

Sam caught the attention of his DIA escort and pointed to the car. He wanted to see Darcy, and the fact he was only miles from her raised that urgency.

The DIA escort drove him to the hotel and slipped him in through the side entrance being used by the groundskeeping staff. "I'll be back at 11:45."

"I'll meet you here." Sam took the stairs two at time. The corner room where Darcy was supposed to be was to the left as he came out of the stairwell. He tapped on the door.

"Stay put, Gabriel. I'll get it," Darcy called from inside. The doorknob turned with a brisk twist. "Sam."

He caught the breadstick she dropped. "Hi, honey."

Her surprise turned to a laugh. "Warn me next time you're going to show up unannounced and I'll make sure I'm not wearing the modern art shirt Gabriel calls a collision."

He absorbed her laughter and relished the chance to study her. "The shirt does give the concept of color new meaning."

She tugged him inside the room. He nodded a greeting to Gabe sitting in front of the bank of monitors. Darcy's partner hadn't known he was coming, but the man didn't look the least bit surprised. Sam handed Darcy back her breadstick. "An early lunch or a late breakfast?"

"Probably both. The definition of time has become rather mixed up." She crossed over to the dresser that held an assortment of trays to put the breadstick down. "Pull up a chair if you can find one. We're in the watching game right now. I'm on shift for another forty minutes."

Sam found one not stacked with paper. "What are we watching?"

"Gabriel was kind and gave me the hotel lobby. It's easier to pay attention when there's something to watch beyond a closed elevator door." Darcy settled sideways onto her chair, putting her feet up on a cardboard box she'd fit into a niche between the monitors. "This chair is a misery device after the first few hours." She pointed to the left monitor. "The hotel's special guests check in there; these two monitors show the general lobby. I'm watching for anyone who seems familiar."

Sam had seen a lot of Darcy's expressions during the past months. The focus to her work absorbed her in a new way, and the lightness disappeared when she wasn't looking at him. This grief . . . it was new and deep.

"Something is wrong. What's happened, Dar?"

"Sergey is dead," she said softly. "He went after Luther, and he didn't come back."

"I'm sorry, honey. I hadn't heard."

"It's been kept quiet, so that Luther doesn't find out we're around."

Sam reached over and rubbed her shoulder. "When?"

"Sometime between Wednesday and Friday." She looked back at him. "You had to let the shipment of explosives go through. I'm sorry."

"The Navy is tracking the boat. We'll still be able to pick it up."

She squeezed his hand. "Will you be part of this takedown?"

"Wolf and I are going to be in the tail."

"I'm actually relieved you'll be involved; we have to stop these guys." She pointed to the monitor with red tape across the top. "Luther's up there on the penthouse level, probably eating breakfast. Just looking at that screen makes me furious. He can afford that room because of profits from terrorist acts." She pointed to the schematic. "Vladimir is in this room. He has a pattern of sorts to his security walkaround. Although no two days have been alike, the

435

places he checks are somewhat predictable. He's getting relaxed."

"The party guests are here."

She nodded. "Nine guests are now on the penthouse level and Reservations have the others arriving throughout today. Jerry remains the wild card. We're not sure if he died stopping Sergey. All we know is that he didn't arrive with Luther." She reached for her glass. "Could you get me a refill? Cold sodas are in the ice chest we temporarily left in the tub."

"Glad to. Have you been getting any sleep?"

She smiled. "Sleep. What's that?"


August 16
Friday, 8:12 p.m.
Pierre Hotel / Nassau, New Providence
  Island, Bahamas


Renee's birthday party was well underway. Darcy pushed off her headphones. "I can't listen to this, Gabriel." The listening devices planted in the flower vases gave them good audio of the main rooms in the suite. Too good. They had Luther on tape now, in conversation about a soccer game, talking about stocks, commenting on the weather and pleasant travel.

Gabe nodded toward Sam. "Go take a walk. All of this is streaming to tape. It's not likely we'll hear where he stashed all his money. I'll call if there are any movements we haven't already anticipated."

She nodded. They weren't going to take Luther in the suite with so many guests present. But if Luther tried to leave, they would stop him. "I want him, Gabriel."

"So do I. This party works to our benefit — they are going to be tired and less alert. The guests will leave, then we'll take Luther."

Another day, another two days of waiting. She could endure this; she had no choice.

Sam held out his hand. "Come on, Dar. We can walk the stairs if nothing else."

The room was crowded with agents keeping an eye on the monitors. Privacy wasn't to be found here. She grasped his offered hand. "Is your partner going to tag along to watch your back?"

Tom, stretched out on the bed, shifted the magazine he had spread over his face to provide some darkness. "Cougar, are you going to get lost?"

"Don't plan to."

Tom moved the magazine back up. "Then have fun, kids. I'm enjoying this article."

Darcy laughed.

"What's it about?" Sam asked.

"Ask me when I figure out how to read German. The pictures show cool-looking cars. They are fueling a few dreams."

Sam picked them up two sodas and held the door for her. Darcy followed him to the stairs where there was some privacy from any possible guest or staff who might be working for Vladimir. She took a seat on the stairs.

"Don't want to walk?"

"Not stairs. I don't mind going down, but it's the coming back up that I hate."

He settled beside her.

She opened the soda he handed her and let herself relax for the first time since this shift began. "This desperately needs to be over. They are up there partying; I want them behind bars for the rest of their lives. Just don't get hurt up there. I don't think I could handle going up several floors to see you getting patched up after being shot."

He wrapped his arm around her shoulders. "You know I will. And Dar — the party we are going to have after Luther's captured will make theirs seem tame."

"I bet SEALs throw good parties." She leaned her head against his shoulder. She was worn out and grateful he let the silence between them stretch out. "Have you been able to call home recently?"

"I got through to my mom yesterday. What about you? Have you talked with Amy?"

"A couple times. A tree blew down and took out part of my new fencerow. She said the oak chest I ordered is in. I'm homesick."

"It's a good thing to be."

She closed her eyes. He could watch out for trouble for the next few minutes. "Would you wake me in a bit?"

He rubbed her back. "Sure."

She let herself drift to sleep.

Sam shifted Darcy to a more comfortable position. She had fallen deeply asleep quickly; the last few days had worn her out. He studied her as she slept, smiling. Even her eyelashes were beautiful. The ring in his pocket would have to wait for another time. He wanted to give her a more impressive memory for the occasion than a stairwell. Maybe a day or two from now this would be over, and that would be possible.

The logistics of making it work . . . They had both overcome tougher problems than geography. She might struggle to find words for the deep emotions she felt, but she excelled at adapting. They would find a workable plan. He'd found the perfect partner for his future. He kissed her forehead and settled back to let her sleep as long as she could.

August 19
Monday, 9:45 a.m.
Pierre Hotel / Nassau, New Providence
  Island, Bahamas

Darcy unwrapped a piece of gum, her eyes never leaving the monitor. Her chair had been relegated to the other side of the room. It was game time, and she was one of the people directing what was about to unfold.

A faint hum in her ear sounded as someone came on the secure communication link. "The last guests have just cleared the lobby. They didn't forget anything that would have them coming back upstairs. I've seen everything from golf bags to luggage going down."

"Roger that."

The penthouse level now held just their critical three people: Renee, Vladimir, and Luther. This mission was a go. Darcy looked at the clock. Renee had an appointment for a facial. They would go in as soon as she left the penthouse. Darcy saw movement on the security camera they had tapped into for the penthouse level.

"Renee is leaving. Stand ready," Darcy informed the leader of the assault team. "She's in the elevator. Hold for doors closed." These seconds mattered; they didn't want Renee coming back up for some reason right in the middle of this, but they also needed to use the cover of the moving elevator noise to their advantage. "Doors are closed." She touched her stopwatch. "Twenty seconds of sound cover is now running."

"Go teams one and two," the team leader ordered.

The monitor in the stairwell caught the movement as the assault team rushed up the stairs. The second team came down from the roof, using the temporarily suspended service elevator shaft so they could fast-rope down to the exact distance.

Darcy paced two steps in one direction, rocked on her heels, then paced two steps back, keeping her focus on the monitors.

Their team had done everything they

could to ensure they were in control for this. Renee had given them the perfect moment to act. They were going in to take the two men and end this now. She could only watch how it played out.

*Lord, please don't let anyone on the team get hurt; don't let Sam and Tom get into trouble. I want Luther, but not at the cost of someone I love.*

"Move in!" the team leader ordered. Men rushed through the stairway doors and the bells clanged as the service elevator door was jammed open. Battering rams crashed and splintered wood. Darcy braced for the sound of gunfire. The monitors on the penthouse level didn't extend into the rooms and suites. She could only listen as agents called rooms clear to have a sense of the progress.

"Clear!"

"Clear in the east room."

The voices rumbled in a quick sequence as the plan executed and then the words came more slowly. The team leader began calling off names checking the floor. One by one they reported back clear. It was what she wasn't hearing that had Darcy biting her knuckles.

The team leader spoke on the secure net, "They aren't here!"

"You're sure?" Gabriel demanded.

"This floor is empty," the man replied. "Luther and Vladimir somehow got away. Look around, Gabe. How did they get by us and when?"

Gabe pushed the pager alarm, triggering the contingency plan they had hoped never to use, rushing agents into the lobby, restaurants, and hallways of the hotel. "What did we miss?"

Darcy scrambled to run back tapes. They had Luther and Vladimir on tape early this morning seeing out some of the guests. She ran back through the video of Renee going downstairs and saw nothing. Over the secure communication link she could hear power screwdrivers whining as ductwork was opened and men tried to find some way Luther and Vladimir had been able to squeeze off the floor unseen.

She fast-forwarded through the tapes of this morning. She stopped the tape showing the last departing group of Renee's guests. Six people, the group from Germany. An older couple, three men, and one woman. She would have to return that Intelligence Star. "The disguise isn't perfect but it's decent. That's Vladimir. That means one of these two must be Luther. This guy, from the general build."

Gabe touched his mike. "Team leader, they slipped out in that last group of guests." Darcy held up the clipboard. "They have . . . fifty-seven minutes on us. That puts them possibly well outside the hotel perimeter.

"Activate the containment plan for the harbor, the airport. They'll likely leave Nassau for a nearby city and depart from there."

"Already done." Darcy was punching in the new code, activating teams around the city.

Gabriel pointed to the city map. Darcy tugged it over for him. "Team leader, finish the search for any communication gear and then egress. We take Renee. She may know where they're heading."

"On it, Gabe."

Darcy circled places on the map where she'd head if she were Vladimir and Luther and getting away was her priority. "I underestimated them. Vladimir is good. I didn't give him enough credit to be able to do something like this."

Gabe pointed to the tape playback. "Look at the time they left — they may not know we are on to them. That close call with Sergey may have taught Luther something about listening to those who know tradecraft. What better way to cover a trail than to stroll out the front door and catch a limousine booked under another name, take a private flight under a new name? They may have intended all along to walk away from this hotel undercover."

She blinked and grabbed hold of the idea, for at least it gave them hope. "Okay. My problem is that Sergey thought like this guy, and I'm still learning. Luther's not rushing to leave. He and Vladimir had a specific destination in mind."

Gabriel went on the net. "Team leader, Luther left disguised, but it may have been part of his original plan. He may not know we're on to him."

"If we have to take him while he's in public . . ." the team leader pointed out.

"I hear you. It can't be helped. We have to stop him here, now." Gabe looked at Darcy. "If he's still in Nassau, what are we missing that will help us find him?"

Darcy hit the rewind to play the segment back again. *I've already blown our best shot to get them, Lord. What's the second best option? What am I missing?* "Breakfast. No one brought breakfast up for Luther this morning."

"Good. He may stop at a favorite restaurant."

"A helicopter pad. He won't fly by plane from here. He'd want to transfer to another island before creating a paper trail because Renee is still here. Tourist charters. Didn't Sergey say that Luther had bought an island and a hotel or an island and a charter service, something like that?"

Gabriel smiled. "He's been ducking us by lingering in the one place we knew he avoided: among tourists."

It was a lead, but how did she get her hands around it given there was no time? "Do you have an idea how many charter services provide helicopter tours within this area?"

The hotel room door opened and Tom and Sam joined them. Gabriel pointed at Tom. "I need some information fast. How many helicopters are departing this island airspace *right now?*"

Tom grabbed the secure satellite phone to DIA to set up a picture relay from the nearest surveillance flight. "It's probably faster just to go on the roof and count them." Tom reached for the case of cables to get the hi-res screen changed over to the satellite feed.

Darcy grabbed binoculars. "I agree." She headed toward the door.

Sam got to the door first and held it for

her. They ran toward the stairs.

"If Luther's already in the air, he can get far enough ahead he can land, change transportation, and melt away on us. We either figure out which flight to chase or this is over."

She broke into bright sunlight on the roof with Sam on her heels. There were numerous planes in the sky. In her first 360-degree pivot, Darcy counted 9 helicopters airborne.

"Give me names, Darcy," Gabe asked over the security circuit.

It was hard to read the words even with powerful binoculars that could pick out details up to half a mile away. "Ashburn Flights, something Hafford."

"Whitcomb Charters, Sea & Air," Sam added.

"Dar, look for Paradise Flights!" Gabriel broke in. "Two men, the limousine driver remembers the golf clubs, and one had a Russian accent. They are only a precious few minutes ahead of us. Tom, are our guys in the air yet? We need an intercept."

"They're on it," Tom replied over the communication link.

Sam pointed to a helicopter. "Two o'clock, Darcy. It's got a scripted *P* and a rainbow painted stripe on the side."

"Heading?"

"East," Sam replied to his partner. "You should be able to look out the window and see it. I put it just past the marina."

"Got it, Chief. Paradise with a scripted *P.*"

"Dar, we've got confirmation," Gabe called. "The receptionist at Paradise Flights confirms the faxed photos are them. The flight just took off. She noticed them because one of the two men was allowed to act as his own pilot, which is rare. It's a day booking; there isn't a filed flight plan. They aren't required between island hops."

The helicopter exploded in midair.

Darcy watched stunned, as burning pieces of the helicopter rained down on the water. "What was *that?*"

"A Stinger. Fired from along the flight-path of the helicopter," Sam answered.

"Gabriel, was that us?" Darcy asked.

"I swear it wasn't. We don't have Stingers in-country. I'm looking out the window at the same thing you are."

"Someone knew his destination." Sam lowered his binoculars. "Dar, someone was already ahead of Luther and Vladimir; someone knew their plans."

This didn't make sense. "Sergey's friends?"

"If it was, they were well connected. Someone had to have literally phoned ahead the moment the helicopter lifted off to allow such a quick setup and shoot."

"Is there any possibility this is a trick? A diversion?"

"I'm asking the same questions, Darcy," Gabe replied. "Or maybe his explosives buyer didn't like leaving a loose end who knew their plans."

"We need to get out to the site."

Sam pointed out to sea. "We're already there." While she watched, two helicopters began to circle the crash site. "They'll recover whatever they can of the debris." Sam touched her arm. "Come on, let's get downstairs, collect gear, and get out there."

She took one long last look, lowered her binoculars, and headed after Sam. Luther was dead, but this had ended wrong. It really felt wrong.

Sam held the roof stairwell door for Darcy, then moved fast down the stairs. Ticking through his mind was the memory of the flight of that missile. He and Wolf could track down the location of the shot if they moved fast. It had been a well-executed attack, and there had to be at least two people involved. Someone called ahead Luther's travel plans to the guy waiting with that missile. Who had that kind of access to Luther's plans? Vladimir. Who alive had that kind of access to Luther's plans?

Sam held the door to the hotel room for Darcy. "Wolf, we need a communication case, diving equipment, and a good map of the area. Let's see what we can find while the trail is there."

His partner handed Major Hamilton his binoculars and stepped away from the window. "The hotel should be able to arrange the diving equipment. How many air tanks?"

"Make it eight sixty-minute cylinders to give us some margin. Gabe, what do you have on Paradise Flights and the limo driver? Someone had to alert the shooter they were taking off."

"And Gabriel, the guy who fired the Stinger has to leave the area somehow. We need the airports covered," Darcy added, heading over to join Major Hamilton.

The window shattered.

Sam dove across the room tackling Darcy and rolling her toward the wall. Wolf was down, but it was the hollow thud of the impact and the blood on the floor that told him the major bought it. "Wolf?"

"Breathing," his partner gasped. "It punched through him and into me."

Sam rolled onto his back, looking up at the window and the explosive pattern of the shot. A low-velocity high-caliber round, for he hadn't heard that distinct snap as it broke the sound barrier. The sniper was a good shooter — the major had been struck between the eyes.

*Jerry.*

"Stay down," Sam ordered Darcy, pushing her down as she tried to turn. *"Please."* They were lying on glass, but he couldn't let her move until he got this sorted out. He elbow crawled his way across the room. "How are you doing, Gabriel?" The man was sweating, his color wasn't good, but he was reaching up to the desk to get his radio mike.

"The doctor warned me against falling like this. What's the plan?"

A sniper focused on this hotel room . . . ducking was a pretty good plan. "I don't care how quiet that sniper gets, he's sitting out there watching and waiting. Tell everyone even remotely connected to this to enter into the hotel only through the back and under cover. Wolf and I are heading to the roof to try and spot this guy."

"I'm afraid I'm not in any shape to take that assignment," Wolf whispered, as Sam leaned over him.

The bullet had killed the major and then hit Wolf high on the shoulder. Sam yanked two pillowcases free and folded them into a thick bandage. "You'll be fine." Sam held his friend's gaze. "I need your eyes."

Wolf tried to smile. "Okay, but you're carrying me up those stairs."

"Darcy —" Sam tightened the belt securing the bandage as Wolf groaned — "you'll have to figure out a way to get Gabe to the hall without standing, crouching, or otherwise getting far off the floor."

"I've got that part down."

"And stay away from that outside wall; a bullet can punch through it." Sam grabbed Wolf's good hand and pulled him back toward the hall. Only when they were well back from line of sight to the windows did Sam take a deep breath, stand, and pull his partner up. Wolf leaned against the wall for balance, sucking in air. Sam kept a tight hold and waited until he stopped swaying.

"Get the cases," Wolf said.

"I'll get a doctor up to the roof."

"You better believe it, and a pillow and about a dozen energy bars."

Sam tapped his fist against his partner's clenched hand and moved.

The assault team had a lockbox for the gear, and Sam left the cases secured there and spun the padlock. Darcy had crawled to join Gabe after she had paused long enough to cover Major Hamilton. He should have at least done that for her. Sam tossed aside the padlock and pulled out the hard cases with his sniper rifle and Wolf's spotter gear. "How's Gabriel doing?"

"I'm fine."

"He badly hurt his back," Darcy replied. "Be careful, Sam. Please."

"Promise." He looked at her, in pain at the sight of her in this place with shattered glass and blood on the floor. "I've gotta go."

"I know."

"I love you." He turned and headed to join Wolf.

As he moved to the corner of the hotel, Sam felt the heat of the roof through the heavy gear he wore from the morning's assault. The sniper rifle could let him hit a dime at a thousand yards. They just had to find where to put the shot. He let Wolf have the only point of shade on the roof in the shadow of an industrial-size air conditioner. Sam could shoot the dime, but Wolf was best at finding the dimes. They worked as a team.

"Where do you think this guy is going to perch?"

"As high as he can get without risking an obvious sniper perch," Sam said. "He'll trust his skills to make the less optimal place his choice."

As Sam began to scan with the rifle, Wolf raised the powerful glasses. "He's already got his cave. He'll be sitting far back in one of those facing hotel rooms with the window open, and we'll never see him until he fires again."

"I know." Sam had meant it when he once demonstrated to Darcy how hard it was to stop a sniper once he or she got into position. "But he'll want to watch the street as well as the hotel room we used as a command center. He'll want to be watching this roof. It's not his sniper skills that will give him away; it'll be his decision not to disengage."

"We'll need security men sweeping those rooms."

Tom's breathing was becoming labored. The doctor needed to get here soon or they would have to disengage from the search to get him help. "We just need a glimpse. I can hit him with the first shot. Time is on his side, not ours. Find us that break."

"If this is Jerry, why did he stay?"

"We take him alive and I'll ask him. Maybe he simply got mad that we marred his perfect track record and got his boss killed, and he's trying to rebuild his reputation the same day he lost it. The guy always was a little off balance."

Concrete chipped and flew up beside him. Sam snapped the rifle back to his left, instinctively tracking back to the source of the shot, ignoring the fact he was under fire. "A west corner hotel window, something high."

"Third floor down from the roof."

The opposing sniper rifle sight reflected sunlight and Sam pulled the trigger.

"Maybe," Wolf said, watching for any signs it had impacted.

Sam chambered another round. "Wait him out."

A shot shattered through a window in the room below them, and Sam's heart stopped. Someone had come to the window at the sound of the first gunshots and just gotten shot. This time Sam saw the muzzle flash. The sniper had moved too far forward. He fired.

"Hit."

"Darcy!" Sam yelled on the communication net.

"I'm here; I'm fine," her shaky voice replied. "It was a police officer who got too close and was grazed. Did you get the shooter?"

"Maybe. Stay down."

Wolf worked the radio to guide the Brits to the right hotel room to search.

Five minutes later a British sniper appeared at the suspect's window. The radio cracked. "The sniper is dead; it looks like your Jerry. And he's got enough explosives here to blow up this hotel. I'd say he had a sample from that shipment."

Sam lowered the rifle.

"That was shaving things a bit too close," Wolf said.

Sam looked at his partner. "Hey, we both got out of this alive."

The doorway to the roof slowly opened and several men from the assault team moved cautiously onto the roof. Sam spotted Darcy and motioned her to join them.

This operation was finally over.

# Twenty-nine

August 21
Wednesday, 10:45 a.m.
Pierre Hotel / Nassau, New Providence
   Island, Bahamas

The hotel conference room had become their new headquarters. It had acquired a set of encrypted phones and computers taken from Luther and Vladimir's rooms, and even one ruggedized laptop recovered from the helicopter crash site, found in Luther's luggage in a secure waterproof case. The laptop was proving to be Luther's brain trust for his operation. Darcy translated the Russian documents for the man beside her, struggling to keep her focus on the present and not the gunshots of two days ago.

"The explosives were destined for oil refinery attacks against the complex in northern Idaho and the gas pipeline coming from Winnipeg, Canada, down through North Dakota. There are no dates, but there are travel documents. From these notes it looks like Luther helped with some of the fake permits needed to get that explosives shipment into Canada. The terrorists were going to come into Vancouver and then drive them into the U.S. Look at the dates on these files. He's been working on this plan for months."

Darcy drank more coffee, trying to stay alert. There weren't many fluent Russian translators available, so she was going hoarse trying to read while an agent annotated Luther's notes. There was keen interest in knowing which terrorist cells this information would help them stop before they could act. At least grabbing the shipment of explosives the military was tracking could disrupt this mission against gas refining capabilities.

Sam joined her and replaced the cup of coffee with a glass of ice water and held out two aspirin. "How many directories are on that computer?"

She gratefully took them. "There are fifteen folders in this section for missions; Luther was methodical in his planning. He was much more deeply involved in the planning than we realized. The financial folders number in the hundreds. When is your team going after the shipment?"

"I talked to the assault team. It's set for an hour from now, as soon as the winds die down."

"They need you with them."

He nudged the glass up, encouraging her to drink it all. "Not as much as you and Tom need me here. Joe wouldn't have joined us here last night if there was a question of manpower for the assault. He and I located where the missile was fired from: a hilltop north of the marina. Local authorities are trying to track down the eyewitness who called in a report of a van that nearly hit him as it came down that side road."

Gabriel came into the room on crutches; willpower was about the only thing keeping him moving given the jarring shock to his spine. "We just got DNA results. They've confirmed it's Luther, and Vladimir is a tentative positive. Definitive tests for him should be out in an hour."

*Thank You, Lord. This is almost over.* She'd been hoping for this level of assurance, for there had been no hope of getting a visual identification. "Renee has got to tell us where their home base is."

"Now that she knows the last hope that someone is coming to the rescue is gone, she's started cooperating. We'll have a location of the island shortly. She's not good at maps — a ten-minute flight from Salina Point leaves a lot of sea and uninhabited islands to check out. The local cops don't recognize the name she used for the island, but that may simply be part of its charm. It really was Luther's private domain. But from the luxurious home she described, it won't take long to locate the place from the air."

"When it's located, Bear and I are going with the assault team. We assume Vladimir and Luther didn't leave the front door unlocked. It'll be treated with some care."

"There is no need to hurry, no need to take risks."

Sam squeezed her shoulder. "We won't. Wolf is insisting that I pull him from the hospital so he can see it."

"I'd like to come out too."

"Once it's secured, we'll probably need both you and Gabriel there. I'll arrange it for you."


August 21
Wednesday, 3:45 p.m.
Bahamas Waters / Pirate Place Island

Sam braced as the helicopter tilted rotors to gain speed. Luther's island was southwest of Salina Point. He had named it Pirate Place Island as a tribute to the pirates of decades past who had roamed these waters. It was fitting. The assault team wanted to get to the island with enough daylight left so they could assess the situation.

The ownership paperwork of the two-mile-by-one-mile island was buried within a trust that owned a set of six uninhabited islands kept for wildlife habitat. The area was hard to reach by boat for the currents went against it flowing back toward Nassau, and it was set out well past the local tourist area. Other than some shipwrecks in the deep waters that had attracted some archaeological dives, the area was rarely visited. He wished the ride were longer so there wouldn't be as much time to think.

He'd killed a man. He had been protecting his partner, the woman he loved, but it didn't diminish the reality of what he'd done. It was one more thing he would have to live with and carry with him because it was a responsibility he had assumed. He'd chosen to be a soldier so that others could be safe.

*Lord, it's hard. I'm sorry I didn't care more for who Jerry was and the fact he didn't know*

*You. I kept my distance from thinking about him to protect myself. Now he's dead, and the opportunity to pray for him is gone. Forgive me for not caring more.*

Bear leaned over to confer with the door gunner. Sam had to focus on the job at hand. The time to process the weight of the deployment was after he was home and on leave, not while he was still in the field. A distraction would get him killed, possibly others too.

They didn't know what security personnel were still on the island or what kind of traps had been placed for unexpected visitors. The helicopter slowed and began to circle the island, looking for any indications of antiaircraft missiles. It was a beautiful island with hills and valleys and a rich soil developed from years of pounding weather against the ancient lava. Sam could see stretches of tall grasses intermixed with the heavy tropical foliage.

The house was set atop a knoll above a lush green valley going down to a pristine beach. Only from the air was it possible to appreciate the size of the estate. There were three wings to the multilevel house, and the sun reflected off the windows along the front of the home.

Set across the valley were several buildings that looked like support structures. Two boats were moored in the harbor. The only people visible were three working on the grounds behind the house, but the appearance of the estate suggested a much larger staff. Renee had given names of twelve of them, but there looked to be more.

Two helos set down on the lawn away from direct view of the house. Weapons off safety but checked, they spread out and provided cover as the last men stepped from the helos. For the next half hour the only good guys would be one of their men. The security sweep began.

Sam looked around the grounds as a sniper would. If he had to defend this place, he wouldn't try from inside the house but rather take a position outside where he could pick off people moving around. He was very glad Jerry was dead. This house would have been a hunting box.

Sam entered the house behind Bear. A lady who looked to be the cook was excitedly trying to make some point in Portuguese. A soldier from Major Hamilton's unit answered in the same language and took her arm, pointing her to the spacious living room where she would be out of the way.

Bear signaled him to the east wing. Sam nodded and headed there with Frank at his heels. They went into the rooms with weapons ready, clearing them one by one. This was the office wing of the house. There were secretary offices and file cabinets and at the end of the wing, a huge open office with a view of the grounds. No one was present, a reflection of the fact Luther had been away for several days.

Over the secure communication network he heard the men searching the grounds call off names as they identified people on the known staff list. There was general chaos at what was happening. To the staff, Luther and Renee had simply been a very wealthy European couple who loved to travel.

Sam entered what had to be Luther's office from its size. "The east wing is secure, Bear. The house doesn't appear to have even the security I would have expected."

"Agreed. The staff knows Vladimir, but he stayed here only occasionally. They recognized Jerry's photo but only saw him here twice. Have you seen any weapons so far?" his boss asked over the security loop.

"None."

Outside came the sound of a third helicopter landing. Sam broke off his search to meet the incoming men. Wolf had insisted on coming with the second group of security officers. Sam met his partner. "You're looking a little green."

"You know I get airsick when these guys fly low," Wolf replied with a grin. His arm was in a sling, and he looked like he'd lost ten pounds in two days. But he was on his feet and determined to head back to the States on his own feet. "Where do you need me?"

"Paperwork."

"I knew I should have stayed in the hospital until morning."

"Luther's office is in the east wing." Sam led Wolf to the office.

"Wow, now this is an office."

"You can tell his priorities." Sam opened file cabinets to get a sense of the type of records Luther had gathered. There were dossiers on individuals, DIA-type files. He pulled half a dozen names at random — politicians, soldiers, intelligence officers, local cops. They came from several countries and some files were begun recently; others had information going back a decade. On one U.S. soldier there was actually a copy of his security clearance paperwork.

"I wouldn't want my name in Luther's

files," Wolf remarked, reading pages.

"You can bet he has one on you if he learned something. He was Czech intelligence; this was how he worked. Luther was recreating his own intelligence service. No wonder he kept his organization to himself, Vladimir, and his wife. Knowledge is power, and controlling who knows something is how he had learned to keep his own security."

Wolf sat at the desk and opened the bottom drawer of the credenza behind it. "Chief, you'll want to see this drawer. Folders, several with names having red lines through them."

Sam walked over to take a look. He read off the names, stopping at the folder with Darcy's on it. He removed it but didn't open it. "Several of these people have been awarded the Intelligence Star for Valor; Sergey was right on Luther's priority in scheduling the hits."

Sam opened the top credenza drawer and saw folder after folder with names of known terrorists. He tugged one free. "Do you think he has intel on the people we've been hunting over the years?" He opened one folder and found it very much like a personnel file with photo, name, aliases, addresses, and a list of events the terrorist had been part of. "We need Darcy and Gabriel here looking through this data."

"I'll go find Bear and let him know."

August 21
Wednesday, 7:17 p.m.
Pirate Place Island

Sam watched Darcy circle Luther's office, scanning files and forming an overview of what was in each file cabinet, deciding her place to start. She had arrived with Gabe shortly before seven, carrying not a briefcase and notebook but a soda and her opera cassette. "These files are extensive, and several of the terrorists in these files we've never heard of," Sam commented.

She just nodded and surprised him by starting with Luther's desk calendar. She looked back three months and forward four. "What else did you find beside files?"

He blinked at the soft question. "This isn't enough?"

She looked up from the calendar and over at him. "It's a great find; I'm sure it will be very useful. But the fact Luther collects information about people and uses it to his advantage is nothing new. That was his role for decades. I would have been more surprised if you hadn't found something on this scale. So what else did you find?"

"Like what?"

"I was hoping for a journal to explain his motives."

Sam had been focused on this discovery and what this room of data represented; he'd missed the fact Darcy wasn't at the same place. "I'm sorry; there wasn't something like that." He leaned against the desk. "You're tired, Dar."

"No, now I'm depressed." She ran her hand through her hair and gave him a rueful smile. "I thought I'd feel like celebrating this moment, but I don't."

Sam had no idea how to help her. She'd given everything she had; there was nothing left. And it added to the reasons why he loved her. "How is Gabe doing on finding the money?"

"The thing Luther valued most — it's ironic isn't it, that he left it all behind? We've seized enough cash already to pay for the last year of our time to hunt Luther down. I suppose there's some justice in that."

"Not enough."

"No, not enough." She sighed and

moved away. "What do you need to do to finish up here? I'd like to go back to the hotel."

He crossed over to join her and wrapped his arms around her. "I'll take you. You'll be back in the States in a matter of days, and then you can get home to see your sister, walk away from this. You need that right now."

"Home used to be a very safe place, my bolt-hole. No matter how hot the world got, I could always go home and be safe. Now I'm wondering what is going to follow me back there."

He rubbed her back. "I'll follow you home."

She tipped her head back and smiled at him.

"I can't say you don't have a reason to be uneasy. This war isn't over, but why worry about dying, Dar? There's a verse in Romans 14 that says: 'If we live, we live to the Lord, and if we die, we die to the Lord; so then, whether we live or whether we die, we are the Lord's.' Death is kind of like being born: It happens to everyone. God knows the right time, and He'll be there."

"I know. I'll get over this disquiet eventually. I guess I'm more tired than I thought."

Sam tipped her chin up and kissed her,

taking his time. "I love you."

She turned her face into his shirt. "I love you, too." She stepped back. "Please take me to the hotel."

He hesitated and then reached for the portfolio on the desk. "I'm sorry; there's no easy way to do this. I've got some news for you that'll probably be very hard to hear, but it can't wait until tomorrow."

Darcy held Sam's gaze, the change in him warning her it was indeed going to be hard news. "Don't worry about it," she said. "What do you have?"

"They found Sergey's boat floundering at sea a couple hours ago."

She blinked. "They did? Was it that cutter he bought when he moved to the British Virgin Islands?"

"Yes."

Her gaze searched his. "Was Sergey's body found?" She would like to give him a decent burial.

"No, the boat was empty. They're towing it back to the harbor now. But there was a note for you." Sam held out the envelope. "A military courier brought it to Joe."

Darcy slipped the single sheet of paper from the envelope and saw a page of numbers. "Who wrote it? Sergey? Luther after he had Sergey killed? I don't know what he used to encrypt it." She tapped the envelope against her palm, and then walked to the desk, picked up her briefcase, and opened it. She retrieved the book she had been reading that first night at the Florida hotel. "Sergey knew I was trying to finish this." She opened pages, compared letters to the note, and nodded. She sat down at the desk and transcribed the note.

I hate to spoil the novel's ending, but the butler did it. And Darcy, I am very hard to kill. The Stingers are as good as advertised. Enjoy your retirement. Samuel is a good man.

Sergey was alive.

She felt optimism return for the first time in days.

"What?"

She shook her head, refolded the note, and slipped it back into the envelope. "Sergey was playing with the open code Luther was using. He enjoyed the book I was reading. He must have intended to drop the note into the mail one day." She owed Sergey a personal favor. This note would never make her reports. Until Sergey chose to make his presence known, he would remain missing at sea. She opened the concealed pocket in the back cover of her book, slipped in the note, and returned the book to her briefcase. "I'm ready to go."

"Gabriel said he would arrange a flight back to Virginia."

She slid her hand under his arm as they walked. "I'm going back long enough to rescue my new guppy and say good-bye to my favorite bomb dog, then I'm heading to North Dakota."

"It's a good plan, Darcy."

"What about you?"

Sam tugged an official piece of paper from his pocket, signed by his boss. "Hawaii. SEAL Team Nine is heading for some shore duty stateside. And Wolf is using that location to smooth things over with Jill for having gotten hurt."

She paused, thinking about that. "I need to work on my tan."

"It's going to be snowing soon in North Dakota," Sam pointed out.

She laughed. "I like snow."

"I don't. Come, Dar. I'll show you paradise. I can convince you to love the water as much as you do the snow. It will be a vacation you won't regret."

"Will you buy me the perfect pineapple ice slush?"

"I'll even make it for you."

September 2
Monday, 10:00 a.m.
Honolulu, Hawaii

What Darcy knew about Hawaii before flying into the islands wasn't much more than what was in the tourist guide she had skimmed. The islands were full of flowing lava fields from active volcanoes, lush tropical areas, pristine beaches, rich coral reefs, and numerous world-class hotels to visit. Having just come from the Caribbean it looked very familiar, with the exception that now she could step out of her hotel in Honolulu without worrying about who might be targeting her.

She had a room at one of those hotels, compliments of Sam, and seven days without a single commitment on her calendar. Staying longer than that didn't feel right, not when Amy hadn't seen her in months and there were loose ends that Gabriel had to deal with alone.

She loved the sun. It baked into her bones and quickly became a cocoon of warmth around her, taking any desire to move away and leaving her relaxed to the point of slumber. She turned over on her beach towel and rubbed on more sunscreen.

She narrowed her eyes against the glare and spotted Sam. He rode a surfboard in the swelling waves and disappeared from sight as the wave toppled over and crashed into the sand. Tom was windsurfing farther out, trying to steer and balance it with one good arm, the other strapped to his chest. He and Sam were partners. Where one was at, the other was likely close by.

Tom's wife Jill was here somewhere nearby with Joe's wife Kelly. The two SEALs were doing their best to make up for a year of constant deployments with the best vacation they could put together for their wives. Sam had good friends; it was nice to be considered part of the group. Darcy closed her eyes and let herself drift.

Drops of water landing on her arm roused her from a light doze. Sam sat on the beach towel beside her, drying his hair. "Hi, handsome."

"Hey, there." Sam held his hand up to shade the sun from her eyes. Darcy smiled her thanks. "You've been sleeping the last hour," he mentioned.

"Probably. It's what a warm sunny day is for."

"One of the things," he agreed, dropping his towel and picking up a bottle of water. "Looking at my beautiful woman in a bathing suit isn't half bad either."

She pushed him, about knocking him over.

He laughed. "Careful, honey. I might retaliate with a dunking in the sea." He set down the water bottle. "I think my goddaughter wants to move here."

Darcy glanced to her left. Bethany was covered with sand, scooping and throwing it with glee as the waves rolled in and water crept up the sand, tickling her toes. "She thinks this entire sandbox was created just for her." Joe was building the trench for a huge castle. "Don't SEALs ever do anything in half measures?"

"Not Bear, which is why he's the boss." Sam dangled the key on his wristband over her face. "Let's go up to the hotel. I owe you a swimming lesson, and since everyone appears to be at the beach, we'll have the pool to ourselves."

"I'm enjoying a chance to relax."

"Four days is relaxing; five you are stalling; and six you're chicken. We're a few hours from day six."

She snapped the wristband. "What do you say I learn to swim when Bethany does?"

He planted his hands on either side of her head, trapping her and smiling down.

"I do a lot of swimming, Dar. It's kind of important you at least know how. I won't let your head come even close to going underwater if that's what you want. You'll notice I'm not asking you to jump out of an airplane. I do a lot of that too."

"How long is this lesson going to last?"

"I can teach you to swim in ten minutes if you trust me. It will take five if you don't."

"What's the technique for if I don't trust you?"

"I throw you in over your head."

She laughed and tugged him down and kissed him. "I'll give you an hour because I'm a lousy student, but only if you come back to North Dakota and help me move a tree."

"Move it where?"

"It's big and old and has to come down. Sound too hard for you?"

"Can I bring Wolf?"

"Jill too if she wants to come."

"You've got a deal." Sam got to his feet and offered a hand. "First rule of learning to swim: You have to remember how to relax. Can you remember what right now feels like?"

She let him pull her up. "Boneless?"

"You'll get this down in no time."

She gathered up her towel and sunscreen

and headed with him up toward the hotel. It was the best kind of vacation — one spent without any schedule.

"The second rule is equally simple: You have to learn to breathe."

"What's wrong with how I breathe?"

Sam paused to look from her face to her toes and back up. "Not a thing from where I'm standing. Just remember to breathe deeply when you can and not to breathe when your head is underwater."

"I think I've got that second part down."

"Seriously, why haven't you ever learned to swim?"

"I'm a coward."

Sam blinked and then his laughter shook his chest. "Sure, Dar. I think the correct answer is you didn't learn when you were young, and then you got too old to admit there was something you couldn't do. I'm going to enjoy this swimming lesson."

She snapped her towel at him. "Just because you like to make water your second home . . ." She left him at the hotel side door and went to her room to change.

Sam sat at the poolside and tossed two inflated rings into the water. "Here are your floaties. You know we could do this in the ocean where the saltwater will naturally make you more buoyant."

Darcy stuck her right foot in the pool. "At least it's warm enough so I won't get pneumonia. I think we'll start counting your ten minutes."

"Why don't you have a seat right where you are? And remember, the first rule is to relax."

Darcy sat on the edge of the deserted pool and reached down to slap the water, sending up a spray toward him. "The second was to breathe when my head was out of the water. I mastered that rule some time ago."

Sam dropped into the pool, and the water came up to his shoulders; she'd struggle to touch bottom. "The third rule is also easy. Give me your foot."

"What?"

His hand settled around her right ankle and he tickled the bottom of her foot. Laughing, she tried to pull back and only managed to come close to kicking him as he kept tickling her. "That's the kick you need. If you get into trouble underwater and need to get to the surface to breathe, just remember what it's like to have your feet tickled. You'll shoot to the top." He reluctantly released her ankle.

"A very vivid illustration. What's rule number four?"

"Sorry, only three easy rules. After that you just jump in and swim. Give me your hand and slide into the water. I won't let you go under."

She hesitated.

"This won't be like the Florida dunking where you stepped into the deep end and had to fight everything including your shoes to get back to the side," Sam reassured.

She dropped into the water. Sam kept a firm grip on her arm until she had a good hold of the side of the pool. He pulled over the rings. "Hold on to them and just kick. I'll race you to the other side of the pool."

"It won't be much of a race; you'll just walk across."

Sam grinned. "True. But I won't use my hands."

She was competitive enough to try and make it a race. He beat her to the other side and waited for her and the inflated rings to touch the side. "You've got a good kick. Turn around and go back without the rings. Just remember to kick hard and use your arms like you're parting curtains at a really elegant store's dressing room."

"If I go down, you promise to pull me up?"

"I won't let you drown."

She made a face at him and then set out for the opposite side of the pool, kicking hard and working her arms back and forth to keep her head out of the water. She eventually reached the other side and gripped it hard. "Swimming is tiring."

Sam put one hand on the side of the pool near hers and leaned over to study her face. "Relax and breathe."

"If you said that halfway across the pool I would have sunk."

"Take a deep breath, close your eyes, and simply relax, let yourself sink below the water. Get used to it. Use your hand on the side to pull yourself up whenever you like. There's nothing to fear about having your head underwater."

Darcy relaxed and went beneath the surface. Sam took a breath and dropped below the water, curious to know if she would have the courage to open her eyes underwater. She did on the third time down and started in surprise at seeing his face near hers. His hand took her arm and propelled them both to the surface, not wanting her to accidentally swallow water. "Good job."

"How long can you hold your breath?"

"A while."

"Show me."

He smiled, took a deep breath, relaxed, and sunk below the surface. He sat down on the bottom of the pool and began cleaning his fingernails. After about forty-five seconds Darcy came underwater, her eyes open, and he waved at her. She didn't look too confident about smiling underwater and went back to the surface.

Sam began counting tiles at the bottom of the pool. The hotel had put its signature initial in every tenth tile. Darcy came back underwater as it approached two minutes, looking a bit worried. He smiled at her.

At two-minutes-thirty she swam toward him to touch his arm and point up. He slid his knuckles across her cheek but shook his head. She looked at him, shook her head, and pushed off the bottom to go back to the surface.

Next time she came down . . . What would she do? She was really getting worried.

He started counting. Thirty-four, thirty-five, thirty-six . . . A surge of water and Darcy came down again. She grabbed his hair and tugged; he winced and let her pull him to the surface.

He sucked in a deep breath and rubbed his head. "Did you have to do that?"

"Over three minutes and you just sit down there and let me worry about you?"

He laughed, leaned over, and kissed her outraged face. "You went underwater and hauled out a man who weighs twice as much as you. Not bad, gorgeous. I'd say you're not only a swimmer, you are lifeguard qualified."

She shoved his head underwater. He came up sputtering, coughing up water.

She was out of the pool and stalking toward the hotel.

"Darcy —"

"The lesson is over. And you still owe me a pineapple ice slush."

Sam floated on his back to recover his breath. "I'll make you two."

"One pineapple ice slush made to perfection." Sam offered it to Darcy as she sat on the lounge chair on the back patio of the hotel, overlooking the beach. She'd changed into a pair of shorts and a simple white shirt that showed off her tan. He moved her feet over and settled on the same chair, stretching his legs out and putting one hand across her to keep the chair from tipping.

"Thank you."

"You've got freckles beginning to show from the sun. They look cute."

She didn't take his lead, her expression still serious. "How long can you actually hold your breath?"

"As long as I need to."

She ran her hand along the front of his shirt. "I'm relieved to hear it." She settled back against the chair, twirled her drink, then smiled. "It was a memorable swimming lesson. I should have grabbed your ear."

He winced. "That would have worked too."

She laughed.

"Let's go take a walk on the beach. It's a perfect day and I need to stretch my legs. Bring the drink." He offered his hand and pulled her from the chair. They headed toward the beach.

"Will you teach me to surf today?"

"I suppose I could try." They walked the sand past where a beach cookout was being prepared and the night's musical entertainment would take place.

"Are we going to that tonight?"

"I think so. If Bethany stays awake she'll love it."

"Why don't you offer that we baby-sit her tonight so Joe and Kelly can have some time alone?" Darcy asked.

"You'd like to?"

"Sure."

"Maybe another night. I think we'll be otherwise occupied this evening."

She looked at him, curious. Sam decided the spot was right. The beach was gorgeous; the day was perfect. He turned her toward him and reached into his pocket. "I have something for you."

He held his hand out palm up, the piece of velvet tied with a pink ribbon. Darcy's hands trembled slightly as she unwrapped it. She lifted the diamond engagement ring, blinking hard. He tenderly tipped up her chin. "I love you, Darcy St. James. Would you marry me?"

Joy overwhelmed her smile. "Yes."

He slid the ring on her finger and closed his hand around hers. "Soon."

He nearly lost his balance as she strangled him in a hug. He laughed. He'd managed to make her nearly speechless. He would have to remember this. "I want to go to North Dakota with you and see Amy, see again the place we'll always call our home base." Darcy needed more than the permanence of a ring; she needed the permanence of a place. He wanted to provide her with that, and so much more.

"Okay."

"Are you crying?"

The top of her head hit his chin. Sam smiled and picked her up to more easily kiss her. Her arms wrapped around his neck. "I like the fact you get quiet when you're overwhelmed. I get to do all the talking. I was thinking we could go back to the hotel, find us a notebook, and make some wedding plans over dinner."

"Amy will be my maid-of-honor."

"Wolf's my best man."

She giggled. "The decisions are made. Let's elope."

"My mom will insist on pictures — lots of them."

She leaned back. "Set me down."

"You're lighter than the gear I haul around."

"Samuel —"

He reluctantly let her feet touch the sand again.

"We'll call people tonight," she decided.

"Probably a good idea."

She tugged him back the way they had come. "We'll start with telling your boss."

He laughed and tugged her back. "And end our privacy for the night? We don't need to tell the guys yet." He tucked her under his arm. "Come on, Dar. Let's go find the perfect place to watch the sunset instead. I don't want to share you."

485

# Thirty

September 7
Saturday, 11:09 a.m.
Shelton, North Dakota

It was good to be home. Darcy leaned against the triple-rail fence she had painted the day before and watched as Sam and Tom tried to figure out what to do with the evergreen that threatened to collapse onto her garage. She was glad it was them and not her.

She turned the engagement ring on her finger. *Lord, thanks for Psalm 55. The verse this morning was right on target. 'Cast your burden on the Lord, and he will sustain you; he will never permit the righteous to be moved.'* A year ago she never would have imagined this much change in her life — a hard-fought victory, a wartime romance, a best friend and a lovely future, a chance to live her dreams. She watched Sam and Tom wrestle with the tree. Life was so good.

The phone rang, interrupting her thoughts. She reached for the sheepskin jacket and tugged out the phone. "Hello."

"Dar, I'm looking at a clean desk and I already miss you."

She rested her forearms against the railing, relaxing at the pleasure of hearing from Gabe. "Absence makes the heart grow fonder."

"I'm glad to hear you're missing me too. You got some mail in."

"Do I really want to read it?"

"You got a postcard from Sergey. It's postmarked from the British Virgin Islands."

"Read it."

"It's typical Sergey, short and to the point: 'Darcy, surprised by message. The answer is yes.' Is something going on?"

"I invited him to my wedding," Darcy replied.

"I thought you weren't going to mix business and your personal life?"

"Business is inevitably personal." She watched the tree sway and heard a sharp crack as wood gave way. The tree came down on the garage roof. There were only so many miracles two SEALs could work. Cutting out a tall dead evergreen safely apparently wasn't one of them.

"Gabe, let me call you back in about ten minutes, okay?"

"Sure."

"Thanks." She hung up the phone and headed over to join the guys.

She stopped beside Sam and folded her arms across her chest to match the way he stood just looking at the tree. She tilted her head, studying the way the tree had crashed. They had done a great job. The crown line of the roof had been broken.

"We decided that you needed a new garage," Sam remarked.

"That's a good idea because as it turns out I do."

He traced a finger down her cheek and smiled. "We'll fix this. I'm thinking something with more than one garage door and a high ceiling, so we can park something taller and wider than a breadbox."

"Good idea."

"Since we've figured out how to take out a building, if you want that shed to go as well just let us know. We can topple another tree."

She leaned against him, sharing his quiet amusement. She loved this man. "Suck it in, sailor, and get back to work."

"Your nose is turning red in the cold."

"I hope it gets so cold we have snow. I

want to have a snowball fight with you since I know I'd win."

"Oh really?" He leaned hard against her so that she lost her balance.

She gestured toward the tree. "Now what?"

"We play loggers."

Tom reappeared from the damaged garage carrying an ax and a handsaw. "Want to make our own version of Old Misery?"

"A legendary telephone pole at the SEAL's BUD/S course," Sam explained. "It weighs an awful lot."

"That's the understatement of the year," Tom added.

Sam accepted the ax. "Let's leave an Old Misery size log and I'll make a bench for the porch."

"Don't you think a chainsaw would be faster?" Darcy asked.

"But not nearly so much fun," Sam pointed out as he stripped off his jacket.

She accepted the jacket and folded it across her arm. "You're going to show off."

Sam stepped over to the tree and buried the ax in the trunk. "Just a little."

She settled down near the flowerbeds and watched them work. They were a good team: Tom clearing off branches while Sam attacked the trunk. She would enjoy being part of the special club of women who called a SEAL *husband*.

*I'm so glad this has come full circle, Lord, that You brought me back here safely and introduced me to a man who will make this place truly a home. Sam's a wonderful man. I couldn't have envisioned something this special a year ago. He enjoys life, and I need that in my life.*

The sound of a car coming up the drive interrupted her prayer. Her sister got out. Amy hadn't changed much in the last year. She wore an Old West sheriff's badge, a gift from Sam, as a badge of honor.

"It looks like you had a bit of trouble here."

"They decided I needed a new garage."

"So I see." Amy settled on the ground beside her. "Now this is a sight worth watching."

Darcy just smiled.

Amy handed her a folded piece of paper. "This came for you; I figured special delivery was the fastest route."

The page was red-striped on the edges; it had come from the sheriff's office secure fax.

423 million now seized. Awarded second Intelligence Star for Valor. Congratulations. Gabriel.

Darcy folded the document and slipped it into her pocket. She didn't deserve it, but the CIA rarely asked the recipient.

"Congratulations," Amy said softly.

"I've already got my reward, Amy. I'm home." She didn't need to go back East and be honored for something that was already a memory. She wanted to return to Hawaii and work more on her tan, learn to dive with Sam, come back here and make them a home for their future. The next season of her life was going to be perfect.

"Will you meet his family this weekend?"

"After we drop Tom off at the airport, we're driving over for lunch with Sam's family."

"You'll enjoy meeting Hannah."

"From what you've said, I know I will."

Sam and Tom began stacking the wood they had cut. "You can deliver a load of that to my place if you like," Amy called out. "Evergreens smell so wonderful in a fire."

"We'd be glad to." Sam walked over to join them. "Hi, Amy."

She got to her feet. "I came over to invite you guys to lunch so I can feed you and tug stories out about what Darcy has been up to these past several months."

"We accept," Tom said promptly.

Amy laughed and tipped back her white Stetson. "Good, because I don't have company as often as I'd like. I cooked up a storm."

Sam offered her a hand up. Darcy laced her fingers with his. This was what she wanted more of for her future — family, friends, and the man she loved.

They followed Amy and Tom down the road to her place.

"What?"

She glanced at Sam. "I'm just happy."

"We'll have many more days like this one. That's a promise."

She put her arm around his waist, his sweaty shirt not deterring her from the hug. "I would love to tell Amy today that we're going to get married here in Shelton next month. You think that would work for your family and your SEAL buddies?" They'd talked about several dates, but she'd hesitated to choose one until now, until she got back here and had a better feel of what was happening in Amy's life.

"It would."

"And I'd like to see Coronado on the way back to Hawaii. I want to see where you trained to become a SEAL."

"We could do that too."

Darcy leaned back to see his face. "If I asked for the moon right now you'd say sure."

"I've got what I want. You." Sam hugged her. "Since you're now ready to make decisions, I'll point out you still need to decide on where we go for our honeymoon."

"I'm pretty partial to somewhere with a beach."

"We could make it a long honeymoon and try a few different beaches to compare which is the best."

"Yes, please. As long as you teach me to surf," Darcy said. Life with Sam was going to be such an adventure.

"I'll also teach you to snorkel and dive. Probably dunk you a few times, just in case you were wondering."

She tried to push him off balance but there was no way to budge him. "You're as solid as a tree."

"I think that was a compliment." He picked her up. "I love you, Dar."

"I love you more."

Sam laughed. "We'll debate that for a few years." He kissed her to seal the promise.

Dear Reader,

During the writing of this book, September 11th happened. The event changed my life, as it did for many in America. The result is a book I wrote more for myself than someone who might later read it. This was the story I wanted to tell as I worked through the months of September through December. More than once during those months I came close to stopping and telling my publisher I didn't want to write a military story — let's do something else. Fans were sending their spouses and loved ones to war. Friends in the military were leaving for overseas. As I write this, many are still there.

Max Lucado's book *Traveling Light* talks about the journey we take with God through life as captured by Psalm 23. Releasing burdens and trusting God even in the midst of tragedy is part of His plan for how we cope when life rips apart. God has a way of pulling together even the tough days of our lives into part of a beautiful tapestry.

Despite the external pressures going on through these months, I really enjoyed writing Sam and Darcy's story. They were part of my own recovery of a sense of hope. Darcy is a warrior as much as Sam.

Darcy was the endurance. She put her head down, accomplished the next objective, and kept going until the job was done. Sam is the trust. He waded into the fight confident he'd win, trusting God for the outcome. Together they were the right kind of team.

There are many like Darcy and Sam working today. This is my tribute and thanks to them. They are indeed heroes.

As always, I love to hear from my readers. Feel free to write me at:

Dee Henderson
c/o Multnomah Fiction
P.O. Box 1720
Sisters, Oregon 97759
E-mail: dee@deehenderson.com
Stop by on-line at:
http://www.deehenderson.com

Thanks again for letting me share Sam and Darcy's story.

Sincerely,

*Dee Henderson*